MELANIE MILBURNE

First Published in Great Britain 2016
By Mills & Boon, an imprint of HarperCollins*Publishers*
1 London Bridge Street, London, SE1 9GF

TEMPTED BY A CAFFARELLI © 2016 Harlequin Books S. A.

Never Say No To A Caffarelli, *Never Underestimate A Caffarelli* and *Never Gamble With A Caffarelli* were first published in Great Britain by Harlequin (UK) Limited.

Never Say No To A Caffarelli © 2013 Melanie Milburne
Never Underestimate A Caffarelli © 2013 Melanie Milburne
Never Gamble With A Caffarelli © 2013 Melanie Milburnen

ISBN: 978-0-263-92087-1

05-1116

Our policy is to use papers that are natural, renewable and recyclable products and made from wood grown in sustainable forests. The logging and manufacturing processes conform to the legal environmental regulations of the country of origin.

Printed and bound in Spain
by CPI, Barcelona

From as soon as **Melanie Milburne** could pick up a pen she knew she wanted to write. It was when she picked up her first Mills & Boon at seventeen that she realised she wanted to write romance. After being distracted for a few years by meeting and marrying her own handsome hero, surgeon husband Steve, and having two boys, plus completing a Masters of Education and becoming a nationally ranked athlete (masters swimming), she decided to write. Five submissions later she sold her first book and is now a multi-published, bestselling and award-winning *USA TODAY* author. In 2008 she won the Australian Romance Readers' Association's award for most popular category/series romance, and in 2011 she won the prestigious Romance Writers of Australia R*BY award.

Melanie loves to hear from her readers via her website, www.melaniemilburne.com.au or on Facebook: www. facebook.com/pages/Melanie-Milburne/351594482609.

NEVER SAY NO TO A CAFFARELLI

BY
MELANIE MILBURNE

To my husband Steve. I dedicate this 50th novel to you for always believing in me, for always encouraging me, for putting up with my highs and lows, for patiently listening on our walks with the dogs about my latest plot and characters, but most of all for just being you— the most wonderful hero of them all.

Love you to pieces. xxx

CHAPTER ONE

'WHAT DO YOU MEAN, she won't sell?' Raffaele Caffarelli frowned at his London-based secretary.

Margaret Irvine turned her palms over in a 'don't blame me' gesture. 'Miss Silverton flatly refused your offer.'

'Then make her a bigger one.'

'I did. She refused that too.'

Rafe drummed his fingers on the desk for a moment. He hadn't been expecting a hiccup like this at this stage. Everything had gone smoothly up until now. He'd had no trouble acquiring the stately English countryside manor and surrounding land in Oxfordshire for a bargain price. But the dower house was on a separate title—a minor problem, or so he'd been led to believe by his business manager, as well as the estate agent. The agent had assured him it would be easy enough to acquire the dower house so that the Dalrymple Estate could be whole once more; all he would have to do was to offer well above the market value. Rafe had been generous in his offer. Like the rest of the estate, the place was run down and badly needed a makeover, and he had the money needed to bring it back to its former glory and turn it into a masterpiece of English style and decadence. What was the woman thinking? How could she be in her right mind to turn down an offer as good as his?

He *wasn't* going to give up on this. He had seen the property listed online and got his business manager, James—who was going to be fired if this didn't get sorted out soon—to secure it for him.

Failure was not a word anyone would dare to associate with the name Raffaele Caffarelli. He was not going to let a little hurdle like this get in the way of what he wanted. 'Do you think this Silverton woman's somehow found out it's me who's bought Dalrymple Manor?'

'Who knows?' Margaret shrugged. 'But I wouldn't have thought so. We've managed to keep the press away from this so far. James handled all the paperwork under cover and I made the offer to Miss Silverton via the agent, as you instructed. You don't know her personally, do you?'

'No, but I've met her type before.' Rafe curled his lip cynically. 'Once she gets a whiff that it's a wealthy developer after her house, she'll go for broke. She'll try and milk every penny she can out of me.' He let out a short sharp expletive. 'I *want* that property. I want *all* of that property.'

Margaret pushed a folder across the desk to him. 'I found some news clippings from the local village from a couple of years ago about the old man who owned the manor. It seems the late Lord Dalrymple had rather a soft spot for Poppy Silverton and her grandmother. Beatrice Silverton was the head housekeeper at the manor. Apparently she worked there for years and—'

'Gold-digger,' Rafe muttered.

'Who? The grandmother?'

He shoved his chair back and got to his feet. 'I want

you to find out everything you can about this woman Polly. I want her—'

'Poppy. Her name is Poppy.'

Rafe rolled his eyes and continued. 'Poppy, then. I want her background, her boyfriends—even her bra size. Leave no stone unturned. I want it on my desk first thing Monday morning.'

Margaret's neatly pencilled eyebrows lifted but the rest of her expression remained in 'obedient secretary' mode. 'I'll get working on it right away.'

Rafe paced the floor as his secretary gathered a stack of documents to be filed from his desk. Maybe he should head down and have a little snoop around the village himself. He'd only seen the manor and the surrounding area from the photos James had emailed him. It wouldn't hurt to have a little reconnaissance trip of his own to size up the enemy, so to speak.

He snatched up his keys. 'I'm heading out of town for the weekend. Anything urgent, call me, otherwise I'll see you on Monday.'

'Who's the lucky girl this time?' Margaret gathered the bundle of paperwork against her chest. 'Is it still the Californian bikini-model or is she yesterday's news?'

He shrugged on his jacket. 'This may surprise you, but I'm planning to spend this weekend on my own.' He stopped pulling down his left shirt cuff to glower at her. 'What's that look for?'

His secretary gave him a knowing smile.' You haven't spent a weekend on your own since I don't know when.'

'So?' He gave her another brooding frown. 'There's a first time for everything, isn't there?'

Poppy was bending over to clear table three when the door of her tearoom opened on Saturday afternoon. Even with her back to the door she knew it wasn't one of her regulars. The tinkling chime of the bell sounded completely different. She turned around with a welcoming smile, but it faltered for a moment as she encountered an open shirt-collar and a glimpse of a tanned masculine chest at the height she'd normally expect to see someone's face.

She tilted her head right back to meet a pair of brown eyes that were so intensely dark they looked almost black. The staggeringly handsome face with its late-in-the-day stubble seemed vaguely familiar. A movie star, perhaps? A celebrity of some sort? She flicked through her mental hard-drive but couldn't place him. 'Um, a table for…?'

'One.'

A table for one? Poppy mentally rolled her eyes. He didn't look the 'table for one' type. He looked the type who would have a veritable harem of adoring women trailing after him wherever he went.

Maybe he was a model, one of those men's aftershave ones—the ones that looked all designer stubbly, masculine and bad-boy broody in those glossy magazine advertisements.

But who went to old-world tearooms on their own? That was what the coffee chain stores were for—somewhere to linger for hours over a macchiato and a muffin and mooch through a raft of the day's papers.

Poppy's stomach suddenly dropped in alarm. *Was he a food critic?* Oh, dear God! Was she about to be savaged in some nasty little culinary blog that would suddenly go viral and ruin everything for her? She was struggling to keep afloat as it was. Things had been deadly quiet since that swanky new restaurant—which she couldn't even name or think of without wanting to throw up—

opened in the next village. The down-turn in the economy meant people weren't treating themselves to the luxury of high tea any more.

They saved their pennies and went out to dinner instead—*at her ex-boyfriend's restaurant.*

Poppy studied the handsome stranger covertly as she led him to table four. 'How about over here?' She pulled out a chair as she tried to place the faint trace of an accent. French? Italian? A bit of both, perhaps? 'You get a lovely view of Dalrymple Manor and the maze in the distance.'

He gave the view a cursory glance before turning back to her. Poppy felt a little shock like volts of electricity shooting through her body when that dark-as-night gaze meshed with hers. God, how gorgeous was his mouth! So masculine and firm with that sinfully sensual, fuller lower lip. Why on earth didn't he sit down? She would have a crick in her neck for the rest of the day.

'Is that some sort of tourist attraction?' he asked. 'It looks like something out of a Jane Austen novel.'

She gave him a wry look. 'It's the *only* tourist attraction, not that it's open to the public or anything.'

'It looks like a rather grand place.'

'It's a fabulous place.' Poppy released a wistful little sigh. 'I spent most of my childhood there.'

A dark brow arched up in a vaguely interested manner. 'Oh really?'

'My grandmother used to be the housekeeper for Lord Dalrymple. She started at the manor when she was fifteen and stayed until the day he died. She never once thought of getting another job. You don't get loyalty like that any more, do you?'

'Indeed you don't.'

'She passed away within six months of him.' Poppy

sighed again. 'The doctors said it was an aneurysm, but personally I think she didn't know what to do with herself once he'd gone.'

'So who lives there now?'

'No one at the moment,' she said. 'It's been vacant for over a year while the probate was sorted out on Lord Dalrymple's will. There's a new owner but no one knows who it is or what they plan to do with the place. We're all dreading the thought that it's been sold to some crazy, money-hungry developer with no taste. Another part of our local history will be lost for ever under some ghastly construction called—' she put her fingers up to signify quotation marks '—modern architecture.'

'Aren't there laws to prevent that from happening?'

'Yes, well, some people with loads of money think they're above the law.' Poppy gave a disdainful, rolling flicker of her eyes. 'The more money they have, the more power they seem to expect to wield. It makes my blood boil. Dalrymple Manor needs to be a family home again, not some sort of playboy party-palace.'

'It looks rather a large property for the average family of today,' he observed. 'There must be three storeys at least.'

'Four,' she said. 'Five, if you count the cellar. But it needs a family. It's been crying out for one ever since Lord Dalrymple's wife died in childbirth all those years ago.'

'I take it he didn't marry again?'

'Clara was the love of his life and once she died that was that,' she said. 'He didn't even look at another woman. You don't get that sort of commitment these days, do you?'

'Indeed you don't.'

Poppy handed him a menu to bridge the little silence

that had ensued. Why was she talking about loyalty and commitment to a perfect stranger? Chloe, her assistant, was right: maybe she did need to get out more. Oliver's betrayal had made her horribly cynical. He had wooed her and then exploited her in the worst way imaginable. He hadn't wanted *her;* he'd used her knowledge and expertise to set up a rival business. How gullible she had been to fall for it! She still shuddered to think about how close she had come to sleeping with him. 'Um, we have a special cake of the day. It's a ginger sponge with raspberry jam and cream.'

The dark-haired man ignored the menu and sat down. 'Just coffee.'

Poppy blinked. She had forty varieties of specialty teas and he wanted *coffee?* 'Oh…right. What sort? We have cappuccino, latte—'

'Double-shot espresso. Black, no sugar.'

Would it hurt you to crack a smile? What was it with some men? And who the hell went to a *tearoom* to drink *coffee?*

There was something about him that made Poppy feel prickly and defensive. She couldn't help feeling he was mocking her behind those dark, unreadable eyes. Was it her Edwardian dress and frilly apron? Was it her red-gold curly hair bunched up under her little mobcap? Did he think she was a little bit behind the times? That was the whole point of Poppy's Teas—it was an old-world experience, a chance to leave the 'rush, rush, rush' pace of the modern world behind while you enjoyed a good old-fashioned cup of tea and home baking just like your great-great granny used to make.

'Coming right up.' Poppy swung away, carried her tray back to the kitchen and put it down on the counter top with a little rattle of china cups.

Chloe looked up from where she was sandwiching some melting moments with butter-cream. 'What's wrong? You look a little flushed.' She narrowed her gaze to slits. 'Don't tell me that two-timing jerk Oliver has come in with his slutty new girlfriend just to rub salt in the wound. When I think of the way he pinched all of those wonderful recipes of yours to pass them off as his own creation I want to cut off his you-know-whats and serve them as an entrée in his totally rubbish restaurant.'

'No.' Poppy frowned as she unloaded the tray. 'It's just some guy I have a feeling I've seen somewhere before…'

Chloe put down her knife and tiptoed over to peek through the glass of the swing door. 'Oh. My. God.' She turned back to Poppy with wide eyes. 'It's one of the Three Rs.'

Poppy screwed up her face. 'One of the what?'

'The Caffarelli brothers,' Chloe said in a hushed voice. 'There's three of them. Raffaele, Raoul and Remy. Rafe is the oldest. They're French-Italian squillionaires. The seriously-silver-spoon set: private jets, fast cars and even faster women.'

Poppy gave her head a little toss as she went to the coffee machine. 'Well, for all that money it certainly hasn't taught him any manners. He didn't even say please or thank you.' She gave the knob of the machine a savage little twist. 'Nor did he smile.'

Chloe peeked through the glass panel again. 'Maybe you don't have to be nice to horribly common people like us when you're filthy rich.'

'My gran used to say you can tell a lot about a person by the way they respect people they don't *have* to respect,' Poppy said. 'Lord Dalrymple was a shining example of it. He treated everyone the same. It didn't matter if they were a cleaner or a corporate king.'

Chloe came back to the melting moments and picked up her butter-cream knife. 'I wonder what he's doing in our little backwater village? We're not exactly on the tourist trail these days. The new motorway took care of that.'

Poppy's hand froze on the espresso machine. 'It's *him*.'

'Him?'

'He's the new owner of Dalrymple Manor.' Poppy ground her teeth as she faced her assistant. 'He's the one who wants to turf me out of my home. I knew there was something funny about that woman who came by the other day with that pushy agent. I bet *he* sent her to do his dirty work for him.'

'Uh-oh…' Chloe winced. 'I know what this means.'

Poppy straightened her shoulders and pasted a plastic-looking smile on her face. 'You're right.' She picked up the steaming double-shot espresso as she headed towards the door leading out to the tearoom. '*This means war.*'

Rafe cast an eye around the quaint tearoom. It was like stepping back in time. It gave him a sort of spooky time-warp sensation where he almost expected a First World War soldier to walk in the door with an elegantly dressed lady on his arm. The delicious smell of home baking filled the air. Fresh cottage flowers were on the dainty tables—sweet peas, forget-me-nots and columbines— and there were hand-embroidered linen napkins on each place setting. The teacups and plates were a colourful but mismatched collection of old china, no doubt sourced from antique stores all over the countryside.

It told him a lot about the owner-operator. He presumed the flame-haired beauty who had served him was Poppy Silverton. She wasn't quite what he'd been expecting. He had pictured someone older, someone a little more hard-boiled, so to speak.

Poppy Silverton looked like she'd just stepped out of the pages of a children's fairy-tale book. She had a riot of red-gold curls stuffed—rather unwillingly, he suspected, given the tendrils that had escaped around her face—under a maid's mobcap; brown eyes the colour of toffee, and a rosy mouth that looked as soft and plump as red velvet cushions. Her skin was creamy and unlined, with just the tiniest sprinkling of freckles over the bridge of her nose that looked like a dusting of nutmeg over a baked custard. She was a mix between Cinderella and Tinkerbell.

Cute—but not his type, of course.

The swing door to the kitchen opened and out she came bearing a steaming cup of coffee. She had a smile on her face that didn't show her teeth or quite reach her eyes. 'Your coffee, *sir.*'

Rafe caught a faint trace of her flowery perfume as she bent down to place his coffee on the table. He couldn't quite place the fragrance…lily of the valley or was it freesia? 'Thank you.'

She straightened and fixed him with a direct stare. 'Are you sure you wouldn't like a piece of cake? We have other varieties, or cookies if you're not a cake man.'

'I don't have a sweet tooth.'

She pursed her full mouth for a brief moment, as if she took his savoury preference as a personal slight. 'We have sandwiches. Our ribbon ones are our specialty.'

'The coffee is all I want.' He picked up his cup and gave her one of his formal smiles. 'Thank you.'

She leaned over to pick up a fallen petal from one of the columbines and he got another whiff of her intriguing scent and a rather spectacular view of her small but delightful cleavage. She had a neat, ballerina-like figure, curves in all the right places and a waist he was almost certain he could have spanned with his hands. He could sense she was hovering, delaying the moment when she would have to go back to the kitchen.

Had she guessed who he was? She hadn't shown any sign of the instant flash of recognition he usually got. She had looked at him quizzically, as if trying to place him, when he'd first come in but he had seen confusion rather than confirmation in her gaze. It was rather comforting to think that not *everyone* in Britain had heard about his latest relationship disaster. He didn't set out deliberately to hurt any of his lovers, but in this day and age a woman scorned was a woman well armed with the weapons of mass destruction more commonly known as social media.

Poppy Silverton moved over to one of the other tables and straightened the already perfectly straight napkins.

Rafe couldn't take his eyes off her. She drew him like a magnet. She was so other-worldly, so intriguing, he felt almost spellbound.

Get a grip. You're here to win this, not be beguiled by a woman who's probably as streetwise as the next. Don't let that innocent bow of a mouth or those big Bambi eyes fool you.

'Are you usually this busy?' he asked.

She turned and faced him again but her tight expression told him she didn't appreciate his dry sense of humour. 'We had a very busy morning. One of the busiest we've ever had. We were run off our feet. It was bedlam…. I had to make a second batch of scones.'

Rafe knew she was lying. This tiny little village was so quiet even the church mice had packed up and left for somewhere more exciting. That was why he'd wanted the manor. It was the perfect place to build a luxury hotel for the rich and famous who wanted to secure their privacy. He took a measured sip of his coffee. It was much better than he'd been expecting. 'How long have you been running this place? I'm assuming you're the owner?'

'Two years.'

'Where were you before?'

She wiped an invisible crumb from the table next to his. 'I was sous chef at a restaurant in Soho. I decided I wanted to spend some time with my gran.'

Rafe suspected there was more to her career change than that. It would be interesting to see what his secretary managed to unearth about her. He sat back and watched her for a moment. 'What about your parents? Do they live locally?'

Her face tightened and her shoulders went back in a bracing manner. 'I don't have parents. I haven't had since I was seven years old.'

'I'm sorry to hear that.' Rafe knew all about growing up without parents. When he was ten, his had died in a boating accident on the French Riviera. A grandparent had reared him, but he got the feeling that Poppy Silverton's grandmother had been nothing like his autocratic, overbearing grandfather Vittorio. 'Do you run this place by yourself?'

'I have another girl working for me. She's in the kitchen.' She gave him another rather pointed look. 'Are you just passing through the village or are you staying locally?'

He put his cup back down in the saucer with measured precision. 'I'm just passing through.'

'What brings you to these parts?'

Was it his imagination or had her caramel-brown eyes just flashed at him? 'I'm doing some research.'

'For?'

'For a project I'm working on.'

'What sort of project?'

Rafe picked up his cup again and surveyed her indolently for a moment. 'Do you give every customer the third degree as soon as they walk in the door?'

Her mouth flattened and her hands went into small fists by her sides. 'I *know* why you're here.'

He lazily arched a brow at her. 'I came in here for coffee.'

Her eyes flashed at him; there was no mistaking it this time. They were like twin bolts of lightning at they clashed with his. 'You did not. You came to scope out the territory. You came to size up the opposition. I *know* who you are.'

He gave her one of his disarming smiles, the sort of smile that had closed more business deals and opened more bedroom doors than he could count. 'I came here to make you an offer you can't refuse.' He leaned back in the chair; confident he would find her price and nail this in one fell swoop. 'How much do you want for the dower house?'

She eyeballed him. 'It's *not* for sale.'

Rafe felt a stirring of excitement in his blood. So, she was going to play hard to get, was she? He would enjoy getting her to capitulate. He thrived on challenges, the harder the better—the more satisfying.

Failure wasn't a word he allowed in his vocabulary.

He would win this.

He gave her a sizing-up look, taking in her flushed cheeks and glittering eyes. He knew what she was doing—ramping up the price to get as much as she could out of him.

So predictable.

'How much to get you to change your mind?'

Her eyes narrowed to hairpin-thin slits as she planted her hands on the table right in front of him so firmly his fine-bone china cup rattled in its saucer. 'Let's get something straight right from the get-go, Mr Caffarelli: you *can't* buy me.'

He took a leisurely glance at the delectable shadow between her breasts before he met her feisty gaze with his cool one. 'You misunderstand me, Miss Silverton. I don't want *you*. I just want your house.'

Her cheeks were bright red with angry defiance as she glared at him. 'You're *not* getting it.'

Rafe felt a quiver of primal, earthy lust rumble through his blood that set off a shivery sensation all the way to his groin. He couldn't remember the last time a woman had said no to him. It spoke to everything that was alpha in him. This was going to be much more fun that he'd thought.

He would *not* stop until he got that house, and her with it.

He rose to his feet and she jerked backwards as if he had just breathed a dragon's tongue of fire on her. 'But I will.' He laid a fifty-pound note on the table between them, locking his gaze with her fiery one. 'That's for the coffee. Keep the change.'

CHAPTER TWO

'Grrhh!' Poppy shoved the kitchen door open so hard it crashed back against the wall. 'I can't believe the gall of that man. He thought he could just waltz in here, wave a big fat wad of notes under my nose and I'd sell my house to him. How…how *arrogant* is that?'

Chloe's blue eyes were wider than the plates she'd been pretending to put away. 'What the hell happened out there? I thought you were going to punch him.'

Poppy glowered at her. 'He's the most detestable man I've ever met. I will *never* sell my house to him. Do you hear me? *Never.*'

'How much was he offering?'

Poppy scowled. 'What's that got to with anything? It wouldn't matter if he offered me gazillions—I wouldn't take it.'

'Are you sure you're doing the right thing here?' Chloe asked. 'I know your house has a lot of sentimental value because of living there with your gran and all, but your circumstances have changed. She wouldn't expect you to turn down a fortune just because of a few memories.'

'It's not just about the memories,' Poppy said. 'It's the only home I've ever known. Lord Dalrymple left it to Gran *and* me. I can't just sell it as if it's a piece of furniture I don't want.'

'Seriously, though, what about the bills?' Chloe asked with a worried little frown.

Poppy tried to ignore the gnawing panic that was eating away her stomach lining like caustic soda on satin. Worrying about how she was going to pay the next month's rent on the tearoom had kept her awake for three nights in a row. Her savings had taken a hit after paying for her gran's funeral, and she had been playing catch-up ever since. Bills kept coming through the post, one after the other. She'd had no idea owning your own home could be so expensive. And, if Oliver's rival restaurant hadn't impinged on things enough, one of her little rescue dogs, Pickles, had needed a cruciate ligament repair. The vet had charged her mate's rates but it had still made a sizable dent in her bank account. 'I've got things under control.'

Chloe looked doubtful. 'I wouldn't burn too many bridges just yet. Things have been pretty slow for spring. We only sold one Devonshire tea this morning. I'll have to freeze the scones.'

'No, don't do that,' Poppy said. 'I'll take them to Connie Burton. Her three boys will soon demolish them.'

'That's half your problem, you know,' Chloe said. 'You run this place like a charity instead of a business. You're too soft-hearted.'

Poppy ground her teeth as she started rummaging in the stationery drawer. 'I'm not accepting *his* charity.' She located an envelope and stuffed the change from the coffee into it. 'I'm handing his tip back to him as soon as I finish here.'

'He tipped you?'

'He *insulted* me.'

Chloe's expression was incredulous. 'By leaving you

a fifty-pound note for an espresso? I reckon we could do with a few more customers like him.'

Poppy sealed the envelope as if it contained something toxic and deadly. 'You know what? I'm not going to wait until I finish work to give this to him. I'm going to take it to him right now. Be a honey and close up for me?'

'Is he staying at the manor?'

'I'm assuming so,' Poppy said. 'Where else would he stay? It's not as if we have any five-star hotels in the village.'

Chloe gave her a wry look. 'Not yet.'

Poppy set her mouth and snatched up her keys. 'If Mr Caffarelli thinks he's going to build one of his playboy mansions here, then it will be over my dead body.'

Rafe was in the formal sitting room inspecting some water damage near one of the windows when he saw Poppy Silverton come stomping up the long gravel driveway towards the manor. Her cloud of curly hair—now free of her cute little mobcap—was bouncing as she went, her hands were going like two metronome arms by her sides and in one hand she was carrying a white envelope.

He smiled.

So predictable.

He waited until she had knocked a couple of times before he opened the door. 'How delightful,' he drawled as he looked down at her flushed heart-shaped face and sparkling brown eyes. 'My very first visitor. Aren't I supposed to carry you over the threshold or something?'

She gave him a withering look. 'This is your change.' She shoved the envelope towards his chest.

Rafe ignored the envelope. 'You Brits really have a problem with tipping, don't you?'

Her pretty little mouth flattened. 'I'm not accepting anything from you.' She pushed the envelope towards him again. 'Here. Take it.'

He folded his arms across his chest and gave her a taunting smile. 'No.'

Her eyes pulsed and flashed with loathing. He wondered for a moment whether she was going to slap him. He found himself hoping she would, for it would mean he would have to stop her. The thought of putting his arms around her trim little body to restrain her was surprisingly and rather deliciously tempting.

She blew out a breath and, standing up on tiptoe, stashed the envelope into the breast pocket of his shirt. He felt the high voltage of her touch through the fine cotton layer of his shirt. She must have felt it too, for she tried to snatch her hand back as if his body had scorched her.

But she wasn't quick enough for him.

Rafe captured her hand, wrapping his fingers around her wrist where he could feel her pulse leaping. Her lithe but luscious little body was so close he felt the jut of one of her hipbones against his thigh. Desire roared through his veins like the backdraft from a deadly fire. He was erect within seconds; aching and throbbing with a lust so powerful it took every ounce of self-control he possessed to stop from pushing her up against the nearest wall to see how far he could go.

She sent him an icy glare and tugged against his hold, hissing at him like a cornered wild cat. 'Get your hands off me.'

Rafe kept her tethered to him with his fingers while he moved the pad of his thumb over the underside of her wrist in a stroking motion. 'You touched me first.'

Her eyes narrowed even further and she tugged again. 'Only because you wouldn't take your stupid money off me.'

He released her hand and watched as she rubbed at it furiously, as if trying to remove the sensation of his touch. 'It was a gift. That's what a tip is—a gesture of appreciation for outstanding service.'

She stopped rubbing at her wrist to glare at him again. 'You're making fun of me.'

'Why would I do that?' He gave her a guileless half-smile. 'It was a great cup of coffee.'

'You won't win this, you know.' She drilled him with her glittering gaze. 'I know you probably think I'm just an unworldly, unsophisticated country girl, but you have *no* idea how determined I can be.'

Rafe felt his skin prickle all over with delight at the challenge she was laying before him. It was like a shot of a powerful drug. It galvanised him. And as for unsophisticated and unworldly... Well, he would never admit it to his two younger brothers, but he was getting a little bored with the worldly women he associated with. Just lately he had started to feel a little restless. The casual affairs were satisfying on a physical level, but recently he'd walked away from each of them with an empty feeling that had lodged in a place deep inside him.

But, even more unsettling, a niggling little question had started keeping him awake until the early hours of the morning: *is this all there is?*

Maybe it was time to broaden his horizons. It would certainly be entertaining to bring Miss Poppy Silverton to heel. She was like a wild filly who hadn't met the right trainer. What would it take to have her eating out of his hand? His body gave another shudder of delight. *He could hardly wait.*

'I think I should probably warn you at this point, Miss

Silverton, that I'm no pushover. I play by the rules, but they're *my* rules.'

Her chin came up at that. 'I *detest* men like you. You think you're above everyone else with your flash cars and luxury villas in every country and yet another vacuous model or starlet hanging off your arm, simpering over every word that comes out of your silver-spooned mouth. But I bet there are times when you lie awake at night wondering if anyone loves you just for who you are as a person or whether it's just for your money.'

He curled his lip mockingly. 'You really have a thing about well-heeled men, don't you? Why is success such a big turn-off for you?'

She gave him a scoffing look. 'Success? Don't make me laugh. You inherited all your wealth. It's not *your* success, it's your family's. You're just riding on the wave of it, just like your party-boy, time-wasting brothers.'

Rafe thought of all the hard work he and his brothers had had to do to keep their family's wealth secure. Some unwise business dealings his grandfather had made a few years ago had jeopardised everything. Rafe had marshalled his brothers and as a team they had rebuilt their late father's empire. It had taken eighteen-hour days, working seven days a week for close to two and a half years to bring things back around, but they had done it. Thankfully, none of Vittorio's foolhardiness had ever been leaked to the press, but hardly a day went by without Rafe remembering how terrifyingly close they had been to losing everything. He, perhaps a little more than Raoul and Remy, felt the ongoing burden of responsibility, to the extent that he had earned the reputation in the corporate world of a being a rather ruthless, single-minded workaholic.

'You are very keen to express an opinion on matters

of which you know nothing,' he said. 'Have you met either of my brothers?'

'No, and I don't want to. I'm sure they're just as detestable and loathsome as you.'

'Actually, they're vastly nicer than me.'

'Oh really?' She raised her brows in a cynical arc.

Rafe leaned indolently against the sandstone pillar, his arms folded loosely across his chest, one of his legs crossed over the other at the ankle. 'For instance, they would never leave a young lady standing out here on the steps without inviting her in for a drink.'

Her eyes narrowed in warning. 'Well, if you're thinking of asking me in, then don't bother wasting your breath.'

'I wasn't.'

Her expression faltered for a nanosecond but then she quickly recovered her pertness. 'I'm quite sure I'd be a novel change from the women you usually invite in for drinks.'

He swept his gaze over her lazily. 'Indeed you would. I've never had a redhead before.'

Her cheeks coloured and her mouth tightened. 'It's not red. It's auburn.'

'It's very beautiful.'

Her gaze flashed with venom. 'If you think flattery is going to work with me, then think again. I'm not going to sell my house to you no matter how many insincere compliments you conjure up.'

'Why are you so attached to the place?' Rafe asked. 'You could buy a much bigger place in a better location with the money I offered you.'

She gave him a hard little look. 'I don't expect someone like you to understand; you've probably lived in luxury homes all your life. The dower house is the first place I've ever been able to call home. I know it's not flash, and that it needs a bit of work here and there, but if I sold it would be like selling part of myself.'

'No one is asking you to sell yourself.'

Her brows arched up again. 'Are they not?'

Rafe held her gaze for several beats. 'My plans for the manor will go ahead with or without your cooperation. I understand the sentiments you expressed, but they have no place in what is at the end of the day a business decision. You would be committing financial suicide to reject the kind of offer I've made.'

Her posture was stiff and defensive, her eyes slitted in hatred. 'You know nothing of my financial affairs. You don't know *me*.'

'Then I will enjoy getting to know you.' He gave her a smouldering look. 'In every sense of the word.'

She swung away with her colour high and stomped back down the steps. Rafe watched her disappear into the distance with a smile on his face. One way or the other he was going to win this.

He would stake money on it.

Poppy was still fuming when she got back to her house. Her three little dogs—Chutney, Pickles and Relish— looked up at her with worried eyes as she stormed through the gate. 'Sorry, guys,' she said bending down to give them all a scratch behind the ears. 'I'm just so cross I can hardly stand it. What an arrogant man! Who does he think he is? As if I'd fall for someone like him. As if I'd even *think* about sleeping with him.'

Well, maybe it was OK to *think* about it a teeny weeny bit. There was no harm in that, was there? It wasn't as if she was going to act on it. She wasn't that type of girl.

Which kind of explained why her ex-boyfriend was now shacked up with another woman.

Poppy knew it was ridiculously old-fashioned of her to have wanted to wait a while before she consummated her relationship with Oliver. It wasn't that she was a prude… Well, maybe a bit, given she'd been raised by her grandmother, who hadn't had sex in decades.

The trouble was she was a soppy romantic at heart. She wanted her first time to be special. She wanted it to be special for the man who shared it with her. She'd thought Oliver Kentridge was going to be that special man who would open up the world of sensuality to her, but he had betrayed her even before they'd been dating a couple of months.

Poppy couldn't say her heart had been broken, but it had definitely been heavily bruised. Men were such selfish creatures, or at least that was how it had seemed in her life so far. Her well-heeled but wild playboy father had deserted her mother as soon as she had told him she was pregnant. And then, to rub more salt in the wound, within weeks of Poppy's birth he had married a wealthy socialite who stood to inherit a fortune to prop up his own. Her mother had been devastated by being cast aside so heartlessly and, in a moment of impulsivity, no doubt fuelled by her hurt, had turned up at his high-society wedding with her 'child of scandal', as Poppy had been called. The press attention had only made her mother's suffering worse and horribly, excruciatingly public. Poppy had frighteningly clear memories from during her early years of running down back-alleys holding tightly to her mother's hand, trying to avoid the paparazzi. During that time her mother had been too proud to go to her own mother for help and support for fear of hearing the dreaded 'I told you so'.

Poppy still remembered that terrifying day when the grandmother she had never met came to collect her from the hospital where her mother had drawn her last breath after taking an overdose. Her gran had seemed a little formidable at first, but over time Poppy realised it was her way of coping with the grief of losing her only child, and her regret at not having stepped in sooner to help her daughter cope with the heartbreak and shame of being cast aside by a rich man who had only used her.

Her gran had done her best to give Poppy a happy childhood. Growing up on the Dalrymple Estate had been a mostly happy but rather lonely existence. Lord Dalrymple rarely entertained and there were no children living close by. But it had gradually become home to her, and she had loved spending time with her gran in the kitchen at the manor.

The decision to study hospitality had been born out of Poppy's desire to own and run her own tearoom in the village one day, so she could be close to her gran and all that was familiar. When she moved to London to do her training she felt like she was the odd one out in her peer group. She didn't have much of a taste for alcohol and she had no interest in casual flings or partying all night in nightclubs. She'd studied hard and managed to land a great job in a hip new restaurant in Soho, but it had all turned sour when her boss had made it clear he wanted her in his bedroom as well as his kitchen.

Her gran's severe bout of bronchitis during the winter two years ago had given Poppy the perfect excuse to move back home and follow her dream. Setting up the tearoom had been a way of bringing in a modest income whilst being able to keep an eye on her gran, and not for a day had she regretted doing it.

Poppy blew out a breath as she made her way inside

the house. Maybe she did have a bias against successful men, as Raffaele Caffarelli had suggested. But why
shouldn't she resent him for thinking he could buy whatever or whoever he took a fancy to? He might be incredibly good-looking, with bucket loads of charm, but she
was *not* going to be his next conquest.

She would stake money on it. Well, she would if she
had any, of course.

Rafe strode into his London office on Monday morning.
'Did you get that information for me?'

Margaret handed him a folder. 'There's not much, but
what I've got is in there. So, how was your weekend?'

'Average.' He started flicking through the papers as he
walked through to his office. 'Hold my calls, will you?'

'What if Miss Silverton calls?'

Rafe thought about it for a beat. 'Make her wait.'

Margaret's brows lifted. 'Will do.'

He closed his office door and took the folder over to
his desk. There wasn't much he didn't already know.
Poppy Silverton had grown up with her grandmother in
the dower house on the Dalrymple Estate and had been
educated locally before moving to London in her late
teens. She had trained as a chef and had worked in a
restaurant in Soho he'd been to a couple of times. She'd
been running the tearoom in the village for the last couple of years. Her grandmother, Beatrice, had died a few
months ago, exactly six months after Lord Dalrymple,
and the house he had left to Beatrice had subsequently
passed to Poppy.

Rafe leaned back in his chair. There was nothing
about her private life, about who she was dating or had
dated. He couldn't help a rueful smile. If a similar search

had been done on him or one of his brothers, reams and reams of stuff would have come spilling out.

He'd driven away from the manor late on Saturday night but he hadn't stopped thinking about her. It wasn't just her house that was playing on his mind. He'd never met a more intriguing woman. She was so spirited and defiant. She must realise she hadn't a hope of winning against him, but she stood up to him all the same. That was enormously attractive. He was so used to women tripping over themselves to please him.

But Poppy's comment about him not knowing who genuinely cared for him had resonated a little too well with him. Apart from his brothers, who really gave a toss about him? His grandfather certainly didn't. His members of staff were respectful and mostly loyal, but then he paid them generously to be so.

He frowned at where his thoughts were heading. He wasn't interested in love and commitment. Losing his parents had taught him to keep a very tight lid on his emotions. Loving someone hurt like hell if you lost them. He never lost anything or anyone now. He did the hiring and the firing in all of his relationships.

They lasted as long as he wanted and no longer.

Rafe leaned forward to press the intercom on his desk. 'Margaret? Find out who owns the building Miss Silverton operates her tearoom out of. Make them an offer they can't refuse. Get them to sign a confidentiality agreement.'

'Right away.'

'Oh, and one other thing… Cancel all of my appointments for the next couple of weeks. I'm heading out of town.'

'A holiday?'

Rafe smiled to himself. 'You could call it that.'

CHAPTER THREE

POPPY WAS WAITING on one of her regulars when Raffaele Caffarelli came in the following Monday. She tried to ignore the little skip of her pulse and focused her attention on Mr Compton who came in at the same time every day and had done so ever since his wife of sixty-six years had died. 'There you are, Mr Compton,' she said as she handed the elderly gentleman a generous slice of his favourite orange-and-coconut cake.

'Thank you, my dear,' Mr Compton said. 'Where's your offsider today?'

'She's visiting her mother,' Poppy said, conscious of Raffaele's black-as-night gaze on her. 'Can I get you a fresh pot of tea? More cream for your cake? Another slice to take home for your supper?'

'No, love, you'd better serve your other customer.' Mr Compton gave her a wink. 'Things are finally looking up, eh?'

Poppy gave him a forced smile as she mentally rolled her eyes. 'I wish.' She went to where Raffaele was standing. 'A table for one?'

His dark eyes glinted. 'Thank you.'

She led him to a table near the window. 'A double-shot espresso, no sugar?'

His mouth twitched at the corners. 'You have a good memory.'

Poppy tried not to look at his mouth. It was *so* distracting. So too were his hands. She could still feel the imprint of those long, tanned fingers around her wrist. She felt shivery every time she recalled them against her white skin. His touch had been unforgettable. Her body still hummed with the memory of it.

He was dressed casually in blue denim jeans and an open-necked white shirt with the sleeves rolled up past his strong, tanned wrists. He had twelve to eighteen hours of stubble on his jaw. He smelt divine—a hint of wood and citrus and healthy, potent, virile male. He oozed with sex appeal. She felt the invisible current of it pass over her skin. It made her heart pick up its pace as if he had reached out and touched her.

Poppy put her chin up to a pert level. 'I don't suppose I can tempt you with a slice of cake?'

His eyes smouldered as they held hers. 'I'm very tempted.'

She pursed her lips and spoke in an undertone in case Mr Compton overheard, which was highly unlikely, given he was as deaf as the proverbial post, but still. '*Cake*, Mr Caffarelli. I'm offering you cake.'

'Just the coffee.' He waited a beat. 'For now.'

Poppy swung away to the kitchen, furious with him, but even more furious with herself for being so affected by him. She'd been expecting him to come back. She had tried not to watch out for him but every morning she had looked towards the manor to see if his flashy sports car was parked out front. She had tried her best to ignore the little dip of disappointment in the pit of her belly when it had failed to appear. She knew he wasn't going to give up on trying to acquire the dower house any time soon.

She had read up on him in some gossip magazines Chloe had given her. He had a reputation for being ruthless in business. 'Single-minded, stealthy and steely in terms of determination', one reporter had said.

Poppy suspected he was equally ruthless in his sensual conquests. His latest mistress was a bikini model with a figure to die for. Poppy couldn't imagine a slice of cake or a chocolate-chip cookie ever passing through those filler-enhanced lips.

She carried the coffee out to him. 'Will there be anything else?'

'What time do you close?'

'Five or thereabouts,' she said. 'I try to be flexible in case I get late-comers. No one likes being rushed over their cup of tea.' She gave his cup a pointed look before adding, 'Or coffee.'

His coal-black gaze glinted again. 'I have some business I'd like to discuss with you.'

Poppy stiffened. 'I'm not selling my house.'

'It's nothing to do with the dower house.'

She looked at him guardedly. 'So…what is it about?'

'I'm spending a couple of weeks at the manor to get a feel for the place before I start drawing up plans for the development,' he said. 'I don't want to employ a housekeeper at this stage. Are you interested in providing dinner each day? I'll pay you handsomely, of course.'

Poppy chewed at her lower lip for a moment. She could do with the money, but cooking him dinner each night? What else would he expect from her—her body dished up as a dessert? 'What's wrong with eating at the village pub? They do a pretty good bar snack. *There was no way she was going to recommend he try Oliver's restaurant.*

He gave her a droll look. 'I don't eat bar snacks.'

She gave her eyes a little roll. 'Of course you don't.'

'Blame my mother. She was French. You know what the French are like with their food.'

Mr Compton shuffled over on his walking frame. 'Do it, Poppy. It'll be a nice little earner for you to tide you over this rough patch.'

Poppy wished she hadn't let slip to Mr Compton a couple of weeks ago how tight things were. She didn't want Raffaele Caffarelli gaining any sort of advantage over her. He was ruthless and calculating. How far would he go to get what he wanted? 'Can I think about it and get back to you?' she said.

Rafe handed her a business card. 'Call me tonight.'

She put the card in her apron pocket and turned to speak to her only other customer. 'I'll just get that slice of cake for you to take home, Mr Compton.'

Rafe held out his hand to the elderly gentleman once Poppy had disappeared into the kitchen. 'Rafe Caffarelli,' he said.

'Howard Compton.' The old man shook his hand. 'So, you're the new owner of Dalrymple Manor.'

'Yes. I've had my eye on it for a while. It's a great piece of real estate.'

'It is at that,' Mr Compton said. 'What do you plan to do with it?'

'I'm turning it into a luxury hotel and spa.'

'Don't go telling Poppy that.' Mr Compton gave him a twinkling smile. 'She wanted a family to buy the place. It's a long time since one lived there, mind you.'

'Were you acquainted with Lord Dalrymple?'

'His wife and mine were best friends since childhood,' Mr Compton said. 'It was a terrible day when Clara died. Henry became reclusive after that. If it weren't for Poppy's grandmother Beatrice he would have curled up and died. We thought it was a nice gesture of his to leave the dower house to her and Poppy. A lot of the locals thought he would leave the whole estate to them, but there would've been too much of an outcry from the extended family if he'd done that. As it was probate took over a year to come through. So messy when there isn't a direct heir.'

Rafe thought about his own situation. He had no direct heirs other than his brothers. Who would inherit his vast fortune? He hadn't really thought about it until now... Why was he working so hard if he had no one to leave it to?

He pushed the thought aside. There was plenty of time to think about marriage. He was only thirty-five. It wasn't like he had a biological clock to worry about. Some time in the future he would select a suitable woman, someone who knew how to move in the circles he moved in, someone who wouldn't encroach on his freedom too much.

Poppy came back carrying a foil-wrapped parcel. 'Here you go, Mr Compton.'

'You're a pet,' Mr Compton said. 'I don't know what I'd do without you.' He turned back to Rafe. 'Nice to meet you, Rafe. Drop by some time and have a wee dram with me. I'm at Bramble Cottage in Briar Lane. You can't miss it.'

'I'd like that very much,' Rafe said and was almost surprised that he meant it. He gave himself a mental shake. What was he thinking? He wasn't here to make friends. He was here to make money.

The bell over the door tinkled as the old man left.

'I can see your charm isn't exclusively aimed at the

female of the species,' Poppy said, casting him a cynical look.

'He's a lovely old man,' Rafe said. 'And quite lonely, I suspect.'

'He is…' Her shoulders went down on a little sigh as she sank her teeth into her lower lip for a beat. 'I do what I can for him but I can't bring back his wife. They were best friends. It's so sad. I guess that's the downside of finding the love of your life. Eventually you have to lose them.'

'Isn't it supposedly better to have loved and lost than never to have loved at all?'

She turned away and began clearing Mr Compton's cup and saucer and plate with brisk officiousness. 'What about your latest girlfriend? Is she coming to stay with you at the manor?'

'I'm currently unattached.'

She glanced back at him over her shoulder with a raised eyebrow. 'Your choice or hers?'

'Mine.' It was *always* his choice. He wouldn't have it any other way.

'She was very beautiful.'

'Until she opened her mouth.'

She gave him an arch look. 'Couldn't you think of other ways to keep her mouth occupied?'

Right now Rafe could only think of Poppy's mouth, how it was so rosy and plump and totally natural. His groin began to thrum with desire as he thought of her velvet lips around him, her soft little tongue licking or stroking him. He wanted to taste her mouth, to sample the texture of her lips, to taste the sweetness of her, to stroke into the warm moistness of her.

What was it about her that was so damn alluring? She wasn't his type at all with her feisty little looks and combative poses. Most of the time she looked like she wanted to scratch his eyes out, but now and again he would catch a glimpse of something else in her gaze, something much more exciting—earthy, primal lust. She tried to hide it but he could sense it in her body: the way she carried herself, holding herself stiffly as if she was frightened her body would suddenly do something out of her control.

Her buttoned-up sensuality was intoxicatingly attractive. He suspected she would be dynamite once she let herself go. Her touch had electrified him the other day. He still felt the buzz of where her fingers had brushed him. He wanted those dainty little fingers all over his body. He wanted to be *inside* her body. He was rock-hard just thinking about how she would feel wrapped tightly around him. It would be a conflagration of the senses, a combustible explosion of fire meeting ice. 'What about you, Miss Silverton?'

Her expression became guarded. 'What about me?'

'Are you currently involved with anyone?'

Her gaze narrowed. 'I find it hard to see why it could be of any interest to you if I am or if I'm not.'

'*Au contraire,*' he said. 'I find it immensely interesting.'

Her cheeks flared with colour but her eyes were glittering with spirited defiance. 'Would you like more coffee, Mr Caffarelli, or shall I get your bill?'

Rafe held that sparkling toffee-brown gaze and felt his blood heat up another notch. He could smell her light fragrance. He was close enough to touch her. He felt the tension in her body; it was pulsing just below the surface. She was doing everything she could to hide it but he was aware of it all the same. Hate and lust were swirling in the air like a powerful, heady aroma. 'You don't like me very much, do you?'

Her mouth tightened primly. 'My job is to serve you coffee, not become your best friend.'

He gave her a lazy half-smile. 'Haven't you heard that saying, "keep your friends close, but your enemies closer"?'

Her eyes flashed at him as she pointedly handed him the bill for his coffee. 'Haven't you heard the saying, "there's no such thing as a free lunch"?'

Rafe chuckled as he took out his wallet, peeled off a tenner and placed it on the table beside her. 'Until we meet again, Miss Silverton. *Ciao.*'

Poppy was about to go to bed when she noticed Chutney was missing. The three dogs had been out in the garden while she had a bath, but when she called them back in only Pickles and Relish appeared. 'Chutney?' she called out from the back door. 'Chutney? Here boy. Come and get a treat.'

There was no sign of him in the garden. He seemed to have completely vanished. It was hard not to worry after what had happened to Pickles. Poppy had found him injured after finding a gap in the hedge leading to the field in front of Dalrymple Manor. It had been so harrowing to find him lying in the long grass, whimpering in pain.

Her heart began to stammer. Chutney had a tendency to wander, especially if he got the scent of a rabbit. Even though she had got the gap in the hedge fixed, she suspected there were other places he could have squeezed through, being so much smaller than the other two dogs. What if he had got out on the road? Although there wasn't much traffic along this particular lane, it only took one speeding car to do the damage.

Poppy looked at the manor in the distance. Raffaele Caffarelli's top-notch sports car was parked out the front. There were lights on downstairs, which meant he must be still awake.

She glanced at the business card on the kitchen table. Should she call him to see if he had seen any sign of Chutney? The three dogs were used to walking up to the manor. Before Lord Dalrymple had died she had taken them up every day to visit, and she had only stopped walking them in the grounds of the manor once the 'sold' sign had gone up.

She picked up the business card and ran her index finger over his name. She took a little uneven breath, reached for her phone and quickly typed in the number before she changed her mind. He answered on the third ring.

'Rafe Caffarelli.'

Poppy felt the base of her spine shiver at the sound of the deep burr of his voice. 'Um…it's Poppy Silverton here.'

'I've been expecting you to call.'

'I'm not calling about the dinner thing. I wondered if you'd seen a little dog up at the manor.'

'What sort of dog?'

'He's a cavoodle.'

'A *what?*'

Poppy rolled her eyes at his tone. 'He's a cross between a miniature poodle and a King Charles cavalier. He's called Chutney.'

'You named your dog after a condiment?'

She pursed her mouth in irritation. 'Have you seen him or not?'

'No.'

'Fine,' she said. 'I'm sorry to bother you so late. Goodni—'

'I'll have a look around outside. Would he have wandered into the maze, do you think? I haven't figured it out yet so you might have to come and rescue me from the minotaur if I get stuck.'

'I'm sure you're quite adept at getting yourself out of complicated situations.'

He gave a little chuckle. 'You've been reading up on me, haven't you?'

'If you find Chutney, please call me.'

'I'll do even better than that. I'll deliver him to your door.'

'I wouldn't want to put you to any bother.'

'Will he come to a stranger?'

'He's a shameless glutton,' Poppy said. 'He'll do anything for food.'

Her spine shivered again as he gave another deep chuckle. 'I know the type.'

The doorbell rang a few minutes later. Poppy had only just come back inside after doing another round of the garden. She shushed Pickles and Relish, who were bouncing up and down on their back legs like string puppets being controlled by a hyperactive puppeteer. 'Down, Pickles; you too, Relish. Sit. I said *sit*.' She opened the door to find Rafe standing there with Chutney under one arm. 'Oh, you found him! Where was he?'

He handed the dog to her. 'He was sitting at the back of the manor near the kitchen door.'

Poppy put Chutney on the floor where his two friends immediately besieged him with frenzied licks and whimpers of delight, as if he'd been away for a month instead of an hour. She straightened to face Rafe. 'I'm sorry about that. I think he still misses Lord Dalrymple. We used to go up to visit him every day.'

'I noticed he seemed quite at home.'

'Yes, well, I made a habit of wandering past with the dogs to check the place wasn't vandalised while it was vacant,' Poppy said. 'I'm not going up there now, of course.'

His eyes glinted knowingly. 'Of course.'

She straightened her shoulders. 'Thank you for returning him. You didn't have to. I would have come to collect him. All you had to do was call me.'

'Have you thought about my dinner proposal?'

Poppy felt that funny little shiver again as his dark eyes held hers. She wasn't exactly dressed for visitors. She was wearing the oldest, shabbiest tracksuit she possessed and a pair of scruffy old trainers that had holes over her big toes where Pickles had chewed them. Her hair was tied up with a ribbon and her face bare of make-up. It made her feel at a distinct disadvantage. It made her feel about ten years old. Why, oh why hadn't she changed into something a little less unsophisticated? 'Um, I think you should ask someone else,' she said.

'I want you.'

Heat flowed into her cheeks as that coal-black gaze smouldered against hers. 'I'm not available.' To her chagrin her voice sounded throaty and husky...*sexy, even*.

'You know you want to say yes. I can see it in your eyes.'

Poppy glowered at him. 'I can see why you fly everywhere by private jet—you'd need all the extra cabin space for your ego.'

A smile lurked around the corners of his mouth. 'You're a stubborn little thing, aren't you?'

'I did warn you.'

'Likewise.' His black-as-pitch gaze held hers with a glint of implacable determination. 'When I want something, I don't give up until I have it.'

'Thank you for bringing Chutney home,' she said holding the door open for him. 'Don't let me keep you.'

Those dark-as-night eyes lowered to her mouth for a moment before returning to mesh with her gaze. 'Aren't you going to do the neighbourly thing and invite me in for a nightcap since I so gallantly returned your dog?'

Poppy knew it would appear churlish of her to refuse him entry. But wouldn't inviting him in so late at night send him the message she actually *wanted* his company?

Of course she didn't want his company. She had plenty of company. She had her three little dogs, didn't she? 'I'm kind of busy right now.'

'I'm house-trained, if that's what's worrying you.' His hint of a smile was devastatingly attractive. 'I won't cock my leg on the furniture or try and bury bones in the backyard.'

'I'm not in the habit of inviting men I barely know into my house late at night.'

Was that a glimmer of respect she saw in his eyes? 'Are you worried about what the neighbours will think?' he asked.

'You're the only neighbour for miles,' she pointed out.

A more serious note entered his voice and was reflected in his gaze as it held hers. 'You're quite safe with me, Miss Silverton. I might have a reputation but I have the utmost respect for women and always have.'

'How reassuring.'

'You don't believe me.'

'Some of the comments your ex-mistress posted online about you were rather derogatory,' Poppy said.

'It's not my best character reference, that's for sure. But she was unhappy about being made redundant, so to speak. I'll get my secretary to send her a parting gift to soften the blow. It was remiss of me not to think of it earlier. I bet once Zandra gets several thousand pounds' worth of rubies or sapphires she'll take the comments down.'

Poppy arched her brow at him. 'Why not diamonds?'

'I never give diamonds.'

'Why not? It's not as if you can't afford them.'

'Diamonds are for ever,' he said. 'When I find the right girl to give them to, I'll buy them, but not before.'

Poppy gave him a sceptical look. 'So you're actually planning to give up your partying and playboy lifestyle at some point?'

His shrug was noncommittal. 'It's not on my immediate agenda.'

She couldn't keep the derision from her tone or from the angle of her chin. 'Too busy out there sowing your wild oats?'

His eyes glinted as they held hers. 'There are a few fresh fields I have yet to plough. After that, who knows? Don't they say reformed rakes make the best husbands?'

'What sort of wife will you require?' Poppy asked. 'A plaster saint with a blue-blooded background similar to your own?'

A sparkle of playfulness entered his gaze. 'Are you thinking of auditioning for the post?'

She pulled her chin back in against her throat. 'You must be joking. You're the very last person I would ever think of marrying.'

He gave her a mock bow before he turned to leave. 'The feeling is mutual, Miss Silverton. *Bonsoir*.'

CHAPTER FOUR

'I JUST RAN into Mr Compton on my way to work,' Chloe said the following morning. 'He said Rafe Caffarelli came in again yesterday.'

'He just had coffee.' Poppy turned to put the cream she had just whipped back in the fridge. 'Quite frankly, I don't know why he bothers. What's the point of going to a tearoom if you don't drink tea and you don't eat cake?'

'Mr Compton also told me Rafe asked you to provide evening meals for him up at the manor.' Chloe picked up her apron and began to tie it around her waist. 'That's exciting. The way to a man's heart and all that. What are you going to cook for him?'

'I'm not cooking for him.'

Chloe blinked. 'Are you crazy? He's going to pay you, isn't he?'

Poppy set her mouth stubbornly. 'That's not the point.'

'*I'll* cook for him, then,' Chloe said. 'I'll do three meals a day and morning and afternoon tea. I'll even give him breakfast in bed. God, I'm having a hot flush just thinking about it. I bet he's amazing between the sheets. He looks like he pumps some serious iron. I bet he could go all night.'

Poppy gave her a withering look. 'There is more to a

man than how he looks. What about intellect and morals? What about personal values?'

Chloe grinned at her. 'You fancy him like rotten, don't you? Go on—admit it. And I reckon he fancies you. Mr Compton reckons so too. Why else would he come in for coffee two days in a row?'

Poppy stalked over to put the cupcakes on the glass cake-stand. 'Raffaele Caffarelli has had more lovers than you and I have had hot dinners. He thinks that just because he wants something or someone he can have it. His sense of entitlement is beyond arrogant. It's deplorable.'

Chloe's eyes began to twinkle. 'You really are all fired up over him, aren't you? This can't just be about your house. Why do you dislike him so much?'

Poppy carried the cake-stand out to the tearoom. 'I'd rather not talk about it.'

Chloe followed close behind. 'Mr Compton said Rafe's going to turn Dalrymple Manor into a luxury hotel and spa. It could be really good for the village if he does. There'd be heaps of jobs for the locals, and we might even get a bit of extra business as a result.'

Poppy plonked the cake-stand down and turned to glare her. 'For the last four-hundred-and-seventy-five years, the manor has been a family home. Generations of the Dalrymple family have been born and have died there. Turning it into a plush hotel will totally destroy its character and desecrate its history.'

'I expect Rafe Caffarelli will do a very tasteful conversion,' Chloe put in. 'I checked out some of his other developments online. He's big on keeping things in context architecturally. He draws up most of the preliminary plans himself.'

Poppy was still on her soapbox and wasn't stepping down any time soon. The thought of the paparazzi hiding in the hedges in her beloved village to get their prized shot of hedonistic celebrities partying up at the manor was sickening. 'Lord Dalrymple will be spinning in his grave if this preposterous project goes ahead. What was his cousin thinking of, selling to a developer? Why couldn't they have sold to a private family instead? Another family could bring life and vibrancy to the place instead of filthy rich people wining and dining and partying at all hours.'

'You really love that old place, don't you?'

Poppy blew out a long breath. 'I know it sounds ridiculously sentimental but I think Dalrymple Manor needs a family to make it come alive again. It's spent the last sixty years grieving. You can feel the sadness when you walk in there. It's almost palpable. The stairs creak with it, sometimes even the foundations groan with it.'

Chloe's eyes rounded. 'Are you saying it's haunted?'

'I used to think so when I was a kid, but no, it's just a sad old place that needs to be filled with love and laughter and family again.'

'Maybe Rafe Caffarelli will settle down there with one of his lovers,' Chloe suggested.

'I can't see that happening,' Poppy said with an expression of disdain. 'He doesn't keep a lover more than a month or two. Playboys like him don't settle down, they just change partners.'

Chloe gave her a speculative look. 'So I take it I'm not the only one who's done a little online searching on the illustrious Rafe Caffarelli?'

Poppy went back to the kitchen with her head at a haughty height. 'I'm not the least bit interested in what that man does or who he does it with. I have much better things to do with my time.'

* * *

Just before lunch Mr Underwood, Poppy's landlord, came in to the tearoom. He usually came in on a Friday afternoon for a cup of tea and a slice of the cake of the day. Poppy desperately hoped this Tuesday visit wasn't a business one. She had a list of expenses to see to on the dower house. The place needed painting inside and out, and the garden needed urgent attention. There was an elm tree close to her bedroom that needed lopping as it was keeping her awake at night with its branches scratching at the window. Even a modest rise in rent at the shop would just about cripple her financially now.

'Your usual, Mr Underwood?' she said with a bright and hopeful smile.

'Er, can I have a word, Poppy?' John Underwood asked.

'Sure.' Poppy's smile tightened on her face. *Please don't ask for more rent*.

'I thought I should let you know I've been made an offer on the building,' John said. 'It's a good one, the best I've had, so I'm going to take it.'

She frowned. 'But I didn't realise you were even thinking of selling.'

'I've been toying with the idea for a while. Jean wants to travel a bit more. We've got three young grandchildren in the States now and we want to spend a bit more time with them. I'm selling this building and another investment property I have in Shropshire.'

Poppy felt suspicion move up her spine like a file of sugar ants. 'Who made the offer?'

'I'm not at liberty to say,' he said. 'The buyer insisted on total confidentiality until all the paperwork is done.'

She pursed her lips as the rage simmered inside her. 'I just bet he did.'

John looked uncomfortable. 'I didn't want to do the wrong thing by you, Poppy. You and Chloe are the best tenants I've had. But at the end of the day this is a business decision. It's not personal.'

Oh yes it is, Poppy thought sourly. 'We've still got another year on the lease. That won't change, will it?'

'Not unless the new owner wants to redevelop.'

'Did he say what he intended to do with it?'

'No, he just seemed really keen to acquire this particular building. He said he instantly fell in love with its old-world charm.'

'Ruthless' didn't even come close to describing Rafe Caffarelli, Poppy thought. He was clever and calculating, much more than she had realised. But she wasn't going down without a fight. There was no way she was going to let him have things all his own way. Did he really think he could twist her arm? Blackmail her into his bed by charging her an outrageously high rent? What sort of woman did he think she was? 'Will the new owner expect a rise in rent, do you think?'

'You'd have to discuss that with him.'

She gave him an ironic look. 'How can I if he wants to remain anonymous?'

'I expect the rent will be handled through an agency,' John said. 'Anyway, I just thought I should let you know I've sold. I'm not one for keeping secrets but he seemed to think it was necessary.'

Poppy ground her teeth behind her tight smile. 'I'm sure he has his reasons.'

She stalked out to the kitchen once John Underwood had left. 'Grrrh! I'm going to punch him on the nose. I'm going to scratch his eyes out. I'm going to give him a black eye. I'm going to kick him in the you-know-where.'

Chloe blinked in confusion. 'But I thought you liked

Mr Underwood. What's he done—put up the rent or something?'

'Not Mr Underwood,' Poppy said through clenched teeth. 'Rafe Caffarelli. He's bought the shop. I know it's him, even though Mr Underwood didn't actually say so. It's supposed to be a secret. And I know why—Rafe Caffarelli wants to blackmail me into his bed.'

Chloe's eyes nearly popped out of her head. 'Hey, have I missed something somewhere? Back up a little bit. Did you say he wants to *sleep* with you? Did he actually say that out loud?'

'Not in as many words, but I can see it in his eyes every time he looks at me.' Poppy clenched her hands into fists. 'I *won't* do it.'

'*I'll* do it,' Chloe said. 'What are you thinking, Poppy? He's gorgeous. He's rich. He's everything a woman could want in a man.'

Poppy set her mouth. 'Not *this* woman.'

'You're mad,' Chloe said. 'What would it hurt to have a little fling with him? He would probably give you heaps and heaps of ridiculously expensive jewellery at the end of it. You could sell them and retire.'

Poppy threw her a look of reproach. 'I had no idea you were so shallow.'

Chloe shrugged. 'Not shallow, just pragmatic. Think about it. When are you going to get the chance to move in his sort of circles? It'd be worth it just for the publicity. It'd really put the tearoom on the map.'

'I am *not* going to sleep with Rafe Caffarelli in order to bring more customers in the door.' Poppy folded her arms tightly across her chest. 'I have far more self-respect than that.'

'You're stuck in the dark ages,' Chloe said. 'Who waits for Mr Right these days? Most girls lose their virginity before they leave school. You're twenty-five for God's sake. Think of all the sex you're going to have to have to catch up.'

'I don't think about sex.' *Well, not until recently.*

'That's because you don't know what you're missing. It's not wrong to have sex before you get married. Not in this day and age.'

'I'm not necessarily waiting until I get married,' Poppy said. 'I'm waiting until I feel sure it's really what I want, and that the man is right for me.'

'It's because of what happened to your mum, isn't it?' Chloe said. 'It's made you gun-shy.'

'Maybe a bit,' Poppy confessed. 'OK, more than a bit. It ruined her life to be cast aside like that. She *never* got over it. She was truly heartbroken. She loved my father and he treated her like a silly little toy he had grown tired of. And it didn't just wreck her life, it ruined my gran's life because she got landed with a little kid to bring up.'

'Your gran loved bringing you up.'

Poppy let out a sigh. 'But my mother died so young and she didn't get to do all the things she wanted to do. I don't want that to happen to me. I want to have control over my future.'

'There are some things in life that you just can't control.'

'I know, but I'm going to focus on the ones I can.' Poppy untied her apron and tossed it on the nearest chair. 'Starting right now.'

Rafe was working on some preliminary sketches in the makeshift study he'd set up at the manor when he heard a car rumble up the driveway. He knew who it was without looking through the window. Only someone with an axe to grind would slam their car door, stomp across the gravel, to put their finger on the doorbell and leave it there. He smiled as the tinny sound assaulted his eardrums. How boring had his life been before meeting Poppy Silverton?

This was the most fun he'd had in years.

'We have to stop meeting like this,' he said as he opened the door. 'People will talk.'

Her toffee-brown eyes were slitted, her hands were fisted and her slim body was rigid. 'You...you calculating, low-life swine.'

He raised a brow at her. 'It's nice to see you too.'

She vibrated on the spot like a battery-operated tin soldier. 'I can't believe how ruthless you are. You bought my shop!'

'So? I'm a property developer. I buy property.'

Her pretty little mouth was white-tipped with fury. 'I know what you're doing but it won't work.'

Rafe leaned casually against the doorjamb. 'What is it you think I'm doing?'

'You're going to blackmail me.' She glowered at him darkly. 'You must know I can barely afford the rent as it is. But it won't work. I won't prostitute myself to someone like you.'

He tapped his index finger against his lips for a moment. 'Mmm, I can see I have some work to do to improve the impression you have of me. What makes you think I'm going to raise the rent?'

She looked at him warily. 'You mean...you're not?'

He shook his head.

'But why did you buy the shop?'

'I like it.'

She narrowed her eyes again. 'You...*like* it?'

'It's unique.'

'What do you mean?'

'I like the idea of a traditional tearoom. It's classy. It makes a nice change from the somewhat impersonal and boring coffee chains.'

A little pleat of scepticism appeared between her eyes. 'You don't even drink tea.'

'That's true, but maybe I haven't tasted the perfect cup. A cheap, dusty tea bag jiggled in a Styrofoam cup is probably nothing like the real deal. Maybe you could educate me in the art of drinking proper, high-quality leaf tea.'

She was still looking at him in suspicion. 'Why do I get the feeling you're not really talking about tea?'

Rafe gave her a lazy smile. 'What else could I be talking about?'

Her cheeks went a deep shade of rose and her soft mouth flattened primly. 'If you want to taste proper tea, then come to the tearoom four o'clock this afternoon.'

He held her gaze in a smouldering little lockdown. 'I'd prefer a private lesson. I don't want to be distracted by other customers. It might ruin the experience for me.'

She gave him a flinty 'I know what you're up to' look. 'All right,' she said. 'Come at five-thirty. I'll put the closed sign on the door.'

'It's a date.'

Rafe watched as she turned on her heel and stomped back to her car. He gave her a wave as she drove away but she didn't return it. With a toss of that fiery head, she put her car into gear and rattled off down the drive, leaving a billowing cloud of dust in her wake.

CHAPTER FIVE

CHLOE UNTIED HER apron at five o'clock. 'I just got a call from my mum. She wants me to pick up some of her asthma medication at the pharmacy on my way home. Do you mind if I leave now?'

Poppy tried to ignore the little flutter of alarm in her belly. She didn't mind giving Rafe Caffarelli a private lesson in the art of tea drinking, but she hadn't planned on it being *that* private. She had banked on Chloe being in the background in case he wanted to have his cake and eat it too, so to speak. 'No, you go,' she said, releasing a little breath of resignation. 'Say hi to your mum from me. Take her some of that double-chocolate slice she likes so much.'

Chloe's smile was teasing. 'Will you be all right entertaining the deliciously ruthless, rich and racy Rafe Caffarelli on your little ownsome?'

Poppy put on a confident smile that in no way reflected how she was feeling. 'Of course.'

The door chime sounded at five-thirty-five. Poppy had been watching the clock ever since Chloe had left. As each minute had crawled by, her heart rate had gone up. She came out of the kitchen as casually as she could even though her stomach was pitching and falling like a paperboat in a jacuzzi.

Rafe stooped as he came in the door. He was dressed a little more formally this time in charcoal-grey trousers and a crisp white shirt teamed with a dark-blue blazer and a silver-grey tie. He had shaved since she had seen him earlier that day. He had showered too, as his hair was still damp and had the groove marks in it from a brush or comb.

'I'm sorry I'm late.'

Poppy couldn't read his expression, but she knew one thing for certain—he wasn't one bit sorry. 'I've set up the table by the window. Take a seat while I put the kettle on.'

'Can't I watch?'

She pursed her lips at him. His dark eyes were pools of black ink but there was a hint of amusement lurking there; she was sure of it. 'I can assure you there's nothing remotely interesting in watching a kettle come to the boil.'

'There is if you're the one boiling it.'

She gave him a schoolmarmish look. 'Are you flirting with me, Mr Caffarelli?'

'Call me Rafe.'

'Rafe…' Poppy felt like she had crossed an invisible line by calling him by his preferred name.

His eyes held hers in an intimate tether. It felt like another line had been crossed, a far more intimate one. Her gaze went to his mouth, as if pulled there by a powerful magnet. Her lips tingled as she wondered what it would feel like to have his pressed against them. Would he kiss firmly or with seductive softness? She felt a tiny shiver pass over her skin as her thoughts continued on their erotic journey… What would it feel like to have his hands cup her breasts or stroke between her…?

'Poppy.'

'Yes?' Her tongue made a quick darting movement over her lips.

His mouth tilted in a sexy smile. 'It's a cute name. It suits you.'

Cute? He didn't think she was stunningly beautiful or gorgeous, just cute, like a puppy or a kitten. 'Thank you.' She gave him a tight, on-off smile. 'Um…the kitchen's this way.'

Poppy went through the motion of putting on the kettle but the whole time she was aware of Rafe's impossibly dark gaze resting on her. She told him how it was important to fill the kettle with fresh cold water each time, and how it was important to warm the teapot before spooning in the leaves—one for each person and one for the pot. 'Tea always tastes nicer from a china cup,' she said. 'Cheap thick, chunky mugs just don't cut it, I'm afraid.'

He was looking at her with a smile lurking in those coal-black eyes. 'Fascinating.'

'Yes, well, I admit I'm a bit old-school about it, but there you go.' She put a hand-knitted cosy on the teapot and placed it on the tray she had laid out earlier.

'Let me carry that for you.'

She felt the brush of his fingers against hers as he took the tray. It felt like a charge of electricity shooting to that secret place between her thighs.

Her eyes locked with his for a pulsing moment.

His eyes were so dark she couldn't see where his pupils began or ended. She could smell the clean, male scent of him—the subtle hint of lemon and lime with an understory of something woody and fresh, like a native pine forest. This close she could see the individual pinpoints of his cleanly shaven jaw. Within a few hours it would be dark and prickly around that sculptured mouth and determined chin. Even now it would rasp if she touched it with the softness of her fingertips…

Poppy curled her fingertips into her palm and shifted her gaze away from his. 'Right… Well, let's go and have tea.'

Once the table was set up, Rafe guided her to her seat with a hand at her elbow. Poppy felt another shiver shimmy up her spine at the contact of his skin on hers. She couldn't recall a time when she had been more acutely aware of a man. Everything about him stirred her senses until she could hardly get her brain to focus on the task at hand.

'Um…do you take milk?'

'I don't know.' He gave her a wry smile. 'Should I?'

'It rather depends on the type of tea,' Poppy said. 'I drink English breakfast with milk, but I drink Earl Grey, Darjeeling, Russian Caravan and Jasmine black. But at the end of the day, it's all a matter of personal taste.'

'Give it to me straight, just like my coffee.'

She poured him a cup and watched as he took a taste. He wrinkled up his nose and put the cup back down in its saucer.

'Well?'

'It's a bit flavourless.'

'*Flavourless?*'

'Bland.'

'It's the highest quality Ceylon tea, for God's sake,' Poppy said. 'What is *wrong* with your taste buds?'

'Nothing's wrong with my taste buds. I just don't like tea.'

'How about if you try it with some milk and sugar?'

'I'll try the milk but not the sugar.' He gave her a heart-stopping smile. 'I'm sweet enough.'

Poppy rolled her eyes. 'Here.' She handed him his cup again. 'Taste it now.'

He went through the same routine, wrinkling up his nose as he took a tentative sip. He put the cup back down again. 'Doesn't float my boat, I'm afraid.'

'You don't like it?'

'It's nondescript.'

'It's not nondescript,' she said. 'It's subtle.'

'It's just not my cup of tea.' He flashed her that grin again. 'Sorry, no pun intended.'

Poppy shook her head at him, trying not to smile. He could be incredibly charming when he put his mind to it. She would have to be careful not to let her guard down. He was the enemy. It wouldn't do to think of him as anything else. 'You're incorrigible.'

'That's what my mother used to say.'

There was something almost wistful about his tone. She wondered if he was close to his family. She picked up her own cup and took a sip. 'Where do your parents live? In France or Italy?'

The light had gone out of his eyes. 'They don't.'

'Pardon?'

'They don't live anywhere. They're dead. They were killed when I was ten.'

'I'm sorry…' Poppy bit her lip. Maybe she should have done a little more research on him. The article she had come across had mentioned nothing about his childhood, only about his playboy status, wealth and the latest lover he'd been with.

'It was a long time ago.'

'What happened?'

He picked up his teaspoon and began toying with it between his finger and thumb like one would do a pen. 'They had a high-speed collision with another motorboat on the French Rivera. My mother was killed instantly. My father died in hospital three days later from internal injuries.'

'I'm so sorry... It must have been a terrible time for you and your brothers.'

A flicker of pain passed through his eyes before he lowered them to look at the spoon he was holding. 'Yes. It was.'

'What happened afterwards? I mean...where did you go? Who looked after you and your brothers?'

'My paternal grandfather took us in.' He put down the spoon, picked up his teacup and cradled it in his hands.

'Is he still alive?'

'Yes.'

'Are you close to him?'

His lip curled but not in a smile. 'No one is close to my grandfather.'

Poppy could tell he wasn't keen to reveal too much about his background. But his cryptic comment about his grandfather was rather intriguing. What sort of man was Vittorio Caffarelli? Had he made the lives of the three bereaved boys even more miserable in his handling and rearing of them? 'What about your grandmother? Was she involved in your upbringing?'

'No, she died of cancer when my father was a teenager.'

'What about your maternal grandparents?'

Rafe turned the cup around in its saucer. 'They died before I was born.' He picked up the cup and took a sip, grimacing at the taste before he put it back down again. 'Tell me about your childhood. You said you lost your parents when you were seven. How did they die?'

Poppy looked down at her hands for a moment as she began folding and refolding her napkin. 'I never met my father. He deserted my mother before I was born. Apparently she wasn't good enough for him so he married someone else.'

'So your grandmother raised you?'

She nodded as she met his gaze again. 'She was wonderful, stepping in to take care of me after my mother died. I had a good childhood, all things considered. Lord Dalrymple was incredibly kind to me. He was a bit of a recluse but he always had time for me.'

'Were you disappointed he didn't leave you and your grandmother the manor as well as the dower house when he died?'

Poppy blinked at him in shock. 'Of course not. Why would we be? We weren't blood relatives. My gran was just his housekeeper.'

He gave a shrug of one broad shoulder. 'Your grandmother worked for him a very long time.'

'She loved working for him. She loved him.'

He arched an eyebrow. '*Loved* him?'

Poppy let out a breath in a little whoosh. 'I think maybe she did love him a little bit like that. Not that he would ever have noticed. He was living in the past, grieving for his dead wife Clara. But my gran never expected anything from him. She wasn't like that. It was a total shock to her when he left us the dower house. It was a nice gesture. It meant a lot to her. She'd never owned anything in her life, not even a car. She had grown up dirt poor and relatively uneducated. She'd been a cleaner since she was fifteen. To suddenly find herself the owner of a house was such a dream come true.'

'It must have been a shock to his family that he left the dower house to his housekeeper and her granddaughter.'

'Yes, there was a bit of a fuss over the separation of the deeds.' Poppy looked at him again but his expression was inscrutable. 'But Lord Dalrymple had made it clear in his will that we were to have it.'

'And then when she died her share of the house went to you.'

'Yes.'

There was a loaded silence.

'It's just a house, Poppy.'

She threw him a flinty look. 'It's not just a house. It's much more than that.'

'You can buy a much better place with the money I'm offering you. A place three times the size and with little or no upkeep.'

Poppy resented how he had gone from attentive listener to hard-nosed businessman in a heartbeat. She had been momentarily lulled into thinking he had a softer side underneath that ruthlessly tough exterior.

He was not soft.

He was as hard as steel and she had better not forget it. 'Why is the dower house such an issue for you? Isn't the manor enough? You have properties all over the globe. Why are you being so pigheaded and stubborn about a little dower house in a tiny little village in the English countryside?'

His mouth was set in an intractable line. 'I *want* that house. It belongs to the estate. It should never have been taken off the deeds.'

Poppy gave him a challenging glare. 'That house belongs to me. You can't have it. Get over it.'

His diamond-hard eyes bored like a drill into hers. 'Don't mess with me, Poppy. You have no idea how ruthless I can be if I have to.'

She got to her feet with an ear-piercing screech of chair legs against the floorboards. 'Get out of my shop.'

He gave her an imperious smile. 'It's my shop now—remember?'

Fury coursed through her body like a flash of hot fire. She wanted to slap him. She had never felt so tempted to resort to physical violence. She clenched her hands into fists, her body shaking with impotent rage. 'What are you going to do—charge me an exorbitant rent? Go ahead. Make me pay. I'll go public with it. I'll tell everyone you tried to blackmail me to sleep with you. I'll speak to every newspaper. Don't think I won't do it, because I will.'

He laughed, which made her all the more furious. 'I really like your spirit. No one has ever stood up to me quite like you do. But you're not going to win this. I *always* get what I want.'

Poppy glowered at him. '*Get out.*'

His eyes glinted at her goadingly as he leisurely got to his feet. 'Call the papers. Tell them what you like. They'll just think you're another wannabe gold-digger after money and fame. You'll be the one with mud on your face, not me.' He took out his wallet. 'How much do I owe for the tea?'

Poppy gave him a look that would have stripped graffiti off a wall. 'It's on the house.'

He held her gaze for a long, throbbing moment. 'I meant what I said about the rent. I don't intend to make any changes to the arrangements you made with John Underwood.'

She flashed him another caustic glare. 'Am I supposed to thank you? Kiss your feet? Prostrate myself before you? Go on, lay one finger on me and see what happens. I dare you— *Oomph*!'

His hands had grasped her upper arms so quickly she

didn't have time to do much more than snatch a quick breath before his mouth came down on hers.

It was a hard, possessive kiss, a hot fizzing pressure against her lips that made them tingle as if high-voltage electricity was passing directly from his body to hers.

Poppy had intended to fight him, but somehow as soon as his mouth connected with hers her lips softened and became totally pliant, melting beneath the fiery purpose of his. She opened to his command and tasted the full potent heat of him, the bold thrust of his tongue going in search of hers with erotic intent. He explored every corner of her mouth with spine-tingling thoroughness, leaving her breathless and barely able to stand upright.

But, even more *mortifying*, she gave a soft little whimper of approval just before he broke the connection.

It was of some slight consolation to her that he looked just as shocked as she felt. His eyes were almost black and a frown had appeared between his eyebrows as he dropped his hands from her upper arms and took an unsteady step back from her.

Poppy tried to think of something witty or pithy to say but her mouth was still hanging open in stupefaction.

He inclined his head in a formal nod, his expression now unfathomable. 'Thank you for the tea lesson. It was very…' He paused over the choice of a word. 'Entertaining.'

Poppy let out her breath in a flustered rush once he had gone. She knew the battle was far from over.

It was just beginning.

CHAPTER SIX

'I THINK YOU'RE being very pig-headed about this,' Chloe said a couple of days later. 'I keep thinking of that poor man starving up there at the manor.'

Poppy snorted. 'He's probably got a bevy of blonde bombshells to peel his grapes for him. Anyway, what's wrong with a microwave dinner every now and again?'

'I can't believe I'm hearing this,' Chloe said. 'You— the cooking-from-scratch queen of the kitchen.'

Poppy couldn't stop a reluctant smile from forming. 'I'm not averse to the odd bit of convenience food. I had baked beans on toast last night.'

Chloe covered her ears. 'Don't use such filthy language in my hearing.'

The chime on the door sounded and Poppy's heart gave a little stumble. 'You get that. I've got to get the cookies out of the oven.'

Chloe snatched the oven mitts out of Poppy's grasp. 'He's not here to see me, more's the pity.'

'How do you know it's him?'

Chloe gave her a knowing look. 'Because you don't blush like a rose when anyone else opens that door.'

'It's only because I dislike him so much.'

'Yeah, and I hate chocolate.'

Poppy threw her shoulders back and walked briskly

out into the tearoom. 'Good morning, Mr Caffarelli. Your usual?'

'I'm not here for coffee.'

She gave him a pert look. 'Tea?'

An enigmatic smile played at the edges of his mouth while her mouth tingled in memory of his hot, hard kiss. 'Are you free for dinner tonight?' he asked.

Poppy drew in a tight little breath as she put her hands on her hips. The hide of him! Where on earth did he get access to so much arrogance and confidence? Was it coded in his DNA? 'You don't give up easily, do you?'

'It's not in my nature.'

Chloe popped her head around the door. 'She'd love to go out to dinner. She's not busy. She hasn't been out on a date with anyone for more than three months.'

Poppy swung back and threw Chloe a livid glare. 'Do you mind?'

'What harm will it do to have a meal with him?' Chloe said. 'You know you want to.'

'I do not want to!'

'She *does* want to,' Chloe said with authority to Rafe. 'It will do her good. She needs to get out more.'

'I swear to God I'm going to—'

'So it's a date,' Rafe said. 'I'll pick you up at seven. I thought we could go to that new restaurant in the next village everyone is talking about.'

'I'm *not* go—'

'What should she wear?' Chloe said before Poppy could finish spluttering her protest.

'Surprise me.' He gave them both a smile and walked back out the door.

'You're fired,' Poppy said, flashing Chloe another deadly glare.

'You don't mean that,' Chloe said. 'Anyway, what

could be more perfect than going to Oliver's restaurant with the seriously rich, staggeringly handsome Rafe Caffarelli as your date? How cool a payback is that? I wish I could be a fly on the wall when that two-timing pig sees you walking in on Rafe's arm. It's a perfect way to show him you're over him.'

'I didn't have to get over him in the first place,' Poppy said, folding her arms across her chest.

'Sure you didn't.' Chloe gave her another knowing look. 'You cried your heart out for a week. And you ate a whole cheesecake.'

'*Half* a cheesecake.' Poppy scowled at her. 'And I only cried because I really wanted to have someone in my life...someone to belong to. Ever since Gran died, I feel like I don't belong to anyone any more.'

Chloe gave her a big squishy hug. 'You belong to this village, Poppy. Everyone loves you. We're your family now.'

Poppy chewed at her lip as she walked back to the kitchen. Maybe Chloe was right—it would be a good way to demonstrate to Oliver she had moved on.

But Rafe Caffarelli?

He was crafty and clever. Everything he did was with a specific purpose in mind. She knew he wanted her house, but what if it wasn't just the house he had set his mind to possess?

Especially after that explosive kiss...

She refused to think about that kiss. She had tried to block it from her mind. Every time she thought of it she cringed at how *willing* she had been, almost desperate, practically hanging off him like a limpet, before he'd put her from him.

She couldn't make him out. He had bought her shop,

yet he hadn't raised the rent and had told her he wasn't going to. Could she trust him not to suddenly change his mind? Was he trying to charm her by stealth?

He could hardly be in doubt of her attraction to him now. She tried her best to hide it but he was so damnably attractive! His casually tousled hair and the dark stubble on his jaw would have looked dishevelled or scruffy on someone else. On him it looked sexy and it made her fingers twitch to reach up and thread through those dark, silky strands or to stroke that chiselled plane of his jaw.

And his mouth… She gulped as she thought of the contours of his lips, how they were so finely sculptured and yet so utterly masculine; how he had tasted; so warm and yet so fresh. Would he kiss her again? Was that why he was taking her out to dinner? Would she have the strength of will to resist him?

Of course.

She'd been caught off-guard before. He had taken advantage of her momentary lapse of concentration. She would be better prepared this time. He could dazzle her with whatever strength of charm he liked.

She was back in control.

Rafe pulled up at the dower house just at seven. There was a cacophony of mad barking from inside the house as he raised his hand to the knocker. He heard Poppy shushing the dogs with limited success and then she opened the door.

'You look…' He was momentarily lost for words. 'Amazing.'

She was wearing a slim black cocktail dress that was simple but elegant, highlighting her trim figure without in any way exploiting it. The subtle sexiness was heartstopping. Rafe swore his heart actually did miss a beat.

She had her hair up in one of those artful twists that looked both casual and elegant at the same time. She had a simple string of pearls around her graceful neck and matching earrings, that he suspected weren't terribly expensive, but with her creamy skin as a backdrop they looked as if they had just come out of a bank vault. Her make-up was light and yet it highlighted every one of her girl-next-door features: the high cheekbones, the cinnamon-brown eyes and the perfect bow of her mouth, which had a fine layer of shimmery gloss on it.

He still couldn't get his mind to stop revisiting that kiss. It was on permanent replay in his head. He couldn't remember a time when a kiss had affected him so much. He had kissed dozens, probably hundreds of women. But something about Poppy Silverton's sweet mouth melting into his had sent an arrow of longing deep inside him that had nagged at him like a toothache ever since.

He wanted her. *Badly.*

'I'll just get my wrap and purse.' She ushered the little mutts back with a shooing gesture and bent to pick up her belongings from the hall table.

Rafe's gaze travelled the length of her legs, from her thin ankles encased in sexy high heels to the neat curve of her bottom. One of the little dogs—the one with a patch of black over one eye, like a pirate—growled at him warningly.

'Down, boy,' Poppy said.

'Are you talking to me or the dog?' Rafe asked.

A delicate blush bloomed over her cheeks as she put her wrap around her shoulders. 'Pickles is a little shy of strangers. But once he gets to know you he'll be all over you like a rash.'

'I can hardly wait.'

Her blush deepened a fraction. 'So…you like dogs?'

'I love dogs.' Rafe bent down and scratched behind Chutney's ears. Relish came over and pushed his mate out of the way to get in on the action, but Pickles was maintaining his beady-eyed stand-off, eyeing Rafe with the sort of suspicion a protective father might cast upon a suitor who had come to collect his teenage daughter for her first date.

'Do you have a dog at home?' Poppy asked.

Rafe straightened. 'No, I travel too much. It wouldn't be fair to leave it with household staff.'

'Where do you base yourself? Italy or France?'

'I have a villa in Umbria and one in Lyon. A have apartments in Rome and Paris I use for business trips. Our family owns a few villas in other locations around the globe. I won't bore you with listing them.'

She gave him a look. 'Which do you love the most?'

Rafe had loved the smallish but comfortable villa just outside Rome he and his brothers had grown up in before their parents were killed. Conscious of the extreme wealth she was marrying into, his mother had insisted on a more normal upbringing for her boys, reducing household staff to a minimum and even doing a lot of the cooking herself.

But his grandfather had sold the villa after Rafe's parents had been killed. He hadn't consulted Rafe or his brothers about it. It had been delivered to them as a fait accompli. It had been devastating to lose not just their parents but their home as well. It was as if everything they had held most secure had disappeared. As a result Rafe tried not to get too attached to people or places or things. His brothers were exactly the same.

'I don't have a favourite,' he said. 'They each serve their purpose.' He held the door open. 'Shall we go?'

Rafe settled her in the car before he got behind the wheel. 'So, three months since your last date?'

'Chloe had no right to tell you that.'

'I'm glad she told me. I wouldn't want to be cutting in on anyone's territory.'

She sent him a narrow-eyed look. 'This isn't a date.'

'What is it then?'

She clutched her purse tightly on her lap. 'It's just a dinner between two…um…'

'Friends?'

'Associates.'

Rafe gave a little chuckle of amusement. 'I'm surprised you didn't say enemies. I must be improving a little in your estimation.'

'Not that much.'

'Come now, Poppy,' he chided. 'Let's not spoil our first date with bickering like children.'

'It's not a date!'

Rafe smiled as he pulled into a space outside the restaurant. 'Sure it's not.'

Poppy forced herself to stop scowling as she entered the restaurant with Rafe. She also had to stop herself from shivering in reaction when he put a gentle guiding hand to the small of her back. The electric sensation of his touch burned through the fabric of her dress. The sharp, citrusy scent of him made her nostrils flare. He was dressed in a dark-grey suit but he hadn't bothered with a tie. His shirt was a pale shade of blue, which brought out the olive tone of his skin. He was simply the most gorgeous man she had ever laid eyes on.

But it wasn't just his looks. It was the way he carried himself that was equally attractive. He had a commanding presence, an aura of authority that made people stop in their tracks.

The *maître d'* was a case in point. Poppy watched as Oliver's new girlfriend Morgan practically swooned when she came over to greet Rafe. 'Mr Caffarelli, it's wonderful to welcome you here,' she gushed. 'We've saved the very best table for you.' She cast a cooler look towards Poppy. 'Hi, Poppy. How's the teashop going?'

'Hello, Morgan,' Poppy said. 'It's going just fine. We've been flat out just lately. I've been run off my feet.'

Morgan gave a tight smile. 'Come this way.'

Once they were seated at their table and Morgan had left them with menus, Rafe raised his brows at Poppy. 'Friend or foe?' he asked.

Poppy picked up the menu with a huffy shrug of one shoulder. 'I'd rather not talk about it if you don't mind.'

'Let me guess.'

'I'd rather you didn't.'

He leaned forward and pushed the menu she was using as a screen down with his index finger so he could mesh his gaze with hers. 'The guy who runs this place… Oliver Kentridge…he and you were an item, what, about three months ago?'

Poppy pressed her lips together without responding.

'And the Morag girl—'

'Morgan.'

'Sorry, Morgan—is the one who lured him away from you, right?'

Poppy let out a breath that sent her stiff shoulders down in a little slump. 'I don't think it's fair to blame Morgan for all of it. Oliver wasn't getting what he wanted from me so he went to her. If he cared about me he wouldn't have strayed. Obviously he didn't care enough.'

A little pleat of a frown pulled the skin together over his eyes. 'What wasn't he getting from you?'

Poppy shifted in her seat. This wasn't exactly the conversation one had in a public restaurant, was it? Not that anyone was sitting nearby, but still… 'Um…'

'Sex?'

She looked at his incredulous expression and felt a blush steal over her cheeks. 'Why are you looking at me like that?'

'You refused to have sex with him?'

Poppy leaned forward and hissed at him, '*Will you please keep your voice down?*'

He leaned forward as well, resting his forearms on the table so his hands were within reach of hers. His gaze was very dark and very focused as it held hers. 'How long had you been going out?'

'A couple of months.'

His frown deepened. 'So what was the problem? You didn't fancy him or something?'

'I sort of did.'

'What does that mean?'

Poppy gave a helpless shrug. 'I think I wanted it to be more than it actually was… Our relationship, I mean. I was lonely after my gran died. I wanted to be with someone. I'd known Oliver for years. He was one of the guys I'd gone to school with. We had a lot in common, or so I thought. We both moved to London to do hospitality training. When he came back a few months ago we sort of got together.'

'So why didn't you sleep with him?'

Somehow one of his hands had found one of hers. Poppy looked down at the way his long, tanned fingers had curled around her lighter-toned ones, creating a circle of intimacy that would make any onlookers automatically assume their relationship was a sexual one. It made an involuntary shiver trickle down her spine. It made a liquid heat pulse between her thighs.

She took a scatty little breath. 'I wanted to wait a bit...'

'For what?'

'To see if the chemistry was right.'

'Clearly it wasn't.'

'No...'

The approach of Morgan with the list of the day's specials put a pause on the conversation. But, instead of leaning back in his chair, Rafe kept hold of Poppy's hand across the table. She was conscious of his warm, dry fingers curled around hers in an embrace that had an undercurrent of sensuality to it. She felt the slow stroke of his thumb against the underside of her wrist. It was a mesmerising movement that stirred her blood to fever pitch.

Morgan's eyes went to their joined hands before she addressed Rafe. 'Would you care for a pre-dinner drink?'

'Champagne,' Rafe said with an easy smile. 'Bring us your best.'

Morgan's eyes widened but she maintained her professional stance and nodded.

Poppy looked at him pointedly once Morgan had left. 'Champagne?'

He gave her a twinkling look that was devastatingly attractive. 'I finally convinced you to go out on a date with me. I think that's worth celebrating, don't you?'

'You didn't convince me.' She gave him a slitted look. 'You *coerced* me.'

He brought her hand up to his mouth, holding it against the slight graze of his newly shaven chin, causing a frisson of delight to pass through her entire body from head to toe. 'You wanted to come. Go on—admit it. You wouldn't be here now if you didn't. You would've found some excuse or slammed the door in my face when I arrived to pick you up. But no, you were ready and waiting for me.'

Poppy was annoyed with herself for being so predictable. Why *hadn't* she slammed the door in his face? 'I don't trust you, that's why. How do I know you're not going to suddenly change your mind about the rent?'

'Because that's not the way I do business.'

'But a teashop is hardly at the top of your list of must-be-acquired assets,' she said. 'It's nothing like your normal investments.'

'I'm all for a bit of diversifying.'

Poppy tried to read his expression but he was a master at keeping his cards close to his chest. She knew she was a novelty to him, hence the little quip about diversifying. She was probably the first woman who had ever said no to him. The trouble was she wasn't sure how much longer she *could* say no. Even now her eyes kept tracking to his mouth. She had felt his smile against the sensitive skin of her hand and it had set every nerve fizzing. What would it feel like to have that mouth press against hers again? Was that where tonight was heading?

Would he settle for just a kiss this time?

Would *she* settle for just a kiss?

Expectation, excitement, nervousness and anticipation were a heady mix in her bloodstream.

Would he expect *more* than a kiss?

There was no denying the chemistry that sizzled between them. It had been there right from the moment he had walked through the door of her tearoom. The problem was, what was she going to do about it?

Morgan came out with their champagne. 'So, what are we celebrating?' she asked as she popped the cork.

Rafe gave her another laid-back smile. 'Nothing special—just dinner between friends.'

Morgan's expression was sour around the edges as she directed her gaze to Poppy's. 'I didn't realise you moved in such elevated circles. There's been nothing in the press about you being involved with each other.'

Rafe's hand tightened warningly as it covered Poppy's. 'We're trying to keep a low profile. We'd appreciate your discretion.'

'Of course.' Morgan gave another one of her stiff smiles before she left.

Poppy glowered at him. 'What the hell are you doing? She'll phone the nearest journalist and give an exclusive. I bet she'll even tell them what we ate and drank.'

'So?'

'*So?* How can you be so casual about this? You deliberately gave her the impression we were seeing each other. I'll be laughed at and mocked in the press. I'm nothing like the women you usually date. Everyone will make horrible comments about me and call me a gold-digger or something equally offensive.'

Just like they had done to her mother.

Poppy had found some of the news clippings in her gran's things after she had died. It had been devastating to find out a little more of her mother's back story. How a normal, mostly sensible girl had been lured into a rich man's world and dropped when she'd ceased to be of interest to him. Poppy was sure that was what had shattered her mother—the public humiliation of being rejected, discarded like a toy that no longer held any appeal. Poppy's playboy father had denied paternity when her mother had told him she was pregnant, and in those days it hadn't been as easy to prove or disprove as it was today when you could buy a testing kit online. Her mother had been painted as a social-climbing, gold-digging slut who wanted to land herself a rich husband.

Wouldn't the same be said about Poppy if she were seen in the press with Rafe Caffarelli?

'Why are you so worried about what people will think?' he asked.

Poppy chewed at her lower lip. 'It's all right for you. You're used to it. I bet hardly a day goes by without an article appearing somewhere with you at the centre of it. I hate having my photo taken even when I'm prepared for it. Some unscrupulous photographer will probably catch me off-guard with parsley stuck in my teeth, or without make-up, or dressed in my shabbiest tracksuit or something.'

He was looking at her with a smile tilting the edge of his mouth. 'I quite liked how you looked in that tracksuit the other night.'

'It had lint balls all over it.'

'I think you looked stunning in it.'

Poppy picked up her champagne flute for something to do with her hands. He was lethally charming in this playful, flirty mood. But she mustn't forget she had something he wanted—the dower house. He had tried other means to get her to sell it to him. Maybe this new approach was nothing to do with how attractive or unique or *cute* he found her, but rather another clever ploy of his to achieve his goal. 'I suppose you think that if you flatter me enough I'll change my mind and sell you my house?'

'I think you're mistaking my motives.'

She gave him an arch look. 'Oh really? So you're going to sit there and tell me you asked me out to dinner, not as a ploy to get me to change my mind, but just because you find my company scintillating?'

That sexy half-smile was still lurking around the edges of his mouth. 'I find your company electrifying. You're so unlike anyone I've ever met before.'

Poppy felt her belly do a complicated tumble turn as his wicked gaze held hers. 'I guess I must be even more of a challenge to you now.'

'Why's that?'

'Because I'm…you know…what I told you before.'

He cocked his head quizzically. 'What did you tell me before?'

Poppy blew out a breath. Did she really have to spell it out for him? She felt the heat of embarrassment ride up from her neck as the silence continued.

Finally, she let out a little breath and dropped the V-bomb. 'I'm still a virgin.'

CHAPTER SEVEN

RAFE PICKED HIS jaw up from the table where he felt it had dropped. 'Are you serious?'

'I told you before…'

'You told me you hadn't slept with your ex. You didn't tell me you hadn't slept with *anyone*.'

Her expression was defensive. 'Go on—call me a dinosaur. Call me a pariah.'

Rafe couldn't get his head around it. He had slept with dozens of women and not one of them had ever been without experience. Some had had much more than him, particularly those he had slept with in his teens.

He liked to think he didn't operate a double-standard; he liked to think he was as twenty-first-century, open and progressive about sex as everyone else. But something about Poppy's inexperience struck a chord of something terribly old-fashioned deep inside him that he hadn't even been aware of possessing until now.

A virgin.

In this day and age!

Rafe looked at her taking careful sips of her champagne, her toffee-brown gaze meeting his every now and again, as if she was trying to act normal in a totally abnormal situation. Or at least, it was abnormal for him.

He had the routine down pat: dinner and sex. It was

a combo that always worked. He couldn't remember a time when it hadn't.

He always got the girl.

But Poppy Silverton was another story. From the moment he had walked into that tearoom of hers he had seen her as the enemy that he would eventually conquer, but somehow she had the edge on him now. It was laughably ironic. He was known for his steely determination, for his merciless intent, yet in this case he felt totally ambushed.

He had not seen this coming. He had been totally unprepared for it. She was the most fascinating and intriguing woman he had ever encountered.

And she hated him.

OK, so that was a minor problem, but he could work on that—get to know her, charm her a little and get her to feel a little more comfortable around him.

Get her to sell him her house.

That was still his goal. Nothing was going to sway him from it. He didn't back down from his goals, not for anyone. He wanted that house because without it the Dalrymple Estate would not be complete. He didn't do things in half-measures. When he set his sights on something he got it. It didn't matter what or who was standing in the way of it. The fact that a mere slip of a red-haired girl was standing in his way was immaterial. There had to be a way around this so he could win.

He always won.

Losing would be playing into his grandfather's belief about him—that he was not good enough, not strong enough to withstand the opposition. Vittorio had instilled in him and his brothers the sense that, like their late father, they were just paltry imitations of him. That *he* was the patriarch that no one could or would dare to outshine.

His grandfather's arrogance had fuelled Rafe's determination since childhood. It was like a river of steel in
his blood. He abhorred failure. It was a word that didn't
exist in his mind, let alone his vocabulary.

Rafe wasn't supposed to *like* his enemy. He wasn't
supposed to respect her, or be intrigued by her, or want
her like he had wanted no other woman. Desire was a
pulsating force inside him even now. Just watching the
way her lips cupped around the rim of her glass as she
sipped from her champagne flute made him hard. He
watched the rise and fall of her slim throat as she swallowed and wondered what it would feel like to have those
rosy-red lips suck on him, to bring him to the brink of
primal pleasure…

'So how did you get to the age of…?'

'Twenty-five.'

Twenty-five! He'd lost count of the number of lovers
he'd had by the age of twenty, let alone twenty-five. 'How
did you get to that age without having sex?'

'I didn't want to end up like my mother, falling for
the first guy who paid her a compliment,' she said. 'I
guess it made me overly cautious. I just wanted to be
sure my first time was with the right person. It's not that
I'm hankering after a wedding ring or anything. And it's
not because of religious beliefs, although I have a lot of
respect for those who have them.'

Rafe wished he could say the same. But the God of
his childhood hadn't answered his prayers the day his
parents had been killed. He had felt alone in the universe
that day and the feeling had never quite left him. 'I don't
think you're a pariah at all,' he said. 'I also think there's
nothing wrong in being selective about who you sleep
with. To tell you the truth, I wish I'd been a bit more selective at times.'

She gave him a tiny 'let's change the subject' smile. 'What do your brothers do?'

Making neutral conversation was good. *He could do that.* 'Raoul's involved in the family business on the investment side of things but he also runs a thoroughbred stud in Normandy. He's a bit of an extreme sportsman; not only does he ride horses at breakneck speeds, he's a daredevil skier on both snow and water. And Remy is a business broker. He buys ailing businesses, builds them up and sells them for a profit. He loves his risks too. I guess it's the gambler in him.'

'You must be constantly worrying about both of them. I'm almost glad I'm an only child.'

Rafe had survived the loss of his parents but the thought of losing either of his brothers was something that haunted him. They were both so precious to him. He didn't tell them—he rarely showed his affection for them, or they for him—but he would be truly devastated if anything happened to either of them. Ever since he was ten it had been his responsibility to keep watch over them. 'We each have our own lives. We try and catch up when we're in the same country but we don't interfere with what any of us is doing unless it's to do with the family business.'

'What role does your grandfather play in the business?'

'He's taken a bit of a back seat lately, which is not something that comes naturally to him,' Rafe said. 'He had a mild stroke a couple of months ago. If anything, it's made him even more cantankerous.'

She looked at him for a little moment. 'You don't like him very much, do you?'

Rafe shifted his mouth in a rueful manner. 'I try and tell myself it must have been hard for him, suddenly being landed with three young boys to raise, but the truth is he was never really all that interested in us even before our parents were killed. My father and he had always had a strained relationship. But it got worse when my mother came on the scene. My grandfather didn't approve of my father's choice of wife. It wasn't just that my mother was French and lowly born. I think it was more to do with jealousy than anything.'

Poppy's brow lifted. 'Jealousy?'

'Yes, he hated that my father was happily settled with someone while his wife—my grandmother—was lying cold in her grave.'

'Did he ever see someone else or think about remarrying?'

Rafe made a little sound of derision. 'Oh, he had his women; he'd had them while my grandmother was still alive: housemaids, cleaners, local girls who he paid to keep silent with a few trinkets. He had them all from time to time, but what he didn't have was what my father had—a woman who loved him not because he was rich or for what he could do for her but because she simply adored him.'

'That's very romantic,' she said. 'How tragic they didn't get to have more years together.'

Rafe picked up his glass again. 'It was, but in a way it was better they went together. I can't imagine how either of them would've coped if they were the one left behind.'

A thoughtful expression settled on her face. 'Is that what you hope to find? A love like that?'

Rafe refilled both of their glasses before he answered. 'I guess I'll have to settle down one day. Sire a few heirs.'

'You make it sound rather clinical.'

'I come from a long line of Caffarellis. We're meant to marry and reproduce, ideally in our early thirties.

It's a familial responsibility. Romance has very little to do with it.'

It had had nothing to do with his grandfather's marriage, which had been arranged by his grandfather's parents to increase wealth and possession of property. But, from what Rafe had gleaned from staff or relatives of staff who had previously been in the family's employ, it had been a miserable marriage from day one.

'So how will you go about selecting a suitable wife?' she asked. 'Check her teeth and bloodline? Conduct auditions to see if she knows what cutlery to use? Take her for a trial ride, so to speak?'

He chuckled as he lifted his glass to his mouth. 'Hopefully nothing quite as archaic as that.'

'So you plan to fall in love the old-fashioned way?'

Rafe studied her expression for a beat or two. Would he allow himself to fall in love? It wasn't something he had ever planned on doing. He didn't like getting attached to people. Loving someone gave them power over you. The one who loved the most ended up with the least power in the relationship. Falling in love was losing control, and the one thing he didn't like was losing control over anything, especially his emotions. Even during sex he always kept his head. He always kept a part of himself back, which was why that kiss had unsettled him so much.

Control was his responsibility.

Hadn't he spent his childhood protecting his younger brothers from the vitriolic and often terrifyingly violent outbursts of their grandfather? He had taken the verbal hits, and on more occasions than he liked to remember he had taken the physical ones as well. His grandfather's unpredictable temper and emotional outbursts had made his childhood and adolescence hell at times.

It had been better once he and his brothers had been packed off to boarding school in England. At least then it was just the holidays Rafe had to keep his brothers out of the line of fire.

No, falling in love was not something he planned to do any time soon, if ever.

Morgan came over to take their orders for their meals. 'How's the decision making going?' she asked.

'I've decided,' Rafe said. 'How about you, *ma chérie*? Do you know what you want?'

Poppy's eyes widened momentarily at his endearment but she recovered quickly. 'Yes, the pork belly with fennel and lime.'

'And you, Mr Caffarelli?' Morgan stood with pen poised over the order pad.

'I'll have the lamb with redcurrant glaze and red wine *jus*.'

Once Morgan had left Poppy leaned forwards across the table again with a quirked brow. '*Ma chérie?*'

'It means "my darling".'

'I know what it means but why are you calling me that in front of her?'

'You don't like being called darling?'

'Not by someone who doesn't mean it.'

'I'm actually doing you a favour,' Rafe said. 'Think of what Morgan is relaying to your ex-boyfriend in the kitchen right now—here you are, out with one of Europe's most eligible bachelors. That's going to sting a bit, don't you think?'

Her scowl turned into a reluctant smile that made gorgeous dimples form in her cheeks. He suddenly realised it was the first time she had genuinely smiled at him. 'Maybe.'

'Were you in love with him?'

Her smile faded. 'I thought so at the time.'

'But now?'

She gave a little shrug of her shoulders. 'Probably not…'

'So you had a lucky escape.'

She met his eyes across the table. 'Thank you.'

'For what?'

'For making me come out tonight.' She twisted her mouth. 'For making me face my demons, so to speak.'

'You mean the one who's too cowardly to come out of the kitchen and say a simple hello to you?' Rafe said. 'Maybe I should think twice about asking him to cook for me while I'm staying at the manor.'

She jerked upright in her chair. 'You can't ask him!'

He picked up his glass and took a leisurely sip. 'Why not?'

'Because…because I'd like to do it.'

Rafe arched an eyebrow at her. 'You've changed your mind?'

She gave a little toss of her head, which made one of her curls bounce out of its restraining clip. She tucked it behind her ear with one of her hands. 'It makes sense, since I only live next door. Besides, he'd only be using my recipes. I might as well get the credit for them.'

'Indeed.'

'And I need the money.'

'Things have been pretty lean in spite of what you told Morgan, haven't they?'

Her brow crinkled in a frown. 'I know I'm not very good at the business side of things. Chloe's always telling me I'm too generous and give way too much credit to people who could pay if I made them.'

'So why a tearoom?' he asked. 'Why not a regular restaurant?'

'I knew I wanted to open a tearoom when I was about ten. My gran had taught me how to cook and I loved being in the kitchen with her. I thought I should do the right thing and get a proper qualification, but it was very different being in the kitchen in a busy Soho restaurant.'

'So you came back to look after your gran when she got sick.'

'Yes, and I don't regret it for a moment.'

Rafe couldn't help admiring her loyalty and devotion. It was so at odds with how he felt about his grandfather. He couldn't wait to get away from him, and loathed having to visit to fulfil his familial duty, such as for birthdays and at Christmas. He rarely spoke to him unless he had to. 'You must miss her.'

'I do…' She ran her fingertip round the rim of her champagne flute. 'Do you know what I miss the most?'

'Tell me.'

Her caramel eyes met his with deep, dark seriousness. 'Her chocolate brownies.'

Rafe blinked. '*Pardon*?'

She gave him an impish smile. 'Just kidding. I really had you there for a minute, didn't I?'

You had me the first moment I met you.

Hang on, what was he thinking? *Had him? Had him* in what way? Sure, he was attracted to her. What full-blooded man wouldn't be? But she wasn't his type. She was the homespun type. He was the hardboiled, been-around-the-block-too-many-times type. His world was of fast cars, fancy hot spots and easy women who knew the rules and always played by them.

Her world was a small, out-of-the-way village, baking cakes and scones and making cups of tea for lonely old gentlemen while waiting for Mr Right.

She was innocent and sweet; he was jaded and cynical.

It was a recipe for disaster.

'I miss her for her wisdom,' Poppy went on. 'She taught me more about food and cooking than any hospitality college could do. The thing most people don't get about cooking is it's not just a collection of ingredients, and hey presto, out comes a five-star meal. It's so much more than that.'

'So what does make a meal special?'

'The love that goes into it.'

'Love?'

'The best restaurants are where the chefs love the food they prepare and the people they feed,' she said. 'It's a symbiotic relationship.'

'So what you're telling me is you actually love the people who come to your tearoom?'

She gave him a pert look. 'Maybe not *all* of them.'

Rafe laughed. 'So what do I have to do to win your love? Have my cake and eat it too?'

Her eyes narrowed. 'You don't want my love. You just want my house.'

I want much more than your house.

Rafe pushed the thought aside as Morgan approached with their meals. He had to stay focused. The goal was the dower house; that was what he was after. He didn't want or need anything else. He wouldn't be around long enough to invest in anything other than building a top-notch hotel that would make him loads and loads of money.

Goal.

Focus.

Win.

Sure, it would be fun to have Poppy Silverton in his bed for the short time he was here, but he wasn't about to offer her anything else. She was looking for her fairytale prince, someone to sweep her off her feet and carrying her off into a happy-ever-after sunset.

Rafe's princely attributes leaned more to the darker side.

That whole domestic scene women like Poppy were after was nothing like the life he had carved for himself. He didn't do picket fences, puppies and sweet-smelling babies. He was never in the same place more than a week or two. He never stayed with a lover more than a month; six weeks max. He didn't do commitment. Maybe he was more like his grandfather than he cared to admit.

Not evil, but not squeaky-clean either.

CHAPTER EIGHT

AFTER THEY LEFT the restaurant, Rafe drove Poppy back home and walked her to the front door of the dower house. She hadn't expected to enjoy the night out, but Rafe had been nothing but charming, and even though Oliver's restaurant wouldn't have been her first choice of venue, in the end it had given her a sense of closure.

But it niggled at her that yet again Rafe had achieved what he'd set out to achieve. He'd got her to agree to cook for him while he stayed on site at Dalrymple Manor. It showed how incredibly shrewd he was. He knew how to turn things to his advantage, to find an opponent's weak spot and then go in for the kill.

And she'd done exactly as he had hoped she would do. She had snapped up the bait and now was committed to seeing him every night as she delivered his food to his door. Was she so predictable, or was he particularly clever at reading her?

Poppy turned to face him on her doorstep. 'Do you have any preferences for meals? Any particular cuisine you'd prefer over another or are you happy with whatever I come up with?'

His dark eyes flicked to her mouth for a brief moment. 'That's not why I asked you out tonight.'

She arched a brow at him. 'Is it not?'

'No.' His voice seemed deeper than normal, almost husky.

Poppy's eyes were almost on a level with his as she was standing two steps above him, and she was wearing her highest heels. She could see the wide black circles of his pupils in those impossibly deep brown eyes. She could see the way his lips were pressed firmly together as if he was fighting some sort of private internal battle. She could sense the tension in him and in the fragrant night air that circled them. 'Then why?'

'I asked you out so I could sleep with you.'

Poppy's eyes widened at his blunt honesty. 'You don't pull your punches, do you?'

His mouth tilted wryly. 'Your honour is safe, Poppy. I'm not going to have my wicked way with you tonight.'

'That's very reassuring.' It was downright disappointing, but to admit that to him would be rather perverse of her.

He captured one of her loose corkscrew curls and wound it round his finger, his eyes holding hers in an intimate lock that made the base of her spine tingle like sherbet sprinkled in a glass of soda water. 'I had it all planned. I was going to wine and dine you, flatter you with compliments and then bring you back here and have wild, bed-wrecking sex with you.'

Poppy swallowed a gulp. 'Y-you were?'

He unwound her hair and tucked it neatly behind her left ear as if she was about seven years old. 'You're a nice girl, Poppy Silverton. But here's the thing… I don't mess with nice girls.'

Mess with me! Mess with me! 'So…what changed your mind?'

'I've had more lovers than you've cooked hot dinners,' he said. 'I don't even remember most of their names.'

'I bet they don't forget yours in a hurry.'

He gave a rather Gallic shrug, as if to say that was just the way things were. 'I'm not what you're looking for. It would be wrong to give you the wrong impression or mislead you into thinking any alliance between us could turn into something more permanent.'

'You're surprisingly honourable for a playboy.'

He brushed the underside of her chin with his index finger in a barely touching movement that set every nerve alight with longing. *'Bonsoir, ma petite.'*

Poppy snatched in a scratchy little breath as she watched him walk down the path to his car. She'd been expecting another kiss. Her anticipation of it had been building from the moment they had left the restaurant. Actually, it had been building from the moment he had picked her up that evening and looked at her as if she had just stepped off a Paris catwalk. She wanted to feel that firm, cynical mouth pressed against hers again. She had been staring at his mouth all evening, wondering when he was going to do it. Maybe she should have taken matters into her own hands. What would have been wrong with a quick peck on the lips to thank him for a lovely night out?

It wouldn't have been a quick peck, that was why.

Once his mouth connected with hers another explosion would be detonated, and this time one or both of them might not be able to step back. Hadn't she felt that simmering tension from the very first moment he had walked into her tearoom? She had never experienced anything like it before. It was a rhythm in her body that only he was able to set going. For all these years she had been waiting for the right man to unlock her senses. She had wanted to find someone who could make her heart race; someone who could make her skin sing with longing; someone who could make her sizzle with a desire so unstoppable it would totally consume her. Hadn't his potently hot kiss given her a taste of what he was capable of doing to her?

She wasn't without an understanding of the workings of her body. She had explored it and had been rather fascinated by how it reacted to stimulation. But she thought of sex as being like sightseeing—it was far more pleasurable to see the spectacular sights with someone else rather than all on your own.

He had said he wasn't going to act on his desire for her. Did he mean just for tonight, or never? She had seen the way his eyes had been drawn to her mouth time and time again, as if he was remembering how it felt beneath his own. Was he going just to ignore the pull of attraction that pulsed between them? He might have the strength of will to do it, but Poppy wasn't so sure she could. At least, not for much longer.

Chloe was agog when she came bursting through the door of the tearoom the next morning. 'Have you seen the paper?' She thrust a tabloid in front of Poppy. 'Everyone's saying you're Rafe Caffarelli's new love interest. That was fast work! I thought you didn't even like him. What the hell happened last night? Did you sleep with him?'

Poppy snatched the paper out of Chloe's hands. 'Of course I didn't sleep with him. I didn't even kiss him. We had dinner, that's all.'

She looked down at the society section Chloe had opened. There was a photo of them sitting at the table last night. Rafe's hand was covering hers and their gazes were locked as if in a deeply intimate conversation.

'So?' Chloe prompted.

Poppy closed the paper and handed it back to her. 'So nothing.'

'Nothing?'

'Zilch.'

Chloe's brow was knitted. 'Not even a kiss?'

'Nope.'

'A peck on the cheek?'

'No.'

Chloe pursed her lips in thought. 'Did you have an argument with him or something?'

'No. In fact I agreed to provide meals for him while he's here.'

'Gosh, he must have really laid on the charm. I thought you would rather see him starve.'

'Yes, well, it was either agree to it or let Oliver do it.' Poppy tied her apron around her waist. 'Do you know Oliver had *my* passionfruit crème brûlée on the menu last night?'

'Did Rafe order it?'

'No, he doesn't have a sweet tooth.'

Chloe looked at her musingly. 'People's tastes can change.'

Poppy gave a little secret smile as she headed to the kitchen. 'We'll see.'

Rafe looked at the preliminary plans he'd drawn up but something wasn't sitting well with him. He couldn't put his finger on it. Normally he was so clear-cut on this stuff. He bought a property with development potential and sketched out plans to present to his design team to fine tune.

But this time something wasn't quite right.

The doorbell rang and he got up wearily from his chair. He'd lost track of time. He'd been sitting for hours going nowhere fast. He scraped a hand through his hair to put it in some semblance of order and opened the door.

'I have your dinner.' Poppy was standing on the doorstep with her three little dogs at her feet like miniature bodyguards. She was holding a tray in her hands from which delicious savoury smells were emanating.

Rafe had never seen a more beautiful sight, and it had nothing to do with the fact that he was starving. 'It smells divine,' he said. 'But it looks like you've got enough here to feed a football team.'

'I wasn't sure how big your appetite was.' Her cheeks immediately turned a deep shade of pink.

'Why don't you join me?' He pushed the door open a bit wider with his shoulder as he took the tray from her. 'You'd be doing me a favour. I've been having one of those incredibly frustrating unproductive days. I could do with some company other than my own.'

She hesitated on the doorstep. 'I wouldn't want to intrude.' She glanced at the dogs at her feet. 'And I've got the guys with me.'

Rafe put the tray on the hall table as Chutney had already rushed up to greet him, wriggling his little body in glee. Relish was whining in delight in case he got overlooked. But Pickles, with his cute overshot jaw that looked like a drawer that hadn't been closed properly, was eyeing him with that same beady look. However, Rafe thought he saw his stumpy tail wag just the once as he bent down to administer pats and scratches to the other two. 'The guys are more than welcome.' He finally straightened and met her gaze once he had closed the door. 'I guess you saw the paper? I think it was only in the one.'

She bit down on her lip and then released it. Rafe felt a punch of lust slam him in the groin. Her mouth was so full and ripe, so incredibly sweet. He had dreamt of those lips. It had kept him awake thinking how much he wanted to feel them on his again.

'Yes…' she said. 'But can't we make them retract it or something?'

He picked up the tray and carried it through to the kitchen. 'No point. They'd just make something else up. I ignore it mostly. They'll soon find someone else to target. Our "affair" will be tomorrow's fish-and-chips wrapper.'

'But I don't want people thinking I'm…you know… sleeping with you, when I'm not.'

He smiled down at her lopsidedly. 'Ironic, don't you think?'

Her big brown eyes looked up at him with a twinkle of amusement. 'Very.'

How was he going to resist her?

'Where would you like me to dish up dinner?' she asked, suddenly turning brisk and housekeeper-efficient. 'Lord Dalrymple used to take most of his meals in the morning room but I can set up here in the kitchen, or the formal dining room if you'd prefer.'

'This will probably come as a bit of a surprise to you but I can't remember the last time I ate in the kitchen,' Rafe said. Actually he could, but the memory of it was too painful to recall: his pretty mother, just two days before she had died, dressed in a flowery apron with a swipe of flour across one cheek as she'd bent down to offer him a teaspoon of thick, sweet cake batter to taste…

He pushed the vision away and added, 'It wasn't the way my brothers and I were brought up. Our grandfather didn't believe in fraternising with the domestic staff. Not in the kitchen at least.'

'He doesn't sound like a very nice person to me,' Poppy said as she set about laying the table in the kitchen.

Rafe watched as she set two places with the cutlery neatly aligned before turning to find glasses and napkins. She seemed to know her way about the place, but then he recalled she had spent a great deal of her childhood there. 'Would you like a drink?' he asked. 'I have wine, both red and white.'

She looked up from placing napkins on the side plates. 'Do you have lemonade?' But before he could answer she said, 'No, of course you wouldn't. It's far too sweet.'

'I have mineral water or soda water.'

'That would be lovely.'

Rafe wondered if she was avoiding alcohol in order to keep a clear head. God knew he should take a leaf out of her book. He was having trouble keeping his hands off her as it was. She was dressed in a cotton skirt that emphasised the slimness of her waist. Her three-quarter-length-sleeved sweater skimmed her small perfect breasts lovingly. She wasn't wearing much make-up—just a hint of shadow, mascara that made her lush lashes look all the more Bambi-like and a light shimmer of lip-gloss on her mouth. She was wearing ballet flats on her feet, making the height ratio between them all the more disparate. Her daintiness made him feel far more aware of his masculinity than any other woman he had ever encountered before.

The trouble was, he was feeling more than a little conflicted about acting on it. Would it be right to seduce Poppy, knowing he was not the man to give her what she was truly looking for?

A vicious war was raging inside his body. Desire wrestled with his conscience like they were two mighty, well-matched gladiators in a ring. His blood ran thick and strong with the need to touch her. Even the way she moved about the kitchen ramped up his desire to fever pitch.

Rafe fetched her drink and poured himself half a glass of red. 'So, what have you prepared for me?'

'I have a light starter, as I didn't want to overload your palate for the main course.' She put a pear, rocket, walnut and blue-cheese salad in front of him. 'It's a nice blend of flavours without being too filling.'

'It's delicious,' Rafe said after taking a few mouthfuls. But it wasn't the food that was so captivating. He watched as Poppy daintily speared a sliver of pear and popped it in her mouth. He had to drag his gaze away and, reaching for his glass, took a deep sip of his wine to control the rapacious hunger that was raging in him— and that had nothing to do with the desire for food.

'How did your family make their money?' she asked after a little silence.

'My great-grandparents on my father's side were property kings,' Rafe said. 'Farms, villas, hotels, businesses—you name it, they were in on it. They bought low and sold high. My brothers and I do the same.'

'Do you enjoy what you do?'

Up until spending such a frustrating day, Rafe would have answered an emphatic yes. But somehow today had made him question everything about his plans for the manor—even, to some degree, his plans for his life. 'Like any career there are good and bad sides to it,' he said. 'I love the challenge of finding a rundown property and following it through the various stages as it develops into a luxury hotel. But the hassles with local councils or development authorities can be incredibly tiresome.'

'Not to mention difficult neighbours.'

He gave her a wry look. 'I almost sacked my property manager over you.'

She looked aghast. 'Oh, surely not?'

Rafe twirled the wine in his glass, watching as it swirled against the sides in a blood-red whirlpool of contained energy. 'I'd seen Dalrymple Manor online and liked the look of it. James thought it would be a good investment. He did all the research and emailed me the photos of inside and I agreed. It had large acreage and the manor itself needed a rapid injection of funds to bring it to its former glory. It ticked all the boxes.'

'But?'

He met her eyes across the scrubbed and worn centuries-old kitchen table. 'There was an unexpected five-foot-five obstacle in my way.'

Her cheeks pooled with a light shade of pink, the point of her tongue sneaking out to deposit a layer of moisture across her lips as her eyes slipped out of reach of his. 'That would be me.'

Rafe felt a smile pull at his mouth. Of all the enemies he'd had to face over the years Poppy Silverton had to be the most delightful.

The most desirable.

'I think you're making a very big mistake with the manor,' she said. 'It's not cut out to be a playboy mansion.'

'Why do you think that's what I have planned for it?'

She gave him one of her cynical looks. 'You and your brothers have glamorous starlets coming in and out of your lives as if there are revolving doors on each of your bedrooms. Do they take a numbered ticket, like at one of those dispenser machines at the delicatessen, to see whose turn it is to warm the sheets of your bed?'

Rafe knew he and his brothers had been portrayed as having rather colourful lives. But what was portrayed in the press was just a fraction of the truth. Most of the time they spent working in hotel rooms on their own, trying to meet impossible deadlines, trying to please people who were impossible to please—most notably their grandfather.

Raoul compensated for it by taking life to the extreme. He set physical challenges that would make the average man shrink in cowardice. It was as if he had no fear. He had ice in his veins instead of blood. He didn't just stare death in the face every time he took on another seemingly insurmountable challenge—he laughed at it, *mocked* it. 'Take me down if you dare' seemed to be his credo.

Remy took risks that were more cerebral than physical, but no less terrifying. He won more than he lost, but Rafe worried that the day might come where fate would step in and make his youngest brother lose in a very big way.

Rafe threw himself into his work with a similar passion, but just lately he had become increasingly restless. He wanted more, but he wasn't sure what it was he wanted. He had money, more money than his father or grandfather had ever had. Even without the input of his younger brothers, he had built an empire that rivalled some of the most notable in Europe. If he never worked again his investments would see him out. But was it enough? What legacy was he leaving?

Who would he leave his wealth to?

Rafe couldn't stop thinking of Lord Dalrymple in his stately manor with no one but his housekeeper and her little red-gold-haired, fairy-like granddaughter to keep him company—and the greedy, grasping extended family waiting on the sidelines to get what they could for the place once he had died.

Had they ever visited him? Had they supported him after his wife had so tragically died?

'I don't plan to live here myself,' Rafe said. 'Once the redevelopment is completed I'll appoint a manager. I'll probably only visit once or twice a year after that. I have other projects to see to.'

'So I suppose Dalrymple Manor will be just another notch on your financial belt,' she said as she came around to his side of the table to clear his plate, her expression tight with disapproval.

'Here. Let me help.' Rafe rose from his chair but as he turned he suddenly found himself a whole lot closer to her than he'd intended.

She took an unsteady step backwards and he instinctively put out a hand to stop her from tripping. The sparks against his fingers where they were wrapped around her wrist were like little fireworks popping off underneath his skin.

He met her gaze and felt a stallion's kick of lust strike him in the groin. He smelt her perfume; it was like a draft of some exotic potion that inflamed him with instant longing. He relaxed his grip, but as her fingers left his hold they moved softly across his palm in a trailing movement that made the blood roar through his veins. He felt a surge of lust-driven blood thicken him, heat flowing over his skin like the path of a flame.

Rafe slid a hand into the thick curtain of her hair, loving the feel of those bouncy curls moving against his skin like dainty, springy, fragrant blossoms of jasmine, each one caressing him, intoxicating him.

He would allow himself one kiss.

Just to see if it was as he remembered. Maybe he'd imagined the sparks of electricity shooting up and down his spine as his lips had come in contact with hers. Maybe her mouth would just be another woman's mouth today. It wouldn't make his head spin and his desire race like high-octane fuel through his veins.

He brought his mouth down within reach of the perfect bow of hers, taking his time, letting their breaths mingle.

'What are you doing?' Her voice was soft and husky, her warm, sweet breath dancing against his lips like a teasing spring breeze.

'What do you think I'm doing?' But before she could answer, or the controlled and sensible part of him could change his mind, Rafe did it.

CHAPTER NINE

POPPY HAD THOUGHT his kiss the other day was electrifying, but this time it was completely off the scale. As soon as his lips settled over hers it was as though fireworks had gone off under her skin. She had never felt such a surge of primal male energy before. It touched on something deep and essential to her as a woman. It was like breaking a secret code that had never been solved until now. Her flesh sang with delight as his mouth explored hers in intimate detail—the way his tongue came in search of hers in a brazenly, commanding gesture that had her belly quivering as soon he made contact.

She tasted the hot, hard, thrusting heat of him; tasted the hint of ruthlessness in his mouth; felt the chivalry in his touch that could so easily be put aside if the situation warranted it. It was that edgy, dangerous element about him that so totally captivated her. Hadn't she felt that from the first moment she had met him? He was a man who always got what he wanted. He didn't let anyone stand in his way.

His mouth ravished hers, plundering its depths with dips and dives of his masterful tongue against hers. Poppy shivered as she kissed him back, her tongue duelling with his in a heart-racing chase that made her toes curl inside her shoes. His mouth was hot, determined and purposeful, and she clung to him as she kissed him back just as passionately.

He gave a deep growl of pleasure and cupped her bottom in both of his hands, tugging her against the heated trajectory of his body.

Poppy slithered against him wantonly; her body aching for the pleasure his body was promising in that erotic embrace. She made a mewling sound beneath his passionate mouth, her arms going up to loop around his neck, to hold him to her.

For a moment she thought he was going to reach for her breast. She actually felt his hand move up her body, but then suddenly he broke the kiss and put her from him, moving some distance away as if he didn't trust himself not to reach for her again.

He scraped a hand through his hair and let out a colourful expletive. 'Sorry.' He was breathing heavily. 'I lost my head there for a moment.'

'Is that such a bad thing?'

He gave her a grim look. 'I never lose my head. *Ever.*'

'Maybe it's time you did.'

He shoved his hands in his trouser pockets and moved even further away, turning his back on her. 'This isn't going to work, Poppy. You know it isn't. It was a mistake to kiss you. I should've known better.'

Poppy felt herself bristling in affront. 'I'm not asking you to marry me.'

He turned and threw her a black look. 'You're not my type. Do I have to spell it out any plainer than that?'

Self-doubt crept up and tapped her on the shoulder, mocking her with its cruel little taunts: *you're unattractive. You're rubbish at kissing. You've got no pulling power, that's why Oliver and every other date you've ever had moved on to the next girl as soon as they could.*

Poppy straightened her spine and swung around to the door. 'I'll just get the rest of your dinner for you.'

'Forget about it.'

'It won't take a minute.' She turned back to look at him. 'I just have to dish it up. I won't stay, if that's what's—'

'I'm not hungry.'

She forced herself to hold his unreadable gaze. 'Will you be hungry tomorrow night, do you think?'

His eyes moved away from hers. 'I'll make my own arrangements with regards to food in future.'

'Fine.' She let out a stormy breath. 'I'll just get the dogs and be on my way.'

'So how did the meal go down last night?' Chloe asked the next morning. 'Did you tickle Rafe Caffarelli's taste-buds?'

Poppy kept her gaze averted as she went about getting the tearoom ready for business. She had used concealer that morning when she put on some make-up but it hadn't done much to disguise the stubble rash on her chin. It looked like she'd been scrubbing at her face with a hand-ful of steel wool. 'There is something terribly defective about that man's tastebuds,' she said as she swished back the last of the curtains to let the watery sunshine in.

'But you didn't make anything sweet for him, did you?'

'No, of course not.' *Had her mouth been too sweet for him?* Poppy pushed the thought aside as she crossed the room to get the napkins out of the old pine dresser drawer. 'He's just one of those difficult to please cus-tomers we get from time to time.'

Chloe's gaze narrowed. 'What happened to your face?'

'Nothing, just a bit of an allergy,' Poppy said shutting the drawer firmly. 'I probably leant too close to the honeysuckle or something.'

'Since when have you been allergic to honeysuckle?' Chloe came over and peered at Poppy's chin like a scientist examining a ground-breaking discovery in the laboratory. 'You've got beard rash!'

Poppy jerked her head away. 'It's not beard rash.'

'It so *is* beard rash.' Chloe grinned at her. 'He kissed you, didn't he? What was it like?'

Poppy pursed her lips and started placing the napkins by each setting. 'I'd rather not discuss it.'

'Did he want to sleep with you?' Chloe asked. 'Is that why you're all uppity about it? Did he put the hard word on you or something?'

'No, he did not put the hard word on me,' Poppy said tightly. 'He told me kissing me was a mistake, or words to that effect.'

Chloe blinked. 'A mistake?'

'I'm not his type.' Poppy leaned over the table near the window to put the last napkin down and straightened. 'Not that I want to be his type or anything—it's just there's a way to let a girl down gently without savaging her self-esteem in the process.'

Chloe angled her head quizzically. 'So, let me get this straight: y*ou* wanted to sleep with him but *he* knocked *you* back?'

'I'm not saying I would've slept with him, exactly…'

'But you were tempted.'

'A little.'

Chloe raised her brows.

'OK…a lot,' Poppy said as she exhaled a breath.

'I expect he's a very good kisser.'

Poppy's insides gave a funny little tug and a twist

as she thought about Rafe's determined mouth on hers. 'The best.'

'Which you can say from such a position of authority because you've kissed…how many men is it now?'

'Six…no, seven. I forgot about Hugh Lindley in kindergarten, but I guess a peck on the cheek doesn't count.'

'That many, huh?'

Poppy let out her breath on another long sigh. 'I know, I know. I have some serious catching up to do.'

'Maybe Rafe Caffarelli isn't the right place to start,' Chloe said, glancing at Poppy's chin again with a little frown. 'You could get yourself really hurt.'

Tell me something I don't already know. 'I'm not planning on going anywhere near Rafe Caffarelli,' Poppy said. 'He's made his position clear. I don't need to be told twice.'

A couple of days later a deafening clap of thunder woke Rafe up during the middle of the night. The wind whipped around the manor like a dervish. It howled and screamed around the eaves and rafters, making the manor shake and shudder as if it was being rattled like a moneybox.

He went over to close the window the wind had worked loose from its catch just as a flash of lightning rent the sky into jagged pieces. The green-tinged light illuminated the dower house in the distance. His stomach clenched when he saw that one of the branches of the old elm tree had come down over the roof, crushing it like a flimsy cardboard box.

He quickly threw on some clothes and found a weatherproof jacket and a torch. He pressed Poppy's number—his phone had recorded it when she'd rung about Chutney being missing—but she didn't answer. He didn't bother leaving a message. He snatched up his keys and raced out to his car, calling the emergency services on the way.

The wind almost knocked him off his feet. He hunched over and forged through the lashing rain, his mind whirling with sickening images of Poppy trapped under a beam. Which room was her bedroom? He tried to recall the layout of the house. There were three bedrooms, all of them upstairs. Wouldn't the main one be the one where the elm tree was?

He hammered at the front door once he got there. 'Poppy? Are you in there? Are you all right?'

There was no power so he couldn't see anything, other than when the lightning zigzagged or from his torch, which was woefully low on batteries. 'Poppy? Can you hear me?'

The sound of the dogs yapping inside lifted his spirits, but only just. What if they were all right but Poppy wasn't? *'Poppy?'* He roared over the howling gale.

'I'm up here.'

Rafe looked up and shone the torch at the pale oval of Poppy's face next to the gaping hole in the roof. Relief flooded him so quickly he couldn't get his feet to move at first. He felt like his legs were glued to the porch. 'I'm coming up,' he called out. 'Keep away from the beams. Don't touch any power outlets or wires.'

He picked up a rock, smashed the glass panel beside the front door and reached inside to unlock the lock. He went upstairs, carefully checking for live wires or debris, but it seemed the branch had cut cleanly through the old roof and done little else but let the elements in.

The three little dogs—even Pickles, the unfriendly one—came rushing up to him, whining in agitation and terror. He quickly ushered them out of harm's way into the bedroom on the other side of the house. 'Later, guys,' he said and closed the door before he headed to Poppy's bedroom.

Poppy was pinned against the wall near the window by the beam that had almost sliced her bed in half. Rafe's stomach pitched when he thought of how close she had come to being killed. She looked so tiny and frightened, her face chalk-white, her eyes as big as saucers.

'Are you all right?' His voice was hoarse from shouting.

'I—I'm fine…I think.'

'Don't move until I check it's safe,' he said, shining the torch around.

'I'm scared.'

'I know you are, *ma petite*,' he said. 'I'll get you out.'

'Are the dogs OK?'

'They're fine,' he said. 'I locked them in the other bedroom.'

Once he'd established it was safe, he climbed over the fallen beam and grasped Poppy's ice-cold hands. He pulled her close, wrapping his arms around her as she shuddered in reaction. 'It's all right,' he said. 'You're safe now.'

'I got up to close the window. If I hadn't, I would've been right where that beam is…'

'Don't even think about it,' Rafe said, stroking her back with soothing movements, trying to ignore the way his body was responding to her. 'I called the emergency services on my way down. They should be here any minute.'

The sound of a fire engine and an ambulance approaching could only just be heard over the howl of the wind. Rafe stayed with Poppy until the fire crew came up and led them to safety, along with the dogs, who were now safely on their leads so they couldn't bolt at the sound of thunder.

Once they were outside, Rafe draped his weather-proof coat around Poppy's shoulders. She was shivering uncontrollably but he had a feeling it was shock rather than cold.

'You'll have to spend the rest of the night some place else,' one of the fire officers said. 'That roof doesn't look too safe. Another gust of wind and the whole lot could come down.'

'I'll take her home with me,' Rafe said.

What did you just say? Are you out of your mind? It was too late to take it back, as the fire officer had already given a nod of approval and moved off to talk to one of the other officers.

Poppy glanced up at Rafe with a frown. 'I can stay with Chloe and her mother. I'll just give her a call...' Her face suddenly fell. 'Except my phone is upstairs by the bed.'

'It's two in the morning,' Rafe said. 'We'll sort out more permanent accommodation later.' *You think that's going to happen once you've got her under your roof?* 'Right now you need a hot drink and a warm comfort-able bed.'

He led her to his car, got her settled in the passenger seat and put the dogs in the back before taking his place behind the wheel. The voice of his control centre was still nagging at him like an alarm bell that hadn't been at-tended to: *what are you doing, man? Take her to a hotel.*

But somehow he managed to mute it as he turned over the engine and glanced at Poppy sitting beside him. 'All right?' he asked.

Her toffee-brown eyes seemed too big for her small

white face. 'I think my phone is crushed under that branch.'

He reached over and gave one of her hands a gentle squeeze. 'Phones are easy to replace. They're a dime a dozen.'

She gave him a weak smile. 'Thank you for rescuing me and the dogs.'

He gave her hand a little pat before returning his to the steering wheel. 'Don't mention it.'

Poppy was still wearing Rafe's jacket as she sat at the kitchen table half an hour later, her hands cupped around a mug of hot chocolate. There wasn't a single tea leaf in the manor, not even a tea bag. The dogs were settled in the laundry on a pile of blankets Rafe had found. Pickles had even licked Rafe's hand instead of snarling at him.

'Do you need a refill?' Rafe asked as he came in from giving the dogs a bowl of water.

'No, this is perfect, thank you,' Poppy said. 'I'm starting to feel almost normal again.'

His dark gaze narrowed in focus. 'What's that on your chin?'

She put a hand to her face. 'Oh…nothing. Just a little allergic reaction…'

He took her chin gently between his finger and thumb. Something moved behind his eyes, a softening, loosening look that made her belly turn over. He ever-so-gently passed the pad of his thumb over the reddened area. 'I've got some cream upstairs to put on that.'

Poppy gave him a pert look to disguise her reaction to his closeness. 'I suppose you have to keep an industrial-size container by your bedside, along with a giant box of condoms.'

The edge of his mouth lifted in a wry smile. 'I only have three on me. They're in my wallet.'

'You surprise me,' she said. 'I thought you'd have them strategically placed all around the house.'

His hand fell away from her face, his expression becoming shuttered. 'The stuff you read about me and my brothers is not always true. We're not the partying time-wasters we're made out to be.'

'Haven't you heard the expression "no smoke without fire"?'

'Yes.' His eyes glinted as they came back to hers. 'I've also heard the one about playing with matches. Do I need to remind you of it?'

Poppy schooled her features into icy hauteur. 'Do you really think I would've slept with you the other night?'

'Undoubtedly.'

His arrogant confidence irked her into throwing back, 'I was interested in kissing you again, I will admit that, but that's as far as I was going to take it. But then, I suppose you assume every woman you kiss is yours for the taking. Obviously, I'm the exception to the rule.'

'That's something we could easily test—' he paused for a heart-stopping beat '—if you're game.'

Poppy didn't know if he was calling her bluff or not. Either way, she wished she hadn't been so foolishly reckless in brandishing about a self-confidence she didn't even possess. He had kissed her twice now and she had practically melted in his arms. What would another kiss do?

Make her fall in love with him?

She pushed her chair back and got to her feet. 'I'd like to go to bed.' She gave him a pointed look. 'Alone.'

'Wise of you.' He smiled a fallen angel's smile.

Poppy felt a shiver go down her spine as she thought

of how that mouth had felt against hers, how his hard body had felt. He was sin and temptation wrapped up in one hell of a hot package. She was playing with fire, striking up a conversation with him, let alone anything else. She just didn't have the defences or the sophistication to deal with someone like him.

'Goodnight,' she said as primly as Mother Superior to one of her novices.

'Goodnight, *ma petite.*' He paused for a beat as his gaze held hers in a lock that sent a shudder straight to her core. 'Sweet dreams.'

CHAPTER TEN

POPPY DIDN'T EXPECT to sleep a wink with the wind still howling outside, but somehow the sound of rain drumming on the roof combined with the warm, cosy comfort of the bed in the Blue Room at the manor and the hot chocolate she had consumed was a somniferous cocktail that had her asleep as soon as her head touched down on the fluffy pillow. She woke to sparkling bright sunshine and that fresh, clean, washed smell of the earth that comes after a storm. She stretched her limbs and lazily glanced at the little carriage clock that was sitting on the bedside table.

Ten o'clock!

She threw off the covers and quickly threw her clothes back on. There wasn't time for a shower; she didn't have any toiletries with her in any case. She raced downstairs with her hair still awry when she encountered Rafe coming in from outside. The three dogs were at his heels, their tongues hanging out of the sides of their mouths as if they'd just run a marathon.

Rafe looked disgustingly healthy and fit, dressed in stone-coloured chinos and a white shirt, his hair brushed back, his jaw freshly shaven and his eyes clear. It was impossible not to feel a little dishevelled in comparison. Poppy knew her eyes weren't clear—she'd caught a glimpse of them in the mirror on the way down—and as for her hair… Well, the less said about that the better. She'd tried finger-combing it but it had been like trying to comb a fishing net.

'Good morning,' he said with irritating cheerfulness. 'Did you sleep well?'

'Why didn't you wake me?' Poppy asked, glowering at him. 'I should've been at work two hours ago.'

'I drove down and spoke to Chloe about what happened,' he said. 'She said to take your time. She's got things sorted at the shop.'

'I need to get home to shower and change.' Poppy pushed back her matted hair with an agitated hand. 'And I need to call someone about getting the roof fixed.'

'Already sorted.'

Her hand dropped back to her side. 'What do you mean?'

'I've called a local roofing expert,' he said. 'He's starting on it early next week.'

'*Next week?*' Poppy said. 'Why not this week? Why not *today?*'

He gave a loose shrug. 'Your roof was not the only one damaged by the storm. You'll have to be patient. Look on the bright side—at least you have somewhere to stay.'

'I can't stay here. What will people think?'

His dark eyes glinted. 'They'll think I'm being a very charitable neighbour in offering you a bed for as long as you need it.'

Poppy's eyes narrowed to the size of coin slots. 'You know darn well what everyone will think. They'll think it's *your* bed you're offering.'

He gave a disarming smile. 'You worry too much about what other people think.'

'I'll find a hotel.'

He hooked a brow upwards. 'With three dogs in tow?'

Poppy chewed her lip. 'Maybe you could mind them for a few days until—'

'No.'

'Why not?' she asked. 'They're following you around like disciples anyway.'

'I don't want the responsibility of looking after them,' he said. 'I sometimes have to travel at a moment's notice. I don't mind you being here with them, but I'm not running a boarding kennel. What if the roof takes longer than expected?'

Poppy could see his point. But if she were to find proper boarding kennels that would be another expense she could do without right now. How long before the village got talking about her sharing the manor with Rafe Caffarelli?

How long before the world got to hear of it?

'How long does the roofing guy say it will take?' she asked.

'A week or thereabouts.'

That meant two weeks staying with Rafe at Dalrymple Manor unless she could come up with an alternative. But what alternative accommodation could offer a kitchen the size of the manor? 'If I can't find anywhere else, is it OK if I use your kitchen while I'm here?' she asked. 'I do a lot of the baking for the tearoom at home.'

'Of course,' he said. 'It's not as if I'll be using it.'

Poppy worried her lower lip again. 'I know you said you'd make your own arrangements about food...'

'You don't have to cook for me,' he said. 'I won't be here for much longer in any case. I have other projects to see to.'

Poppy wondered if his other projects were female. She pushed her feelings of disappointment aside. It wasn't as if he was the man of her dreams or anything. She didn't even like him. Well, she hadn't up until last night, when he'd been so gallant at rescuing her, putting his own safety at risk to get her out. The way he'd held her in his arms and comforted her had made her feel so safe and protected…

She gave herself a good, hard mental slap. She had no right to harbour such whimsical thoughts. He was a player, not a stayer. Even if he did agree to a fling with her it wouldn't last more than a week or two. He had made it abundantly clear she wasn't his type. If he did happen to sleep with her, it would be for the sheer novelty of it. He'd probably joke about it with his brothers or friends in the future. How he'd found a home-spun village girl who'd never had sex before.

But then, why *wasn't* she his type?

It rankled that he had dismissed her so easily. She was female, wasn't she? Sure, a top modelling agency wouldn't be calling her any time soon for a photo shoot, but as far as she was aware she hadn't broken any mirrors just lately. What was his problem?

'What about rent or payment for board and expenses? How much do you—?'

'I don't want your money, Poppy.'

What do you want? The question was left unspoken in the silence.

Rafe undid a spare key from his keyring and handed it to her. 'I have a meeting in London this afternoon. I might not make it back until tomorrow or the next day. Make yourself at home.'

Poppy took the key and closed her fingers around it as he moved past her. 'Hey, guys,' she called out to the dogs who were slavishly following Rafe. 'Remember me? The owner who loves and feeds you?'

Their toenails clicked on the polished floor as they came back to her with sheepish looks and wagging tails.

'Traitors,' she muttered as she bent down to tickle their ears.

'I'd love to have you and the dogs stay, but Mum's allergic to dogs,' Chloe said at work an hour later. 'Anyway, why are you so against staying at the manor? You lived there with your gran for years and years.'

'I know, but it's different now.'

'Yes, because you've got the world's hottest, most eligible bachelor sharing it with you,' Chloe said with a mischievous sparkle in her eyes.

Poppy frowned as she put on her apron. 'It's not what you think. Anyway, he's not going to be there much longer. He's off to London this afternoon. He has other fish to fry.'

'Are you sure about that?' Chloe asked. 'Anyone can see you two have a little thing going on.'

'We do *not* have a little thing going on,' Poppy said. 'I don't even like the man. He's too arrogant for my liking.'

'That's confidence, not arrogance,' Chloe said. 'He knows what he wants and goes out and gets it. And I reckon it's not just the dower house on his acquisition list. You're right up there at the top of his must-have items.'

Poppy shrugged off Chloe's comment. 'I don't think so. I told you before, I'm not sophisticated enough for the likes of him.'

'Ah yes, so you keep saying, but I was watching him when he came to see me this morning,' Chloe said. 'He was so concerned about what happened to you last night. I could see it in his eyes. I think he's more than halfway to falling in love with you. He just doesn't realise it yet.

Maybe that's why he's heading back to town. He's trying to get his head around it.'

Poppy choked out a scornful laugh. 'Men like Rafe Caffarelli don't fall in love. They fall in lust and they just as quickly fall out of it, too.'

'Call me a hopeless romantic, but I think you're exactly the sort of girl a hardened playboy like him would fall for,' Chloe said. 'He hasn't been seen with anyone else since he met you. That's a bit of a record, since he usually has a new lover every week or so.'

'I bet the papers tell a different story tomorrow,' Poppy said. 'He'll probably have a couple of wild nights of sex with some glamorous starlet or model. He won't give me a second thought.'

Rafe called an end to the board meeting at six p.m. but his middle brother Raoul hung back to speak to him after the others had left. 'A no-show from Remy as usual.'

Rafe grunted. 'One day I'm going to throttle him, I swear to God. He could have sent a text or an email. Where the hell is he?'

'I think he's in Vegas.'

Rafe rolled his eyes. 'Let's hope it's a showgirl he's with this time, not sitting at a gaming table with a billionaire oil baron ready to toss for the lot.'

Raoul grimaced in agreement. 'Wouldn't be the first time. Don't know how that boy wins more than he loses.'

'He'll lose one day,' Rafe said.

Raoul arched a brow in mock surprise. *Lose?* That word doesn't exist in our vocabulary, remember? You've been drumming that into us since we were kids: goal. Focus. Win. The Caffarelli credo.'

Rafe frowned as he recapped his fountain pen. 'I worry about Remy. He's like a loose cannon.'

'You worry too much about both of us, Rafe,' Raoul said as he perched on the edge of the boardroom table. 'You're our brother, not our father. You don't need to take so much on your shoulders. Loosen up a bit. You seem overly tense today. What's happening with that dower house in Oxfordshire you were after? Have you convinced the owner to sell it yet?'

Rafe gathered his papers together with brisk efficiency. He didn't want to get drawn into any discussions about his private life, even with his brother. He'd only been in the city a couple of hours and all he could think of was getting back to the manor. He refused to acknowledge it was because Poppy was staying there.

He liked the place. It had a homely feel about it. He enjoyed the space and the peace of it. He wanted to keep working on the plans *in situ*.

'I'm still working on it.'

'I saw your photo with her in the paper a few days back,' Raoul said. 'She's not your usual type, is she?'

Rafe snapped the catch closed on his briefcase. 'Definitely not.'

'You looked pretty cosy in that restaurant,' Raoul said. 'You slept with her yet?'

Rafe's brow jammed together. 'What sort of question is that?'

Raoul leaned back as he held up his hands. 'Hey, don't bite my head off.'

Rafe clenched his fist around the handle of his briefcase as he lifted it off the table. Normally he would have no trouble with a bit of ribald humour between his brothers over his latest lover, but talking about Poppy like that felt totally wrong. 'I'm not sleeping with her.'

Raoul raised his brows. 'You losing your touch or what?'

Rafe gave him a look. 'So who are you sleeping with?' he asked. 'Is it still that tall blonde with the endless legs?'

Raoul grinned. Slipping off the desk, he punched Rafe on the upper arm. 'You got time for a beer?'

Rafe pretended to glance at his watch. 'Not today,' he said. 'I have some more paperwork to see to when I get home.'

'Home being where the heart is?' Raoul said with a teasing smile.

'You're a jerk,' Rafe said, scowling. 'You know that, don't you?'

Raoul dodged his older brother's playful punch. 'Always said you'd be the first to go down.'

'The first to go down where?'

'Down the aisle.'

Rafe felt his spine tighten. 'I'm not going down the aisle.'

'You're the eldest,' Raoul said. 'Makes sense that you'd be the one to set up a family first.'

'Why would I want to do that?' Rafe said. 'I'm fine the way I am. I like my life. It's a great life—I have total freedom; I don't have to answer to anyone. What more could I want?'

Raoul gave a little shrug. 'I don't know… I've been thinking lately about what *Mama* and *Papa* had. It was good. They were so happy.'

'Hindsight is always in rose-coloured vision,' Rafe cut him off. 'You were only eight years old. You remember what you want to remember.'

'I was nine. My birthday was the day of the funeral, remember?'

How could he forget? Rafe had watched his brother bravely hold himself together as their parents' coffins had been carried out of the cathedral. Remy had been crying and Rafe had put an arm around him, but Raoul had stood stoically beside him, shoulder to shoulder, not a single tear escaping from his hazel eyes. He often wondered if the roots of his brother's death-defying pursuits had been planted that day. They were a way of letting off steam from all that self-containment. 'I remember.'

'You don't think they were happy?'

Rafe let out a breath. 'They were happy, but who's to say what they would've been like in a few more years?'

Raoul shifted his mouth from side to side in a reflective fashion. 'Maybe…'

'What's brought this on?'

'Nothing.' Raoul gave a smile that looked a little forced.

'Come on,' Rafe said, putting his briefcase down again. 'Something's eating at you. You hide it from most people but I can always tell. You're like a Persian cat with a fur-ball stuck in its throat.'

'I don't know…' Raoul picked up a glass paperweight and passed it from one hand to the other. 'I guess I've been thinking about things. I don't want to end up like *Nonno*. He has to pay people to be with him.'

'You've seen him recently?'

'I spent the weekend there.'

'And?'

Raoul lifted a shoulder in a non-committal shrug. 'It was sad…you know?'

Rafe *did* know. He had been having the same thoughts. His grandfather spent most of his time alone with just a band of people he employed to take care of the villa and his needs. It was a sterile life. There was no love or mutual enjoyment. His grandfather went from meal to meal with no real social contact, no real affection or connection. He got what he paid for: obsequious and obedient service.

'He's brought it on himself,' he said with the rational part of his brain. 'He's pushed everyone who cared about him aside. Now he has to make do with the people who will only do it for the money.'

Raoul put down the paperweight and slid off the boardroom table with a little frown. 'Do you ever think about it…about life? About what it's all about?'

Rafe hid behind his usual shop-front of humour. 'Of course I do. It's about making money and making love. It's what us Caffarellis do best.'

'We make money and have sex, Rafe. Love has nothing to do with it.'

'So?'

Raoul looked him in the eye. 'Do you ever wonder if the woman who is with you is with you because of who you are or because of what's in your bank account?'

Rafe felt an eerie shiver move over the back of his neck at the chilling familiarity of those words. Hadn't Poppy asked him the very same thing the first day she met him? 'Come on, man. What's going on?' he asked. 'Last time I looked, you were out there partying like the best of them. What's changed?'

'Nothing. But I've been thinking about Clarissa, the girl I've been dating recently.'

'You're *not* serious about her?' Rafe gave his brother an incredulous look. 'I admit she's attractive but surely you can do better than that?'

'It solves the gold-digger problem, though, doesn't it?' Raoul said. 'Clarissa wouldn't be marrying me for my money because her old man has plenty of his own and she's his only heir.'

Rafe picked up his briefcase again. 'One beer, OK? After that I have to get going.'

[faint text from previous page showing through]

CHAPTER ELEVEN

POPPY WAS IN the smaller of the two sitting rooms, wiping copious tears from her eyes as the credits rolled on one of her favourite classic romance movies, when Rafe suddenly appeared in the doorway.

'What's wrong?' he asked, frowning as he came towards her. 'Why are you crying? Has something happened?'

Poppy sprang off the sofa guiltily. She stuffed her sodden tissue up the sleeve of her pink teddy-bear pyjamas and wished she didn't have a red nose and red eyes to match her cheeks, not to mention her hair. 'It's just a movie. I always cry even though I've watched it about a gazillion times.'

He bent down and picked up the DVD case. *'An Affair to Remember...* I don't think I've seen that one. What's it about?'

'It's about a spoilt, rich playboy who meets this girl on a cruise...' Poppy felt her blush deepen. 'Never mind. You wouldn't like it. It was made decades ago. I bet you only like movies with lots of car chases and heaps of CGI and over-the-top action.'

He put the case down again, his expression unreadable. 'I didn't think you'd still be up. It's almost one in the morning.'

'I had to bake some extra things for one of my cus-tomers,' Poppy said. 'She's having some guests over for a dinner party tomorrow. I made the desserts for her.'

'That's sounds like a good little money-spinner for you.'

Poppy averted her gaze as she popped the DVD back in its case and clicked it shut. 'I wasn't expecting you back tonight. I thought you'd make the most of the night-life in London while you were there.'

'After my meeting I had a quiet beer with my middle brother, Raoul.'

'So, no hot date or shallow pick-up?'

'No.'

'You must be losing your touch.'

His look was unreadable. 'That's what my brother said.'

There was a little silence.

'You do charge people for cooking those extras, don't you?' he asked.

Poppy blew out a little breath. 'I always say I'm going to…'

'But you're trying to run a business, for God's sake,' he said. 'Your goal is to make a profit. That should be your focus, not trying to be everyone's best friend.'

'I know, I know. Do you think I haven't been told this a hundred times?'

'Do you want me to help you?' he asked. 'I can have a look over your books. I can see where the leaky holes are and put the necessary plugs in place. You won't have to lose any sleep or friends over it.'

She looked up at him gratefully. 'Would you do that?'

He gave her a slow smile that made her legs go weak. 'I'd be glad to.'

Another little silence fell between them.

Poppy hugged her elbows with her crossed over arms. 'It's been funny being here tonight—funny weird, not funny hilarious.'

'Why?'

'Because I spent so much of my childhood here, right in this room. Lord Dalrymple let Gran and me use it. He said it was because the television reception was better here than at the dower house, but I think he liked having us around in the background.' She gave a little sigh. 'This is the first time I've been in here since Gran died.'

He came over and placed his hands gently on the tops of her shoulders. 'I should've realised it might be tough coming back here. I should have postponed my meeting and stayed with you.'

Poppy looked up into his deep, dark eyes. He was standing very close; close enough to smell the citrus base of his aftershave and the hint of late-in-the-day male sweat that was equally intoxicating. 'I don't need babysitting.'

A corner of his mouth lifted in a wry smile. 'So says the pint-sized girl who's wearing pink teddy-bear pyjamas, and hippopotamus slippers on her feet.' One of his hands moved from her shoulder to cup the nape of her neck. 'Which should be enough to stop me doing this.'

She swallowed. 'Doing…what?'

His mouth came down towards hers. 'I think you know what.'

'I thought you said you didn't want to…?'

He pressed a soft-as-air kiss to her lips. It barely touched her but it set every nerve longing for more. 'I want to,' he said in a rough, sexy tone. 'I want to very much. I've thought of nothing but you the whole time I was in London. How you taste, how you smell, how you feel.'

Poppy's breath hitched on something sharp in her chest as his mouth came back down to hers. The kiss was longer this time and deeper. She felt the first brush-stroke of his tongue against her mouth and her spine liquefied. She opened to him on a little whimper of approval, her hands winding up around his neck, her body pressing closer to the hard warmth of his.

His tongue played with hers, cajoling it into a dance that was brazenly erotic. He moulded her to him, his hands pressing against her bottom to hold her against his aroused body. He felt so thick and strong pulsing there against her neediness. The empty, achy feeling inside her was almost unbearable, especially when the answer to it was so temptingly close.

He broke the kiss to move his lips down to the side of her neck where a thousand nerves were trembling in anticipation. 'You should tell me to stop before this gets out of hand.'

'What if I don't want you to stop?' She angled her neck to give him better access.

He framed her face in his hands, looking deep into her passion-glazed eyes. 'I could hurt you.'

Her heart kicked against her ribcage at the concern in his gaze. 'I'm sure you won't.'

He leaned his forehead against hers, his warm breath mingling intimately with hers. 'This is crazy…' He drew in a breath as if to steady himself. 'Everything about this is crazy.'

'I feel a little crazy around you,' Poppy confessed as she planted a soft, teasing kiss to his mouth.

He kissed her back, a light play of his lips upon hers, pressing, nibbling, caressing. 'Do you have any idea how out of my depth I'm feeling right now?'

She gave him a wry look. 'Isn't that what I'm supposed to be feeling?'

He cupped her face in his hands again. 'How *do* you feel?'

Poppy shivered as his dark eyes centred on her mouth. 'Nervous, excited… A little worried I might disappoint you…'

His gaze held hers with a look that was surprisingly tender. 'You have no need to be worrying about that. This first time is all about you. I don't want you to feel concerned about anything else but your needs.'

Poppy touched his lower lip with the tip of her finger. 'I do know what an orgasm is. I've had them…you know…? By myself…'

His eyes darkened. 'Do you want to show me what works for you or would you prefer me to discover it for myself?'

Poppy felt a hot blush storm into her cheeks. 'I think I'd feel more comfortable with you discovering it…'

His thumbs stroked her cheeks in a slow and gentle caress. 'Making love with someone for the first time is all about discovering what works and what doesn't. I want you to tell me if you want to stop at any point. If you don't feel comfortable then we can call a halt. You're the one in control, OK?'

Poppy wondered if she could have chosen a better first lover. He seemed so concerned for her, so adamant that she was not to be pressured or frightened or pushed out of her depth. For someone with such a racy reputation, he was showing a softer, gentler side that was powerfully seductive. She wanted to melt into his hard male body, to lose herself in his sensual expertise.

She didn't want to think about the dozens of women who had been with him before. In a strange way, it felt as if it was the first time for both of them. She felt it in the slight hesitancy of his touch, the way his hands moved over her in almost reverent discovery. Like how he explored her breasts, as if they were the most precious, sensitive globes he had ever touched.

She shuddered as he slid his hand under her pyjama top, shaping her, the warm cup of his palm making every hair on her head tingle at the roots. He brushed the pad of his thumb over her tight nipple and a shower of sensation cascaded down her spine. A hot spurt of longing fired between her legs and she pressed herself closer, wanting more of him, wanting his skin on her skin without the frustrating barrier of their clothes.

His mouth covered hers in a searing kiss; it burned and sizzled every nerve-ending until she was breathless. He pushed aside her pyjama top as if it was nothing more than a scrap of tissue paper, his hand cupping and shaping her possessively as his mouth bewitched hers. She felt the drag of desire deep and low in her belly, the slow but delicious ache that tugged and pulled, drawing her towards him like a magnet. Her loins pulsed and ached with the need for more. She pressed herself even closer, her insides melting as she felt the hard, insistent press of his body against her.

He brought his mouth to her breast in a hot, moist caress that made her quake with desperate need. His tongue laved her tightly budded nipple, playing with it, teasing it, tantalising it until she was whimpering in soft little gasps of want.

'Not here,' he said. 'We need a bed.'

Poppy's breath came out in a startled whoosh as he scooped her up in his arms. 'I'm too heavy to carry upstairs.'

'You're a featherweight. I'm twice the weight of you. I'm worried I'm going to crush you.'

Poppy had never felt more feminine in her life. She wrapped her arms around his neck and gave herself up to the thrill of being swept off her feet. Each step he took on the staircase made her heart thump harder. It was one step closer to him taking her into his full possession. Her skin danced with the anticipation of it, every nerve in her body alert and finely tuned to the radar of his.

It seemed like for ever yet it was no time at all before her back was pressed against a firm mattress. He came down over her, his mouth hot and insistent on hers, his hands moving over her in gentle caresses that peeled off her night clothes with a slow deliberation that made her blood tingle in her veins. She reached for his shirt buttons, undoing them with fevered concentration. She wanted to kiss every inch of his hot flesh, to feel it shiver and shudder under the ministrations of her lips and tongue.

He shrugged off his shirt as her hands reached up to explore the carved muscles of his chest and shoulders. 'You work out.'

'A bit.' His mouth found the underside of her breast, his lips moving lightly over the sensitive skin like a maestro with an instrument he has never played before. 'You are so beautiful.'

The hot press of his naked chest against hers made her body react like a wanton. Her bones melted, her limbs unhinged, her spine loosened. She ran her hands over his taut buttocks, pressing him against her need, wanting to feel the hot, hard probe of his flesh in her aching centre. She went for his buckle and blindly unfastened it as her mouth met his in a fiery kiss. She felt him against her, so erect, so ready for her it made her insides shift like tectonic plates beneath the earth. She touched him through the fabric of his trousers, stroking the thick length of him while his tongue played with hers.

He briefly broke the kiss so he could shuck off his trousers and underwear. Poppy faintly registered the thud of his shoes hitting the floor. She was mesmerised by the male beauty of his body. It wasn't that she hadn't seen a naked man before but she had never seen one who looked so magnificent. She touched his tanned flat abdomen with an experimental glide of her hand. 'You're so…' she swallowed convulsively '…big.'

'Don't be frightened, *ma belle*.' He took her hand and placed it against his erection. She wrapped her fingers around him, getting to know his shape and feel. He was both satin and steel, power and potency, yet vulnerable too. She felt the pulse of his blood against her hand, the need there thundering so similarly to what was happening in her own body. There was even a bead of moisture forming at the head of his erection; just like the slippery dew she could feel secretly gathering between her thighs.

He gently pulled her hand away and pressed her back down against the mattress, his limbs in a sexy tangle with hers. 'My turn to explore you.' He laid a hand on her belly, just above her pubic bone.

Poppy shivered at the intimate contact; those long fingers were *so close* to where she most ached and throbbed. Her breath caught in her throat as he gently separated her with his fingers as if she was a delicate hothouse flower that needed careful handling. Her nerves quivered and shook as he delicately traced her form, not touching her anywhere too hard or for too long, his slow but sure process building up a delicious tension inside her.

'I want to taste you.'

Poppy saw the intent in his coal-black eyes and shuddered in nervous anticipation. She felt him move down her body, his warm breath caressing her folds, his tongue stroking the seam of her body in a gentle sweep that had her sucking in a sharp breath and shrinking back in startled surprise. 'Oh!'

He paused. 'Don't back away from it, *ma petite*. Relax; let yourself go.'

'I don't think I can...' Poppy suddenly felt exposed and inadequate. What if she was hopeless at this? What if he thought she was ugly or different down there? She hadn't waxed as neatly as her peers. She found the thought of being totally bare down there a little unsettling. Was she supposed to look like a little girl or a woman? What did men want? Was he comparing her to all his other lovers?

'Hey.' Rafe captured her chin and made her look at him. 'You're beautiful. You taste beautiful. You smell beautiful.'

Poppy covered her face with her hands. 'This is why I'm still a virgin at twenty-five. I'm hopeless at this.'

He tugged her hands away from her face. 'You're not hopeless at this. Relax, *ma petite*. We're not in a hurry. Take all the time you need.'

'But what about you?'

He stroked the flank of her thigh with a slow, caressing touch. 'I can come in two minutes or forty-two. It's in my control.'

She frowned. 'But I thought...'

He pressed the pad of his thumb over her lips. 'Stop thinking, *ma chérie*. Your job right now is to feel.'

Poppy let out an uneven breath as he stroked her thigh again. His touch was like a velvet glove against her skin. She closed her eyes and gave herself up to the moment, to the feel of his hand on her thigh, her belly and her breasts in gentle glides that were almost reverent. He came back to her with his mouth, soft as a feather landing on her, waiting for her to feel comfortable before progressing to firmer, more intimate caresses. She felt the slow stroke of his tongue, the sensations ricocheting through her, but instead of fighting them this time she embraced them. It was like a giant wave coming down over her. It swept her up in its vortex, tumbling her over and over in a dizzying whirlpool that made her feel disoriented. She heard a high, keening cry split the air and realised with quite some embarrassment that it had come from her.

It sounded so primal, *so carnal.*

He brushed the damp hair away from her forehead, a smile that was just shy of smug playing at the edges of his mouth. 'See? You're not hopeless at this. You're a natural.'

Poppy trailed a fingertip down his sternum rather than meet his triumphant gaze. 'So…forty-two minutes, huh? Did you set a stop-watch or something?'

He pushed her chin up so her gaze was level with his. 'Being a considerate lover is a responsibility I take very seriously as a man. No woman should feel rushed to meet a timetable that isn't hers. Your body will have different moods and needs. What works well one time may not work so well another time.'

Poppy traced her index finger over the contour of his lower lip, her softer skin catching on his stubble like silk on sandpaper. 'You seem to know your way around a woman's body.'

'I'm still getting to know yours but what I've discovered so far is delightful.' He captured her fingertip with his lips and sucked it into his mouth. She shivered as she felt the intimate pull of his warm mouth, his eyes glittering with primal intent as they held hers.

Poppy sank back with a blissful sigh as he moved over her, balancing his weight on his arms so as not to crush her. The sexy abrasion of his masculine leg hair against her smoother skin was a potent reminder of how different he was from her. His mouth covered hers in a sizzling-hot kiss that fired up all of her nerve-endings all over again. His tongue played with hers in a commanding way, taming hers into submission, then backing off, making her come in search of him, encouraging her to be bolder, more daring. She took up the challenge, enjoying the deep murmurs of approval that came from his throat as her tongue danced with his.

His hands glided over her breasts, touching, teasing in unhurried strokes that made her heart race. He worked his way down her abdomen, those lazy caresses over her belly, hips and thighs making her skin tremble all over with need. She felt his erection move against her and got a sense of the urgency that was building in him from the increased rate of his breathing. It excited her that she was the one doing that to him, that she could have that sensual power over him.

He reached for a condom from the bedside drawer and tore the little packet with his teeth before applying it. He was not only a sensitive lover, but also a safety-conscious one. How different from her mother's experience with her father, who had only wanted to slake his lust without a thought for the consequences.

'Are you still sure you want to go ahead with this?' Rafe asked.

Poppy touched his steely length, her body already pulsing with a longing so intense it was like a pain deep inside. 'I want you to make love to me.'

His eyes meshed with hers for a long moment of intimacy that made her feel as if she was the only woman in the world he had ever wanted or would ever want. 'I'll go really slowly,' he said in a gravel-rough voice. 'Tell me if I'm hurting you.'

She put her arms around his neck and kissed his mouth, breathing in the male scent of him, the raspy feel of his stubble on her softer skin making her celebrate her femininity in a way she had never done before.

He moved against her, guiding himself as he gently nudged her apart. 'All right so far?'

Poppy nodded. 'I'm OK.'

'Relax, *ma petite*.' He waited for her to let go of her tight muscles before he tried again. 'You're in control, remember?'

She felt the glide of his body within hers, her own moisture making the passage far easier than she had thought possible. He was so big, yet her body stretched to accommodate him. She was feeling really proud of herself, but then he went that little bit deeper and a sharp pain tugged at her. 'Ouch!'

He stopped and held her steady, his deep-brown eyes full of concern. 'Sorry, *ma chérie*. That was too deep, yes?'

'No...I'm OK.' She took a little breath. 'I'm sorry for being such a drama queen.'

'You're not being a drama queen.' He brushed the hair back from her forehead. 'You're tiny. Just try not to tense up. Your muscles need to be relaxed to accommodate me. Let your legs go.' He kissed her softly on the mouth, making her melt into him as he slowly went deeper. Her tender flesh caught on him but it didn't hurt as much this time. She lifted her hips and he went in with a smooth, gliding thrust that made her gasp in pleasure.

He paused again. 'All right?'

'Mmm…' Poppy caressed his back and shoulders, getting used to the feel of him deep inside her. He started to thrust, the friction of his body within hers stirring sensations that spiralled out from her core. She felt the tight ache of want building inside her; it was a thrumming pulse that reverberated throughout her body.

Taking his cue from her, he gradually increased his pace, using his fingers to enhance her pleasure. She felt the exquisite goal approaching but it was just out of her reach. She shifted restlessly against him. 'I'm sorry. I can't do it.'

'Shhh,' he soothed her gently. 'Take all the time you need. I'm not going anywhere.'

Poppy gave herself up to his slowly measured thrusts, each one deeper and more exquisite than the one before. He caressed her intimately, varying the speed and pressure until she was hovering on the edge of a scarily high precipice.

'Go with it, *ma petite*,' he coaxed her gently. 'Don't hold back from it.'

Poppy gasped as the first wave of her orgasm smashed into her. She felt stunned by the velocity of it. It was like being on an out-of-control fairground ride. She was spinning around and around; she didn't know which way was up or which way was down. Every cell of her body seemed to be concentrated at that one point in her body. She threw her head back against the pillows as the sensations coursed through her. It went on and on, thrashing her about until she felt like she was being shaken alive.

He waited until she was coming out of it to take his own pleasure. She felt the increase of tension in him, felt the bunching of his muscles underneath her hands as he pitched himself into oblivion with a deep groan that was thrillingly, unmistakably male.

There was a long moment of silence.

Poppy wasn't sure what to say. What did you say after the most stunning experience of your life? 'Thanks' didn't seem quite appropriate somehow. Her emotions were scattered like the pieces of a jigsaw puzzle that had been shoved out of place. She didn't know what to think or feel. He had been so tender with her, so caring and considerate. How could she have thought she hated him? Her feelings were a little closer to the other end of the spectrum, but she didn't want to think about that right now. Falling in love with someone just because they were a fabulous lover wasn't a good enough reason, in her opinion. Loving someone had more to do with having similar values, and trust and commitment on both sides; knowing they would always be there for you, no matter what. Rafe Caffarelli wasn't making those sorts of promises. This was a fling and the sooner she got her head—and her body—around it the better.

He propped himself up again to look down at her. 'How do you feel?'

Poppy felt a little tug on her heart at the tender concern she could see in his gaze. 'I'm fine,' she said. 'No worse for wear…I think.'

He picked up one of her stray curls and tucked it behind her ear. 'You were amazing.'

She gave him her version of a worldly look. 'I bet you say that to all the girls.'

A frown pulled at his brow. 'I know you probably won't believe this, but it was different for me.'

'How?'

'Just…different.'

Poppy searched his features for a moment. 'I thought you were pretty amazing too.'

He gave her a slow smile that made her insides melt all over again. 'It's not like you have anyone to compare me to.'

'Not yet.'

His brows snapped together as he moved away and disposed of the condom. His movements seemed almost too controlled, stiff almost, as if he was trying to contain his emotions and not quite managing it. 'I might be a playboy, but I insist that my partners—no matter how temporary—are totally exclusive.'

Poppy sat up and hugged her knees to cover her nakedness. 'Touchy.'

He threw her a hard little glare. 'I mean it, Poppy. I am not unfaithful in my relationships and I won't tolerate it in a partner.'

'*Am* I a partner?'

He drew in a breath and released it in a rush as if he had come to a decision in his mind. 'You are now.'

'For how long?'

His eyes met hers, searing hers with hot longing and unbridled lust. 'This will burn itself out,' he said. 'It always does.'

'Give me a ballpark figure,' Poppy said. 'A week? A month?'

'I'm not planning on being down here for too much longer.' He scraped a hand through his hair to push it back off his forehead. The sexily tousled look made him look even more staggeringly gorgeous. 'And I'm not a great believer in long-distance relationships.'

She rested her chin on the top of her bent knees as

she wrapped her arms around her ankles. 'I guess you don't stay in one place long enough to form lasting attachments.'

'I don't want to give you false hopes, Poppy. I know girls like you want the whole package, but I'm not interested in that right now. I have too many other responsibilities to sort out first before I even think about settling down.'

'That's fine,' Poppy said, even though it wasn't. Could she settle for a short-term fling and leave it at that? How would she feel when it was over? Would she be so deeply in love with him by then her heart would be shattered when he walked out of her life for good?

Wasn't she already a teensy bit in love with him?

He came over and tipped up her chin so his eyes meshed with hers. She had to work hard not to show how conflicted she felt. Emotions she had never felt before were bubbling inside her. It felt like a vicious tug-of-war between pretence and honesty was pulling her in two. She wanted to tell him how she felt, that she loved him and wanted to be with him for ever, but the practical, sensible side of her resisted.

If she told him how she felt he would end their affair before it had even started. At least if she kept her feelings to herself she would have a few precious memories to treasure once he had moved on. And he would move on. Didn't his track record prove it?

'The press will probably hassle you for a few days,' he said. 'Try not to let it get to you.'

'I won't.'

He leaned down and pressed a lingering kiss to her mouth. 'You taste like spun sugar.'

Poppy gave him an arch look. 'I thought you didn't have a sweet tooth?'

His dark eyes glinted as he pressed her back down on the bed. 'I do now,' he said and covered her mouth with his.

CHAPTER TWELVE

POPPY WOKE TO the sound of birdsong at dawn. She stretched her legs and winced when she felt the tug of her tender feminine muscles. Rafe had been incredibly gentle with her last night, which had made it so much harder for her to keep her emotions in check. She had lain in his arms, feeling satiated, yet strangely dissatisfied. They were so close physically—she seriously wondered if two people could be closer—and yet she felt as if a chasm of difference separated them.

His world was so disparate from hers. He had the money to buy whatever he wanted, wherever he wanted, whenever he wanted. He could travel the globe and not have to stop and count the pennies. He had casual affairs that left no lasting impression on him. He probably didn't even remember their names after a few weeks or months had passed.

Would he remember her after this was over? How long before he forgot her name or what she looked like? How long before someone else took his fancy?

Poppy turned her head and looked at him lying beside her. He was lying on his back, one of his arms loosely around her shoulders, the other hanging over the edge of the bed. His breathing was deep and even, his body relaxed, yet there was a slight frown between his closed eyes, as if his mind was mulling over something complicated.

Before she was even aware she was doing it, she reached up with her fingertip and smoothed away the tiny three-pleat crease.

His eyes opened and met hers. 'Hasn't anyone told you before that you should let sleeping dogs lie?'

She moved her fingertip to his stubbly jaw, tracing a line from the side of his nose to the base of his chin. 'I'm not the least bit scared of dogs, even big scary ones who look like they might bite if cornered.'

He took her finger into his mouth and gently nipped it with his teeth, his eyes holding hers in a sexy little lock down that made the base of Poppy's spine tingle. 'You'd better stop looking at me like that.'

'How am I looking at you?'

'Like you want me to pin you to the bed and make mad, passionate love to you.'

Poppy felt a frisson of delight pass over her skin. 'Why shouldn't I look at you like that?'

He rolled her onto her back and entangled his legs with hers. 'Because I don't want to make you sore.'

She looked into his espresso-black gaze and felt another shackle around her heart slip away. How could she not love this man? He was so thoughtful and gentle, yet so passionate and attentive. How was she supposed to resist the feelings that were burgeoning inside her?

He was everything she had ever wanted in a partner.

From the first moment his mouth had met hers, she had felt a seismic shift in her body. How would she ever be satisfied with anyone else? Wouldn't she always compare them with him? His touch was like magic. His kisses were hypnotic, his gaze mesmerising and his possession captivating and cataclysmic. She would never be the same now she had shared this incredible intimacy with him. It wasn't just that he was her first lover; he had touched on something deep inside her that spoke to her on a primal level.

Poppy touched his face again, smoothing away the frown that had appeared again between his brows. 'When I met you for the first time when you came into the shop that day, I thought you were the most arrogant, unfeeling person I had ever met.'

'And now?'

She gave him a little smile that had a hint of reproof about it. 'You're still arrogant.'

He shrugged self-deprecatingly. 'It's my middle name.'

'I kind of figured that.' She trailed her fingertip over his lower lip. 'Are your brothers the same?'

'Raoul less so, Remy more so,' he said, looking at her mouth. 'I guess I fall somewhere in between.'

Poppy felt the rise of his body against her belly. The roar of his blood incited her own to race frenetically through her veins. Her heart began to thump when she saw the glittering intention in his dark-as-night gaze. Her body gave an involuntary shiver as his mouth came down and covered hers in a kiss that awoke every feminine instinct in her. Her tongue met his in an urgent tangle of lust that made her pelvis throb for his possession. She shifted against him, urging him to complete the erotic dance he had started.

He eased his mouth off hers and went in search of her breasts, trailing his hot, moist tongue over their sensitive peaks in turn. Each roll and glide of his tongue against her flesh escalated her desire. She felt the pull of it between her legs, the pulse of longing that was like a fever building in her blood.

He moved down her body, his mouth a hot, searing trail that made her back arch in delight. He lingered over her belly button, dipping the tip of his tongue into its tiny cave before going lower to where she ached and pulsed with feverish want.

Poppy sucked in a sharp breath as she felt him stroke her apart. His breath was a warm caress, his touch on her most sensitive point triggering a maelstrom of feeling. He read her body so well, timing the strokes and the pressure until her body responded in a turbulent wave of release that rocketed through her. She clung to the bed with clawing fingers to anchor herself against the avalanche of sensations that shuddered through her body, leaving her spent once it was over.

He stroked his hand down the length of her thigh as he looked into her eyes. 'You're so beautifully responsive.'

Poppy gazed back at him, dazed. She felt stunned by the way he made her feel. Her body was tingling from head to foot, her nerves dancing in delight at what they had experienced under his touch. 'I want to pleasure you,' she said, shyly reaching for him.

He drew in a breath when she curled her hand around his length. She saw the flash of pleasure in his eyes, felt too the rising tension in him as she moved her hand in a rhythmic motion up and down his shaft. She ran her thumb over his moist tip and watched as he fought to control his response. It spurred her on to be even more adventurous. She gave him a sultry look and slithered down his body, breathing over him first, tantalising him with what was to come.

He gripped the sides of her head with his hands. 'If you're not comfortable with doing that...' He let out a short sharp expletive as her tongue found him. 'At least let me put on a condom.'

Poppy pulled back as he fished out a condom. She took the little packet off him and set about putting it on him. He drew in another harsh-sounding breath, his abdomen contracting as she smoothed it over his length. His raw male beauty took her breath away. He was so thick with desire. She could feel the thunder of his blood against her fingers.

She lowered her head to him again, licking him at first, letting him feel the warmth of her tongue through the thin barrier of the condom. She became bolder as her confidence grew, taking him into her mouth, sucking on him with varying degrees of pressure to see what he preferred. He gave her all the encouragement she needed with deep, growly groans of pleasure as the tension built inside him.

It was much more pleasurable than Poppy had been expecting. She had always imagined the act to be a very one-sided affair, and to some degree subservient, perhaps even slightly demeaning.

But it was nothing like that.

The feminine power she had over him thrilled her and excited her. Her lips and mouth registered every subtle change as he hurtled towards the final moment of release. The tension in him rose to a crescendo, his breathing becoming more rapid and uneven, his hands clutching at her head with a desperation that made the blood fizz and sing with delight in her veins. She felt that final cataclysmic explosion; it made the fine hairs on the back of her neck lift up to sense the monumental power of his response to her.

He pulled away from her and dealt with the condom, his breathing sounding ragged in the silence.

'Was that...OK?' Poppy asked.

He cupped one of her cheeks in his hand, his look tender. 'You were wonderful. Perfect.'

'I have a lot of catching up to do,' she said, tracing a fingertip over his collarbone. 'Chloe told me I'd have to have heaps of sex to catch up with other girls my age.'

The smile went out of his eyes and his hand fell away from her face as he got off the bed. 'It's not a competition, Poppy.' He stepped into his trousers and zipped them up almost savagely. 'There's no prize for the person who's bedded the most partners.'

Poppy watched as he shrugged himself back into his shirt. His movements seemed tense, angry almost. 'Do you know how many lovers you've had?'

His frown carved deep into his forehead. 'I stopped counting a long time ago.'

'Have there been any stand-outs?'

He looked at her quizzically. 'Stand-outs?'

'You know…women who've left a lasting impression on you.'

He let out a breath and began to hunt for his shoes. 'No one that springs immediately to mind.'

Not even me? Poppy's heart sank like a stone. She wanted him to see her differently. She didn't want to be just another nameless notch on his bedpost. She wanted to *matter* to him.

To have him love her.

Was it foolish of her to hope he would fall in love with her in spite of the very real differences in their backgrounds? Their physical compatibility was unquestionable, even given her limited experience. She sensed a much deeper connection, one that he might not be ready to admit to, but it was there all the same. Hadn't it been there right from the start? That clock-stopping moment when their eyes had met for the first time when he'd stepped over the threshold of her tearoom. That single moment in time had changed everything. She had thought she was sparring with her worst enemy but instead he had turned into the love of her life.

Their first kiss, the way their mouths had communicated a need that was unlike anything she had felt before; once his mouth had met hers she knew she would never be the same. How could she be? He had unlocked sensations and responses she had not even known she possessed.

Their first time joined together as lovers had felt much more than a physical union. She had felt as if he had reached deep inside her and touched her soul. She would never be able to look back on their time together as just a casual fling. It wouldn't matter how many times she made love with other partners, she would never forget Rafe's tender touch and mind-blowing passion.

Would he come to think of her the same way?

Poppy swung her legs over the edge of the bed, wincing as her tender inner muscles protested at the movement.

Rafe was beside her in an instant with a frown tugging at his brow. 'Are you all right?'

'I'm fine.'

He slid a gentle hand down the length of her bare arm, encircling her wrist with his fingers.

Poppy looked up into his concerned gaze, her love for him feeling like a clamp around her heart. How was she supposed to navigate her way through an affair with him? She wanted the whole package. She would never be satisfied with a few weeks with him.

She wanted for ever.

She lowered her gaze in case he saw the desperate longing there. 'I'll be fine…'

He brushed her cheek with the back of his knuckles. 'When was the last time you took a break from work?'

'It's been a while…' She frowned as she thought about it for a moment. 'Not since I came back to look after my gran.'

'Can Chloe hold the fort for a few days?'

She met his gaze again. 'How many days?'

He stroked the underside of her chin with a lazy finger. 'Four or five, maybe we could stretch it to a week. I'd have to check my diary.'

'Where are you thinking of going?'

'Paris.'

Poppy's heart swelled in hope. *The city of love…*

'I have a meeting there early next week,' he said. 'But afterwards I thought we could spend a few days doing touristy things. By the time we get back, your house should be fixed.'

Did that mean their affair would be over when they got back? Was this his way of indulging his desire for her without letting her take too permanent a place in his life?

As far as she knew he had never lived with a lover before. But then, strictly speaking, she wasn't living with him. He had offered her a roof over her head until hers was repaired. He wasn't going to make the manor his home. It was a profit-making exercise, a money-spinner that held no sentimental value to him at all.

Poppy rolled her lips together uncertainly. *Could she do it?* Could she step outside of her normal, rather mundane life and spend a few days in his exotic world of untold riches and privilege? 'I'd have to check with Chloe first.'

'Let me know tonight.' He brushed her mouth with a brief kiss. 'I've got to dash. There's a landscaper coming to see me this morning about the gardens. I want to sketch out a few more plans before he gets here.'

Poppy frowned. 'What sort of plans do you have in mind?'

'I want to get rid of the wild garden,' he said. 'It's too rambling and chaotic. I want more structure and formality. It will better suit the overall feel for the hotel I have in mind.'

'But the wild garden is one of the most beautiful features of Dalrymple Manor,' she said. 'How can you possibly think of changing it?'

He gave her the sort of look a parent gives to a child who hasn't quite grasped right from wrong. 'How can you possibly think of leaving it the way it is? It's full of weeds and nondescript plants.'

'Those weeds and nondescript plants have been there for hundreds of years,' she said. 'You can't just waltz in and rip them all out.'

'I can and I will,' he said with a challenging glint of determination in his gaze. 'It's called possession and progress.'

Poppy clenched her jaw and her hands. 'It's called desecration and bad taste.'

His mouth tilted. 'You think I've got bad taste?'

'You have appalling taste.'

He arched a brow. 'In women?'

She gave her head a little toss. 'I definitely think you could lift your standards a bit. That last mistress you had was clearly after money and notoriety. It was pretty obvious she didn't like you as a person; she just liked your money.'

He gave an indifferent shrug. 'She was just another woman who came along.'

'Just like me?'

His gaze held hers for a beat. 'I've not made any promises to you, Poppy.'

'No,' she said, flashing him a defiant look. 'And I'm not making any to you.'

He took that on board with a half-smile that didn't reach his eyes. 'Let me know what you decide about Paris. I'll get my secretary to make the arrangements.'

Poppy let out a jagged breath once he had left. Would she be making the biggest mistake of her life by going with him to Paris? Or would it be an even bigger one to deny herself a precious few days with him before he called an end to their affair?

Rafe tried to give the landscaper his full attention but his mind kept drifting back to Poppy. She had looked so gorgeously tousled this morning after spending the night in his arms. He had watched her sleep for a couple of hours after they had made love. She had curled up against him like a little cat, her soft skin warm and sensual against his.

His stomach gave a little free fall every time he thought of how tender she was after his possession. When he'd disposed of the first condom, he had seen a smear of blood on it. He hadn't thought he would be so moved by the experience of sharing her first time with her. He had thought himself far too modern and progressive to consider a woman's virginity as some sort of prize to gloat over. But the intimacy he had shared with Poppy had made him realise how mundane and predictable his sex life had become over the years. His encounters were little more than physical transactions of mutual pleasure. There was no sentiment attached, no feeling that life would never be the same if that person were never to return to his bed...

'And over here we could do a fountain or water fea-
ture.' The landscape designer pointed to the middle of
the wild garden. 'We could pave it with sandstone.'

Rafe gave himself a mental shake. 'Right… I'll have
a think about it and get back to you.'

'I've had a look at the maze,' the designer said. 'It's
going to be a big job to restore it. It's been neglected
for years, by the look of it. And that storm the other
day didn't help things. It needs replanting in a couple
of places.'

'I don't care about the expense,' Rafe said. 'Do what
needs to be done.'

'Cute dogs.' The landscape designer crouched down
and made 'come here' noises to Chutney, Pickles and
Relish who had been following Rafe like devoted slaves
since he had walked out of the manor that morning.
'My wife has a couple of Maltese poodly things. Never
thought I'd be one to go gaga over a fluffy mutt, but
there you go. They worm their way into your heart, don't
they?'

'They're not mine,' Rafe said. 'Watch out for the grey
and white one. He'll nip at you if you come too close.'

Pickles immediately took shelter behind Rafe's left
leg, peering out with his beady gaze. The man straightened after ruffling Chutney and Relish's ears. 'I'll get
back to you with a quote on the development and the
maze in a day or two,' he said. 'Say hi to Poppy for me.'

Rafe frowned. 'You know her?'

'My mother and her gran were best friends. She's a
sweetheart, isn't she? Got a heart of gold. Does a lot for
the village—in the background, like. When my wife had
a caesarean with our twins, Poppy came by every day
with a hot meal prepared. Even took home the washing
and brought it back all neatly folded and ironed.' He gave

Rafe a man-to-man wink. 'She'll make some lucky guy a fabulous wife one day.'

Rafe stretched his mouth into a tight smile. 'I'm sure she will.'

CHAPTER THIRTEEN

'Paris…' Chloe gave a wistful sigh. 'You do realise you're living every girl's dream? Being taken to the city of love with a handsome billionaire to be wined and dined and passionately wooed.'

Poppy chewed her lip as she put some pieces of sultana-and-cherry slice on a flowered plate ready for the display cabinet. 'It's mostly a business trip for Rafe. I'm just tagging along as entertainment.'

'I don't believe that,' Chloe said. 'He's falling for you, big time. Next thing you know, he'll be down on bended knee. You see if I'm not right. And what better place to propose to you than Paris?'

'He's not going to propose to me,' Poppy said with a heavy heart. 'He's going to send me on my way once this week in Paris is over with a bit of jewellery as a consolation prize. I bet he won't even choose it himself. He'll get one of his secretaries to do it.'

Chloe sucked in one side of her cheek as she studied Poppy's downcast features. 'You really are in love with him, aren't you?'

Poppy let out a serrated sigh. 'When he came into the shop that first day I thought he was the biggest jerk I'd ever met. It just goes to show you can't trust first impressions. Underneath that cold, hard business front he puts up, I suspect he's a really caring person.'

'So what's the problem?'

Poppy's shoulders dropped. 'He doesn't care about me…or at least, not the way I want him to care.'

'What's the hurry?' Chloe said. 'You've only known him, what, a week or two? Give him time.'

'But what if it's not me he's really after?' Poppy finally voiced the fear that had been lurking in her mind ever since Rafe had made love to her. 'What if he's only involved with me to charm me into selling him the dower house?'

Chloe's forehead wrinkled. 'Do you really think he'd do something as low as that?'

'I don't know… Look at what Oliver did. I didn't see that coming. Maybe I just attract the type of guys who think they can pull the wool over my eyes.'

'You *are* a bit of a babe in the woods,' Chloe said, but not unkindly. 'Be careful, hon. Just take it one day at a time. Enjoy what's on offer while it's on offer. That's all you can do.'

'Do you fly *everywhere* in a private jet?' Poppy asked Rafe the following Monday as they were about to leave London.

'I hate waiting around gate lounges,' he said. 'It's such a waste of time.'

She rolled her eyes at him. 'I hope you realise that, now the dogs have been placed in those plush boarding kennels you organised for them, they'll never be happy staying anywhere else. They'll probably turn their little noses up at their stainless steel dishes when they get back. I'll have to get them gold or silver ones, or maybe diamond-encrusted ones.'

He gave her a bone-melting smile. 'I don't see why they can't have a good time as well as us.'

Poppy had no doubt she was going to have a good time while she was away—a *very* good time. The last few nights with him had left her body tingling with delight. This morning he had joined her in the shower, leaving her quivering with ecstasy. Just looking at him now made her insides slip like a drawer pulled out too quickly. His dark eyes contained a sensual promise that made her toes curl up and her heart race.

There was one attendant on the flight who served them champagne and canapés and then pulled and locked the sliding door across the cabin to give them privacy.

Poppy took a sip of her champagne. 'Do your brothers have private jets too or do you share this one?'

'We each have our own. My grandfather has two.'

She studied him for a moment. 'Do you ever think of how different your life would be if you'd been born into another family? One without loads and loads of money to burn?'

A frown settled between his brows. 'I don't *burn* money for the sake of it, Poppy.'

She toyed with the stem of her glass. 'Maybe not, but I bet you've never had to worry about where your next meal is coming from.'

'I know that anyone looking from the outside would think people with enormous wealth have it easy, but having money brings its own issues,' he said. 'The one you mentioned the first day we met, for instance.'

Poppy screwed up her face as she tried to remember. 'What did I say?'

'You said I probably lie awake at night wondering if people liked me for me or just for my money.'

She pulled at her lower lip with her teeth. 'I probably

shouldn't have said that. I didn't even know you then. I was just making horrible assumptions about you.'

He stroked a finger down the back of her hand resting on the armrest between them. 'I made a few about you that weren't all that accurate too.'

Poppy met his gaze. 'I want you to know I like you for you, not for your money. We could've come to Paris by car or even by train or bus and I wouldn't have minded one little bit.'

His smile was lopsided as he brushed the curve of her cheek with an idle fingertip. 'You're very sweet, Poppy Silverton.'

'I expect what you really mean is I'm terribly naïve.'

His smile was exchanged for a frown. 'Why would you think that?'

Poppy gave him a direct look. 'How do I know this trip to Paris isn't part of your plan to get me to relinquish the dower house?'

His frown deepened. 'Is that what you really think?'

'You can't deny you still want it.'

'Of course I still want it,' he said. 'But that's got nothing to do with our affair.'

Poppy wanted to believe him. She *ached* to believe him. But how could she be sure what his motives were? He had been upfront about his intentions over the dower house from the very first day. He wasn't one to be dissuaded from a goal.

He played to win, not to lose.

A compromise would be anathema to someone as task-oriented as him. He would see that as failure, as a weakness.

'I'm not going to sell it to you, Rafe. I don't care how many private jets you take me on, or how much champagne you give me to drink. I'm not selling my house to you, or to anyone.'

He unclipped his belt and stood up, raking a hand through his hair in a gesture of frustration and impatience. 'Do you really think I would stoop that low?' he asked. 'What sort of man do you think I am?'

'A very determined one.' She eyeballed him. 'Stealthy, single-minded and steely, or so the press would have us believe.'

He gave a cynical bark of laughter. 'And you take that as gospel, do you?'

'I want to believe your motives are honourable,' Poppy said. 'But how can I be sure you want me for me?'

He came over to her and lifted her chin so her gaze meshed with his. 'I'm not going to deny I want the dower house. I can't go ahead with my development plans for the manor without it. But this thing between us is entirely separate.'

Was it? Was it really?

He unclipped her belt and drew her to her feet. 'I want *you, ma chérie*. I've wanted you from the very first moment I laid eyes on you.'

But for how long? The words were a mocking taunt inside her head. His track record of quickly turned-over relationships didn't bode well for her hopes of marriage and babies and a happy-ever-after. It was the hopeless romantic in her that hoped she would be the one to change him.

How many women just like her had been burnt by the same deluded dream?

Poppy pushed her doubts aside and gave him a little teasing smile as she started working on the knot of his tie. 'So…just how private is this jet of yours?'

His eyes glittered as he tugged her against him. 'Very,' he said and lowered his mouth to hers.

Rafe's apartment was more like a villa than an apartment. It was a six bedroom luxuriously appointed property not far from the Ritz Hotel overlooking *Jardin des Tuileries*. It was definitely the top end of town. For Poppy, who had only ever travelled on a shoe-string budget, it was certainly an eye opener. She tried not to act too star struck or over-awed but it was impossible not to feel a little envious of the wealth Rafe had at his fingertips.

Rafe had organised dinner at Moulin Rouge in Montmartre and Poppy sat transfixed as the can can show Paris was famous for played out so vibrantly and colourfully before her. After the show he took her to another venue where there was live music and dancing.

'But I'm rubbish at dancing,' Poppy protested when he took her by the hand to lead her to the dance floor.

'Just follow my lead,' he said, drawing her close against him.

It was hard at first not to think everyone was looking at her tripping over her own feet, but after a while she started to relax as Rafe led her in a slow waltz to the tune of a romantic ballad.

'See?' he said against her hair. 'You're a natural.'

'You're a very good teacher,' Poppy said, looking up at him.

His pitch-black eyes glinted. 'You're a very fast learner, *ma petite*.'

She moved against him and shivered in delight when she felt his arousal. 'I guess I should make the most of my limited time under your tutelage,' she said flippantly.

His lips pressed together and his eyes lost their light

spark. 'We should get going,' he said, dropping his arms from around her. 'It's getting late and I have an early meeting in the morning.'

Poppy mentally kicked herself for spoiling a perfectly good evening. What was the point of reminding him their relationship was temporary? She trudged after him with her spirits sagging like sodden sheets on a clothes line. Why couldn't she just be satisfied with what she had rather than what she didn't have? Most girls would give anything to have a week or two with someone like Rafe. She had seen the envious looks from other women all evening. Rafe's good looks and aura of power and authority were incredibly head-turning. What right did she have to insist on more from him when they had only known each other such a short time?

The problem was she *knew* he was 'the one'. She had known that the first time he had kissed her. His love-making had only reinforced her conviction. She couldn't imagine being with anyone else. She didn't want to be with anyone else.

Once they were out on the street, Poppy touched him on the forearm. 'Rafe, I'm sorry. I'm being a cow. It must be the jet lag.'

His fingers enveloped her hand and gave it a tiny squeeze. 'I understand you want to feel more secure, *mon coeur*. Let's just take it a day at a time, hmm? I have a lot on my mind right now with my work.'

'I'm sorry…I didn't realise,' she said. 'Is your meeting tomorrow worrying you?'

He tucked her arm through his as they walked back to the car. 'There are always worries when you are responsible for people's jobs and careers. Tomorrow's meeting is with one of my accountants based here. For a while now I've had some concerns that he's been fudging the books now and again. I've had an independent audit done. The results will be put on the table tomorrow. It's not looking good.'

'Oh no, that's awful,' Poppy said.

'Yes.' He gave her a brief glance before turning his gaze ahead, resigned. 'I'm not looking forward to it. He's got a wife and young family. He's worked for me since he graduated from university. It's hard not to feel betrayed.'

'There's no worse feeling, is there?' Poppy said. 'That someone you trusted has exploited you.'

He stopped walking and turned to look at her. 'Is that what happened with your boyfriend?'

Poppy grimaced. 'I hate even thinking of him as my boyfriend now. Thank God I didn't sleep with him. I'd have been feeling even more foolish now if I had.'

He tucked a curl of her hair behind her ear, a thoughtful expression on his face. 'I was talking to Howard Compton about you the other day.'

Poppy lifted her brows. 'I didn't know you two were friends.'

He gave her a sheepish smile. 'I drop in every day or so for a wee dram, as he calls it. I can't stand whisky but I haven't got the heart to tell him. I enjoy his company. He's a nice old chap. Nothing like my grandfather, which is probably why I like him so much.'

'What did you say to him about me?'

'I told him I had drawn up a business plan for you, the one I showed you the other night.'

Poppy bit her lip. She hadn't actually got around to looking at it too closely and she was pretty sure Rafe knew it.

'You have to learn to say no, *ma petite*,' he said. 'You'll go under if you don't learn to stand up for yourself. People will respect you for it.'

'I'll try.'

He looped an arm around her shoulders and, drawing her towards him, kissed the top of her head. 'Good girl.'

Back at his apartment, Rafe came out of the bathroom and found Poppy busily taking pictures of the art deco furnishings with her mobile phone. 'If you like them so much I'll buy you some,' he said.

She swung around guiltily, blushing like a kid caught with her hand in the cookie jar. 'It's a lovely apartment. You have wonderful taste.'

Rafe came over, took the phone out of her hand and tossed it on the bed. 'I want your hands free for the next little while.'

'Oh really?' She gave him a sparkling smile. 'What did you have in mind?'

He unclipped her hair and watched as it tumbled around her shoulders. The honeysuckle fragrance of it wafted towards him. He threaded his fingers through its thick, silky tresses, loving the feel of it against his fingers. He brought his mouth to hers, tasting her sweetness, losing himself in the lush softness of her lips and the shy response of her tongue as he summoned it into play with his.

Her body moved against him in that delightfully instinctive feminine way, fitting against the hard planes of his frame as if she had been tailor-made for him. He put a hand at the base of her spine and pushed her against his erection. His need for her was a throbbing pulse that drove every other thought out of his head. The desire to ravish her was almost overwhelming, but the gentleman in him would not rush her or push her beyond her comfort zone.

She gave a little whimper as he skated a hand over the

globe of her breast. He loved the shape of her, the way her breast fit so neatly into his hand, how soft her skin was, how sensitive to his touch.

'You're wearing too many clothes,' he murmured against her mouth.

'So are you.' She tugged his shirt out of his trousers and moved her soft little palm over his chest.

A surge of lust almost knocked him off his feet. He found the zip at the back of her dress and lowered it. Her dress slipped to the floor and she stepped out of the circle of fabric, still with her mouth clamped on his and her slim arms looped around his neck.

Rafe smoothed his hands over her back, deftly unhooking her bra in the process. He slipped off her lacy knickers, running his hands over her neat bottom, teasing her with a feather-light touch on her feminine folds. He felt for her slickness, his insides coiling with desire when he found her ready for him.

She undid his belt and unzipped him with ruthless purpose. He sucked in a breath when she finally uncovered him. Her touch was mind-blowing. The blood roared through his veins, his desire at fever pitch. When she started caressing him in bolder and bolder strokes he thought he was going to disgrace himself.

He pulled her hand away and took a steadying breath. 'Not so fast, *ma belle*.'

'I want you.' Her toffee-brown eyes held his in a sultry little lock that made his heart race. She walked into him until he had nowhere to go but lie on the bed, taking her down with him.

Her body was draped temptingly over him as she took both of his hands and put them above his head. 'What are you doing?' he asked.

'I'm tying you up.'

Rafe laughed as she wrapped his tie around his wrists and anchored it to the bedpost. Did she really think that flimsy piece of silk was going to restrain him? He'd let her play her little game, but he would be free before she could say 'cupcake'. He was the one in control here, not her. But it would be fun to let her think she was on top, so to speak.

She slithered back down his body, her thighs trapping his between hers, the look in her eyes making his blood heat to boiling. She picked up the fullness of her hair and flung it over her shoulder so she could get down to business.

Rafe's insides quivered as she put her lips around him. *No condom.* He tested the hold on the tie but it was surprisingly—*terrifyingly*—firm.

Her first tongue stroke was long, hot, wet and nearly sent him over the edge.

He struggled against the bonds. 'What the hell?'

She looked up from beneath her lashes from where she was poised over his painfully thick erection. 'That's what you get for insisting on a designer brand. You should have settled for a cheap chain-store one.'

Rafe sucked in another breath as she teased him some more with her tongue. He tried to count backwards; he thought of all the distracting things he could, like the mounds of paperwork that needed to be dealt with, but none of it worked. She began to draw on him as if she was going to turn him inside out with the hot, wet suction of her mouth. He felt himself lift off and soar. He lost all sense of himself as he pumped himself into a mindless oblivion that surpassed anything he had felt before.

She gave him a naughty smile as she untied his wrists. 'So, Mr Must Have Control At All Times. How did that feel?'

'Amazing.' Rafe pushed a finger into her and watched as her face gave a spasm of pleasure. She pushed against him, urging him on, inciting him. He withdrew his finger and flipped her around so her back was to him. He pressed up against her, letting her feel the growing, hot, hard heat of him from behind. She gave a sensuous wriggle against him, searching for him with a sexy little hitch of her hips. It was all he could do to stop from thrusting into her without protection. 'Wait,' he said, stalling her with a hand on her left hip. 'I need a condom.'

Once it was on he came back to her, sliding his hands down her slim sides, breathing in the aroused fragrance of her. 'Are you comfortable with this?' he asked against the back of her neck.

She gave a little murmur of assent and wriggled against him again.

Rafe thrust in slowly, gauging her response, trying to keep control when all he wanted to do was explode inside her tight warmth. She urged him on with little kittenish mews that made his skin come up in goose bumps. He started to move, his thrusts going deeper and deeper, then harder and faster. She was with him all the way, her body accepting him, responding to him with such frenzied passion it made him teeter on the edge of control all over again.

He slipped a hand between her legs to give her that extra friction, and within seconds she was convulsing around him, her cries of pleasure and the tight contractions of her body triggering his own spectacular release. He emptied himself, shivering all over in that blissful aftermath.

He didn't want to step away from her and break that intimate connection. He felt his erection subsiding but knew it wouldn't take long to get it going again. His desire for Poppy was increasing rather than abating. Usually by this stage in a relationship he was getting a little restless, even a little bored. But with Poppy every time was so completely different, more exciting, more satisfying....more *addictive*.

Her glib comment about making the most of her time with him had annoyed him. He wasn't ready to commit to anything without some serious thought. Choosing a life partner was a big deal. He had seen too many marriages come unstuck because they had been forged out of lust rather than common sense.

He was a planner, a strategist, not an impulsive fool. He was not at the mercy of his loins.

At least, not unless he was tied up.

His conversation with Raoul had got him thinking, however. He didn't want to end up like his grandfather, having to pay people to be with him in his old age. The thought of a wife who would be a lover, friend and confidante was rather attractive. So too was the thought of children. Only that evening they had walked past a young couple pushing a pram. Rafe had seen Poppy's covert glance at the cute baby inside. It had got him thinking of how beautiful she would look if she were pregnant. With her coltish limbs and ballerina-like figure, she would be all baby. He hadn't realised how sexy a pregnant women looked until now... Or, at least, how sexy Poppy would look.

What are you thinking? You've known her how long—two weeks?

He had to get a grip on himself. Maybe it had been a mistake to bring her to Paris. It wasn't called the city of love for nothing.

Love.

That was one four-letter word he didn't like to think about too much.

Rafe moved away from her and disposed of the condom. She turned and looked at him in that coy way of hers he found so incredibly endearing. She had played the game of temptress with stunning aplomb, but deep down she would always be an old-fashioned girl. He felt a string being plucked deep inside him as she picked up her dress and used it like a shield against her nakedness. 'You don't have to hide yourself from me, Poppy.'

Her teeth bit into her lower lip. 'I know. It's just I can't help thinking you're probably comparing me to all the other women you've slept with.'

The irony was Rafe could barely recall the names, let alone the features, of his previous lovers. He came over to her and cupped her face in his hands. 'You are the most beautiful woman I have ever been with—not just in terms of looks, but in terms of who you are as a person. And let me tell you, that's far more important.'

'Do you really mean that?'

He pressed a lingering kiss to her mouth. 'I mean that.'

CHAPTER FOURTEEN

POPPY WAS WAITING outside the building where Rafe had his meeting when he came out. He had been expecting her to go shopping for the morning. He had even given her a credit card to use. She had slipped it in her purse without argument, but he had seen the way her lips had pressed together momentarily, as if she had felt compromised in some way. Her reaction had been completely different from any other woman he had been with. Some had barely contained their excitement at being given carte blanche. It was a refreshing change to think Poppy had not taken his generosity for granted.

She stepped up and slipped her hand into his. 'Are you OK?'

'I need a drink.'

'That's not always the best solution.'

He pushed a hand through his hair. 'I know. I hate myself right now. I just sacked a man who has a wife and three little kids.'

She gave him a sympathetic look. 'Was there no alternative?'

Rafe looked down at her heart-shaped face. She was so innocent, so unjaded. 'He's got a gambling problem. He's ripped me off for hundreds of thousands of euros.

It's been going on for a couple of years. I should be pressing criminal charges.'

A little worried frown pulled at her brow. 'But you're not going to do that, are you?'

He let out a long, jagged breath. 'No.'

'There are programs, you know? For problem gamblers,' she said. 'What about if you offered to sponsor him through one? You could strike a deal with him. He has to do the program while you support his wife and kids, or he has to go to jail.'

Rafe gripped her by the shoulders and pulling her towards him, pressing a brief, hard kiss to her mouth. 'You are absolutely brilliant. Do you know that?'

She gave him a shy smile. 'I wouldn't go as far as saying that.'

He took out his phone and started scrolling through his contacts. 'Give me five minutes. Once I get this sorted, we are going to have a night to remember.'

It did turn out to be a night to remember, but for all the wrong reasons. Poppy was sitting in an award-winning restaurant with him when Rafe's phone rang. She had seen him switch it to silent as they entered the premises, but even with the subtle background music the vibration of it was still audible. He gave her an apologetic look and took it out of his breast pocket.

His face dropped right in front of her. Her heart contracted in panic as she saw the way his features tightened.

'Is he going to make it?'

Poppy felt her stomach tighten in dread. Whose life was hanging in the balance? Rafe's face was pinched and white with shock. Was it his grandfather; one of his brothers or one of his friends; one of his employees?

'I'll get there as soon as I can.' He ended the call and looked at her, ashen-faced. 'My brother Raoul has had an accident whilst water skiing at Lake Como. He's got suspected spinal injuries.'

'Oh no…'

'I have to go to him.' He got up so abruptly the glasses rattled on the table. 'I'm sorry about this week. I'll have to cut it short. I'll get my Paris secretary to organise your flight home.'

'Can't I come with you?' Poppy asked as they left the restaurant. 'You'll need support and I can—'

'No.' The word was clipped and hard, intractable. 'I want you to fly home. I'll deal with this on my own.'

'But surely it would be better if you—?'

He gave her a frowning glare. 'Did you not hear what I just said? I don't want you with me. This is about my family. It's my responsibility, not yours.'

Poppy flinched. 'I know you're upset, Rafe, but—'

'But what?' he asked. 'You knew this was how it was going to be, Poppy. I never said this was for ever. We both have our own lives. And mine just reared its big, ugly head.'

Her stomach dropped in despair as they made their way back to their hotel in a taxi. What did this mean? Did he mean it was over between them? She wasn't brave enough to ask. She sat in a miserable silence, feeling his tension and worry in the air combining with her own in a knotty tangle that seemed to be pulling on her heart.

When they got back to their hotel, Rafe barely paused long enough to gather his passport and a change of clothes. Poppy felt so helpless. She wanted to reach out to him but it was like an invisible fortress had formed around him. He was closing off from her. She could see it in the tight set of his features, as if something deep inside him was drawing him away from her inch by inch.

'Is there anything I can do?' she asked when she could bear it no longer.

He looked up from his phone after sending another text, one of many he had sent in the last few minutes. 'What?' The one word was sharp and his frown deep, as if he had already forgotten who she was and why she was there.

Poppy felt her heart contract again. 'I said, is there anything I can do for you while you're away?'

'No.' He pocketed his phone, his expression closing off even further. 'There's nothing. I have to do this alone.' He took a short breath and then released it. 'It's over, Poppy.'

'*Over?*' She looked at him numbly. 'You don't really mean that, do you?'

His look was even more distant. 'Look, I have to go. My brother needs me. I'll get Margaret to send you something to make up for this abrupt end to our affair.'

She drew herself up straighter. 'Please don't bother.'

He reached for his jacket. 'I'll be in touch about the dower house. Hopefully we can come to some agreement.'

'I'm not going to change my mind.'

He gave her another grimly determined look. 'Nor am I.'

As he closed the door on his exit, Poppy wondered if he was talking about her, the dower house, or both.

It was terrible seeing his younger brother in intensive care hooked up to monitoring machines and IV drips. Rafe's stomach was clenched so tightly he could barely breathe. Remy was standing by Raoul's bedside with a look of such bewilderment on his face it reminded Rafe of the day they had been told their parents had been killed. The weight of responsibility back then was like a leaden yoke on his ten-year-old shoulders. He had realised at that moment he had to take control—that at seven and almost nine his brothers were far too young to understand what had happened and how it would impact on them. He'd had to take charge, to step up to the plate and make them feel someone was looking out for them.

He felt the same now.

'He's not going to die.' Rafe said it without really believing it. It was his role to give assurance, to keep control. To support his brothers and keep the family together no matter what tragedy was thrown at them.

Remy swallowed convulsively. 'What if he can't walk again?'

'Don't even think about it,' Rafe said. He had already thought about it—how it would impact on Raoul, who was the most physically active of them all. His brother would rather be dead than spend his life trapped in a wheelchair; Rafe was sure of it. His job now as his older brother would be to keep him focused on getting as well as he could, to give him hope that he would one day be able to walk again. Medical breakthroughs were happening all the time, admittedly not as quickly as everyone hoped, but it would be crazy to give up hope. He had to keep Raoul positive about a possible recovery.

He looked at his brother lying so pale and broken. He looked at those long, strong legs lying useless in the hospital bed. How would Raoul cope with never feeling the floor beneath his feet, the sand between his toes… the sensuous feel of a lover's legs entwined with his?

It was painfully, torturously ironic that only days ago Raoul had expressed to Rafe over that beer they had shared his desire to settle down. How likely was that going to be now? What if he had no function at all? The doctors had been very cautious in what they had said so far. Perhaps they didn't know until more scans and tests were done. Spinal injuries could be mild or serious and just about everything in between.

'We'll have to tell *Nonno*,' Remy said, pulling Rafe out of his painful reverie.

'Yes.' Rafe stood up and took out his phone. 'He won't be much help, though. He'll just blame Raoul for being such an adrenalin-junkie. You were probably too young to remember what he said when *Mama* and *Papa* were killed. But I have never forgotten and I've never forgiven him.'

'I remember...' Remy's expression was shadowed, haunted. He swallowed again, thickly, as if something hard and misshapen was stuck in his throat. 'Did you know Raoul was thinking about getting engaged to Clarissa Moncrief? I think he was going to propose to her while they were on this trip to the lake.'

Rafe felt his stomach clench again. He had caught a glimpse of Clarissa in the waiting room earlier. She had darted out to the ladies' room rather than speak to him. That didn't bode well in his opinion. Would she stick around for Raoul if things didn't go according to plan?

He couldn't help thinking of Poppy, how she had offered to come with him to support him. He had pushed her away because that was what he always did when he had to focus.

He missed her.

It was hard to admit it, but he did. He missed her in a hundred different ways—her smile her tinkling-bell laugh; the scent of her, a mixture of sugar and spice and all things nice.

But he would damn well have to get used to missing her. He couldn't take her with him back to Italy once this was sorted out. It had been crazy to think of a future with her, or a future with anyone right now. He had even more responsibilities on his shoulders now. How could he possibly think of settling down when Raoul was in such a state? It would be selfish and crass of him to rub his brother's nose in it by announcing his own engagement.

But you love her, you idiot.

Hang on a minute. His sensible control-centre cut in. What fool would fall in love so quickly? It was lust, that was what it was.

He should never have got into an affair with her in the first place. He'd been blindsided by lust. It had affected his judgement. It was uncharacteristic of him to act so impulsively and now he had to deal with the consequences. She would find someone else, someone who was more in her world of hearth and home and cute, fluffy dogs.

But the least he could do was go and see her about the dower house once he got Raoul stabilised.

That was the plan, the goal.

Now he had to focus.

'I know you told me never to mention his name around here again,' Chloe said a couple of weeks later. 'But have you heard how Rafe's brother doing? There's been nothing in the press since the first report of the accident. It's like there's been a block out on it or something.'

Poppy let out a painful sigh. 'I called his secretary a couple of times. There's still some uncertainty about his mobility. He has some feeling in his legs, so at least that's a positive. It could be much worse.'

'God, life really sucks sometimes,' Chloe said. 'Is

Rafe coming back to the manor? Did his secretary say anything about his plans?'

'She said he would be back in a couple of weeks to pick up his things.'

'Don't give up on him yet,' Chloe said. 'Sometimes tragic occurrences make people take stock of their lives. He might want you with him by his side as he helps his brother get through this.'

Poppy wished she had Chloe's confidence but she knew Rafe was a lone wolf when it came to handling difficult things. It had taken a lot for him to tell her about his concerns with the accountant who had been defrauding him. He had told her even less about his childhood, but she suspected it had been desperately lonely, and that he had been given far too much responsibility for a ten-year-old boy when his parents had died. It had left its mark on him. He was used to dealing with things on his own. He didn't want anyone to see the heavy toll it took on him.

Wasn't that why he had pushed her away?

He felt responsible for his family. He wasn't used to sharing that with anyone.

He worked ridiculously punishing hours to keep his and the family's business at the top of its game. She sensed his inner drive was not so much about a desire to be super-successful, but more to compensate for the emptiness he felt at being left an orphan so young.

Was it too much to hope that he would one day see that he didn't have to do it on his own? That he could share the load with someone who cared about him and his happiness?

Of course it was.

She couldn't go on with this idealistic way of viewing

the world that everything would turn out in the end. Life was hard at times and she had to be hard to cope with it.

It was time to toughen up.

CHAPTER FIFTEEN

RAFE DROVE DOWN to the manor three weeks later. He had a pounding headache; he was tired from not having slept properly since he had found out about his brother's accident. Raoul was a lot better physically—the concussion he'd sustained had gone and his right arm that had been broken was healing well—but it was obvious he was having difficulty accepting his spinal injury. He'd had surgery to decompress the spine but the doctors were still a little cagey about how good his overall recovery would be.

When Rafe had left the private rehab unit Raoul had been transferred to, his brother had been sitting in his chair staring blankly out of the window. He had barely spoken a word since he'd left the hospital. It was devastating to witness. Rafe couldn't bear to see his vibrant brother slumped so sullenly and listlessly in that wretched chair.

Rafe blamed Clarissa Moncrief. Raoul had proposed the night before the accident and she had readily accepted. Rafe didn't believe for a second she loved Raoul or that Raoul had loved her, but that wasn't the point. She had ended their engagement with a chilling disregard for his feelings.

Rafe was determined to get Raoul out of this slump

of self-pity. He was in the process of tracking down a specialist he'd read about in an article online, a young English woman called Lily Archer who had worked with the young daughter of a wealthy sheikh who had suffered a horse riding accident. Halimah Al-Balawi had made a stunning recovery that had defied the doctors' prognosis. Rafe was determined to engage Miss Archer's services no matter what it cost and no matter what resistance his brother put up. Raoul could be stubborn when things didn't go his way, but Rafe had a gut feeling Lily Archer was just the person to sort him out.

But before Rafe went back to be with Raoul he had one other thing to sort out. He hadn't heard from Poppy, but then he hadn't expected to. He had made things pretty clear to her. But it niggled at him that he could have handled things a little better. He had been caught off-guard in Paris. He had shut down as soon as he'd heard about his brother's accident. It was how he always handled things, by closing off all distractions and concentrating on the task at hand.

But seeing how Clarissa had walked so callously out of his brother's life had pulled him up short. He hadn't liked what he had seen when he examined himself. How had Poppy felt to be dismissed like that? How could he have done that to her?

The lights were on in the dower house as he pulled up. He saw Poppy moving about the kitchen as he walked up the path to the back door. She was wearing her flowery apron and her hair was tied up on top of her head. There was a streak of flour over one cheek as she carried a tray of something to the oven.

The dogs must have heard him, as they started their maniacal barking, and Poppy immediately stiffened, put the tray back down on the bench and turned to see him through the window near the back door. Her face turned as white as the flour on her cheek, but then she seemed to compose herself. Her mouth tightened as she took off her oven mitts and, placing them on the counter, came over to open the door. 'Yes?'

Rafe knew he deserved a cool welcome but this wasn't like the Poppy he knew. 'Hi. I saw your light on.'

'I do that after dark,' she said. 'It's expensive, but I'm covering all my costs now that I'm following your business plan. No more freebies. No more credit. No more being taken advantage of. Wish I'd done it earlier.'

Rafe gave her a twisted smile. 'Good for you.'

She was like a stranger, a cold, distant stranger who didn't smile, whose toffee-brown eyes didn't light up when she saw him. Even the dogs seemed to sense the change, for they were not jumping around him vying for his attention but standing well back, eyeing him suspiciously. Pickles was giving him that beady look again, as if to say, "I knew I couldn't trust you".

'I should've called to tell you I was coming,' Rafe said.

'Why?' She gave him a hardened look. 'So I could roll out the red carpet for you?'

He frowned. 'No, it's just that I wanted to explain why I left you in Paris like that.'

'You don't need to explain it. I totally got it, Rafe. You didn't need me any more. You wanted to be on your own so you could concentrate on your brother. How is he?'

'He's out of hospital,' he said. 'I'm hoping to take him to his villa in Normandy once he's cleared from rehab.'

'There's been nothing in the press.'

'No, we've been trying to keep things pretty quiet. But I'm not sure how long that will last.'

A silence chugged past.

Rafe couldn't believe how hard this was. He had been expecting… What had he been expecting? He felt out of his depth, out of balance, disoriented. She was so unreachable, so tightly contained, he felt like an invisible wall was around her.

'I've come to a decision,' Poppy said. 'You can buy the dower house. I don't want it any more. It should never have been separated from the manor. They belong together.'

Rafe blinked to reorient himself. 'How much do you want?'

'Twenty-five percent above market value.'

He let out a slowly measured breath. 'You drive a hard bargain.'

'I had a very good teacher.'

He searched her features for any sign of a chink in that shiny new armour but she was as hard as nails. He felt a sinkhole of sadness open up inside him. She'd had a very good teacher indeed.

He had done that to her.

'I'll get my secretary to tee things up,' he said.

'Fine.'

There was another clunky silence.

'Is there anything else?' Her tone was impatient and unfriendly. Rafe recognised it, for he had used it a thousand times when he had wanted to dismiss someone who was taking up too much of his precious time.

'No.' He gave her a tight, formal smile. 'That's about it.'

She didn't return his smile. She didn't even wait until he'd turned his back to go back down the path before she shut the door.

Rafe stared at the wood panelling for a moment. He

toyed with the idea of knocking and starting over, but he dismissed the thought before it took hold.

It was better this way. He'd got what he wanted; she was selling him the dower house.

Goal.

Focus.

Win.

But it was ironic that the victory, now he had it, didn't taste so sweet.

'Any luck on tracking down that rehab woman Lily Archer?' Rafe asked his secretary when he got back to London after he'd taken Raoul to his villa in Normandy.

'Yes, but apparently she doesn't work with male clients,' Margaret said.

Rafe exhaled in irritation. 'Then get her to change her mind. I don't care how much it costs.'

'How is Raoul?'

'The same.' He scraped a hand through his hair. 'Won't eat. Barely drinks. Just sits there brooding all the time.'

'A bit like you, then.'

Rafe's brows snapped together. 'What's that supposed to mean?'

Margaret gave him a knowing look. 'You remind me of one of my sons. He's an all-or-nothing thinker. He doesn't know how to compromise. It doesn't have to be either-or, Rafe. You can help Raoul and be happy in your love life.'

'I don't have a love life.' He strode over to the window and looked at the dismal weather outside.

'You miss her, don't you?'

Rafe swung back to glower at her. 'You might want to have another look at your job description. As far I as recall, it says nothing about you making comments on my private life.'

'You're a good boss, Rafe, and you're a good man,' Margaret said. 'What you've done for Armand, your accountant in Paris, is proof of that.'

'That was Poppy's idea, not mine.' He thrust his hands in his pockets, still scowling. 'I was going to send him to rot in prison.'

'No, you weren't,' Margaret said. 'You'd have found a way to help him. Just like you help lots of people. Like that foundation you set up for kids who've lost their parents. Funny how the press like to report on who you're sleeping with but they never report on all the good things you do.'

Rafe turned back to the window. He couldn't bear the thought of sleeping with anyone but Poppy. His need for her was an ache that had settled around his heart like a set of ten-kilogram dumb-bells. Every breath he took felt painful. It wasn't just the sex he missed, which was ironic, because that in itself was way out of character for him.

It was her smile he missed, the way her gorgeous brown eyes lit up whenever she saw him. The way her touch soothed the wound of loneliness inside him that he had not even realised he'd possessed until she had eased it. The way she gave herself to him with such complete trust.

But he had destroyed the things he loved most about her. She didn't look at him like that any more. She didn't want to touch him. She didn't trust him.

Could he win back her trust? Could he make her smile at him? Could he make her eyes sparkle with delight when he walked into the room?

'Do you want me to send Miss Silverton some jewellery?' Margaret asked. 'Rubies, sapphires or maybe pearls? They'd look rather nice with her colouring, don't you think?'

Rafe turned and faced her. 'No, I'll do it myself.'

Margaret's pencilled brows rose above the frame of her tortoiseshell glasses. 'Are you sure?'

'Absolutely.'

Rafe had never been surer of anything in his life. It was like a stone curtain had lifted in his brain. 'Cancel all of my appointments,' he said. 'I'm heading out of town.'

'Do you need me to book a hotel for you?'

'No, I'm going to stay at the manor.'

'But I thought you were going to sell it.' She swung around in her chair to look at him as he reached for his jacket. 'You told me to contact the agent about putting it back on the market.'

'Sell it? Are you crazy?' He snatched up his keys off the desk. 'I'm going to live there.'

Poppy was emptying the display cabinet at the end of the day when the doorbell chimed. A shiver rose over her skin and her heart started to gallop. She slowly turned around and her breath caught in her throat. Rafe was standing there, looking as gorgeous as ever, if a little tired. There were shadows beneath his eyes and his face looked a little drawn, as if he'd lost weight.

She put on her business face, but it hurt to keep it there. He looked *so* worn out. She had to control the impulse to reach out to him and give him a hug. 'Would you like a coffee?'

'Actually, what I'd really like is a cup of tea.'

She blinked. 'Tea?'

He gave her a wry smile. 'The hospital coffee was

awful. It was even worse at the rehab centre. I had to resort to tea; I got used to it after a while. Now I can't get through the day without a cup or two.'

'I never thought I'd see the day,' Poppy said with forced lightness. 'I don't suppose you'd like a piece of cake?'

'Do you have any butter cake?'

She blinked again. 'Butter cake?'

'Preferably raw.'

Her eyes almost popped. '*Raw?*'

He smiled again but there was hint of wistfulness about it. 'My mother used to bake for us. She didn't want us to grow up with cooks and housekeepers doing everything for us. My favourite cake was vanilla butter-cake. She always used to let me lick the bowl. The day before she and my father were killed, she'd baked one and gave me a spoonful of the batter.'

Poppy blinked again but this time to hold back her tears. 'Oh Rafe…'

'I guess it would be quite a novel thing, having a raw wedding cake,' he said. 'Do you think anyone's ever done that before?'

Poppy's heart sank. 'You're getting married?'

His dark eyes twinkled. 'I hope to very soon.'

She swallowed a tight lump in her throat. She could barely look at him in case he saw the bitter disappointment in her eyes. 'Who's the lucky girl?'

Rafe took her hands in his. 'That's what I love about you, Poppy. You take nothing for granted. You're modest and gracious and so incredibly sweet, I can't bear the thought of spending another day without you.'

Her eyes were so wide they looked like satellite dishes. 'You love me?'

'I think I fell in love with you the first day I walked

in here and met your beautiful eyes. I loved your feistiness, the fact that you were so completely undaunted by
me. You were prepared to fight for what you believed in.
But what I admire even more about you is how you put
your own needs aside for others. The way you realised
the manor and the dower house belong together. I was too
stubborn to see that but, even though you wanted to keep
your house, you saw the greater good in letting it go.'

'I can't believe I'm hearing this…'

Rafe smiled as he drew her closer. 'Marry me, *ma
petite*. Please?'

Her dimpled smile was the most beautiful thing he
had ever seen. 'Yes.'

He could not believe how one simple word could make
him so happy. 'I have something for you,' he said, taking out a velvet box from his jacket pocket. 'I had it de-
signed specially.'

Poppy held her breath as he opened the box to reveal
a princess-cut diamond that glittered brilliantly. 'It's so
beautiful…'

He took it out and slipped it on her finger, holding her
hand in his. 'Diamonds are for ever, *ma cherie*. I won't
settle for anything less from you. I hope you realise that.
And I want babies. At least two.'

She gave him a smile that made her eyes dance. 'I
love you.'

He gathered her close. 'I love you so much. I can't
believe I didn't realise it earlier. I must have hurt you so
much by leaving you in Paris like that—and then when
I came to see you at the dower house. I was so shocked
in the change in you. I thought I'd lost you for ever, that
I'd changed you for ever.'

Poppy rested her head against his chest. It was the
most wonderful feeling in the world to belong to some-

one who loved her. She felt it in his touch, in his gaze, in the strong, protective shelter of his arms. 'It was so hard to be like that with you. I'm surprised you didn't see through it. I was sure you would call my bluff. But you're here now, that's all that matters.'

He lifted her face to press a lingering kiss to her mouth. 'How do you feel about living at the manor?'

Her face lit up with excitement. 'Do you mean it?'

He smiled down at her. 'It'd be a perfect home for a family, don't you think?'

She threw her arms around him and hugged him tightly. 'It would be a dream come true.'

* * * * *

NEVER UNDERESTIMATE A CAFFARELLI

BY
MELANIE MILBURNE

To Sharon Kendrick, a Harlequin Mills & Boon sister
and a dear friend. xxx

CHAPTER ONE

'BUT I NEVER work with male clients,' Lily said to her boss at the south London physical therapies rehabilitation clinic. 'You *know* that.'

'I know but this is such an amazing opportunity,' Valerie said. 'Raoul Caffarelli is from serious money. This four-week live-in post in Normandy will be worth a year's work to you. I can't send anyone else. Anyway, his brother absolutely insisted on you.'

Lily frowned. 'His brother?'

Valerie gave her eyes a little roll. 'Yes, well, apparently Raoul isn't too keen on working with anyone just now. He's become a bit reclusive since coming out of hospital. His older brother Rafe read about your work with Sheikh Kaseem Al-Balawi's daughter. He wants you to help his brother. He's willing to pay you very handsomely. I got the impression from him when he called that you could just about name your price.'

Lily chewed at her lower lip. The money was certainly attractive, especially given her mother's desperate circumstances right now, after yet another failed relationship had drained her bank account dry. But a live-in post with a man—even one currently confined to a wheelchair—was the stuff of her nightmares.

She hadn't been anywhere near a man in five years.

'I'm not doing it,' Lily said, turning to put another patient's file away. 'It's out of the question. You'll have to find someone else.'

'I don't think saying no is a going to be an option,' Valerie said. 'The Caffarelli brothers are known for their ruthless determination. Rafe wants Raoul to be his best man at his wedding in September. He believes you're the best person to get his brother back on his feet.'

Lily closed the drawer, turned and looked at her boss. 'What does he think I am, a miracle worker? His brother might never get back on his feet, let alone in a matter of weeks.'

'I know, but the least you could do is agree to work with him to see if it's possible,' Valerie said. 'It's a dream job— all expenses paid while you get to stay in a centuries-old château in rural Normandy. Do it, Lily. You'll be doing me a huge favour. It will really lift the profile of the clinic. This is exactly what we need right now to build on the work you did with the Sheikh's daughter. We'll be known as the holistic clinic for the rich and famous. Everyone will want to come here.'

Lily swallowed a tight knot of panic in her throat. Her heart was thumping such a rapid and jerky tattoo it felt as if she had just run up a skyscraper's flight of stairs. Her skin was clammy and her head felt as tight as if a vice were pressing against her temples. She tried to think of an escape route but each time she thought of one it was immediately roadblocked by her need to help her mother and her loyalty to her employer.

Could she do it?

'I'll need to see Mr Caffarelli's scans and reports from

his doctors. I might not be able to do much at all for him. It would be wrong to give him or his brother false hope.'

Valerie clicked the mouse at her computer. 'I have the scans and reports here. Rafe emailed them to me. I'll forward them to you.'

Lily looked at the reports a short time later in her office. Raoul Caffarelli had a spinal injury from a water-skiing accident. He had also sustained a badly broken right arm, although that was apparently healing. He had some feeling in his legs, but he was unable to stand upright without aid, and at this point in time he could not walk. The neurosurgical opinion was that he would be unlikely to regain full use of his legs, although they expected some minor improvement in his current mobility. But Lily had read similar reports before and tried not to let them influence her when dealing with a client.

Some spinal injuries could be devastatingly permanent, others relatively minor, and then there was everything in between. So much depended on the type of injury as well as a client's attitude and general state of health.

Lily liked to use a mix of therapies—the traditional things such as structured exercise, strength-training and massage, and some which were considered a little more on the alternative side, such as aromatherapy, dietary supplements and visualisation techniques.

The Sheikh's daughter, Halimah Al-Balawi, was one of her star clients. The young woman had been told by three neurosurgeons that she would never walk again. Lily had worked with her for three months; the improvement had been painstakingly slow at first, but finally Halimah had taken her first steps with the aid of parallel bars and she had continued to improve until she was able to walk unaided.

Lily sat back in her chair and chewed at a ragged end on her pinkie nail. For anyone else it would be a dream job to take on a man as rich and famous as Raoul Caffarelli. To spend a month in the lap of luxury working closely with a man every single woman on the planet would give ten years of her life to have one day or night with, let alone thirty-one of them. They would grab the opportunity with both hands and relish every minute of it.

But for her it would be a form of torture.

Her stomach recoiled at the thought of putting her hands on a hard male body. Working with a client as a physical therapist meant physical contact—*close* physical contact. Hands on flesh. Hands on muscles and tendons, stroking and massaging… *Touching.*

Her mobile rang from where it was sitting on her desk. She saw her mother's face come up on the screen and pressed the answer button. 'Hi, Mum. Are you OK?'

'Darling, I hate to bother you when you're at work, but the bank's been on the phone to me again. They're going to foreclose on the house if I don't come up with the last three months' mortgage payments. I tried to explain that it was Martin who siphoned off my account but they wouldn't listen.'

Lily felt her blood boil at how her mother had been scammed by a man she had met through an online dating service. Never a great judge of character at the best of times—although *she* was hardly one to talk, given what had happened to her on the night of her twenty-first birthday—her mother had foolishly trusted her new partner and was now paying heavily for it. That lowlife pond-scum had hacked into her mother's accounts and stolen her life savings.

Was fate twisting Lily's arm? How could she knock back this job when her mother was in such desperate need of financial support? Her mother had stalwartly stood by her during her lowest point. Those terrible dark days after her twenty-first birthday had almost sent her to the edge of sanity. But her mother had stood by her, putting her own life on hold to help Lily come out of that black hole of despair and self-loathing. Didn't she owe this to her mother?

It was only for a month.

Four weeks.

Thirty-one days.

It would feel like a lifetime.

'It's all right, Mum.' She took a scratchy little breath. 'I'm taking on a new client. It'll mean I'll be away in France for the whole of August but I'll ask them to pay me up-front. That will sort out the bank. You're not going to lose the house. Not if I can help it.'

Raoul scowled at his brother. 'I thought I told you I want to be left alone.'

Rafe blew out a breath of frustration. 'You can't spend the rest of your life holed up here like a recluse. What is wrong with you? Can't you see this is your best chance— maybe your only chance—of a recovery?'

Raoul wheeled his chair with his one good arm so he didn't have to face his brother. He knew Rafe meant well but the thought of having some young Englishwoman fussing over him with her snake-oil remedies was anathema to him right now. 'The best doctors in Italy said this is as good as it's going to get. I don't need to have this

Archer woman wasting my time and your money pretending it's going to be otherwise.'

'Look, I know you're still smarting about Clarissa breaking off your engagement, but you can't hold it against all women just because she—'

'This has *nothing* to do with Clarissa,' Raoul snapped as he wheeled back round.

Rafe gave him a look that spoke volumes. 'You weren't even in love with her. You just thought she ticked all the boxes. The accident showed you her true colours. The way I see it—and Poppy says the same—you had a very lucky escape.'

Raoul's left hand gripped the chair so tightly he thought his knuckles were going to explode through his skin. 'You think I've been lucky? Look at me, Rafe. I'm stuck in this chair! I can't even dress myself. Don't insult me by saying I'm lucky.'

Rafe rubbed a hand over the top of his head. 'Sorry. Bad choice of words.' He dropped his hand back by his side. 'Will you at least meet her? Give her a trial run for a week or even a couple of days? If it doesn't work out then you can call it quits. You'll be the one in control of whether she stays or goes.'

Raoul wheeled back over to the window to look at the view over the fields where some of his most prized thoroughbreds were grazing. He couldn't even go out to them and stroke their velvet noses. He couldn't walk over the soft springy grass. He was trapped in this chair, trapped in his own body, in the body that for the last thirty-four years had defined him as a person—as a *man*. The doctors had told him he was luckier than most; he still had feeling in his legs and full bladder and bowel function. He supposedly still had sexual function, but what woman would want him now?

Hadn't Clarissa made that starkly clear?

He wanted his body back. He wanted his *life* back.

Who was to say this Archer woman was the miracle worker Rafe suggested? She could be the biggest charlatan out there. He didn't want to be taken for a ride, to be given false hopes only to have them dashed in the end. He was slowly coming to terms with his situation. He needed this time at the château to get his head around how life was going to be from now on. He wasn't ready to face the world just yet. The thought of the paparazzi tailing him to get the best pity shot made him sick to his stomach.

He just wanted to be left alone.

'One month, Raoul,' Rafe said into the silence. 'Please. Just give it a try.'

Raoul knew both of his brothers were worried about him. Remy, his younger brother, had been there the day before, doing his best to jolly him along like a male version of Pollyanna. His grandfather, Vittorio, had been less supportive, but Raoul had come to expect that from him. Vittorio was not the sort of man to offer sympathy or support. His speciality was to blame and to castigate.

'I'd like a week or two to think about it.'

There was a loaded silence.

Raoul turned his chair around again, suspicion crawling up his damaged spine like sticky spider's legs as he met his brother's sheepish dark brown gaze. 'You *haven't*.'

'She's waiting in the morning room,' Rafe said.

Raoul let out a string of colourful obscenities in French, Italian and English. Rage raced through his body like a fast-acting poison. He had never felt so powerless, so damned impotent, in his life. What did his brother think he was, a little child who couldn't make a sensible decision?

This was *his* sanctuary.

No one came here unless *he* invited them.

'Cool it,' Rafe said in an undertone. 'She'll hear you.'

'I don't care if she hears me! What the hell are you playing at?'

'I'm trying to help you, since you don't seem to want to help yourself,' Rafe said. 'I can't stand seeing you like this. Sitting around brooding, snapping everyone's head off if they so much as glance at you. You won't even go outside, for pity's sake. It's as if you've given up. You *can't* give up. You have to work through this.'

Raoul glared at his brother. 'I'll go outside when I can get out there under my own power. You had no right to bring that woman here without my permission. This is *my* house. Get her out of it.'

'She's staying,' Rafe said. 'I paid her up-front and I can't get a refund. It was part of her stipulation in accepting the post.'

Raoul flicked his eyes upwards in derision. 'Doesn't that tell you what sort of woman she is? For God's sake, Rafe, I thought you of all people would've had more sense. This is just a money grab. You wait and see— she'll walk out after a couple of days over something I said or did and do a happy dance all the way to the bank.'

'Miss Archer comes on very good recommendation,' Rafe said. 'She's highly trained and very experienced.'

Raoul gave a scoffing grunt. 'I just bet she is.'

'I'm going to leave you to get acquainted with her. I need to get back to Poppy; we have a wedding to organise. I want you there, Raoul, chair or no chair. Do you understand?'

Raoul let out a hiss. 'I'm not going to sit up there in front of everybody like some sort of freak show. Get Remy to be your best man.'

'You know what Remy is like. He'll fail to show up because something far more interesting has come across his radar. I want you to do it, and so does Poppy, and I don't want her disappointed.' Rafe moved to the door, holding it open as he added, 'I'll call you in a couple of weeks to see how you're doing. *Ciao.*'

Lily gripped her handbag on her lap with fingers that were ice cold in spite of the summer temperature. She'd heard shouting, and although she wasn't fluent in French or Italian she understood enough to know Raoul Caffarelli was not happy about her being here. Which was ironic, since she wasn't all that happy about being here, either. But with the money safely in her mother's mortgage account at least one worry had been shelved.

But her biggest worry lay ahead.

Being left alone in this huge old château with a man she had never met before was like something out of a horror movie. Her pulse was racing and her heart was hammering. She could feel the stickiness of perspiration between her shoulder blades and on her palms. The floor of her stomach was crawling with prickly feet of panic and she had to press her knees together to stop them from knocking against each other.

The morning-room door opened and Rafe Caffarelli came in with a grim look on his face. 'He's in the library. Try not to be put off by his surly attitude. Hopefully he'll improve a little on acquaintance. He's just frustrated and angry about his situation.'

Lily rose to her feet, still clutching her handbag like a shield. 'It's fine…' She moistened her paper-dry mouth. 'It must be very difficult for him….'

'It's a nightmare, for him and for me. I don't know how to reach him. He's locked everyone out.' He rubbed a hand over his face in a weary manner. 'He refuses to cooperate. I've never seen him like this. I knew he could be stubborn, but this is taking it to a whole new level.'

'It's still early days,' Lily said. 'Some people take months to accept what's happened to them. Others never accept it.'

'I want him at my wedding,' Rafe said with an implacable look. 'I don't care if we have to drag him or push him there kicking and screaming. I want him there.'

'I'll see what I can do,' Lily said. 'But I can't make any promises.'

'The housekeeper, Dominique, will assist you with anything you need,' he said. 'She will show you to your suite once you meet Raoul. There's a young guy called Sebastien who comes in each morning to help my brother shower and dress. Have you any questions?'

Hundreds, but they could wait. 'No, I think I've got it all under control.'

He gave her a brief nod and held the door open for her. 'I'll show you the way to the library but I think it's best if I leave you to it.' He twisted his mouth ruefully and added, 'I'm not my brother's favourite person right now.'

The library was on the same floor in the centuries-old château, but the sombre dark setting was in sharp contrast to the bright morning room where the sunlight had streamed in through a bank of windows that overlooked the rolling, verdant fields of the Normandy country-side. The library had only one window that let in limited light, and there were three walls of floor-to-ceiling bookshelves that dominated the room, as well as a large leather-topped desk and an old-world globe positioned beside it. The smell of parchment and paper, leather and furniture polish gave Lily a sense of stepping back in time.

But her gaze was immediately drawn like a magnet to the silent figure seated in a wheelchair behind the desk. Raoul Caffarelli had the same breath-snatching good looks of his older brother, with glossy black hair, olive-toned skin and a rather stubborn, uncompromising-looking jaw. But his eyes were a green-flecked hazel instead of dark brown, and right now they were glittering at her in blistering anger.

'You'll forgive me for not rising.' His tone was clipped and unfriendly, his expression stony.

'I… Of course.'

'Unless you are hard of hearing or a complete and utter fool, you must realise by now I don't want you here.'

She lifted her chin, determined not to show him how intimidated she felt. 'I'm neither hard of hearing nor a fool.'

He measured her with his gaze for a long, pulsing moment. Lily could see his French-Italian heritage in his features and in his bearing. There was a hint of the proud aristocrat in him; it was there in the broad set of his shoulders and the way he held himself in spite of being confined to a chair. He was taller than average—she estimated two or three inches over six feet—and was obviously a man who had been intensely physically active prior to his accident. She could see the well-formed muscles of his chest and arms through the fine cotton of the shirt he was wearing. His right arm was still in a plaster cast but his hands looked strong and capable. His face was cleanly shaven but the shadow of regrowth was evident, suggesting potent male hormones. His nose was a little more Roman than his brother's, and there were lines about his mouth that gave him a slightly drawn look, as if he had lost weight recently. His mouth was set in an intractable line, flattened by his mood and temper, and she wondered what it would look like if he smiled.

Lily pulled back from her thoughts with a little start. She was not here to make him smile. She was here to see if she could make him walk, and the sooner she got on with the job, the sooner she could leave.

'I suppose my brother has given you all the gory details of my condition?' he said, still pinning her with that intimidating gaze.

'I've seen your scans and read the doctors' and physiotherapists' reports.'

A dark brow lifted above his left eye, almost accusingly. 'And?'

She rolled her lips together to moisten them, trying to ignore the annoying jackhammer beat of her heart. 'I think it's worth trying some of my methods. I've had some success with clients with similar injuries to yours.'

'So, what are some of your methods?' His top lip curled mockingly. 'Waving incense around? Chanting mantras? Reading auras? Laying on of hands?'

Lily felt a little spurt of anger shoot through her blood. She was used to people rubbishing her holistic approach but somehow his sarcastic tone got under her skin. But he would be laughing on the other side of his face if she got him back on his feet. The challenge to do so was suddenly rather more attractive than it had been before. 'I use a combination of traditional therapies and some complementary ones. It depends.'

'On what?'

'On the client. I take into consideration their diet and lifestyle, their sleeping habits, their mental state and—'

'Let me guess—you read their tarot cards or give them a zodiac reading.'

Lily pursed her mouth to stop herself from issuing a stinging riposte. He was quite possibly the rudest man she'd ever met. Arrogant, too, but she supposed that came from his privileged background. He was a spoilt, over-indulged playboy who had been handed everything on a silver platter. His surly, 'poor me' attitude was just typical of someone who'd never had to work for anything in his life. He had it so good compared to some of her clients. At least he had the money to set himself up. He had people to wait on him, to take care of him. He had a family who refused to give up on him. Didn't he realise that while he was in his luxury château feeling sorry for himself, there were people out in the world who were homeless or starving with no one to care what happened to them from one day to the next?

'I'm a Taurus, in case you're wondering,' he said.

She gave him an arch look. 'That explains the bull-headedness.'

'I can be very stubborn.' He gave her another measuring look. 'But I suspect you can, too.'

'I like to call it persistence,' Lily said. 'I don't believe in giving up on something until I've put in a decent effort.'

He drummed the fingers of his left hand on the arm-rest of his wheelchair, an almost absentminded movement that seemed overly loud in the silence.

Lily felt the slow, assessing sweep of his gaze again. Was he comparing her to all the women he had dated? If so, he would find her sadly lacking. She didn't dress to impress. She didn't wear make-up as a rule and she wore plain Jane clothes that hid her figure and her past.

'I'm not sure what to do with you.' He glared at her darkly. 'It's not like I can physically throw you out.'

Lily sent him a warning in her gaze. 'I can assure you, Monsieur Caffarelli, I would put up a spectacular fight if you laid even a single finger on me.'

One of his brows went up in an arc. 'Well, well, well; the seemingly demure Miss Archer has a sting in her tail. Scorpio?'

She ground her teeth. 'Virgo.'

'Detailed. Nit-picking. Pedantic.'

'I prefer to think of it as thorough.'

A ghost of a smile tilted the edge of his mouth. It totally transformed his features and Lily had to remind herself to breathe.

But the half smile was gone almost as soon as it had appeared. His expression darkened again and his gaze singed hers. 'I've had weeks of physical therapy, Miss Archer, and none of it has worked, as you can see. I can't see how you could succeed where others more qualified than you have failed.'

'It's still early days,' Lily said. 'The body can take months, if not years, to recover from trauma.'

Cynicism made his eyes glitter. 'You're not offering your services for years, though, are you, Miss Archer? My prediction is you'll last one or two days, three at the most, and then you'll be off with a nice fat little wad of cash in your bank account. I've met your type before— you exploit people who are desperate. You've got nothing to offer me and we both know it.'

'On the contrary, I think I can help you,' Lily said. 'You're at a critical stage in your recovery. You should be supervised while exercising—'

'Supervised?' He barked the word at her. 'I'm not a child who needs supervising while playing on the monkey bars.'

'I didn't say that. I just meant that you have to—'

'I will do it *my* way,' he said with indomitable force. 'I don't want your help. I didn't ask for it. And I didn't pay for it. I know what I have to do and I'm doing it, and I prefer to do it alone. Do us both a favour and catch the next flight back to London.'

Lily stared him down even though it took an enormous effort to hold that diamond-hard gaze. His anger was coming off him in waves that sent crackles of electricity through the air. She could even feel her skin tightening all over her body, as if those invisible currents were flowing over and through her. She could even feel her blood heating; it was pounding through her veins as if she had taken a shot of adrenalin. 'You do realise if I leave now your brother will lose a considerable amount of money? There's a no-refund clause in my contract.'

His mouth thinned in disdain. 'Let him lose it. It's no skin off my nose.'

Lily was shocked. Was he really prepared to forfeit an amount most people didn't even earn in a year? And it wasn't even his money. His assumption she would take the money and go made her all the more determined to stay. Her conscience wouldn't allow her to take the money for nothing. He would think she was an unscrupulous gold digger and, given how high profile the Caffarelli name was, it would quite possibly tarnish the reputation of the clinic if word got out that she'd left without doing a day's work.

Besides, she was a little intrigued by his resistance to rehabilitation. Didn't he want to improve his mobility, or had he simply given up? Some clients found it very hard to adjust to the smallest of limitations put on them, while others coped remarkably well in spite of far worse injuries.

He was in good physical health, which was always a bonus in hoping for a positive outcome in rehabilitation, but his state of mind suggested he had not yet come to terms with what had happened to him. He reminded her of an alpha wolf who had secluded himself away to lick his wounds while no one was watching.

But then, hadn't she done the very same thing five years ago?

Lily held his steely gaze. 'I have no way of getting to the airport now that your brother has left.'

'Then I'll get one of the stableboys to drive you.'

'I'm not leaving.'

A muscle worked in his jaw. 'I don't want you here.'

'You've made that more than obvious,' Lily said huffily. 'I didn't expect a red carpet to be rolled out or anything, but the least you could've done is be civil. Or does being filthy rich mean you can act like a total jerk and get away with it?'

His gaze warred with hers for a throbbing moment. 'My brother had no right to bring you here without my permission.'

'So you take it out on me?' Lily tossed back. 'How

is that fair? I've travelled for hours and hours, I'm tired and hungry, and as soon as I set foot in the place I get my head bitten off by a boorish man who has a massive chip on his shoulder because he can't do some of the things he used to do. At least you've got a roof over your head and a family who love you, not to mention loads and loads of money.' She put a hand over her heart theatrically. 'Oh, how my heart bleeds for you.'

His eyes were glacial as they hit hers. 'I want you out of here by lunchtime tomorrow. Do you understand?'

Lily felt strangely exhilarated by their verbal sparring. The atmosphere was electric, the tension palpable. 'Your loss, my gain. Well, I suppose it's your brother's loss, really, but still. Easy come, easy go, as they say.'

He gave her a glowering look before he turned to press an intercom button on his desk and spoke in French to his housekeeper. A fine shiver lifted the hairs on the back of Lily's neck as she listened to the deep timbre of his voice in that most musical of languages. She wondered what his voice would sound like when he wasn't angry. She wondered what his laugh sounded like. He was such a compelling man to look at, so dark and intense, bristling with barely suppressed emotion.

'Dominique will show you to a guest suite,' he said. 'I will arrange to have you driven to the airport first thing tomorrow.'

The housekeeper appeared at the door of the library and escorted Lily to a guest suite on the third floor of the château along a long wide corridor that was lined with priceless works of art and marble statues that seemed to follow her progress with their eyes.

'Monsieur Raoul's suite is that one there.' Dominique pointed to a double-door suite as they walked past. 'He is not a good sleeper so I did not like to put you too close to him.' She gave Lily a pained look. 'He wasn't like that before the accident. I blame that fiancée of his.'

Lily stopped in her tracks and frowned. 'I didn't realise he was engaged.'

Dominique gave her a cynical look. 'He's not. She broke it off while he was in hospital.'

'Oh, but that's awful!'

The housekeeper gave a Gallic sniff of disdain. 'I didn't like her from the moment I met her. But then, I haven't liked any of his mistresses. His brother's fiancée is another story. Poppy Silverton is the nicest young woman you'll ever meet. She's the best thing that ever happened to Monsieur Rafe. I just hope Monsieur Raoul meets someone like her.'

No wonder he was so bitter and angry, Lily thought. How heartless of his ex-fiancée to end their relationship in such a way. It was such a cruel thing to do. Surely she hadn't truly loved him? How could she? Loving someone meant being there for them in the good times and the bad. How could his fiancée live with the fact she'd abandoned him when he was at his lowest point? It explained so much about his attitude. It was no wonder he was so prickly and unfriendly. He was hurting in the worst possible way.

Lily followed the housekeeper into the suite that was decorated in a classical French style. The queen-sized bed was made up in snowy white linen with a fine gold trim that matched the gilt-edged paintwork of the suite. An antique dressing table with a tapestry-covered stool was positioned in front of an ornately framed mirror; there was a chest of drawers on cabriole legs and a discreetly hidden built-in wardrobe lined another wall. The heavily festooned windows overlooked the formal gardens of the estate where neatly clipped hedges, sun-drenched paved terraces and a large bubbling fountain were situated.

'I hope you'll be comfortable,' Dominique said. 'Dinner will be served at eight. I'm not sure if Monsieur Raoul will join you. He's not very sociable these days. He spends most of his time in his study or in his room.'

'How does Monsieur Raoul get up and down the stairs?' Lily asked. 'I didn't see a stair climber on the staircase.'

'There is a proper lift on the ground floor that goes to all four levels,' Dominique said. 'Monsieur Raoul had it installed a few months ago when his grandfather came for a visit after he had a stroke. Not that he got a word of thanks for his effort, mind you. Vittorio Caffarelli is not the nicest person to have around. He spoke to me as if I was the dust under his feet. I had to bite my tongue the whole time he was here.'

Lily was starting to suspect there was a lot more to the Caffarelli dynasty than she had first realised. She had read a bit online about the family—how they had made their wealth in property and a variety of timely and rather clever investments; how Raoul's parents had been killed in a speedboat accident on the French Riviera when he and his brothers were young. The three boys had been raised by their grandfather but had spent most of their school years at boarding school in England.

Raoul had been born to wealth but brought up with tragedy. And now he had yet another blow to deal with. Not that she had read anything of his injuries in the press, which made her wonder what sort of power the Caffarellis had at their fingertips. But how long would it be before some unscrupulous journalist came hunting for a story? It was certainly a juicy one: a rich man rejected by his fiancée after a freak accident that left him in a wheelchair.

In spite of her dislike of the man, Lily couldn't help feeling Raoul had been badly treated. Rejection was always hard, but to be cast aside because of injury went against everything she believed in.

What sort of money would be exchanged for a photograph of him now? Was that why he didn't want anyone he didn't know here at the château?

'It is a pity you aren't staying the month,' Dominique said. 'Even without the physical therapy you offer, I think the company would have been good for Monsieur Raoul. He spends too much time on his own.'

Lily found it ironic that she wanted to stay when only days ago she had been hunting for excuses *not* to come. 'I can't force him to let me stay. It's his call. If he wants to work with me, then I'll be happy to do it. But he seemed pretty adamant he wanted me out of here.'

'He might change his mind, *oui*?' Dominique said. 'You took him by surprise. Perhaps he will have a change of heart overnight.'

Lily walked over to the windows when the housekeeper had left and looked at the view over the estate. It was certainly a picturesque setting with its beautiful gardens and lush, seemingly unending fields beyond.

But the brooding man downstairs, who so resented her being here, reminded her that in any paradise there was always the potential for trouble and temptation.

CHAPTER TWO

RAOUL HAD PLANNED on eating alone in his room or not eating at all, but the thought of spending an hour or two with Lily Archer proved to be the greater temptation. He told himself it was because he wanted to keep an eye on her. Who knew what she might be up to when his back was turned? She might be pilfering the silver or stashing away some of his priceless objects while no one was looking—or, even worse, she might be an undercover journalist planted inside the château to get the prize shot of him.

He was still furiously angry with his brother for bringing her here. He'd planned to spend some time out of the public eye, working on his recovery as best he could. What could she offer that hadn't already been offered by his specialists and doctors? He wanted to be alone to get his head around the possibility that he might never fully recover. He didn't want people fussing around him. He needed time to process what had happened and how he was going to move forward.

Her understated beauty didn't fool him for a moment. That was probably all part of her artifice—to trick people into trusting her. Her nondescript clothing had hung off her slim figure as if she was trying to disguise it, and her brown hair had been tied back severely from her make-up-free face.

It was her eyes that had intrigued him, however. They were the most startling shade of blue, dark like slate, and veiled, as if she were hiding something. Eyes were supposed to be the windows to the soul, but he had a feeling Miss Lily Archer's soul was not for public display.

He heaved himself into his electronic chair even though it annoyed the hell out of him to have to use it. It made him feel even more disabled, hearing that whirring sound as he drove it. He couldn't wait to get this wretched plaster cast off his right arm. At least then he'd be able to keep his upper body in shape by wheeling himself around in the manual chair.

He caught a glimpse of himself in one of the large mirrors as he drove down the corridor towards the lift. It was like looking at someone else. It looked like someone had hijacked him and put him in someone else's body.

A dagger-like pain seized him in the chest. What if this was the best he would ever be? He couldn't bear the thought of spending the rest of his life stuck in this chair, having people look down at him—or, even worse, flicking their gaze away as if the sight of his broken body repulsed them.

He *wasn't* going to give in to this.

He *would* get well.

He would move heaven and earth to get back on his feet and he would do it like he did everything else: *on his own*.

Raoul was on his second glass of wine when Lily Archer came in. She was dressed in a long-sleeved beige dress that was a size too big and did nothing to flatter her colouring. Her face was free of make-up, although she had put on a bit of lip gloss, and perhaps a bit of mascara as her dark lashes seemed more noticeable than they had earlier in the darker lighting of the library. Her hair was tied back, but in the brighter light from the chandelier overhead he could see it was healthy and shiny with natural-looking highlights in between the ash-brown strands.

'Would you like a drink?' He held up the bottle of wine he was steadily working his way through.

She inhaled a sharp little breath and shook her head. 'I don't drink alcohol. I'll just have water… Thank you.'

'A teetotaller?' Raoul knew he sounded mocking but he was beyond caring.

She pressed her rather generous lips together as she took her seat to the left of his. Even the way she flicked her napkin across her lap communicated her irritation with him. Why hadn't he noticed how lush her mouth was before? Was the lighting *that* bad in the library? Nor had he noticed how regally high her cheekbones were or the way her neck was swan-like and her pretty little nose up-tilted. She had prominent brows and deep-set eyes that gave her a mysterious, untouchable air. Her skin was clear and unlined with no hint of tan, as if she spent most of her time indoors, out of the sun.

She gave him a school-marmish look. 'I don't need alcohol to have a good time.'

'So, how *do* you have a good time, Miss Archer?'

'I read. I go to movies. I spend time with my friends.'

'Do you have a boyfriend?'

Her face flinched. She covered it quickly, however, adopting a composed façade that would have fooled most people—but then, he liked to think he was not most people. 'No.' Her one-word answer was definitive, like a punctuation mark. Book closed. End of subject.

Raoul picked up his wine glass and took a sip, holding it in his mouth for a moment before he swallowed. 'What's wrong with the men of England that a young woman like you is left on the shelf?'

She lowered her gaze and started fiddling with the stem of her empty wine glass. 'I'm not interested in a relationship just now.'

'Yes, well, I'm with you on that.' He lifted his glass to his mouth and emptied it.

She brought her gaze back to his. Her expression had lost some of its reserve and was now sympathetic. It struck him as being genuine; although he could have been mistaken, given he'd drunk almost half a bottle of wine. 'I'm sorry about your engagement,' she said. 'It must have been devastating to have it ended like that when you were feeling at your most vulnerable.'

Raoul wondered what online blog or forum she'd been lurking on, or whether Rafe or Dominique had told her the details of his failed relationship with Clarissa. He would be lying to say he wasn't upset at having been dumped. He had always been the one to begin and end his relationships. He liked to be the one in control of his life because—like his brothers—having control was an essential part of being a Caffarelli. You didn't let others rule or lord it over you. You took charge and you kept in charge.

No matter who or what stood in your way.

He picked up the wine bottle and recklessly refilled his glass. 'I wasn't in love with her.'

Her pale, smooth brow crinkled in a frown. 'Then why on earth did you ask her to marry you?'

He put down the bottle and looked at her shocked expression. Was she a romantic at heart behind that prim, nun-like façade? He gave a shrug and picked up his glass again. 'I wanted to settle down. I thought it was time.'

She looked at him as if he was speaking gibberish. 'But marriage is meant to be for life. You're meant to love the person and want to be with them to the exclusion of all others.'

Raoul gave another careless shrug. 'In the circles I move in, it's more important to marry the person who will best fit into your lifestyle.'

'So love doesn't come into it?'

'If you're lucky—like my brother Rafe, for instance. But it's not mandatory.'

'That's preposterous!' She sat back in her chair with an exhalation of disgust. 'How could you possibly think of marrying someone you didn't love?'

He met her gaze with his. 'How many people do you know who have married whilst madly in love and yet went on to divorce in bitter hatred a few years later? The way I see it, love doesn't always last. It's better to choose someone you have something in common with. Clarissa was beautiful to look at, she came from a similar background, she was relatively easy company to be in and she was good in bed. What more could I have wanted?'

She rolled her eyes and reached for her water glass. 'I can see now why she ended your engagement. Your attitude is appalling. Love is the only reason anyone should get married. If you love someone you will do anything to support them—to be with them through thick and thin. No woman—or man, for that matter—should marry for anything less.'

'So you're a romantic at heart, Miss Archer.' He

twirled the contents of his wine glass. 'You'd get on well with my brother's new fiancée, Poppy.'

'She sounds like a lovely person.'

'She is. Rafe's very lucky to have found her.'

The look she gave him was pointed. 'But from what you said just a moment ago you don't think their love will last.'

'I said love doesn't *always* last. I think in their case it will. For one thing, his wealth means nothing to her. She loves him for who he is, not for what he has. She is indeed a rare find. But, apart from her, I have yet to meet a woman who doesn't have dollar signs in her eyes.'

She visibly bristled. 'Not all women are gold diggers.'

Raoul nailed her with his gaze. 'Why did you ask for your payment up-front with a no-refund clause?'

She looked momentarily discomfited. 'I—I had an urgent financial matter to see to.'

'Are you a big spender, Miss Archer?' He gave her outfit a cursory glance. 'You don't appear to be, on current appearances.'

Her mouth tightened a fraction and her creamy cheeks developed two spreading circles of colour. 'I'm sorry if my lowly apparel offends your sensibilities, but I'm not a slave to fashion. I have other far more important priorities.'

'I thought all women liked to make the most of their assets.'

She gave him an icy look. 'Are you really so shallow that you judge a woman on what she is wearing rather than who she is on the inside?'

Raoul couldn't help wondering what she looked like underneath those dreadful clothes. He was used to women who shamelessly flaunted their bodies in front of him, wearing the minimum of clothes and the maximum of cosmetics to draw his attention. But Miss Lily Archer, with her dowdy outfits, scrubbed clean face and dark blue secretive eyes intrigued him in a way no woman had ever done before. She held herself in a tightly contained way, as if she was frightened of drawing unnecessary attention to herself.

Maybe you shouldn't have been so hasty to send her packing.

Raoul quickly nudged the thought aside. 'I try not to judge on appearances alone, but it's all part of the package, isn't it? How people present themselves—their body language, how they act, how they speak. As humans we have evolved to decode hundreds of those subtle signs in order to work out whether to trust someone or not.'

She began to chew at her lower lip with her small white teeth. It struck Raoul how incredibly young it made her look. It was hard to gauge her age but he assumed she was in her mid-twenties, although right now she looked about sixteen.

Dominique came in with their entrées at that point. 'Can I pour you some wine, Miss Archer?' she asked, glancing at Lily's empty glass.

'Miss Archer is a teetotaller,' Raoul said. 'I haven't been able to tempt her so far.'

Dominique's black button eyes gave a little twinkle as she placed the soup in front of him. 'Perhaps Mademoiselle Archer is immune to temptation, Monsieur Raoul.'

He moved his lips in a semblance of a smile. 'We'll see.'

The housekeeper left the room and Raoul studied Lily's almost fierce expression. A frown was pulling at her smooth forehead and her mouth was set in a tight line, as if she was trying to stop herself from saying something she might later regret. Her slim shoulders were tense and her right hand was gripping her water glass so firmly he could see the bulge of each of her knuckles straining against her pale skin.

'Relax, Miss Archer. I'm not about to debauch you with liquor and licentiousness. I couldn't do so even if I wanted to, in my present condition.'

She raised her gaze to his, her cheeks still bright with colour. 'Do you usually drink so much?'

He felt the back of his neck prickle with defensiveness. 'I enjoy wine with my meals. I do not consider myself a drunk.'

'Alcohol numbs the senses and affects coordination and judgement.' She sounded like she was reading from a drug-and-alcohol education pamphlet. 'You'd be best to avoid it, or at least limit it, while you're recuperating.'

Raoul put his glass down with a little thwack. 'I'm not "recuperating", Miss Archer. This is what I'm left with because some brainless idiot driving a jet ski didn't watch where he was going.'

'Have you spoken to someone about how you feel about the accident?'

His defensiveness turned into outright nastiness. 'I don't need to lie down on some outrageously expensive psychologist's sofa and tell them what I feel about being mowed down like a ninepin. I feel royally pissed off, or has that somehow escaped your attention?'

Her slim throat moved up and down in a tight little swallow but her eyes remained steady on his. 'It's understandable that you're angry, but you'd be better off channelling that anger into trying to regain your mobility.'

Raoul saw red. It was like a mist in front of his eyes.

He felt his rage pounding in his ears like thunder. What had the last few weeks been about other than trying to regain his mobility? What right did she have to suggest he was somehow blocking his recovery by holding on to his anger at being struck down the way he had been? Letting go of his anger wasn't suddenly going to springboard him out of this chair and back into his previous life.

The life he'd had before was over.

Finished.

Kaput.

'Do you have any idea of what it's like to be totally dependent on other people?' he asked.

'Of course I do. I work with disabled people all the time.'

He slammed his fist on the table so hard the glasses almost toppled over. 'Do *not* call me disabled.'

She flinched and paled. 'I—I'm sorry…'

Raoul felt like the biggest jerk in the world but he wasn't ready to admit it or to apologise for it. He was furious with Rafe for putting him in this invidious position. She was clearly only doing it for the money. It was ludicrous to think she would succeed where others had failed. She was a fraud, a charlatan who exploited the vulnerable and desperate, and he couldn't wait to expose her for what she was.

'Why did you take on this job?'

The tip of her tongue darted out to moisten her lips. 'Your brother requested me. He'd heard about my success with another client. My manager at the clinic encouraged me to take the post and the money was…um… very good.'

'I got the impression from my brother that he had to work rather hard to convince you to come here.'

Her gaze moved away from his as she picked up her spoon. 'I don't usually work with male clients.'

Raoul felt a pique of interest. 'Why is that?'

She scooped up a portion of the soup but didn't manage to bring any of it to her mouth. 'I find them…' She seemed to be searching for the right word. 'Difficult to work with.'

'Uncooperative, you mean?'

She moistened her mouth again. 'It's hard for anyone to suffer a major injury—male, female, child or adult. I find that generally women and girls are more willing to accept help and to work within their limitations.'

Raoul watched her for a moment or two, the way she toyed with her food and kept her eyes averted from his. Her cheeks still had two tiny spots of colour high on her cheekbones. Her teeth kept coming back to savage her bottom lip and there was a little pleat of a frown between those incredibly blue eyes. His gaze went to her hands—they were small and slim-fingered and her nails had been bitten down almost to the quick.

'You don't seem to be enjoying that soup. Would you like me to ask Dominique to get you something else?'

She met his gaze and gave him a tremulous smile but it was so fleeting it made him long to see it again and for longer. 'No, it's fine…. I'm just not very hungry. It's been a very long day.'

Raoul felt a faint twinge of remorse. He certainly hadn't laid on the Caffarelli charm he and his brothers were famous for. What if he allowed her to stay for a week to see if there was anything she could do for him? It wasn't as if he had anything better to do right now.

At least it would be a distraction from the humdrum pattern his once vibrantly active life had been whittled down to. What did he have to lose? If she was a fraud, he would expose her. If she had something to offer, it would be win-win.

'I have a hypothetical question for you. If I agreed to have you here for the next month, what would you do with me?'

A light pink blush stole over her cheeks. 'Your brother told me you have a gym here. I'd work on some structured exercises to start with. We'd start slowly and gradually build up. It would depend on what you could do. It's tricky, given you've got a broken arm, but I'm sure I could work around that.'

'What else?'

'I'd like to have a look at your diet.'

'I eat a balanced diet.'

She glanced at his almost empty wine glass, her mouth set in a reproving line. 'Yes, well, there's always room for improvement. Do you take any supplements?'

'Vitamins, you mean?'

'Yes. Things like fish oil, glucosamine, vitamin D—that sort of thing. Studies have shown they help in the repair of muscles and tissues and can even halt the progress of osteoarthritic change in your joints.'

He gave a bark of scorn. 'For God's sake, Miss Archer, I'm not arthritic. I'm only thirty-four years old.'

Her small chin came up. 'Preventative health measures are worth considering no matter what your age.'

Raoul pinned her with his gaze. 'How old are you?'

Her frown came back but even deeper this time and she seemed to hesitate over her reply. 'I'm…I'm…twenty-six.'

'You looked like you had to think about it for a moment.'

She gave a tight movement of her lips that didn't even come close to being a smile. 'I'm not keen on keeping a record on birthdays. What woman is?'

'You're very young to be worrying about that,' Raoul said. 'Once you're over thirty, or even forty, it might be more of an issue, but you're still a baby.'

She looked down at the soup in her bowl, that same little frown pulling at her forehead. 'My father died on my birthday when I was seven years old. It's not a day I'm used to celebrating.'

Raoul thought of the tragic death of his parents so close to his own birthday. Rafe had been ten; he had been eight, just about to turn nine, and Remy only seven. His parents' funeral had been on Raoul's birthday. It had been the worst birthday present anyone could imagine—to follow those flower-covered coffins into the cathedral, to feel that collective grief pressing down on him, to hear those mournful tunes as the choir sang.

To this day he hated having flowers in the house and he could not bear the sound of choral music.

'I'm sorry,' he said. 'What about your mother? Is she still alive?'

'Yes. She lives in Norfolk. I see her whenever I can.'

'You live in London, yes?'

She nodded. 'In a flat in Mayfair but, before you get all excited about the posh address, let me tell you it's got creaking pipes and neighbours who think nothing of having loud parties that go on until four or five in the morning.'

'Do you live alone?'

Her eyes flickered with something before she disguised it behind the screen of her lowered lashes. 'Yes.'

Dominique came in to clear their plates, ready for the next course. She looked at Lily's barely touched soup and frowned. 'You are not hungry, *mademoiselle*? Would you like something else? I should have asked. Was the soup not to your liking?'

'No, please, it was lovely,' Lily said. 'I'm a bit jet-lagged, that's all. I suspect it's affected my appetite.'

'I have some lovely *coq au vin* for the main course,' Dominique said. 'It is Monsieur Raoul's favourite. Perhaps that will whet your lagging appetite, *oui*?'

'I'm sure it will,' Lily said with a smile.

Raoul felt a spark of male interest when he saw Lily's smile. She had beautiful white teeth, straight and even, and her smile had reached her eyes, making them come alive in a way they had not done previously. He felt a stirring in his groin, the first he had felt since his accident. He tried to ignore it but when she brought her gaze back to his he felt like a bolt of lightning had zapped him. She was stunningly beautiful when she wasn't holding herself so rigidly. Her brief smile had totally transformed her rather serious demeanour. Why did she take such pains to hide her assets behind such drab clothing and that dour expression?

'I hope I haven't offended her,' Lily said once Dominique had left.

'She's not easily offended,' Raoul said with a hint of wryness. 'If she were, she would have resigned the day I returned here after my accident. I wasn't the best person to be around. I'm still not.'

'It takes a lot of adjusting to accept limitations that have been imposed on us,' she said. 'You want your old life back, the one where everything was under your control. But that's not always possible.'

Raoul picked up his wine glass again but he didn't take a sip. It was more to have something to do with his hands, which increasingly felt compelled to reach across the table and touch one of hers. He wondered if her skin felt as soft as it looked. Her mouth fascinated him. It had looked so soft and plump when she'd smiled, yet now she held it so tightly. She gave off an aura of containment, of rigid self-control.

He gave himself a stern mental shake.

He was reading her aura?

'That sounds like the voice of experience,' he said. 'Have you been injured in the past?'

Her expression closed like curtains coming down on a stage. 'I didn't come here to talk about me. I came here to help you.'

'Against my will.'

She gave him a challenging look that put a defiant spark in her gaze. 'I'm leaving first thing in the morning, as you requested.'

Raoul didn't want her to leave, or at least not yet. Besides, his brother had paid a king's ransom for her services. The no-refund clause she'd insisted on irritated him. She would be home free if he let her pack up and leave before she had even started.

No, he would make her stay and make her work damn hard for the money.

He gave her an equally challenging look. 'What if I told you I'd changed my mind?'

'Have you?'

'I'm prepared to give you a week's trial. After that, I'll reassess.'

Her expression was wary. 'Are you sure?'

'When do we start?'

She reached across the table and snatched his wine glass away. 'Right now.'

Raoul tightened his jaw. He knew he was using alcohol as a crutch. Normally he was appalled by such behaviour in others, but he didn't take kindly to being treated like a child who didn't know how to practise self-restraint. 'It helps me sleep.'

'Alcohol disrupts sleep patterns. Anyway, Dominique told me you were a bad sleeper.'

'I wasn't before.'

'Do you have nightmares?'

'No.' He could tell she didn't believe him, but there was no way he was going to tell her about the horrifying images that kept him awake at night. The pain he had felt on the impact would stay with him for life. The fear that he would drown before anyone got to him had stayed with him and made him break out in a cold sweat every time he thought of it. He couldn't bear the thought of being submerged in water now, yet he'd used to swim daily.

'I have a list of supplements I'd like you to take,' she said. 'And I want to introduce some aquatic exercises.'

Raoul held up his plastered right arm. '*Hello?* This isn't waterproof. Swimming is out of the question.'

'Not swimming, per se. Walking in water.'

He gave a disdainful laugh. 'I can't even walk on land, let alone in water. You've got the wrong guy. The one you're looking for died two thousand-odd years ago and had a swag of miracles under his belt.'

She gave him a withering look. 'You can wear a

plastic bag over the cast. It will help your core stability switch on again to be moving in the water.'

Raoul glared at her furiously. 'I want my *life* switched on again! I don't give a damn about anything else.'

She pressed her lips together as if she were dealing with a recalcitrant child and needed to summon up some extra patience. 'I realise this is difficult for you—'

'You're damn right it's difficult for me,' he threw back. 'I can't even get down to the stables to see my horses. I can't even dress or shave myself without help.'

'How long before the plaster comes off?'

'Two weeks.'

'You'll find it much easier once it's off. Once your arm is strong enough, you'll be able to do some assisted walking on parallel bars. That's what I did with my last client. Within twelve weeks she was able to walk without holding on at all.'

Raoul didn't want to wait for twelve weeks. He didn't want to wait for twelve days. He wanted to be back on his feet *now*. He didn't want to turn his house into a rehabilitation facility with bars and rails and ramps everywhere. He wanted to be able to live a normal life, the life he'd had before, the life where he was in the driving seat, not being driven or pushed around by others. The grief and despair of what he had lost gnawed at him like a vicious toothache. How would he ever be happy with these limitations that had been forced on him?

He could *not* be happy.

He would *never* be happy, not like this.

How could he be?

Dominique came in with their main course. 'Would you like me to cut the chicken into smaller pieces for you, Monsieur Raoul?' she asked as she set his plate in front of him.

'No, I would not,' Raoul said curtly. 'I'm not a bloody child.'

Lily gave him a reproachful look once Dominique had left the room. 'You're giving a very convincing impression of one, and a very spoilt one at that. She was only trying to help. There was no need to bark at her like that.'

'I don't like being fussed over.' Raoul glowered at her. 'I refuse to be treated like an invalid.'

'It's always much harder for people with control issues to accept their limitations.'

He let out a derisive grunt of laughter. 'You think I'm a control freak? How did you come to that conclusion? Was my aura giving me away?'

'You're a classic control freak. That's why you're so angry and bitter. You're not in control any more. Your body won't let you do the things you want it to do. It's galling for you to have to ask anyone for help, so you don't ask. I bet you'd rather go hungry than have that meat cut up for you.'

Raoul curled his lip. 'Quite the little psychologist, aren't you, Miss Archer?'

She pursed her mouth for a moment before she responded. 'You have a strong personality. You're used to being in charge of your life. It doesn't take a psychology degree to work that out.'

He gave her a mocking look. 'Well, how about I read *your* aura, since we're playing amateur psychologist?'

Her expression tightened. 'Go right ahead.'

'You don't like drawing attention to yourself. You hide behind shapeless clothes. You lack confidence. Shall I go on?'

'Is it a crime to be an introvert?'

'No,' Raoul said. 'But I'm intrigued as to why a young woman as beautiful as you works so hard to downplay it.'

She looked flustered by his compliment. 'I—I don't consider myself to be beautiful.'

'You don't like compliments, do you, Miss Archer?'

She brought her chin up. 'Not unless I believe them to be genuine.'

Raoul continued to hold her gaze, watching as she fought against the desire to break the connection. Her eyes were dark blue pools, layered with secrets. What was it about her that so captivated him? Was it that air of mystery? That element of unknowable, untouchable reserve? She was so different from the women in his social circles—not just in looks and manner of dress but in her guardedness. She reminded him of a shy fawn, always keeping a watch out for danger—tense, alert, focused. He would enjoy the challenge of peeling back the layers of that carefully constructed façade.

'What time would you like to start in the morning?' he asked.

'Is nine OK? It will be hard work, but hopefully you'll find it beneficial.'

'I certainly hope so. Otherwise my brother is going to be without a best man.'

She frowned at him. 'You mean you won't go to the wedding at all if you're not walking by then?'

'I'm not going to ruin all the photos by being stuck in a chair. If I can't walk, then I'm not going.'

'But you can't not go to your brother's wedding.' Her frown deepened. 'It's the most important day of his life. You should be there, chair or no chair.'

Raoul set his jaw. He was not going to make a spectacle of himself on his brother's wedding day. The wedding would be large and the press would be there in droves. He could just imagine the attention he would receive. He could already see the caption on the photograph: the poor crippled brother. His stomach churned at the thought of it. 'Your job, Miss Archer, is to get me out of this chair. You have one week to convince me you can do it.'

She moistened her lips with another little sweep of her tongue. 'I'm not sure if I can or not. It's hard to put a time frame on the healing process. It could take months or it might not happen at all…'

'That is *not* an option,' Raoul said. 'You've supposedly worked a miracle before. Let's see you if you can do it again.'

CHAPTER THREE

LILY DID HER best with the meal Dominique set before her but the intensely penetrating gaze of Raoul Caffarelli did no favours to her already meagre appetite. He made her feel threatened, but strangely it wasn't in a physical way. He had a way of looking at her as if he was quietly making a study of her, peeling back the layers she had taken such great pains to stitch into place. Those layers were the only things holding her together. She could not bear the thought of him unravelling her, uncovering her shame for the world to see.

She tugged her sleeves down over her scarred arms beneath the table. The multiple fine white lines were not as noticeable as they once had been but she still liked to keep them covered. She hated the looks she got, the questioning lift of eyebrows and the judgemental comments such as, 'how could you deliberately cut yourself?'.

But the external scars were nothing to what she kept hidden on the inside.

Lily hated thinking of herself as a victim. She liked to think of herself as a survivor, but there were days when the nightmare of her twenty-first birthday came back to her in sharp stabs of memory that pierced the carapace she had constructed around herself. Sometimes it felt as if her soul was still bleeding, drop by drop, until one day there would be nothing left…

She looked up from fiddling with her sleeves to find Raoul's hazel gaze on her. She had lost track of time; how long had he been looking at her like that? 'Sorry… Did you say something?'

'No.'

'Oh…I thought you did.'

'You looked like you were miles away,' he said.

She tried to keep her features blank. 'Did I?'

'Are you a dreamer, Miss Archer?'

Lily would have laughed if she could remember how to do it. She had long ago given up dreaming for things that could never be hers. She was more or less resigned to the bitter reality that she could not turn back the clock and make a better choice this time around. 'No.'

He continued to hold her gaze, watching…watching. She forced herself to keep still, to not fidget or shift in her seat. But the tension was making her neck and shoulders ache and she could feel a headache starting at the back of her eyes. If she wasn't careful it would turn into a migraine and she would be even more vulnerable than she was now.

Lily put her napkin on the table. 'Will you excuse me?' She pushed back her chair. 'I need to use the bathroom.'

He gave a formal nod without once disconnecting his gaze from hers. 'Be my guest.'

Lily let out her breath in a stuttered stream once she was inside the nearest bathroom. She caught a glimpse of her reflection in the mirror and flinched. There were still times when she didn't recognise herself. It seemed like another person lived inside her body now. Gone was the outgoing, cheerful, laugh-a-minute girl who loved to party with the best of them. In her place was a drab young woman who looked older than her years.

Lily knew it pained her mother to see her downplay her features, but it was the only way she could cope with the past. She didn't want to be reminded of who she had been back then.

That girl had got her into trouble.

This one would keep her out of it.

When Lily came back to the dining room, the house-keeper was clearing away the plates. 'Monsieur Raoul has retired for the night,' Dominique said, looking up from her task of placing their used glasses on a silver tray.

'Oh…' Lily wasn't sure why she felt a little tweak of disappointment. It wasn't as if she had been expecting him to entertain her. The fact that he'd joined her at table was surprising in itself, given how tetchy he'd been to find out his brother had brought her here. But to leave without even saying goodnight seemed a bit rude. Was it his way of showing her he was still in control of some aspects of his life? Was he reminding her of her place here? She was just an employee, one he hadn't even wanted to hire.

'Would you care for a coffee in the salon?' Dominique asked.

'Coffee will be lovely.' She stepped forward. 'Can I help you with that tray?'

Dominique smiled. 'You are here to work for Monsieur Raoul, not to help me. But thank you for offering. I will bring your coffee to you shortly.'

Lily gnawed at her lip as she made her way to the salon. Why had Raoul changed his mind about having her here? He had said he would give her a week's trial and then reassess.

But what exactly would he be assessing?

Raoul tried to concentrate on some bloodlines on the computer in his study. There was a thoroughbred sale in Ireland he went to every year, but how could he turn up to it like this? It was the most humiliating thing of all, to be so helpless that he couldn't operate his chair with both hands, but until this arm healed he was stuck with it. He had not realised how dominant his right arm was until he had lost the use of it.

As for his legs… He tried to wriggle his toes but it was as if the message from his brain was delayed. He gripped his thigh with his left hand, digging his fingers in to see if the sensation was any stronger than the day before, but it was still patchy and dull in some places.

He let out a frustrated breath and clicked off the website he'd been reading. He felt restless and on edge. He couldn't help thinking of his future yawning out before him like a wide, deep, echoing canyon. Long, lonely nights sitting in front of the computer, or drinking his way to the bottom of the bottle, waiting for someone to fetch and carry for him.

He knew he was better off than most. He knew it intellectually, but on an emotional level he couldn't accept it—wasn't ready to accept it. He wasn't even *close* to accepting it. He didn't want to spend his life looking up at people, watching them get on with their lives while his was stuck on pause. He was used to every head turning when he walked into a room. He and his brothers had been blessed with the good looks, height and build of their Caffarelli forefathers. He wasn't any more vain than Rafe or Remy were but he knew no one would look at him the same way while he was sitting in this damn chair.

He thought back to Clarissa's visit at the hospital. She had barely been able to meet his gaze, yet only days before she had been lying in his arms, her limbs entangled with his.

Now his limbs were as good as useless.

He punched his thigh, as if that would make the nerves inside wake up and take notice. He punched and punched until the heel of his hand was sore, but it made no difference. He raked his throbbing hand through the messy tangle of his hair, vaguely registering that he needed a haircut.

Emotions he had locked down centuries ago rumbled like the tremor of a mighty earthquake inside him. He hadn't cried since he was kid. Not in public; oh, no, not even in front of his brothers, especially Rafe, who had so stalwartly, so unflinchingly modelled courage, strength and stoicism from the moment they had found out they had been orphaned. He still remembered standing shoulder to shoulder with Rafe at their parents' funeral. He had been determined not to cry. And he hadn't. Remy had been sobbing out of bewilderment and Rafe had gathered him close. He had offered Raoul his other arm but he had shrugged it off.

Raoul had waited until he was alone to vent his feelings. He *always* went to ground when he had to deal with things. He didn't need people around, offering their useless platitudes and pitying looks.

But now he had Miss Lily Archer inside his bunker.

He pushed back from his desk and motored his chair to the door, but just as he was coming out of it he saw Lily coming up the corridor. She had her head down and her arms folded across her middle as if she was keeping herself tightly contained. She must have heard the faint whirr of his chair for she suddenly looked up and stopped in her tracks, her cheeks pooling with a faint blush of colour.

'I—I thought you'd gone to bed.'

'Not yet,' Raoul said. 'I refuse to lie down before eleven o'clock and even that's far too early for me.'

Her blush deepened a fraction but the tone of her voice was starchy and disapproving. 'I'm sure it is.'

'Are you a night owl, Miss Archer?'

'No.'

Her answer was so quick and so definitive. Every moment he spent with her piqued his interest a little bit more. What was going on behind the bottomless lake of those dark blue eyes? What was it with her stiff, schoolmarm formality? He couldn't help imagining her without that layer of dowdy, shapeless clothes. She was on the slim side, but even so he could see the jut of her small but shapely breasts beneath that sack of a dress.

What would she look like in a swimsuit?

What would she look like naked?

'Would you care to join me in a nightcap?' he asked.

She looked like he had just asked her to drink from a poisoned chalice. 'No.'

Raoul raised his brows. 'Surely one little tipple won't corrupt you?'

She compressed her lips until they were almost white. 'I told you before, Monsieur Caffarelli, I don't drink.'

'You can call me Raoul. You don't have to be so formal with me.' He gave her an indolent half smile. 'It's not as if it's me paying your wages.'

Her eyes moved away from his. 'I like to keep professional boundaries in place when I'm dealing with clients.'

'So you don't ever get on a first-name basis?'

She huddled into herself again. She reminded him of a porcupine folding in on itself to keep away predators. 'Sometimes, but not always.'

'So, how can I get you to relax the boundaries enough to call me by my first name?'

Her eyes were as chilly as a Scottish tarn as they met his. 'You can't.'

Raoul felt the thrum of his blood as she laid down the challenge. There was nothing a Caffarelli male loved more than a challenge—a seemingly impossible obstacle to overcome. They *thrived* on it. It was like air—as essential to them as oxygen. It was a part of their DNA.

He remembered the pep talk Rafe had given him and Remy when things had turned ugly after their grandfather had jeopardised the family fortune with an unwise deal with a business rival a few years ago.

Goal.

Focus.

Win.

It was the Caffarelli credo.

Raoul looked at her tightly composed features. She didn't like him and she didn't like being here. It was only about the money. This next week could be far more entertaining than he had first realised. He would rattle her cage some more and enjoy every single minute of doing it. 'Good night, Miss Archer.'

Her cheeks were still rosy but her eyes hardened as she raised her chin. 'Goodnight, Monsieur Caffarelli.'

He watched as she walked on past with brisk steps that ate up the corridor like a hungry chomping mouth. The door of her bedroom closed with a snap and the sound echoed for a moment in the ringing silence.

Raoul frowned as he wheeled back into his study. It was a new experience to have a bedroom door closed on him.

He decided he didn't like it.

Lily came down for an early breakfast the next morning to find Dominique talking to a man in his late twenties over coffee and hot, buttery croissants.

'Ah, Mademoiselle Archer, this is Monsieur Raoul's carer, Sebastien,' the housekeeper said. 'Or should I say, ex-carer?'

Sebastien rolled his eyes as he put his coffee cup down on the counter. 'I've been fired as of this morning. Monsieur Caffarelli has decided he no longer needs my help.'

'Oh...'

'I probably should warn you, he's in a spectacularly foul temper,' Sebastien said. 'I don't think he slept at all last night.'

'He's not very happy about me being here,' Lily said.

'Yes, so I gathered.' He gave her a sizing-up look to see if she was up to the task of dealing with such a difficult client as Raoul. 'His bark is worse than his bite, although I have to say his bark can be very savage at times.'

'I have no intention of allowing Monsieur Caffarelli to harangue or intimidate me,' Lily said.

'Good for you,' Sebastien said and, nodding briefly at the housekeeper in farewell, picked up his keys and left.

Dominique wiped away some crumbs from the counter top. 'Monsieur Raoul is not by nature a bad-tempered man.' She stopped wiping to look at Lily. 'You have no need to be afraid of him. He would never hurt anyone.'

'I'm not afraid of him,' Lily said. *Well, maybe a bit.*

The housekeeper's gaze held hers for a moment longer than necessary. 'He is in his study doing his emails. Will you take him his coffee for me? It will save my aching feet one more trip down that corridor.'

'Of course.'

The door of the study was closed and Lily stood outside it for a moment, listening to the sounds coming from inside. She heard the click of a mouse and then a vicious swear word in English. She waited another beat before raising her knuckles to knock on the door.

'Yes?' The word was sharply delivered, like a short but vicious bark.

Lily took a steadying breath. 'I have your coffee, Monsieur Caffarelli. Dominique asked me to bring it to you.'

'Then bring it in, for God's sake.'

She opened the door to find him sitting behind a desk that was almost as large as her bathroom back at home. He was dressed in gym gear, but it didn't take away from his air of authority and command. If anything he looked even more intimidating. His shoulders looked even broader in a close-fitting T-shirt. The stark whiteness of the T-shirt against the tan of his olive skin was another reminder of his love of the outdoors prior to the accident. She saw the carved contours of his pectoral muscles. His strong arms were liberally sprinkled with dark coarse hair that trailed right down over the backs of his hands and to his fingers.

Something shifted in her belly as she thought of those tanned hands touching her smoother, paler ones...

'Don't hover,' he snapped at her.

Lily set her mouth as she stiffly approached his desk. 'Your coffee.' She placed it before him. 'Sir.'

His eyes warred with hers for a tense moment. *'Sir?'*

She gave him an arch look. 'You don't like being called sir?'

'You're not one of the servants.'

'No,' Lily said. 'I'm a human being, just like you.'

'You're nothing like me, Miss Archer.' A flash of irritation fired in his gaze. 'Apart from the obvious male and female thing, you're not currently confined to a wheelchair.'

'Perhaps not, but I am confined to this château to work with you for the next month,' she returned.

'A week, Miss Archer,' he said flatly.

'A week, then.'

A tight silence crackled the air.

Lily glanced at his untouched coffee. 'Is that all you're having for breakfast?'

He gave her a don't-mess-with-me-look. 'I'm not hungry.'

'Your body needs proper fuel. You can't ask your body to improve if you don't give it what it needs.'

His eyes glinted dangerously. 'What does *your* body need, Miss Archer?'

Lily felt the slow burn of his gaze as it lazily traversed the length of her body, a hot, melting sensation pooling deep in her core. His eyes lingered for a moment on her mouth, as if he was wondering how it would taste and feel beneath his own. She felt a strong urge to moisten her lips but somehow refrained from doing so. 'It's not my body that is the issue here. It is yours.'

'My body…' He gave a little grunt. 'I don't even recognise it when I see it in the mirror.'

'Muscle wastage is common after injury,' Lily said. 'We can work on that.'

His hazel eyes roved over her once more. 'Are you going to work with me in the gym wearing that dress?'

She felt her cheeks heat up again. 'No, I have a tracksuit upstairs.'

The sardonic gleam in his eyes was deeply unsettling. 'What do you wear in the pool?'

'Um…a bathing suit.'

Those wicked eyes glinted again. 'Maybe I'll change my mind about the water work. Who knows what delightful surprises will be in store for me?'

Lily pressed her lips together for a moment. 'I'm going to speak to Dominique about making you a protein shake. If you won't eat breakfast, then at least you can drink it.'

He held her gaze in that assessing way of his. 'Are you usually this bossy with your clients?'

'Only the childish ones.'

His brows lifted a fraction. 'You have a smart mouth, Miss Archer.'

Lily held her ground even though his green-flecked eyes were boring into hers. 'I speak as I find.'

'Tell me something…' He paused as his gaze continued to hold hers. 'Has that quick tongue of yours ever got you into trouble?'

She kept her spine straight and her shoulders neatly aligned. 'Not lately.'

A beat of silence passed.

'It won't work, you know.'

She looked at him blankly. 'Excuse me?'

His mouth curled up at one corner in a cynical manner. 'I can almost hear the cogs of that clever little brain of yours clicking over. You think if you're unpardonably rude to me it will make me send you packing before the week's trial is up. You want to take the money and run, don't you, Miss Archer?'

Lily wondered if he could read minds or if he was just much more cynical than she had realised. 'I don't believe in taking money I haven't earned. And, as for being unpardonably rude, I think you've already got the headmaster's prize for that.'

A satirical smile tilted his mouth. 'You're a spirited little thing under that demure façade, aren't you?'

She threw him a haughty look. 'I expect the only spirits you're used to seeing in the vacuous women you surround yourself with are the ones you pour into a glass.'

For a moment Lily thought she had gone too far. She saw his eyes harden and his jaw tighten. But then he suddenly threw back his head and laughed. It was a nice sound, rich, deep and melodic. It made the fine hairs on the back of her neck lift up and do a little jiggle. It made something that was tightly knotted in the pit of her stomach work its way loose.

Careful, the new girl reminded her. *Watch your step. Keep your guard up.*

Lily turned briskly for the door. 'I'll go and see about that protein shake.'

'Miss Archer?'

She turned and faced him. 'Yes?'

He held her gaze for what seemed to her an interminable pause. But, whatever he had planned to say, he left unsaid. His lingering smile gradually faded until it completely disappeared from his mouth and his frown returned. 'Close the door on the way out.'

CHAPTER FOUR

THE GYM WAS in a sunny room on the eastern side of the house. It was well-equipped, with every modern piece of equipment an exercise junkie could wish for. Lily trailed her hand over the state-of-the-art treadmill. She wondered if Raoul would ever use it again as it was intended to be used. He didn't look like the sort of person who would ever be satisfied to walk at a sedate pace. Those long, strong legs were made for hard physical exercise. She had caught a glimpse of his muscular thighs when she had run into him in the corridor last night. If he didn't—or couldn't—do specific exercises to maintain or increase strength, he would lose that impressive definition.

The change to his life was unimaginable. For a man who had chased adventure and women simultaneously, he was going to find any sort of restriction difficult to manage.

Lily thought yet again of his ex-fiancée. What type of woman was Clarissa that she could just walk away from him when he was struck down? It seemed so shallow and selfish. Raoul said he hadn't been in love with her, but Lily wondered if that was a way of dismissing or disguising the hurt he felt. How could he not feel some measure of hurt? It was like being kicked when you were already down.

She had seen many relationships flounder as a result of a person's injury. It wasn't just the injuries that changed people; it was the experience of confronting their own mortality. A period of reassessment nearly always occurred after a traumatic event. Relationships were either severed or secured, lifetime patterns were changed or adjusted, careers were either abandoned or taken in a new direction. It was a very unsettling time for the patient as well as their loved ones.

Was that why Raoul had locked himself away in his secluded château—so he could reflect on what had happened to him?

He was a complex man, deeply layered, with a keen intelligence to match those strong, observant eyes. It would test her sorely to spend the whole month with him. She couldn't help feeling he was toying with her, allowing her a week to prove herself, keeping her on tenterhooks, all the while luring her into his invisible web.

Lily turned when she heard the sound of his chair coming through the door. 'You have an impressive set of equipment,' she said without thinking.

His hazel eyes glinted. 'Yes, so I've been told many, many times.'

She felt her blush travel to the roots of her hair. 'Um… we should probably get started…' She hastily summoned her clinical professional self but she had never felt more flustered. Was he doing it on purpose, playing his double-entendre game so she would blush like a schoolgirl? All she seemed to do was blush around him. It was mortifying.

'Do you want me in or out of the chair?'

'Maybe we could have you sit on the weight bench,' Lily said. 'We can do some light weights and resistance work.' She swallowed tightly as he motored to the bench. 'Do you need help getting out of your—?'

'No.'

Relief flooded her momentarily. She'd been psyching herself up to touch him. She had lain awake the night before wondering what it would feel like to have those hard muscles under her hands.

She watched as he lifted himself out of the chair close to the weight bench. The muscles in his left arm contracted as he balanced himself. She could see the struggle playing out on his face. His mouth was set in a tight line, his forehead creased in fierce concentration as if he was willing every damaged nerve inside his body to respond. He finally sat down on the weight bench and visibly winced as he dragged his legs in front of his body.

'Are you in any pain?' Lily asked.

'I can handle it.'

'You don't have to be a martyr. Taking properly prescribed pain relief is not a crime.'

His hard gaze collided with hers. 'Can we quit it with the pharmacy lesson and get on with this?'

Lily let out a breath and held out a light dumbbell. 'Thirty reps, in three lots of ten.'

He gave the weight a scornful look as if it was nothing more than a dust bunny. 'Are you *serious*?'

'You can't go straight back to what you were lifting before. You could end up with even more damage to your spine. You have to start slowly and gradually build up.'

His jaw locked down stubbornly. 'This is ridiculous. I'm going to kill my brother for this.'

She put one hand on her hip, the other hand holding

the weight out to him. 'You can kill him later. Right now, you do as I say.'

He opened his hand resignedly and she dropped the weight into it. His fingers closed over it and with a little roll of his eyes he started on the repetitions. 'How am I doing?' His tone was unmistakably sarcastic. 'Can you see my biceps bulging?'

Lily was trying *not* to notice anything about his body, especially his biceps. She was having trouble accessing the professional therapist inside her head. In her place was a young woman who had not been this close to a physically gorgeous man for five years. It was hard to think of clinical specifics when a man as well-built as Raoul Caffarelli was sitting within arm's reach. She could even smell him—a hint of spice, grace note of lemon and lime, and a sexy understory of a man in his prime.

'Not so fast,' she said, hoping she didn't sound as breathless as she felt. 'You need to concentrate on the release as much if not more than the contraction.'

Those sinful eyes glinted as they tethered hers. 'I *always* concentrate on the release.'

Lily adopted a prim and haughty manner. 'Right; well, then, let's get working on your deep abdominal stabilisers. They switch off in the presence of back pain or injury. It takes a lot of work to switch them on again. You can feel them if you press a finger to your abdomen—like this.' She put two fingers to her own abdomen covered by her tracksuit. 'You pull them in like you were drawing your belly button back towards your spine.'

'I'm not sure I know how to do that.'

She let out an uneven breath. She didn't trust that

guileless look for a second. 'It's not exactly rocket science. You contract those muscles all the time.'

'Doing what?'

Lily couldn't hold his gaze. He knew exactly what activity activated those muscles. He had probably overused them in his marathon bedroom sessions over the years. 'Let's try some leg lifts. Have you any movement at all?'

'A bit.'

'Show me.'

He lifted his right leg an inch off the floor but it trembled as he did it. It was even worse on the left side. He could barely lift it at all. 'I guess I won't be running a marathon any time soon.'

Lily heard the faint hint of despair behind the quip. He was a man used to relying on his body strength. To have it taken away from him, or even reduced marginally, struck at the very heart of what he believed being a man entailed. 'Let's concentrate on getting you standing and then walking before we even think about running. Can you circle your ankles at all?'

He circled his right ankle easily enough but again his left was slow to respond. A look of frustration tightened his features. 'This is pointless. I can't do this. I don't *want* to do this.'

'You have to be patient,' Lily said. 'You can't expect instant results. This could take months or even years.'

His dark brows snapped together. 'Is that how you make your money? Stringing people along for years on end with a vague hope of a cure?'

'I try to be honest with all of my clients.'

'How about you start being honest with me?' He flashed his diamond-hard gaze at her. 'What are my chances? You can shoot from the hip. You don't need to sugar coat it. I can take it like a man.'

Lily ran her tongue over her sandstone-dry mouth. 'I think it's going to be a long and hard struggle to regain your full mobility.'

'Are you saying I'm *never* going to regain it?'

No one wanted to hear the bad news. That was part of the agony of rehabilitation. No one ever wanted to accept what fate and circumstances had dished out. Life was incredibly cruel at times. Bad things happened to good people. There was no way of getting around it.

'I think it's too early to say,' she said, taking the safe middle ground.

His eyes burned with acrid bitterness. 'You would say that, wouldn't you? It gives you a safety net in case things don't go according to plan. You get your money either way, don't you, Miss Archer? You've made sure of that.'

Lily bitterly resented his summation of her character. She was the very last person who would exploit another's vulnerability. She'd had her vulnerability exploited in the worst way imaginable. The memory of that night was like a cancer inside her head. She tried to radiate it with distractions, she tried to poison it with activity, but still it festered there, waiting for another chance to destroy her.

'I've had to put off several other clients in order to come here,' she said. 'Some financial compensation for that is not unreasonable.'

His green-brown eyes measured hers for a pulsing moment. 'Then we'd best get my brother's money's worth, hadn't we?'

Lily handed him a heavier weight, taking great care

not to encounter his fingers in the exchange. 'Yes. We'd better.'

He cooperated for a while but she could see his impatience simmering inside him. She knew it must be humiliating for someone so used to being in control to have so much of it taken away. But patience was exactly what he needed right now. There was no point going at things like a bull at a gate. Slowly but surely was the best way of managing any crisis.

She was living proof of that.

'I think that's enough for today,' she said, after he worked through a couple more exercises.

He frowned at her. 'Are you joking?'

'No.' Lily picked up the weight he'd left on the floor and took it over to the rack, trying not to notice the warmth of where his fingers had been. 'You've been sitting for more than ten minutes. Didn't your neurosurgeon advise you to limit sitting at this stage?'

'But I've done nothing.' His frown turned into a glare. '*You've* done nothing.'

'On the contrary, I've been observing you the whole time you were doing the reps. I was noting your posture and the activity of your muscles. You have a lot of tension in your neck and shoulders. Your left side is much worse than your right. It's probably a knock-on effect of the injury to your lower discs and, of course, your broken arm.'

'So what's the plan?'

Lily didn't care for the gleam that had so quickly switched places with his glare. 'Um…plan?'

'Are you going to massage me?'

A swooping sensation passed through her stomach.

Stop acting like an idiot. You've massaged hundreds of clients.

Yes, but none of them have been male!

The conversation went back and forth inside her head until she realised Raoul was looking at her quizzically. 'Is everything all right?' he asked.

'Of course…' She forced herself to meet his gaze. 'I'd need to hire a massage table. I didn't bring one with me. It might take a few days to get one. I should've thought, but it was all such a rush and I—'

'I have one.'

Lily gulped. 'You…you do?' *But of course he would.* A man who had everything money could buy would have a massage table. He probably had one for every day of the week. He probably had one in every room of his château. They were probably lined with gold or dripping with diamonds or something.

'It's in the room next to the sauna and Jacuzzi.'

'But of course,' she mumbled, not quite under her breath.

He hooked one brow upwards. 'You find my wealth something to mock, Miss Archer?'

Lily felt the scorch of his gaze as it held hers. 'No… I was just thinking out loud.'

'Then please refrain from doing so in my presence.'

Don't look away. Don't let him win this. He's trying to intimidate you. She held his steely gaze as each throbbing second passed. It was a battle of wills and she knew she was seriously, woefully outmatched but she didn't care. He was looking for a chance to wield some of the power he had lost. It was a game to him. *She* was a game, a toy to be played with until he got tired of pressing her buttons.

And he was pressing her buttons. Big time. Buttons that hadn't been pressed in a very long time—new buttons that had never been pressed before.

Like the one that was deep in her core. It felt like a shot of electricity went through it every time he looked at her with that dark, satirical gaze. Those glinting, *knowing* eyes were seeing much more than she wanted them to see.

She wasn't that wilful, reckless girl any more.

She was sensible and stable now.

She had her head screwed on tightly.

She had her emotions under control.

'What time would you like your massage?' *Had she really said that?* Lily heard the words but they seemed to have come from someone else's mouth. The new girl would never offer to massage a full-blooded man, certainly not one as dangerously attractive as Raoul Caffarelli. Her stomach nosedived as she waited for him to answer. The silence seemed to thrum with an extra layer of tension.

Sexual tension.

Lily smothered an involuntary gasp. Desire was something other girls felt. The new girl didn't have any place for such primal urges. She was literally dead from the waist down.

Or she had been until now…

'Shall we say eleven?' he said. 'I have some things to see to in my study first.'

'Fine. Perfect. I'll go and get set up. Don't rush if you get caught up with work or phone calls or texts or emails or anything. If you need to cancel, then we can always do it later.' *Much, much later. Or what about not at all?*

'I'll see you at eleven, Miss Archer.' A glitter of devilry entered his gaze. 'I'll look forward to a bit of hands-on therapy from you.'

Lily let out a flustered breath once he had left. Could this farce get any worse?

CHAPTER FIVE

LILY'S STOMACH WAS a frenzied hive of nerves by the time Raoul arrived at the door of the massage room. She could barely look him in the eye in case he saw how on edge she was. 'I'll leave you to get undress—I mean, ready.' She tucked a strand of her hair that had come loose back behind her ear and chanced a glance at him. 'Do you need help getting on the table?'

His expression was inscrutable. 'I'll call you if I need you.'

'Right.' She darted out of the room to leave him to it, her heart flapping like a sheet in a tornado inside her chest.

She came back in a few minutes later to find him lying face down on the massage table. She had left a towel for him to drape over his buttocks but due to his mobility issues he hadn't been able to position it correctly. It was a little skewed, giving her a good view of his tan line and the taut curve of his right buttock.

He is totally naked underneath that towel!

'Are you comfortable?' Her voice came out like a squeak as she carefully draped the towel back over him.

'Yes.'

Lily looked at the scar over his L5S1 and L4S2 discs.

It was still red and slightly puckered from where his neurosurgeon had operated to decompress the spinal cord but it would eventually fade to white.

She cast her eyes over the rest of him. He had an amazing physique—broad-shouldered, lean-hipped and well-muscled without being over the top. She could have stood there drinking in the sight of him for hours. It was so long since she had looked at a man—properly looked. He was like a sculptor's model, so beautifully put together it was almost painful to look at him knowing he was unable to walk or stand.

'I must be a whole lot worse than I thought,' he drawled. 'I can't feel a thing.'

Lily felt a reluctant smile pull at her mouth. 'I haven't touched you yet.'

'What's taking you so long?'

'Nothing. I'm just…um…getting to it.'

She drew in a little breath and pumped some oil from the dispenser into her palms to warm it. She put her hands on his feet to begin with—it was an anchoring touch she had used hundreds of times with clients. But never before had she felt such a high voltage surge of electricity from touching someone. It made her palms and fingers tingle as soon as she came into contact with his skin. She felt him flinch as if he had felt the same shock of contact. Then, taking another steadying breath, she moved her hands to his right leg, moving up his calf, working on loosening the tight, stringy muscles there. He flinched again and she heard him smother a curse.

'You can feel that?' she asked.

'Your thumbs feel like corkscrews.'

'Your muscles feel like concrete.'

He grunted. 'You should feel it from my side.'

Lily's mouth curved again. 'Stop whining and relax.'

She continued working on his legs, going up to his thigh and massaging with long, strong movements. She switched to his other leg and did the same. He was hard, hairy, warm and intensely male. His legs were powerfully made, strongly muscled and yet lean, without an ounce of fat on him anywhere.

She carefully lowered the towel from his buttocks so she could work on his attachment muscles. They were incredibly ropy and tight but after a while she felt them start to give a bit under her touch.

His body seemed to take a deep breath and then release it. She felt him relax into the table; his breathing gradually becoming slow and even.

Lily moved up his spine, careful to leave his damaged discs alone, working instead on the muscles and ligaments that supported them. He was tight in the neck and shoulders as she had observed earlier, but again after a while his muscles seemed to let go. His skin was smooth and warm, scented by the oil she was using and his own particular smell. It was a heady combination that stirred her sleeping senses.

She looked at the thick, black glossy hair on his head as she worked on his shoulders. Her fingers itched to feel it, to comb it, to tidy it. He had a tousled, couldn't-be-bothered-with-grooming look about him. She could see the traces of a style that was distinctly European— parted in the middle but long enough to sweep back over his forehead if the mood took him, the back long enough to curl beyond his collar.

Without even knowing she was doing it until she was actually doing it, Lily trailed her fingers lightly through the thickness of his hair. It felt springy, silky, soft and smelt like fresh apples.

'Do I have muscles there?' His deep voice was muffled from relaxation and from being pressed face down on the table.

Lily was glad he wasn't face up for he would have seen her fiery blush. 'No, but your scalp does.' She moved her fingers over the crown of his head, stroking and kneading to release the tension she could feel residing there. 'Do you get tension or cluster headaches?'

'Occasionally.'

'Migraine?'

'Once or twice.'

'What do you do to relax?' she asked.

'Is that a trick question?'

She felt that little smile tug at her mouth again. 'I'm serious. What do you do to unwind?'

There was a little silence.

'If you'd asked me that a month ago, I would have said sex.'

Lily removed her hands from his head and wiped them roughly on a towel. She didn't know what to say so said nothing. It seemed easier than making a fool of herself.

He turned his head so one eye could fix itself on her. 'Don't you find sex relaxing, Miss Archer?'

What could she say? That it was the most *unrelaxing* thing she could think of? He would no doubt laugh at her, make her feel silly, gauche and unsophisticated.

But then, if she told him the reason why she felt that way, she would have to confront her shame all over again. Stir up all those ghastly memories, set off a chain of nightmares that took months to go away.

Instead she snatched on the lifeline he'd inadvertently handed her. 'Does that mean you can no longer…?' She left the sentence hanging. It was devastating for anyone to lose sexual function but for a young man in his prime it was surely the most shattering blow of all.

'I have yet to find out.' He pulled himself up into a sitting position. 'The doctors seem to think things will be OK in that department.'

Lily was completely tongue-tied. She felt a fool just standing there staring at him. She could feel her face glowing with heat as the silence stretched and stretched.

'Don't look so shocked, Miss Archer,' he said dryly. 'I'm not asking you to rehabilitate me.'

'I wouldn't agree to it if you did,' she threw back quickly.

A glint of something indefinable entered his gaze as it tussled with hers. The massage room seemed suddenly smaller. The air thinner and tighter. Her breathing faster and more uneven. More audible.

She couldn't stop her gaze from drifting to his mouth. It was quite possibly the most sensual-looking mouth she had ever laid eyes on. She hadn't been kissed in years. She had almost forgotten what it felt like to have a man's mouth moving on hers.

Raoul Caffarelli's mouth looked like it knew how to kiss. A fuller lower lip hinted at the sensual power at his command; the slightly thinner top one spoke of a man who liked his own way and made no apologies for going out and getting it.

'Find what you're looking for?' His deep voice jolted her out of her stasis.

Her eyes met his briefly before falling away. 'I'll just leave you to—'

Before Lily could bolt he caught her loosely by the wrist. The Taser-like shock of his touch sent tingles down her spine. She looked at his darkly tanned fingers overlapping the slender bones of her wrist. If he so much as pushed up her sleeve an inch he would see the crisscross map of her shame.

She brought her gaze back to his, her mouth dry, her heart hammering like a piston in a faulty engine. Time seemed to stand still as she looked into that green-and-brown gaze. His lashes were thick and plentiful; his pupils were wide and inky black.

A girl could get lost in those eyes if she wasn't careful. 'You have a towel crease.' *Could you not have thought of something a little more sophisticated to say?*

His mouth slanted, making his eyes crinkle up at the corners in a staggeringly gorgeous way. 'Where?'

'On your forehead.'

His thumb moved slowly over the underside of her wrist as he kept her gaze tethered to his. It was the slightest, barely moving stroke, but it caused a tsunami of sensations to erupt like bubbling lava beneath her skin. She was acutely aware of how close she was to him. She was standing between his open thighs in an erotic enclosure that should have terrified her but somehow didn't.

His eyes went to her mouth. Stayed there. Burned there. Tingled there.

Tempted there.

He brought his gaze back to mesh with hers. 'Do you ever smile, Miss Archer?'

Lily moistened her parchment-dry lips. 'Sometimes.'

His thumb located her pulse and measured it. 'You're not very relaxed, are you?'

'I'm not the one who just had a massage.'

His smile tilted his mouth again. 'It was a good massage. Very professional.'

'Thank you.'

He slowly released her wrist. Lily could still feel where his fingers had been long after she had brought her arm back close to her side. It was like a hot brand that had somehow transferred its molten heat all the way to her core. She could feel it swirling there in a tide of longing. Needs she had ignored for years shifted, stirred, stretched. She felt the movement of it in her blood, the way her heart picked up its beat to keep pace with the heady rush of primal, earthy desire.

'Can you push my chair a little closer?'

Lily took a skittering breath. 'Of course.' She brought the chair to him. The towel draped over his lap did little to hide the unmistakable evidence of his erection. Her gaze seemed to be drawn to it like a magnet. She gulped. *Was it getting bigger?*

She finally managed to tear her eyes away. 'I'll just... go and let you get dressed.' She turned and bolted for the door, almost knocking herself out in her haste to open it.

Raoul watched her leave with a smile lingering on his mouth. She was an intriguing mix of sassy-smart mouth and shy schoolgirl. He couldn't make up his mind which persona he liked best.

You like her?

He looked down at the bulge of his erection. *Yeah, it seems I do.*

He pushed back from where his mind was heading, a frown rapidly replacing his smile. He didn't want an affair with anyone until he could be physically whole again. He could not bear the thought of a pity lay. He could just imagine the utter humiliation of it. Could there be a crueller punishment than to reduce a playboy to that?

He was used to taking the lead in sex. He enjoyed sex. He had a strong drive but he knew how to contain it. He was a good lover. He wasn't selfish or self-serving; he wasn't averse to the odd quickie up against a wall or kitchen worktop, but only if the woman was with him all the way.

His gut twisted at the thought of never experiencing that primal power again. Even if he could perform he would be confined to doing it in bed. He wouldn't even be able to carry the woman to the bedroom. He would be old before his time.

He swore savagely as he reached for his clothes. If he still believed in God he would have cursed him, too. He had never been a violent person—not like his grandfather, who could fly off the handle at a moment's notice—but right now he wanted to punch his fist through the nearest wall in frustration. His mood soured like milk that had been left all day in the sun. It curdled his sense of humour; it made rancid every remotely positive thought that entered his head.

You have to get through this.

How? He wanted to shout it until his voice cracked. *How am I supposed to get through this?*

Raoul eased himself off the table, but just as he was about to lower himself into his chair it moved out of reach. He made a grab for it but he only managed to push it further away. Anger and frustration surged like an erupting volcano inside him.

This is not my life.

I don't want to be like this.

He considered calling Lily to help him, but pride forestalled him. Surely he could get back in the damn chair without her help? It was only a step or two away. He held on to the table for balance, willing his right leg to move the short distance. He gritted his teeth and stretched out his hand. Almost there....

Raoul took a half-shuffle, half-hopping step with his right leg but his left leg wouldn't come to the party. It folded under him like a wet noodle and he landed in a crumpled heap on the floor, banging his forehead for good measure against the metal footplate of the wheelchair. The curse he let out cut through the air like a blade.

'Are you all right?' Lily called from the other side of the door.

He ground his teeth as he eased himself up on one elbow. 'I'm fine.'

The door opened and her eyes went wide as she came in. 'What happened?'

'What do you think happened?' He glared at her. 'I thought it'd be fun to look at the ceiling from this angle.'

She crouched down beside him, her slate-blue gaze concerned as she reached out to brush his hair back from his forehead. 'You've cut your forehead.' Her touch was as gentle as a feather and it made his skin lift up in goose bumps.

'Lucky me. A towel crease *and* a cut.'

She got up from the floor to fetch a tissue from a box next to the oil dispenser. She came back to him, kneeling beside him again, the tissue neatly folded into a square as she pressed it like a compress to his forehead just above his right eye.

His gaze meshed with hers.

A timeless moment passed.

Raoul could smell her fragrance—a light, flowery scent that was understated and yet utterly, powerfully feminine. Her eyes were like dark pools, fringed by sooty black lashes that curled up at the ends like a child's. Her skin was flawless, like smooth cream or priceless fine porcelain, her lips soft and a dark pinkishred, just ripe for tasting.

He could feel her warm, vanilla-scented breath on his face. Her breathing had quickened, but then so too had his, along with his blood. It stuttered and then roared through his veins as his latent desire took a foothold and then pressed the pedal down—*hard.*

He slid his left hand beneath her silky ponytail. He heard the rapid little uptake of her breath and felt her hand still on his forehead, but she didn't pull away. Her lashes lowered over her eyes as she darted a quick glance at his mouth. He saw her moisten her lower lip, then the top one, with the tip of her tongue.

He applied the gentlest pressure to the nape of her neck to bring her closer to his slowly descending mouth.

He didn't kiss her straight away. He played with her lips with little pushes, little rubs and little teasing tastes, letting their breaths mingle and mate. She made a soft little sound, not a gasp, not a sigh, but something in between. Her lips were unbelievably soft and warm and tasted like the first harvest of sweet summer strawberries. He felt the shy hesitancy of her touch as one of her hands came to rest against his chest.

He covered her mouth with his, applying the slightest pressure, waiting for her to come back at him with the signal she wanted more.

She did.

He felt it in the way her lips softened against his, yielding to his subtle increase of pressure, opening like a flower to the first slow stroke of his tongue. He swallowed her little whimper and took the kiss deeper, tasting her moist sweetness, familiarising himself with the contours of her mouth, cajoling her tongue into seductive play with his.

She was tentative at first, holding back as if she was frightened of letting herself get out of control. But then the fingers of her hand resting on his chest suddenly curled into his T-shirt and her mouth became an urgent force against his.

He tasted hot female desire. It caused a firestorm in his blood, making him hard, thick and hungry for the slick, wet cocoon of her body.

He flicked his tongue against hers in an age-old rhythm that made her whimper in primal response. She moved against him, seeking more of him, her hands going to his hair, her fingers splaying across his scalp and then digging in as her mouth fed greedily off his.

He had never experienced a more explosive kiss.

It made every nerve in his spine—including the damaged ones—tingle in response. His groin was on fire. He felt like a teenager at his first sexual encounter. His control was shot.

He wanted her and he wanted her *now*.

And given the way her mouth was nipping and sucking at him, she wanted him, too.

But reality suddenly reared its head and its hand and slapped Raoul across the face. *What was he thinking?* How could this go to the next step? He couldn't even get up off the floor, let alone sweep her off her feet and into the nearest bedroom.

Besides, she was the hired help—the physical therapist who was supposed to get him back on his feet, not have him flat on his back while she rode him to Sunday and back.

His insides suddenly knotted.

Had Rafe set him up? Was Lily Archer and her holistic remedies his older brother's idea of getting him back into the saddle?

Raoul pulled back from her mouth with a muttered curse. 'OK, time to stop.'

She blinked at him for a moment. She looked vague, disoriented, shocked. 'Y-yes… Yes, of course.' She bit her lip and shifted her gaze, blinked another couple of times. Frowned. Frowned harder.

He watched as she scrambled ungainly to her feet, tucking a wayward strand of hair back behind her ear where the rest of her ponytail was confined. Her cheeks were pink, her mouth swollen, her gaze still averted. If he were to put money on it he would say she was currently feeling a little out of her depth, but he was not the gambler Remy was, and his money was staying right where he could keep an eye on it.

'Did my brother pay you to do that?' he asked.

Her bluer-than-blue eyes came back to his wide, startled. *'What?'*

He pinned her with a look. 'I know how his mind works. He's keen for me to get back to normal as soon as possible. Is that what he paid you to do? To test the equipment, so to speak?'

Her saw her slim throat move up and down over a swallow and her cheeks fired up another notch. 'I think you've got the wrong idea about me.'

'I don't need a bloody sex therapist,' he bit out as

he hauled himself up against the massage table. 'And I certainly don't need a pity screw to make me feel like a man again.'

There was a ringing silence.

'Excuse me…'

He turned his head to see her dashing out as if there was a fire in the room.

But then, in a way, there was.

His desire.

CHAPTER SIX

LILY WAS BEYOND mortified as she left the room, but angry, too. How dared he suggest she was here other than in her professional capacity? What sort of woman did he think she was? She knew the clinic had a bit of a reputation for being innovative in some of its methods but his assumption was nothing short of ridiculous! As if there was any amount of money that would induce her to sleep with anyone.

It wasn't going to happen.

Not for love nor money.

How could she be intimate with a man with those scars all over her arms and thighs? She could just imagine the look of horror, disgust and revulsion once her scarred flesh was uncovered.

The sad irony was that before her twenty-first birthday party she had been confident in her body, but that night had totally destroyed her self-esteem and taken away every scrap of her self-respect.

The cutting had been a way to release the emotional torment. It had been her way of controlling the shame that resided inside her body at having been taken advantage of by a man she had thought she could trust. Even though the rational part of her acknowledged she hadn't deserved to be treated like that, and the man in question had been very drunk, the emotional part flayed her with recrimination. She should have been more careful. She should have stayed with her friends. She shouldn't have drunk that fourth drink.

She should have told someone.

That was the one thing Lily had never been able to bring herself to do. How did you tell one of your closest friends that her older brother had lured you into another room and forced himself on you while everyone else had been partying next door?

So she had kept silent, and the pain and shame had burrowed deep inside her.

Which made what Raoul Caffarelli thought of her so totally laughable. Even in her partying days she had never been the type to sleep around. She'd only had two relationships—one when she'd been nineteen, which had lasted four months, and another when she'd been twenty that had lasted six. She hadn't felt emotionally ready for a full-on physical relationship.

Throughout her childhood she had watched her mother go from one ill-advised relationship to another, which had made Lily careful in her choice of partner. She often wondered if she had been a bit more streetwise if she might have been able to prevent what happened to her. Her judgement had been skewed by youthful complacency and familiarity.

But she was older and far wiser now.

And angry.

It was good to be angry because it stopped her thinking about that kiss.

How had it happened? One minute she'd been holding a tissue to Raoul's cut forehead, the next she'd been clutching at him as if his mouth was a lifeline. His lips had been like velvet on hers, warm and teasing, commanding and yet controlled. The seductive activity of his tongue had sent shivers rolling down her spine like runaway firecrackers.

You enjoyed it.

Yes, but that's beside the point. Kissing a client—especially one as dangerously, deliciously, lethally attractive as Raoul Caffarelli—was totally out of the question.

N.O.

No.

No!

Lily walked out into the gardens rather than hide away in her room. She needed fresh air and exercise to clear her head and to stop her body from its traitorous impulses. It had been years since she had thought about sex. She had become accustomed to pushing it from her mind because of the shame she always associated with it. But for some reason Raoul's kiss had not made her feel shame, but an intense desire to feel more of his touch.

He had been so gentle.

That had been so utterly disarming. If he had crushed her mouth to his and groped her with his hands she would have shoved back from him and given him a piece of her mind, if not a stinging slap across the face.

But she had been completely ambushed by his mesmerising lip play, the slow but sure stroke of his tongue, his measured pace, as if he'd known she would not like to be rushed or pressured.

It had made the hard, tight, locked away part of her soften and loosen. She had melted under the slow but sure seduction of his very experienced mouth.

She didn't like to think of *how* experienced he was. She knew enough about him to know he was a playboy, who before his engagement had moved from partner to partner with astonishing haste.

The sun was hot on Lily's head and shoulders as she traversed the expansive lawn that fringed the field where some magnificent-looking thoroughbreds were grazing. Their coats were like high-gloss satin, their powerful hindquarters shivering and their tails flicking every now and again as they shook off a fly.

It was a beautiful property with its rolling fields and lush pastures. But she wondered how Raoul was going to manage his arm of the family business while he was confined to a wheelchair. Breeding horses was a very hands-on affair. Attending sales and trials and track meetings would be next to impossible, or at least very difficult—maybe even dangerous. Horses were flighty creatures and thoroughbreds particularly so. It would be difficult for Raoul to have any sort of control over them when he was unable to stand.

One of the horses lifted its head from the grass and looked at Lily with big, soft, intelligent eyes. It blew some air out of its velvety nostrils and came over to the fence, idly swishing its tail as it went.

Lily held out a flat hand and the horse wobbled its soft mouth against her palm in search of a treat. 'I haven't got anything for you. I'll have to ask Dominique for an apple.' She stroked the mare's diamond shaped white blaze and then up behind her pointed ears. 'You're a beauty, aren't you? I wonder how many races you've won.'

'That's Monsieur Caffarelli's favourite brood mare,' a young boy of about fifteen or sixteen said as he came over from the nearby stables. 'Her stable name is Mardi.' He stroked the mare's gleaming shoulder. 'In her day she won all but two of her starts, didn't you, old girl?'

The mare gave the stableboy an affectionate nudge with her head before blowing out her nostrils again.

Lily smiled and gave the mare another stroke. 'She's gorgeous.'

'Do you ride?' the boy asked.

Lily dropped her hand from the horse's forehead, her smiling fading. 'Not in ages. I used to ride at a friend's country estate just about every weekend or during the holidays but we…we sort of lost touch over the years. I'm not sure I'd be very confident now.'

For months after her birthday party she had tried to keep her friendship with Georgina Yalesforth going but in the end the prospect of running into Georgie's older brother Heath had been too upsetting. One of the worst things about it was Heath had seemed to have no memory of what had occurred that night. When she'd next seen him, a few weeks after her birthday, he'd acted as he had always acted towards her—teasing and friendly in a big-brotherly way. All she could conclude was that he had been so heavily inebriated that night that—like so many other binge drinkers—he had no memory of what he'd done or who he'd done it to.

Lily had decided it was easier to sacrifice the friendship than destroy the Yalesforths' good name and reputation. After all, what hope did a working-class girl have over an upper-class moneyed family with a pedigree that went back two hundred years?

She would have been laughed out of court.

'You should get back in the saddle,' the stableboy

said. 'Mardi's quiet as a mouse. You'd be lucky to get a canter out of her.'

Lily gave him another brief smile. 'I'll think about it.'

'How long are you here?'

'A week.'

The boy glanced up at the château, his forehead heavily creased when his gaze came back to hers. 'Monsieur Caffarelli hasn't been down to the stables since he came home from the rehab centre. I don't think he's even come out of the château, not even out to the gardens. He used to spend all of his time out here with his horses. They are his passion. His life. But he refuses to come down because of the chair. He is very stubborn, no?'

'It's a very difficult adjustment for him,' Lily said.

'Is he going to walk again?'

'I don't know.'

'You must help him, *mademoiselle*,' he insisted. 'He is like a father to me, a mentor, *oui*? He got me off the streets of Paris and gave me this job. He's a good man—the very best of men. I trust him with my life. I would not have a life without him. You must *make* him get better. Monsieur Rafe thinks you can do it. So does Dominique.'

'Their confidence and yours is very flattering but I'm not sure what I can do in a week,' Lily said.

'Then you must change his mind so you can stay longer. I, Etienne, will talk to him, *oui*? I will tell him he is to keep you here for as long as it takes.'

Good luck with that, Lily thought as she walked back to the château gardens. Raoul Caffarelli might be a good man but he was one hell of an obstinate one.

An hour or so before dinner Lily went to speak to Dominique who was collecting herbs from the herb garden. 'Can I have a quick word, Dominique?' she asked.

'*Oui, mademoiselle.*' The housekeeper straightened from where she had been picking some tarragon.

'I was talking to Etienne down at the stables earlier,' Lily said. 'He said Monsieur Raoul has not been outside the château since he came home after the accident.'

Dominique gave a heartfelt sigh. 'It is sad but true. He won't go out until he can walk out. He is very stubborn when he puts his mind to things.'

'I have an idea,' Lily said. 'What if we set out dinner on the terrace overlooking the lake this evening? It's a lovely warm night, far too nice to be indoors. It will be a way of getting Monsieur Raoul out of the house without going too far. The fresh air will do him good and perhaps make him want to come out more.'

The housekeeper's black button eyes shone in mutual conspiracy. 'I have the perfect menu for alfresco dining. But how will you get him to come out?'

'I don't know…' Lily chewed at her lower lip for a moment. 'But I'll think of something.'

Raoul was in his study going through some accounts from one of his feed suppliers half an hour before dinner when he heard a soft knock on the door. 'Come.'

The door opened and Lily Archer stepped into the room. 'Is this a good time for a quick chat?'

He dropped the pen he was holding and leaned back in his chair to survey her features for a moment. She was wearing her usual don't-notice-me garb and her face was as clear and clean as a child's.

His gaze drifted to her rosebud mouth.

Big mistake.

His groin stirred and then throbbed with a dull ache of longing. Had he ever felt a more responsive mouth?

Had he ever tasted lips so full, sweet and tantalising? He could still feel the shy movement of her tongue against his. He could still feel the velvet softness of her lips as they'd played with his. What would it feel like to have those plump lips and that little cat's tongue sucking and stroking him on other parts of his body?

Don't even think about it.

He forced his gaze back to her blue one. 'It's as good a time as any, I suppose. What did you want to talk about?'

'I met one of your stableboys today. Etienne.'

'And?'

'He spoke very highly of you.'

Raoul lifted one shoulder up and down dismissively. 'I pay his wages.'

'He said you're like a father to him.'

'Probably because his own father beat the living daylights out of him since he was little more than a baby. Anyone who showed the least bit of kindness towards him would be a saint in his eyes. And there is one thing I am not, Miss Archer, and that is a saint. I would've thought what happened in the massage room earlier today would've firmly established that.'

Those two delightful spots of colour appeared in her cheeks. 'That was just as much my fault as yours.'

He gave her a levelling look. 'Because my brother paid you to service me?'

'No.' Her mouth flattened for a moment before she added, 'Because…I don't know. It just…happened.'

'It must *not* happen again,' Raoul said. 'Do I make myself clear?'

Her chin came up. 'Perfectly.'

A tense silence filled the corners of the room.

'Will that be all, Miss Archer? I have some important paperwork to see to before dinner.'

'That's what I wanted to talk to you about—dinner, I mean.' She twisted her hands together in front of her body, reminding him of a schoolgirl who had been summoned to the headmaster's office and wasn't yet sure of her fate.

'Then please get to the point.'

She gave him a brittle glare. 'You're not making this easy for me. Why do you have to be so…*beastly* all the time? I don't know why the papers say you're the most charming of the Caffarelli brothers. It just goes to show you can't believe a word you read in the press. As far as I'm concerned, you're about as charming as a venomous viper.'

Raoul drilled his gaze into hers. 'Have you finished?'

She ran the tip of her tongue over her lips in a sweeping motion that sent a rocket blast of lust straight to his groin. Her colour was still high, her eyes glittering brightly with antagonism. 'I suppose it's pointless now asking you to have dinner with me on the terrace.'

Raoul raised a brow. 'You're inviting me to dinner in my own house?'

'Not in your house. Outside on the terrace. Dominique's gone to a lot of trouble. It's a nice evening to dine outside.'

'Is this part of your therapy, to have me eaten alive by mosquitoes?'

She pressed her lips together for a moment. 'I just thought it'd be nice for you to have some fresh air. But I can see you're already made up your mind to stay inside and sulk and feel sorry for yourself. Fine. You do that. Have your own private pity party. I'll have dinner by myself.' She turned and stalked over to the door, her back stiff and straight as an ironing board.

'I'll strike a deal with you,' Raoul said.

She turned around and looked at him warily. 'What sort of deal?'

He ran his gaze over her primly pulled back hair. 'I'll have dinner with you out on the terrace if you wear your hair loose.'

Her eyes flickered with something he couldn't identify. 'I never wear my hair loose.'

He gave her a who-dares-wins look. 'Deal or no deal?'

CHAPTER SEVEN

RAOUL KEPT HIS part of the bargain. He used the manual chair even though it took him twice as long because he had made a promise to himself that he would not go outside until he could get there under his own power. Sure, it was bending the rules a little bit, but he'd made a deal with Lily and he wanted to see if she would take him up on it.

He transferred himself to the chair at the table Dominique had set up, complete with starched tablecloth, flowers and candles, and waited for Lily to join him.

He heard the sound of her light footsteps on the flagstones and turned his head to watch her approach. Her hair was longer than he'd thought; it swung in a glossy ash-brown curtain around her shoulders and halfway down her back. It had a bouncy wave to it that her tight ponytail had suppressed, and with her face bare and loose-fitting clothes it gave her an indie-girl look that was surprisingly eye-catching.

'You have very beautiful hair,' he said as she took the seat to his right.

'Thank you.'

Raoul couldn't take his eyes off her. She was so hauntingly beautiful, like a Tolstoy or Brontë heroine—

dark and yet pale, with that air of untouchable reserve. 'When was the last time you let your hair down?'

Something shifted in her eyes before they fell away from his. 'Not for a while.'

He felt an almost irresistible urge to reach out and thread his fingers in those silky thick tresses. He could smell the sweet summer jasmine scent of her shampoo. It teased his nostrils into a flare like one of his stud stallions taking in a new mare's scent. 'You should do it more often.'

'I've been thinking of getting it cut off.'

'Don't do that.'

She shrugged as if it didn't matter either way and picked up her water glass. He watched as she lifted it to her mouth and took a delicate sip. She was so self-contained it was fascinating to observe her. That little taste of her passion in the massage room had spoken to the primitive male in him. Her mouth had communicated what her speech and posture tried to keep hidden.

She wanted him.

He wondered how experienced she was. She certainly didn't look the worldly, confident type. At the age of twenty-six it would be unusual for her to be a virgin, but certainly not impossible. She'd said she wasn't interested in a relationship just now, which could mean she'd not long come out of one. Perhaps it had ended badly and she was waiting until she got over it.

Was that a broken heart she was hiding? She seemed a sensitive girl, in tune with other people's feelings. The way she had spoken to him about his break-up had suggested she had compassion and empathy for others.

The birds in the garden chirruped as they settled for

the evening. The warm air was fragrant with the clean smell of freshly mown grass. It seemed like for ever since he had been outside and yet it had only been weeks.

An ache tightened around his heart at the thought of spending the rest of his life indoors. How would he ever endure it? He didn't feel alive unless he was challenging himself physically. He loved the adrenalin rush of fighting his most primal fears in conquering a terrifying ski slope or climbing a vertiginous precipice. He had lived life on the edge because he felt grounded when he challenged himself physically.

How would he ever settle for anything else?

'Tell me about your life in London.'

'It's probably excruciatingly boring to someone like you,' she said.

'I don't live the hedonistic life the papers like to portray,' Raoul said. 'Compared to my younger brother, Remy, I'm really rather conservative. After all, I was about to settle down and get married.' He picked up his wine glass but didn't raise it to his mouth. 'You can't get more conservative than that.'

She looked up at him with those big dark blue eyes. 'Do you miss her?'

Right now Raoul had trouble even bringing Clarissa Moncrief's features to mind. He realised with a jolt that he didn't even know if her hair was naturally blond or coloured from a bottle. Had her eyes been grey or light blue? 'I miss being in a relationship. I can't remember being single for so long a period. But as to missing her… Not really.' *Not at all, if he were honest.*

Lily's brow was furrowed. 'Doesn't that strike you

as rather unusual, given you were considering marrying her?'

'I make a point of not needing people to that level. My theory of life is that people will always let you down if you give them enough room to do so. It doesn't matter how much they profess to love or care for you, there will always be a situation or circumstances where they will bail on you to serve their own interests.'

Or die on you and leave you lost and abandoned.

'But your brothers are always there for you, aren't they? Rafe seemed very concerned about you. He was so insistent I come here. I got the impression Remy was right behind him in that.'

'Rafe is distracted by his new life of love and his vision of happy-ever-after,' Raoul said. 'He wants me all sorted so he can get married and make babies with Poppy. But don't be fooled by Remy. He might show up occasionally and do and say all the right things but he only does it when it's convenient to him.'

'What part of your family's business does he work in?'

'Remy does investments and shares, as well as buying and selling businesses,' he said. 'He searches for ailing companies, injects funds and puts corporate strategies in place to lift the profile and profit margins, and then he resells them. He got into it in a big way after our grandfather lost one of our major companies a few years ago in a business merger that turned sour. Remy's made it his life's mission to turn things around and get justice, or his version of it, anyway.'

'Do you think he'll be able to do it?'

Raoul frowned as he reached for his water glass. 'I'm

not sure, to be perfectly honest. Rafe and I worry that it's going to blow up in his face. Henri Marchand—the man who duped my grandfather—is smart and incredibly devious when it suits him. His daughter Angelique is even smarter. There will be hell to pay and more if those two ever cross paths again. They hate each other's guts. I can't think of a person Remy would rather avoid than Angelique.'

'Why does he hate her so much?'

'I'm not sure.... Maybe he doesn't hate her as much as he thinks, but he won't admit it. If you think I'm stubborn, wait until you meet him.'

'Obstinacy seems to be a common trait in your family.'

'Yes, but in my experience it's the stubbornly determined people who get things done. Setting goals, working towards them, not stopping until you've ticked them off the list is the only way to get ahead. What's that old saying—if you aim for nothing you hit it every single time?'

'Yes, but not every goal can or should be achieved. It's good to set goals, but they should be realistic. Not everyone can be a Hollywood superstar or a billionaire entrepreneur no matter how much they hope or dream to be.'

He tilted his mouth at her sardonically. 'You're not much of a risk taker, are you, Miss Archer?'

'I suppose compared to someone like you I must seem very circumspect.'

'Do you ever push yourself out of your comfort zone?'

Her blue eyes moved away from his. 'Not if I can help it.'

He studied her for a beat or two. With her long hair

framing her heart-shaped face, she looked ethereally beautiful in the golden light of evening. He had never seen someone so completely unadorned look quite so achingly beautiful.

His eyes kept going to the soft, full bow of her mouth. He could still taste the warm wet sweetness of her in his mouth. He could still feel the shy play of her tongue against his.

Desire pulsed and then pounded in his groin.

She looked up and met his gaze as if he had summoned her with his errant thoughts. He saw the flare of female attraction; saw the way her cheeks were stained with a faint hint of pink and the way her soft mouth glistened after she ran her tongue over it to moisten it, as if she were remembering and revisiting the taste and feel of him against her mouth.

Lust burned hot and strong in his blood. He felt his body swell and thicken beneath the table. He felt the current of attraction tighten the air. He wanted her and yet he couldn't—*wouldn't*—have her. His grandfather's life-long penchant for sleeping with the hired help had made Raoul wary of indulging his senses to that degree. He liked his relationships conducted on equal terms. That was why Clarissa Moncrieff had been such perfect wife material. She came from the same wealthy background; there had been no fears of gold-digging motives because she had just as much wealth—if not more—as he did.

The realisation that he couldn't recall much about the last time—or any time—they had slept together troubled him. He knew he had made sure she'd been satisfied; he had some standards to uphold, after all. Mutual pleasure was the goal in all of his sexual conquests and he always stuck to it, even if some encounters were a little perfunctory in nature.

But the fact that he couldn't remember what Clarissa's kiss tasted like or whether she had ever looked at him with spine-tingling longing was a little disturbing if he were to be truly honest with himself. Being ruled by passion had destroyed many a man and he didn't want to add his name to the list.

Dominique came out with their entrées. She looked rather pleased with herself and exchanged a conspiratorial look with Lily before she set the plates down. 'Isn't it a lovely evening? Perfect for dining outdoors. So romantic.'

Raoul raised his brows at Lily once the housekeeper had left. 'Romantic?'

'The goal was to get you out of the château for an hour or two. There was nothing whatsoever romantic about it.'

'Why do I get the feeling my staff are conspiring against me?'

'They're not against you at all. They care about you, especially Etienne.'

Raoul looked out past the lake to the fields where his thoroughbreds were grazing. He could see his stableboy in the distance lugging a bale of hay to the feeder. That thin scrap of a kid who had come to him late at night on a Paris back street begging for food had turned into one of his biggest assets. Etienne had been brought up in filth and neglect; he had been distrustful of everyone and had hit out at every attempt to get close to him. It had taken Raoul months to get through the boy's thick, impenetrable armour. But now the boy ran the stables like a well-oiled machine. He had an affinity with the horses that was second to none. He preferred horses to people, and to some degree Raoul felt exactly the same.

Horses could be flighty or fearless, strong willed or biddable, yet once he had their trust they would do anything for him. It was so satisfying to see a willful, unruly yearling mature into a true champion. He had sold yearlings to racing syndicates from all over the world. He had bred winner after winner, champion after champion. He had been there from the moment his foals had taken their first spindly steps to watching them thunder past the finish line in some of the world's most prestigious races.

How could he possibly run his business from the sidelines?

But it wasn't just the stud business. He could not think of a worse form of torture than to watch a race while seated. No one sat down when a race was coming to the finish line. Everyone jumped to their feet—the trainers, the owners and the crowd. The cacophony of cheers and shouts as the horses came down to the line always gave him goose bumps.

How could he do it any other way?

Raoul met Lily's gaze. 'I suppose you cooked up this little scheme with Etienne—to lure me out here in the hope that it will make me yearn to get back down to the stables. But dinner on the terrace is not going to change my mind. I will not go down to the stables until I can get there on my own two feet.'

'I think you're being unnecessarily stubborn about this. Plenty of people run very successful businesses in spite of their physical limitations.'

'I don't think you understand what I'm saying, Miss

Archer. I don't want to run my business from a chair. I would rather sell it than do that.'

'But Etienne said the horses are your passion.'

'I have other passions.'

Her cheeks bloomed again with colour, but her voice was tart and full of spinsterish disapproval. 'I'm very sure you do.'

Raoul gave an indolent crook of his mouth. 'You don't approve of indulging one's passions?'

Her expression was tightly composed, almost too composed. 'Only if you don't hurt anyone else in doing so.'

'Have you been hurt in love, Miss Archer?'

'I've never been in love.'

'But you've been hurt.'

Her gaze skittered away from his as she reached for her water glass. 'Hasn't everyone at one time or another?'

Raoul watched as she took a token sip. So measured, so controlled, but behind that cool façade was a passionate, sensual young woman. He had felt that surge of passion against his mouth. He had felt the primal heat of erotic human contact, the mingling of her breath with his, the duelling of their tongues, the carnal desire he felt in her lightest touch.

He wanted to feel it again.

He dragged his gaze away from her mouth, his body still humming with the thought of bedding her. It was crazy even to allow the thought to enter his head. He was probably only tempted because it had been weeks since he'd had sex. Or maybe it was because she was such a fresh challenge to him. She had made it pretty clear she didn't like him or approve of his lifestyle. It could prove rather entertaining to change her mind.

Forget about it. You don't need any more complications in your life right now.

Raoul was getting dizzy from all the mental shakes he'd been giving himself. He wasn't in the mood for an affair even if his body thought it was a good idea. He liked to conduct his affairs with clear focus, with control and purpose. Diving into a fling just for the hell of it wasn't his way. Emotions were something he controlled, even though there was a part of him that kind of liked the thought of falling in love.

He and his brothers had spent their early years surrounded by their parents' love for them and for each other. It had set a standard, perhaps a rather unrealistic one, because not one of his relationships had even come close to what their parents had. Love and commitment had been central to their relationship. They still had their arguments, sometimes quite passionate ones, but they had never let the sun go down on their anger. Conflicts were resolved, slights forgiven, love restored.

Raoul had seen the change in Rafe, how falling in love with Poppy Silverton had given him an extra dimension to his life. Rafe had always been a goal-driven workaholic but now he was talking about taking extended leave for his honeymoon, and there were even baby plans afoot. Rafe had spoken of his and Poppy's desire for a family to love and nurture together.

Raoul knew his brother would be a fabulous father. He had been such a protective big brother, always putting Raoul's and Remy's interests ahead of his own. He had taken the brunt of their grandfather's anger countless times, even taking the blame for misdemeanours that Raoul or Remy had committed in order to shield them from Vittorio's harsh and unpredictable temper.

For the last twenty-five years Rafe had been the family anchor, but now it was time for him to launch into his new life. Finding Poppy—the love of his life—in a quiet little village in the English countryside had transformed his older brother into a man who embraced and expressed love with the same force of determination he previously used to avoid it.

You want that, too: love, commitment, children.

Did he?

He tried to picture it: a beautiful wife, two or three children, a dog or two…

A wheelchair.

His insides clenched and twisted at the thought of not being able to walk alongside his children from when they took their first steps or to walk with them into their first day of school. Not to be able to carry them in his arms, or to kick a football with them or teach them to swim, ski and water-ski as his father had done with him and his brothers.

If he had a daughter he would not be able to walk her down the aisle one day.

If he had a son he would not be able to stand shoulder to shoulder with him to teach him everything he knew about being a man.

It was impossible for him to imagine being a father without the full use of his legs.

He didn't want to be a father if he couldn't be a whole one.

How cruel was fate to snatch something away from

you just when you realised you wanted it? Raoul didn't want to spend the rest of his life pining for what he had lost. He didn't want to end up bitter and twisted like his grandfather. But how could he possibly settle for a life without the very things everyone else took for granted?

He would always be the one sitting to one side while everyone else was up and dancing through life. He would be the one everyone privately pitied or stayed well clear of in case the blow of fate was somehow catching.

'Are you in pain?' Lily's voice jolted him out of his reverie of misery.

'Why do you ask?'

'You were frowning so heavily I thought you must be uncomfortable. You've done a lot of sitting today.'

'I can hardly work at my computer if I can't sit or stand,' Raoul said with a fresh wave of frustration at his situation.

'Have you got a laptop? You could lie down and work on that. It would take the pressure off those discs.'

'I use my bed for sleeping or for sex, although lately I'm doing neither.' He scraped his hair back with his left hand. 'I can't remember the last time I slept more than an hour or two in one stretch.'

'Have you tried taking some sleeping medication for a couple of nights, just to break the cycle?'

Raoul gave her a quelling look. 'I'm not going to be turned into a pill popper, Miss Archer. Dependency is not my thing, in spite of what you might think about my current use of alcohol. I've only been drunk a couple of times in my life and both times I hated the loss of control.'

'I just thought it might help if—'

'You know what would help?' he clipped back. 'Being able to exercise properly. I like being physically active. I don't feel alive unless I get my blood pumping. I don't know any other way to live.'

She gave him one of her compassionate looks that made Raoul feel a brute for snapping at her. 'I'm sorry…'

He let out a muttered curse as he put his napkin on the table next to his plate. 'I'm the one who should be apologising.' Not that he was going to, of course. *He never apologised.* Besides, he hadn't asked for her to be here. It wasn't helping him one little bit having her to witness his pain and frustration. He wanted to be alone. He needed to be alone. 'I'm not the most convivial company right now.'

'I'm not here to be entertained.'

'No, you're here for the money, right?' Just like his grandfather's domestic minions, obsequiously pretending they cared about him just so they could collect their wage at the end of the day. He would be a fool to be taken in by her mask of empathy. She was just like everyone else, out for whatever she could get.

Her gaze lost its compassionate softness and her small, neat chin came up to a combative height. 'Unlike you, Monsieur Caffarelli, I don't have squillions in my bank account. So yes, I'm here for the money. I'm sorry if you find that hard to stomach but, quite frankly, if it weren't for the money your brother is paying me I wouldn't spend another minute of my time with you.' She put her napkin down like someone throwing down a gauntlet and pushed her chair back from the table to stand up.

'Sit down, Miss Archer,' he commanded.

Her slate-blue eyes flashed mutinously. 'Why, so you can continue to snip and snarl at me like a bad-tempered dog? No, thanks. I can think of much better ways to spend the evening.'

Raoul clenched his jaw so hard he felt his teeth grind together like granite against a grindstone. 'You will do as I say. Do you hear me? *Sit down.*'

She gave him glare for glare. 'I think I can see why your fiancée broke off your engagement. It had nothing to do with your accident or your injuries. It's your my-way-or-the-highway personality that's the problem.'

Had he ever met a more headstrong, opinionated woman? Raoul was used to people—and women, in particular—doing what he said even before he said it. Lily Archer was wilful and defiant and was a little too ready to express her opinions. Having her here reminded him too much of the power he had lost. She was rubbing his nose in it every chance she could. What had his brother been thinking, getting her to come here? The sooner she left—and to hell with the money—the better.

'Get out of my sight,' he ground out.

'See what I mean?' She gave him a pert look. 'You chop and change like the wind. You're moody and unpredictable. No woman in her right mind would put up with that, no matter how filthy rich you are.'

'I want you out of here by morning,' Raoul said through tight lips.

'Fine.' She gave him an airy thanks-for-that smile. 'I'll go up and pack right now.'

You just gave her what she wants. She wanted to get out of jail free and you just signed the release slip.

Dominique came out with the main course just as

Lily breezed past. The housekeeper turned and looked at Raoul with a crestfallen expression. 'What's going on? I thought you two were getting on like a house on fire.'

Raoul wheeled back from the table with an angry scowl. 'Don't ask or I'll fire you on the spot.'

CHAPTER EIGHT

It was too hot to sleep. Or maybe it wasn't the summer temperature at all but rather Lily's overheated temper. She was packed and ready to leave, as Raoul Caffarelli had so rudely commanded, but a part of her was struggling with taking the easy way out.

To leave would be admitting defeat.

Raoul was certainly a challenge, with his forceful personality and stubborn ways, but underneath that brooding, angry and resentful exterior she sensed he was essentially a good man. Didn't his care and support of the former street kid Etienne prove it? He treated all of his staff cordially, if a little distantly. He had not said a bad word about his ex-fiancée, publically or privately, even though she had clearly hurt him by rejecting him the way she had. Didn't that suggest he was at heart a decent and honourable man?

He was angry and bitter and finding it hard to cope with what had happened to him. Lily understood that far more than he could ever realise. She had railed at the world, too. She had pushed everyone who cared about her away. She had felt so dreadfully alone but she had sabotaged every attempt to reach her emotionally.

Wasn't he doing the same?

What if she *could* help him? It seemed a shame to walk out and leave him to his own devices. Like a lot of men with an achievement-based personality, he had a tendency to overdo things, which could compromise his recovery. But he had more feeling in his legs than the Sheikh's daughter Halimah had at the start, and he was incredibly fit and strong.

But he had made up his mind, and she couldn't see him changing it any time soon. She had her money and that was all that mattered. It would be embarrassing going back to London so soon, but that was hardly her fault. Raoul Caffarelli would test an angel's patience, and she knew she was no angel, or at least not in his presence. He seemed to bring out the worst in her. She hadn't realised she had a sharp tongue until he had made her use it.

He was rude and arrogant and she was glad to be leaving.

Of course she was glad.

She hadn't wanted to come in the first place. Her life was in London. It might be a little predictable and boring at times, but at least she didn't have to deal with brooding, handsome men with foul tempers.

Lily threw off the bedcovers and padded over to the window to look at the moonlit gardens her bedroom overlooked. There was a swimming pool she hadn't noticed before in a sheltered section of the back garden. Its surface shimmered in the silver light of the moon, tempting her with its promise of cool refreshment from the night's sticky and cloying humidity.

It had been a long time since she had swum in public. The work she did with clients in the hydrotherapy pool at the clinic could hardly be called swimming. She spent most of the time standing waist-deep, guiding the client through a range of exercises. Her 'bathing costume' was a modest one-piece suit with a long-sleeved rash vest over the top, which she told her clients was to protect her skin from the chlorine.

The thought of a swim on a hot night in a secluded garden with only the light of the moon was a temptation she was powerless to resist. Given how reluctant Raoul was to come outdoors, it was reasonable to assume he wouldn't witness her midnight dip. It would be her way of putting her nose up at him one last time; her chance of having the last word. She would use his pool without his knowledge or permission and she would enjoy every minute of her little act of rebellion.

Lily picked up her one-piece and vest. Was it her imagination or did the fabric feel thicker and pricklier than normal? After a moment of deliberation she tossed it aside, picked up a matching set of bra and knickers and a lightweight cotton T-shirt to go over the top. If she was going to swim, then she was going to do it properly.

Once she was dressed in her makeshift costume she took a fluffy towel from her en suite bathroom and tiptoed downstairs, keeping an eye and ear out for anyone moving about, but the methodical ticking of the ancient grandfather clock on the second landing was the only sound in the silence.

The flagstones in the private section of the garden where the pool was situated were still warm from the summer sun beaming down on them all day, but the water of the pool was deliciously cool as she tested it with her fingertips.

Lily sat on the edge of the pool and dangled her legs

in the water. The splish-splash movement of the water against her legs seemed deafening in the silence.

She took a breath and slipped into the cool, silky embrace of the water. It lifted the hairs from her scalp, playing with them in a watery dance that made her aware of every inch of her flesh. She duck dived to the bottom of the pool and swam like a mermaid with dolphin-like undulations of her body, feeling free in a way she hadn't felt in years.

She came back up to the surface and swam lap after lap, the rhythmic movement of her limbs lulling her into a state of calm that was both meditative and incredibly soothing.

She had no idea how far or for how long she had been swimming. She had made a vain attempt to count her laps in the beginning, but her mind had drifted into blissful numbness after the first ten or so. She was totally in the moment, feeling the water move over her skin, feeling the contraction and pull of her muscles as she carved through the resistance of the cool, refreshing fluid that surrounded her. She was weightless, yet strong. Her body felt invigorated, tired yet satisfied, her blood singing around her veins in delight at being active after spending so much time indoors.

Lily finally surfaced at one end and threw back the long wet curtain of her hair. But when she opened her eyes she found Raoul sitting in his chair watching her from the side of the pool with an inscrutable expression on his face. Her heart gave a little stutter in her chest but it had nothing to do with the physical exertion she had just performed. 'How long have you been there?' she asked.

'Long enough.'

She focused her gaze on the tiles near her hands rather than meet his gaze. 'I suppose you're thinking what a totally rubbish swimmer I am.'

'On the contrary, you look quite at home in the water. But that T-shirt must be annoying. It's creating quite a drag when you swim.'

Lily met his gaze with a little hitch of her chin. 'I don't like swimming in public.'

He arched a dark brow in a wry manner. 'It's hardly *public* out here.'

'*You're* here.'

His gaze slowly but surely moved over her like a minesweeper, detonating all of her senses in the process. 'Wasn't that your goal, to get me outside of the château?'

She wrapped her arms around her body, hoping the light wasn't good enough for him to see her in too much detail. 'I want to get out. I'm getting cold.'

'So?'

'So you need to leave.'

His dark eyes did another lazy sweep of her upper body, lingering for a moment on the upthrust of her breasts where her crossed-over arms had showcased them as good as any push-up bra. Her flesh tingled where his gaze had rested. It felt like a fire had been lit beneath her skin.

'Last time I looked, this was my château and my pool. If anyone is trespassing it is you.'

Lily set her mouth. 'I'm not getting out until you leave.'

He gave her a devil-may-care smile, his hazel eyes glinting. 'I'm not leaving until you get out.'

The water hadn't seemed cold until he had laid down that challenge. Goose bumps peppered all over her body as she tried to stare him down. Her T-shirt clung to her like a wet sheet and she knew that right at this moment it was probably showing far more than she was trying to hide.

Was the moonlight muted enough that he wouldn't see the roadmap of her pain on her arms? What did it matter if he *did* see it? It wasn't as if she were trying to impress him. She was leaving at first light. She had packed all her things and was ready to go. Dominique had slipped the flight details he had booked under her door only a couple of hours ago.

'Could you pass me my towel?' It was a form of compromise but there was no way Lily was going to let him win this battle.

'Swim a lap without the T-shirt.'

'Pardon?'

His eyes trapped hers. 'Take it off.'

She felt a traitorous frisson pass over her flesh at his authoritative tone. 'I'll take it off if you join me in the water.' As soon as she issued the challenge, she regretted it. *What was she thinking?* He loved a challenge. Didn't she know that by now?

'Nice one.' He gave her a gleaming half smile. 'Clever. Tactical.'

'So…' She swallowed. 'You'll do it?' *Don't do it! Don't do it!*

He moved his chair closer to the side of the pool. His eyes stayed on hers as he unbuttoned his shirt. Her breath stalled as each inch of his chest was revealed. He shrugged himself out of his shirt and tossed it to one side.

Lily gulped as he started on the waistband of his trousers. Was he really going to join her in the water? *Yikes!*

'Um…maybe this is not such a great idea. What about your plaster cast? It'll get soak—'

'I'll get another one put on if it gets wet. Anyway, it's almost time it came off. What's a couple of weeks?'

'You can't just ignore your doctor's orders to do what you like.'

'Water therapy was part of your plan for me, wasn't it?'

'Yes, but you told me you didn't want me to stay,' Lily quickly reminded him. 'I'm officially off duty. You terminated my contract. I don't have to do anything with you if I don't want to— What are you *doing*?'

'I'm getting undressed.'

Lily clamped her hands over her eyes. 'You can't do that!'

'I always swim naked when I'm at home. It's totally private here.'

'But I can see you!'

'So?'

She stole a little peek from between her fingers. 'I don't want to see you.'

'Then don't look.'

How could she *not* look? He looked like he had just stepped down off a plinth in the Louvre, so beautifully carved and sculptured. Everything about him spoke of a man in the prime of his life, strong, virile and staggeringly potent if the proud heft of him beneath the black underwear he was wearing was any indication.

Was he going to take them off?

She opened her fingers a tiny bit wider. The muscles of his left arm bunched as they took his weight as he eased out of the chair but he left his underwear on. She wondered if peeling them off would be too difficult in the chair. Maybe once he was in the water...

Eek! He was in the water!

Lily snatched in a breath as the water his body displaced when he entered the pool moved across her breast like a liquid caress. Her nipples reacted as if he had touched them, tight and aching, so sensitive she could feel them pushing against the lace of her sodden bra.

Her belly quivered as she roved her gaze over his chest. He had the broad and well-defined shoulders and biceps of a regular swimmer. His chest was generously covered with coarse masculine hair that spread from a wide T across his pectoral muscles, narrowing down over the washboard of his flat abdomen to disappear—rather tantalisingly, she thought—beneath his hip-hugging briefs.

OK, my girl, remember that pair of lungs inside your chest? They're for breathing.

Lily drew in a breath but it fluttered against her windpipe like the wings of a moth trapped inside a straw. Her heart was doing a crazy little pitter-pat pitter-pat behind her ribcage and the desire she thought had been dead and buried long ago reared its head and screamed, *I'm alive!*

He was holding on to the side of the pool with his left arm while he kept his other raised just above the water. He moved along the wall until he was in the deeper end so the water could support him, but even so his head and shoulders easily cleared the surface. For the first time Lily got a sense of how tall he was. She wouldn't come up to his chin in her bare feet.

'How does it feel?' she asked.

'Wet.'

Lily couldn't read his expression, as he was in the

shadow cast by the nearby shrubbery, but she got the sense he was not totally at ease being back in the water. She wondered if it was bringing back horrible memories of his accident. A water-based accident always held the terrifying prospect of drowning. How soon had help come to him? How long had he floundered with his arm broken and his spine damaged?

But a challenge was a challenge and he was clearly taking her up on it.

She moved closer to him, her legs treading water to keep her afloat as she got within touching distance. 'Do you need a hand?'

'Right now a pair of legs would be quite handy. The ones I've got don't seem to be working all that well.'

'Can you move them at all? Sometimes the water helps you become more aware of your body.'

'I'm aware of it, all right.'

This time Lily could see his expression and her belly gave another little swoop and dive at the glitter of male desire shining there. She was aware of his body, too.

Very aware.

One of her legs brushed against one of his underneath the water. It sent a shockwave of fizzing sensations all the way to her core.

His gaze went to her mouth, lingering there for a heart-stopping moment before ensnaring hers once more. 'So, you've got me outside and now you've got me in the water. What's the next step in your plan?'

She gave him an arch look. 'I get you to apologise.'

'For what?'

'For telling me to get out of your sight.'

His eyes measured hers for a pulsing moment. She could see the battle playing out on his features: the tiny twitch of a muscle near the corner of his mouth; the tensing of his jaw; the set of his lips into a tight line; the fissure of a frown between his black eyebrows.

'I never wanted you here in the first place.'

'There are much better ways of telling a person their services are no longer required than dismissing them from the table like a misbehaving child,' she tossed back.

'You overstepped the mark.'

'Because I dared to criticise your personality?'

'No.' His eyes were as hard as diamonds. 'Because you wouldn't do as I said.'

'I'm sure you're used to people bowing and scraping to you because you've got truckloads of money, but in my opinion respect has to be earned, not bought. And, just for the record, I don't take orders and I won't be bullied into obedience.'

'We seem to be at somewhat of an impasse, Miss Archer, for I won't apologise and you won't take an order.'

Lily didn't back down even though his look was long and steely and the set to his mouth determined. 'It won't matter come tomorrow. I'll be leaving, as per your instructions. And, let me tell you, I'm *very* glad to be going. Glad, glad, glad. Ecstatic, actually.'

'Of course you are.' His top lip curled in that mocking way he had perfected. 'You've been looking for an escape route from the first moment you arrived. I'm playing right into your hands by telling you to leave.'

Then why did it feel so wrong to be going? 'You're not my preferred type of client.'

'Because I'm male?'

'Because you're arrogant and insufferably rude.'

The warm night air sizzled with electricity as his green-and-brown gaze held hers in silent combat. But it seemed much more than a simple battle of wills. Lily was intensely aware that the same water that surrounded and touched her body was surrounding and touching his. It added a level of intimacy that was disturbing and yet exciting at the same time.

'Why are you wearing a T-shirt?'

The question coming out of the silence threw her for a moment. 'I—I have very sensitive skin.'

'The moon doesn't have UV rays.'

She gave him a withering look as she folded her arms across her chest. 'Ha ha.'

His eyes grazed the shape of her breasts and then narrowed as they came to rest on her forearms. His gaze came back to hers, dark and concerned. 'What happened to your arms?'

Lily dropped her arms back down below the water. 'Nothing.'

'Doesn't look like nothing to me. It looks like you got up close and personal with a razor blade. Did you need stitches?'

'No.'

'Hospitalisation?'

Lily compressed her lips. She didn't want to talk about that time in her life. She didn't want to have to explain why she had felt so compelled to do what she had done. She just wanted to put it all behind her and move on.

She *had* moved on.

'Did you cut anywhere else?' His voice was gentle now rather than judgemental, which totally surprised her. Disarmed her.

She let out a breath of resignation. She was leaving

in the morning; he could think what he liked of her. 'My thighs.'

He winced as if he had personally felt each and every slice of the blades that had marked her flesh. 'What happened to you?'

'I bled. A lot.'

'Not when you cut.' He frowned at her attempt at black humour. 'What happened to make you want to do that?'

Lily put on her tough-as-nails face. 'I was a bit messed up a few years ago. I took it out on myself. Not a great way of handling things, but still.'

'Drugs?'

'No.'

'Relationship problems?'

She gave a little cough of humourless laughter. 'You could say that.'

'Do you want to talk about it?'

'No.'

'Do you still cut?'

Lily flashed him an irritated look. 'No, of course not.'

He held her gaze for longer than she felt comfortable with. He seemed to be seeing right through her façade. *It terrified her.*

'I'd like to get out of the pool.' She gave him a haughty look. 'Do I have to ask permission or are you going to stand there and watch me freeze to death?'

'I'm not standing,' he pointed out wryly. 'I'm leaning. And you're not freezing, you're scared.'

She raised her chin. 'Not of you.'

His gaze held hers in that quietly assessing way that unsettled her so much. 'I'm very glad to hear it. How could we ever work together if you're frightened of me?'

Lily blinked at him. 'You want to work with me?'

'Yes.'

'But… But I thought…?'

'I'd like you to stay for the month. I'll pay you double the amount my brother offered.'

She looked at him in bafflement. Why had he changed his mind? Hadn't her scars put him off? Most people shunned her when they saw her body. He was doing the opposite.

Why?

Who cares? Think of the money. Two years' wages for a month's work!

'But I don't understand…'

'I quite like the idea of getting to know you, Lily Archer. I suspect no one else has achieved that before.'

She gave him a guarded look. 'I suppose you see me as yet another challenge to overcome?'

'No.' His eyes glanced briefly at her mouth before coming back to mesh with hers. 'I see you as a temptation I should resist.'

Her brows lifted. 'Should?'

'Can't,' he said, and before she could move even an inch out of his way he covered her mouth with his.

CHAPTER NINE

THE FEEL OF his mouth on hers made every nerve in Lily's body stand up and quiver in delight. He tasted of mint and male heat, an intoxicating blend that made her senses spin out of control. His tongue found hers and called it into an erotic dance that made her insides do a series of frantic somersaults. It was a much harder kiss than his previous one, more focused, even more ruthlessly determined.

Even more irresistible.

His body was flush against hers, his erection pressing against her stomach. It burned like a brand against her, the primitive need it signalled calling out to her own. She felt the tingling of her desire deep in her pelvis, the throb-ache pulse that pounded in time with her blood.

Had she ever experienced sexual attraction like this before? If so, she couldn't remember it, and nor could her body. It was as if she were experiencing desire for the very first time. Never before had her body felt so in tune with a man's touch. She had never felt a need so strong she couldn't find an excuse to delay its satiation. She softened against him like molten wax against a source of heat, her legs entwining with his.

Male against female, light against dark. It was a potent mix of hormones and needs that swirled and simmered in the water that enveloped them.

She wanted more.

She wanted to feel his hands and mouth on her breasts. She was so out of practice she didn't know how to communicate her need. She made a little mewling sound against his lips, pressing closer; conscious he was only supporting himself with his one good arm.

He kissed her again, slowly first, and then deeply and passionately. She tasted the need that was thundering through his body. It called to everything that was female in her. She kissed him back with such fervour it made her heart race to think he wanted her even half as much as she wanted him.

Somehow they got to the steps so he could sit and she could stand between his open thighs. He cupped her breast with a gentle hand, his thumb rolling over the pebbled nipple as his mouth savoured hers in little nips, sucks and licks that thrilled her senses. Whatever fear or trepidation she had felt had completely dissipated. All she could feel was the desire for completion. It was a bone-deep ache that made her blood hum inside the circuitry of her veins.

He lifted his mouth just a fraction off hers, his voice low, deep and sexy. 'I want to make love to you.'

Lily suddenly realised the implications of what she was doing. Where was her professionalism? Where was her self-control? What was she thinking, kissing Raoul Caffarelli as if her life depended on it? She wasn't the type of girl to have a fling. She didn't know how to be casual about sex; she didn't *want* to be casual about it. It went against everything she had learned over the years.

She pulled back out of his embrace, her gaze shifting away from his. 'I'm sorry…I'm not ready for this. I shouldn't have given you the impression I was…um… interested. I'm not normally so…so forward.'

'You don't have to apologise.'

She met his gaze again. 'You're not…angry?'

'Why would I be angry?'

'You said you wanted to make love…'

'I did. I do. But that doesn't mean I have to do so right this very minute. I might be pretty stubborn and determined in other areas of my life, but I would never force a woman to have sex with me against her will. It's not what a man with any decency does.'

Lily chewed at her lower lip, struck by how calm and in control he was. There was no sign of anger or resentment or any look that said 'how could you do this to me?'. No pushing or shoving, no gripping or grabbing and insisting on having his needs met.

Just respect and quiet calm.

Emotions she thought she had safely locked behind the do-not-open-again door in her mind suddenly sprang out of their confinement like a jack-in-the-box let loose. Tears she had sworn she would never shed again sprouted in her eyes. She choked back a sob and buried her head in her hands.

'Hey…' His gentle tone made her cry all the harder.

'I'm sorry.' She brushed at her streaming eyes with the back of her hand. 'You must think I'm a fool.'

'I don't think that at all.'

She took a shaky breath and tried to get her emotions back under control. 'You're the first man I've kissed in years. I never thought I'd ever want to get close to a man again. I deliberately didn't get close…until now.'

'You were…raped?' His tone was full of indignation, which she found strangely comforting.

'Yes.'

A muscle flicked in his jaw as if he was having trouble containing his outrage at the treatment she had been subjected to. 'Was the man arrested and charged?'

She shook her head. 'I didn't report it.'

His frown was so deep it created a V on his forehead. 'But what if he did it to some other girl?'

Lily crossed her arms over her body. 'I thought about that. A lot. But it was complicated.'

'That lowlife creep should be brought to justice. It's not too late. I can get you a good lawyer. It's not too late to file a charge. I know retrospective cases are much harder to prove but it would be worth it to have your day in court, even if it's only to name and shame him.'

'No, I don't want to do that. I *can't* do that.'

'Why can't you?' His frown was even more severe, his look even more forbidding. 'It's not right that he gets away with it. He hurt you, damn it. He should be made to pay for his crime. Do you have a good description of him? The police have face-recognition data files now. The technology is improving all the time. They might be able to track him on that to see if he's a serial offender.'

'He's not a serial offender.' Lily let out a long breath. 'Or at least, I don't think so. He was my best friend's older brother and he's got a law degree, along with his father, grandfather and great-grandfather.'

'You *know* him?'

'Most sex crimes are committed by people known to the victim. Random acts are still thankfully rare, although they do happen.' She knew she sounded like a police statement but she had heard the words so many times. 'I guess that's why I didn't take any precaution-ary steps. I didn't realise he was a threat until it was too late. Up until that night he'd been like a brother to me. But he was drunk and I was very tipsy. I thought we were just having a bit of a flirt with each other but suddenly everything changed. He got aggressive and before I knew it I was having unwanted sex. There was nothing I could do to stop it. He was very strong and I was under the influence of alcohol. I should have been more careful, but I guess everyone is wiser in hindsight.'

'You're blaming yourself for *his* lack of decency and control?' He gave her an incredulous look. 'How does that work? He should've realised you weren't able to give proper consent. It was his responsibility, not yours.'

Lily couldn't help a part-sad, part-wry smile. 'In spite of being known as a ruthless playboy, you're really a rather old-fashioned man, aren't you?'

His expression was dark and brooding. 'I'm not going to apologise for believing women deserve respect and protection.' He glanced at her arms. 'Is that why you started cutting?'

'Yes.'

'It's nothing to be ashamed of. The shame belongs to the man who took advantage of you. You were just try-ing to cope in the best way you could.'

'It wasn't a great way of coping.' She let out a ragged sigh. 'I wish I'd chosen something a little less perma-nent.'

'What, like drugs or alcohol or smoking? They're just other coping mechanisms, and they can have far more serious and dangerous implications in the long term.'

'I hate my scars.' Lily looked down at the white marks on her arms. 'I wish I could erase them.'

'Scars are a way of reminding ourselves of what we've learned in life. We all have them, Lily, it's just that some are more visible than others.'

Lily looked into his strong yet kind eyes and wondered yet again how his fiancée could have left him. He was such a noble man, so proud and yet so honourable. What woman wouldn't want to be loved and protected by such a man?

But then, he hadn't loved his fiancée, or so he had said. Was he capable of loving? Some men weren't. Neither were some women, and up until very recently she had been one of them.

Love?

You think you're in love with him?

Are you completely nuts?

Lily rubbed her hands over her shivering arms. 'I've been in the water too long…. I'd better go in. Do you need a hand getting out?'

'No, I might stay in for a while. Try some of that walking in water you suggested.'

'Is your cast still dry?'

'So far.'

Lily got out of the pool and turned to look at him. He hadn't moved at all. He was still watching her with a frown pulling at his brow. He looked so normal leaning there against the side of the pool. It was gut-wrenching to think his legs were not able to hold him upright. But maybe his limitations had given him the ability to understand hers. Or maybe he was just a truly wonderful man who didn't deserve what life had thrown his way. Either way she knew she would never forget this night. Being in his arms, feeling normal and desirable, had touched her deeply. He had seen her scars and had wanted her anyway.

He had made her feel beautiful and she hadn't felt that in a very long time.

Raoul waited until Lily had gone back inside the château before he moved from the side of the pool. His insides were churning at what she had gone through. He wanted to fix things for her, to seek justice, to undo the wrong that had been done to her. It seemed so unfair that she had suffered for so long on her own, hiding herself behind shapeless clothes, downplaying her features, living half a life in order to avoid a repeat of what had happened. The scars on her arms did nothing to detract from her beauty, or at least not as far as he was concerned. He had always thought she was stunning, but even more important to him was her inner beauty. She was kind-hearted and gentle, compassionate yet spirited.

He felt deeply ashamed for thinking she had only come for the money. How could he have misread her so appallingly? She had wanted to leave at the first opportunity because she didn't feel safe. He had probably terrified her with his snarly comments and black looks. But, in spite of her fear, she had been drawn to him.

He thought of the way she kissed him, so unrestrainedly, as if for those few moments she had acted purely on instinct and allowed herself to be who she was truly meant to be. What would it take to unlock that frozen passion for good? To get her to come out of her protective shell and live life the way it was meant to be lived?

Was he the man to do it?

How could he help her when he couldn't even help

himself? He was stuck in a chair with legs that refused to work. He had nothing to offer her other than an affair to remember. He could just imagine her telling her friends about it some time in the future—the little fling she'd had with a guy in a wheelchair to get her confidence back. What a story that would be to dine out on.

He couldn't think of anything worse.

Why couldn't he have met her before his accident? They might have had a chance to build on the mutual attraction they felt. If he acted on it now, how could he be sure she wasn't feeling sorry for him? How could he know she wanted him for himself and not as a confidence boost?

Why did it matter? It had never mattered before. Sex was sex. It was a physical experience that didn't touch him emotionally. He'd had dozens of partners and he hadn't once thought of anything but the physicality of making love. It wasn't that he didn't like the women he'd slept with, although admittedly he had liked some more than others.

He wasn't comfortable with getting close to people emotionally. He had been very attached to his parents but the accident had taken them away from him and his brothers, shattering their lives in the blink of an eye. The family unit he had taken for granted had been destroyed. Everything that had been secure and sacred to them had been lost, even the very roof over their heads. The modest villa their mother had insisted they be brought up in to keep them grounded and in touch with those less fortunate than themselves had been sold within days of the funeral. They hadn't been consulted. Their grandfather had taken control and he'd had no time for tears or tantrums. He ruled with an iron fist and it came down on anyone who dared to thwart his will.

Raoul had shut down the feeling part of himself because it was safer to be distant and in control than to be up close and unguarded.

Turning it back on again was out of the question.

Especially now....

CHAPTER TEN

DOMINIQUE WAS BEAMING from ear to ear when Lily came down for breakfast the next morning. 'You have worked a miracle, *oui*?'

'Yes, well, he's agreed to keep me on for the month, but I wouldn't get your hopes up too soon.'

'Not that.' Dominique pointed to the window. 'Look.'

Lily moved over to the bank of windows. Raoul was in his wheelchair down near the stables talking to Etienne who had one of the horses on a lead. It was a huge beast, strong and feisty-looking with a regally arched neck, wide nostrils and jittery stamping feet. But after a moment it quietened, stepped forward and nuzzled against Raoul's outstretched hand and then started rubbing its head against his chest with the sort of familiarity that spoke of deep affection and trust. Even from this distance she could see the smile on Raoul's face. A knotty lump came up in her throat and she had to swallow a couple of times to remove it.

'You are very good for him, Mademoiselle Archer.' Dominique's voice sounded like she had her own prickly lump to deal with. 'I did not think he would ever go outside again. It broke my heart to see him. He bred that stallion himself. People from all over the world pay a lot of money to have him sire their foals.'

'He looks gorgeous.'

Dominique gave her a cheeky look. 'I was talking about the horse.'

Lily felt a blush steal over her cheeks. 'So was I.'

The housekeeper poured Lily a coffee and handed it to her. 'Etienne told me you used to ride.'

'Not recently. I'd probably fall off as soon as the horse took a step.'

Dominique smiled at her. 'They say it is like riding a bike, no? You never forget.'

Lily took the cup and cradled in in both hands. 'Then I must be the exception to the rule because I've completely forgotten.'

'It's just a matter of confidence. The right time, the right horse, *oui*?'

'It's the most dangerous sport of all. It doesn't matter how well trained the horse is, they can still revert to their instincts.'

Dominique gave her a thoughtful look. 'Not all horses are like that.'

Lily put her cup down on the counter as she turned to leave. 'Maybe not, but all the ones I've met so far are.'

Raoul was already in the gym doing some weights when Lily came in an hour later. Although he didn't like admitting it, he felt better for having spent a bit of time outdoors. He had decided to relax his rule about going outside a bit further—just to the stables, not off the property or out in public. It went against every instinct he possessed to compromise, but last night in the pool had made him realise he could be short-changing himself not to stretch and push against every boundary that had been placed on him. It hadn't been easy getting down to the stables but Etienne had helped him down and back and the horses, particularly Mardi and his stallion, Firestorm, had appreciated his efforts.

'Etienne told me you are a former horsewoman.'

'Hardly that.'

'Would you be interested in exercising some of my horses while you are here?'

Her expression closed like a fist. 'No.'

'I have a very quiet mare that you—'

'You're not lifting that weight properly.' She picked up a lighter weight and demonstrated. 'See? You're incorporating the wrong muscles if you don't do it properly. It's a waste of time and effort if you don't do it the right way.'

Raoul didn't even look at the weight. 'What's wrong?'

'Nothing.'

'You're upset.'

She put the weight back down with unnecessary force, clanging it against the others on the rack. 'I'm here to help *you* rehabilitate. That's what you and your brother are paying me to do. I'm not here to get back in the saddle, either figuratively or literally.'

'I thought you might like some time off to relax. I don't expect you to spend all of your time here stuck indoors with me.' He scraped a hand through his hair and frowned. 'God knows it's bad enough for *me* being with me. I can't even imagine what it's like for you.'

There was a little silence.

'I don't find it hard being with you.' Her voice was so soft he almost didn't hear it.

Raoul looked at her. 'What, you enjoy my cutting sarcasm?'

'I think you push people away because you don't want them to see how much you're hurting.'

'Here we go.' He rolled his eyes. 'The psychology lecture. Have I paid for that or is that extra?'

Her chin came up a fraction. 'It's free.'

'Well, guess what? I don't want it. I was doing just fine until you came along.'

She folded her arms across her chest. 'Sure you were. That's why you were stuck inside this great, big old mausoleum with no one but your housekeeper to feed you meals through the tiny gap you allowed in the door. Oh, yes, you were getting on just fine and dandy.'

He glowered at her. 'And just how well are *you* getting on? Why don't you take a dose of your own therapy? Perhaps read your own aura for a change. See what everyone else sees when they look at you.'

She stiffened as if he had thrown something nasty at her; she was determined not to show how much it affected her. 'By "everyone else" I suppose you mean you?'

'What I see is completely different. I see a young woman who is deeply passionate but is too frightened to show it. I see how much you want to grab life with both hands, but those hands have been burnt once and you're too scared to reach for what you want because you don't want to get burnt again. What other people see is a distant, somewhat cold, frumpy woman—that's not who you are, Lily. You will never be happy until you are true to who you are meant to be.'

Her mouth flattened and her eyes flashed at him. 'I don't need you to sort out my life for me.'

'If you can't sort out your own, life what chance have you in sorting out mine?'

She opened and closed her mouth, her cheeks going a deep shade of pink as she turned away. 'I don't think this is going to work. I think it's best if I just leave.'

'You do that a lot, don't you?' Raoul said. 'You run away when things get uncomfortable. But avoiding a problem only means you won't be the one to eventually solve it.'

Every muscle in her back seemed to stiffen before she turned back to face him. 'And how are you going to solve *your* problems? By pushing everyone away who could help you? Good luck with that. I've tried that in the past and, believe me, it doesn't work.'

'Then let's both do it differently this time.' Raoul let out a long breath. 'Let's pretend my brother didn't engineer this. Let's just be two people who might be able to help each other get back on their feet…or back on the horse; whatever metaphor works.'

Her look was guarded. 'I'm not sure what you're suggesting.'

'Just be yourself. That's all I'm asking. I want to get to know the real Lily Archer.' He suddenly realised it was true. He wanted to know *everything* about her. He wanted to understand her and help her to claim back the life that had been stolen from her. She was a beautiful, warm-hearted girl who had been treated badly. She needed to regain her confidence and trust in people— and wasn't he the perfect man to do it?

Are you out of your mind? You can't help her. You can't even help yourself!

Raoul didn't want to listen to the voice of reason. This time he was going to go on his instincts rather than rationality. Spending time with her would make her feel more at ease with herself. Make her less shy, less defensive. It would be a two-way deal. She would be helping him to get back on his feet and he would help her embrace her life once more.

Her teeth sank into her bottom lip again. 'You might be disappointed.'

'I might be surprised. And you might be, too.' He gave her a crooked smile. 'I'm told I can be quite charming when I'm not snapping people's heads off.' He held out his hand. 'Truce?'

She put her small, soft hand in his. His almost swallowed it whole. 'Truce.'

Lily spent the next fortnight working with Raoul in the gym and on parallel bar exercises. She kept things as conservative as she could because she was concerned he was doing too much already. She had caught him a couple of times doing extra sessions in the gym, and she had seen him in the pool each afternoon since his plaster had come off, although she hadn't been brave enough to join him. It worried her that he was pushing himself beyond his body's capabilities. She didn't want to leave him worse off.

Leave him.

Those words made her uneasy every time she thought of them. She had to keep reminding herself that this was a job like any other. She wasn't supposed to get attached in any way to a client. She was supposed to do what she could to help them regain their mobility and strength and then move on to the next person who needed her. She wasn't supposed to daydream about their kisses or touches. She wasn't supposed to hope they would kiss her again or touch her other than incidentally.

He had kept a polite distance after that night in the pool. He had dined with her only a handful of times, mostly preferring to eat in his study while he worked. But she had seen the way his gaze kept homing in on her mouth now and again when he was speaking to her. It was like an involuntary impulse he couldn't control.

She wasn't much better. Only that morning she had helped him stabilise on the parallel bars and had come too close to him. He had momentarily lost his balance and she had stepped in to support him. She felt his warm, minty breath on her face and her heart had given a kick inside her chest in case he closed the small distance and covered her mouth with his.

But he hadn't.

His eyes had locked on hers for a heart-stopping moment. Her belly had flipped and then flopped. She had dropped her gaze to his mouth, instantly recalling how those firm lips and that searching, commanding tongue had wreaked such havoc with her own.

The seconds of silence had pulsed with sensual energy.

'That was a close one.' He gave her a wry smile as he rebalanced. 'I was about to fall flat on my face.'

'I wouldn't have let that happen.'

He looked at her for another long moment. 'Do you want to have dinner tonight?'

She arched a brow at him. 'You mean you don't have pressing paperwork or thousands of emails to see to?'

'Dominique told me you're lonely eating in the dining room all by yourself.'

'I'm not lonely.' Lily knew she had said it too quickly. It sounded far too defensive and prickly.

'I'll get Dominique to pack us a picnic.'

She blinked at him. 'A picnic?'

'You have something against picnics?'

'No, of course not. I love picnics. It's just I thought—'

'Meet me down by the lake. There's a glade on the western side. It'll be sheltered there if the wind picks up.'

'You don't want me to push you down there?'

He gave her a look. 'No.'

'But how will you—?'

'I have ways and means.'

The ways and means had four legs, a mane, a tail and looked terrifyingly skittish. Lily was waiting on a tartan blanket Dominique had packed along with the picnic when she saw Raoul coming towards her astride a glossy black stallion—she assumed it was the one she had seen him with before. He was leading another saddled horse on a rein and she recognised it as the gentle one called Mardi that Etienne had introduced her to that first day. Her heart gave a sudden lurch. What was he doing riding? How had he got on and what if he fell off? She sprang to her feet, almost tripping over the picnic basket as she did so. *Are you out of your mind?*

The stallion gave a snort and danced as if the ground beneath his hooves had suddenly turned to hot coals. Raoul kept his seat and soothed the horse in softly murmured French. The mare did nothing but look with considerable relish at the fresh baguette that was lying on the tablecloth. 'I thought you liked horses.'

'I do, but you're not supposed to be riding!'

'Why not?'

'Because you could fall off!'

'I won't fall off.' He stroked the stallion's satin-like neck. 'This is the perfect solution. I have four good legs instead of two bad ones.'

Lily gave him and the flighty horse a doubtful look. The stallion looked edgy and temperamental. Raoul was flirting with danger if he thought he could ride again as if nothing had changed. If he fell off he could damage his spine even more. The thought of him being injured further made her stomach curdle. Hadn't he had enough to deal with without looking for more tragedy?

'You're mad. You're asking for trouble. It's too soon. You could end up worse off. If you fall off and break both your legs, don't come running to me.' She blushed when she realised the absurdity of what she'd said. 'I meant that figuratively...of course.'

'Of course.' He grinned as he held out the mare's reins. 'Then supervise me. Come with me and make sure I'm being a good boy.'

She gave him a telling look. 'You and that stallion of yours are about as far away from good as it's possible to be.'

His eyes glinted at her. 'He looks mean and he acts mean, but he's a big softy underneath all that bluster.'

Lily took the mare's reins after a lengthy hesitation. The smell of leather and horse took her back to a time in her life when everything had been settled and in order. *Happy.* She stroked Mardi's shoulder as she prepared to mount. 'Good girl. Nice girl. Steady. Steady.' She managed to vault into the saddle without going over the other side like a circus clown, but it was a very near thing.

'You have a good seat.'

'Let's hope I keep it,' she muttered.

It didn't take her long to find her rhythm. The mare was as gentle and quiet as a lamb and her gait steady and sure. Raoul's stallion was anything but. He pranced and snorted but Raoul didn't appear to be having any trouble in keeping his seat. If anything he seemed to be enjoying himself. He looked relaxed and happy, his smile making him appear younger and more carefree than she had ever seen him. Looking at him now, no one would ever know he was unable to walk. He looked utterly gorgeous; fit, strong and devastatingly handsome.

He was the most wonderful, decent, honourable man she had ever met.

Hadn't the last two weeks confirmed that? He'd kept a polite distance, respecting her decision that night in the pool to refrain from committing to a physical relationship. He hadn't pressured her to talk about her past. He had simply given her the space to be herself.

He made her feel safe.

Her heart gave a little squeeze at the thought of going back to her life in London when this appointment was over.

Back to her female clients.

Back to her lonely nights watching something inane on television to fill in the hours until it was time to go to bed.

Back to reading books describing experiences she would never experience first-hand.

Like falling in love.

Lily gnawed at her lip. Maybe she wouldn't have to rely on books for that. Didn't she already feel a little bit in love with Raoul?

It was sheer and utter madness, of course. Deluded wishful thinking. Lunacy.

He wouldn't have looked twice at a girl like her if he hadn't been stuck with her at his château as a physical therapist. She had searched on her smart phone for a photograph of his ex-fiancée, Clarissa Moncrieff. Beautiful didn't even come close to describing the slim blonde woman with endless legs and a toothpaste-commercial smile. Looking at that photograph had made Lily feel like a small brown moth coming face-to-face with an exotic butterfly.

Sure, Raoul had kissed her a couple of times, but that didn't mean anything. Why would it? He'd kissed hundreds of women. He probably would have slept with her, too, if she'd given him the go ahead. He was used to having flings. Up until his relationship with Clarissa he hadn't spent more than six or eight weeks with the same partner. His interest in Lily had more to do with propinquity than anything else.

And she had better not forget it.

'Do you fancy a canter to the copse and back?' Raoul's voice pulled her out of her miserable mind wandering.

'Does Mardi have that particular gear?'

'If you give her plenty of encouragement.'

She gave the mare a gentle squeeze with her thighs and after a slow start the horse went from a trot to a lovely smooth canter. It was exhilarating to feel the breeze against her face as she rode towards the copse of trees. It brought back happy memories of a time in her life when things were hopeful and positive.

Raoul kept his stallion at a sedate pace but after a while he let him open out and stretch his legs. Lily watched as the horse's satin-clad muscles bunched and fired as he shot past. Raoul looked in his element, like a dark knight riding his finest steed.

He brought his horse to a standstill as he waited for her to catch up. 'All good?'

Lily couldn't keep the smile off her face. 'Wonderful.'

'You look beautiful when you smile.'

She *felt* beautiful when he looked at her like that. His eyes were meltingly dark and sexy as they held hers. She felt her stomach pitch when his gaze dropped down to her mouth. It never failed to stir her senses. It felt like a vicarious kiss each and every time.

'Are you hungry?' he asked.

'Starving.' Was he talking about food? *Was she?*

'But first I need to dismount.'

'How will you...?'

'Watch.' He made a clicking noise with his tongue and the stallion bent his forelegs to the ground. He eased himself out of the saddle and, using the horse as a prop, he came down on the picnic rug. For a fraction of a second it looked like he actually took all of his weight on his left leg. Lily was sure she hadn't imagined it, unless it was her wishful thinking back in overdrive. Had he been aware of doing it? He issued an order to the stallion in French and the horse moved away and started grazing as if butter wouldn't melt in his mouth.

'Wow, that is impressive. Has he always done that or did you just teach him?'

'I taught him ages ago. I just didn't realise how handy it would turn out to be.'

Lily could hear the strain of the last few weeks in his voice. Progress of any sort could be demoralising if it wasn't as fast and as perfect as one had hoped for. She had seen so many clients struggle with the emotional side of rehab. That final acceptance of limitation was the hardest thing to deal with. Some people never got there. They just couldn't cope with not being able to do the things they used to do. 'You're doing so well, Raoul. Did you realise you took your weight on your left leg just then? I'm sure I didn't imagine it.'

He gave her a grimace that fell short of being a smile. 'No, you didn't imagine it. I can stand for a few seconds, but I can't see myself walking into that church for my brother's wedding, can you?'

'The only thing that matters is your being there. I'm sure that's all your brother and his wife-to-be want.' Lily slipped out of the saddle and released the mare to graze alongside the stallion. 'You have to be there, Raoul. You don't really have a choice. You'll hurt Rafe and Poppy too much if you don't show up.'

He frowned as he picked a strand of grass and started toying with it. His right arm was still showing signs of the muscle wastage and topical dryness from being inside the cast and, though it was still swollen, his fingers were moving freely and seemingly without pain. 'I stood shoulder-to-shoulder with Rafe at our parents' funeral. It was the hardest thing I've ever had to do.' His frown deepened as if he had time-travelled to that dark, tragic time in his head. 'I put my feelings aside so I could support him. I swore on that day that I would always stand by him and Remy. That's what brothers are supposed to do. They support each other through everything and anything.'

'You don't have to physically stand by someone to support them. There are lots of ways to show you care about someone.' Like taking them on a picnic and arranging a quiet horse to ride so they get their lost confidence back.

Stop it. You're reading far too much into this.

His hazel eyes met hers. 'Rafe relies on me to back him up. Remy is like a loose cannon. I guess it's because we spoilt him so much. He was so young when our parents died. We tried to protect him and as a result he takes a hell of a lot for granted.'

'You did your best under terrible circumstances. No one could ask more of you than that.'

'I can't let Rafe down, but I can't bear the thought of only being half there.'

She reached for his left hand lying on the rug and squeezed it in her own. 'You won't be half there. *All* of you will be there. Can't you see that? You are much more than your physical self. Much, *much* more.'

He picked up her hand and brought it to rest against his chin. She felt the prickle of his stubble against her fingers and a wave of longing rolled through her as his eyes meshed with hers. 'I wish I'd met you before my accident.'

Her heart gave a sudden kick against her ribcage. 'Why?'

'I think I could've fallen in love with you.'

Like you have a choice?

'What's stopping you now?' She could not believe she'd just asked that! What was she doing, asking for a slap down? Hadn't her self-esteem taken enough hits? Why would he fall in love with her?

She was a nondescript brown moth, not a beautiful butterfly.

His fingers moved against hers. They seemed to be relaying a message that was at odds with his words. 'Reason. Rationality. Responsibility.'

'The three Rs.'

'You've been reading about me and my brothers.'

Lily decided there was no point pretending she hadn't. 'Rakes. Rich. Ruthless. Everyone's been calling you and your brothers that for years.'

He frowned as he looked at her fingers encased in his own. 'We're one down on the rakes. Two, if you count me.'

Lily wondered if he was thinking of his ex. Even if he hadn't loved Clarissa he must surely be missing the sex. He was an intensely physical man. Virile. Potent. *Irresistible.*

He brought his eyes back to hers and her belly did a complicated gymnastics manoeuvre. 'Do you realise this is the longest period I've been celibate?'

'Wow, must be some sort of record, huh? What is it, six or seven weeks?' Her face was hot. It felt like it was on fire.

You're discussing his sex life?

What is wrong with you?

He gave her a grim smile. 'Nine.'

'Wow. That's a long time. It's like a decade for someone like you, right? Maybe more like a century. Or a millennium.' *Shut up!*

His thumb traced a lazy circle over the back of her hand. 'I guess it's been even longer for you.'

Lily looked down at their joined hands. Her hand was so small compared to his. Her skin so light. It was like a physical embodiment of everything that was different about the worlds they came from.

Hers was plain and boring.

His was colourful and exciting.

The silence ballooned until it seemed to suck all the oxygen out of the air.

'Have you…?'

'I haven't.'

They had spoken at exactly the same time.

'You go first,' Raoul said.

Lily blushed and looked down again at her hand within his. 'I haven't got back on the horse, so to speak. It wasn't that I was all that good at it to start with. I'd had a couple of relationships but I can't say I ever felt that certain spark everyone talks about.' *Like the one she could feel now as his thumb did another circle on her hand.* 'I guess I'm not a very passionate person. As a sexual partner, I'm what you'd call vanilla, not rocky road.'

His eyes went to her mouth. 'I hate rocky road. Vanilla is simple and uncomplicated. Understated. Elegant. And it's a perfect blend with other flavours. It goes with just about anything.'

Were they still talking about ice-cream?

Lily willed him to look at her. Couldn't he see how much she wanted him? Her body was humming with need. It was a wonder he couldn't hear it. It was like a roaring sound inside her ears.

Her blood was racing with it.

Firing with it.

Heating with it.

Exploding with it.

She wanted him.

It was a powerful, overwhelming feeling that was at odds with everything she had previously clung to. Pride, safety and security were nothing when it came down to the wire.

She wanted to feel like a woman. She wanted to be *his* woman.

He looked at her and the universe seemed to take a breath and hold it.

Lily saw the heat and the longing. She saw the need and desperation she felt in her body reflected in his gaze. She reached for him as he reached for her.

'I want you.' They said it in unison.

'Are you sure?' he said.

She stroked his stubbly jaw, mesmerised by the way his gaze had softened. 'I've never been surer. I want this. I want you. I don't want my bad memories to haunt me any more. Give me good ones to replace them.'

To store away and revisit when this is all over, as it surely will be all too soon.

He cupped her face in with his hands, his gaze dark, concerned. Conflicted. 'I'm not the right man for you. I'm not the right man for any woman right now.'

Lily gazed into his warm green-brown eyes. 'I think you're the perfect man. It will be like the first time for both of us.'

'I can't offer you anything but this.' His mouth was already nudging hers, his breath mingling with hers in that hotly intimate way that made her shiver and shudder with desire. 'You have to understand and accept that.'

'This is all I want.' *Liar. You want the whole she-bang. You want the fairytale you keep reading about: boy meets girl, boy loves girl, boy rides with girl off into the sunset.* 'I want to feel passion again. I want to feel alive again.'

'I want that, too.' His voice sounded deep and tortured. 'You have no idea of how much I want that.'

'Show me.' She breathed the words against his lips. 'Show me...please?'

CHAPTER ELEVEN

RAOUL HAD BEEN making love—having sex was probably a more accurate way of putting it—with women since he was seventeen. He knew their bodies. He knew what turned them off and what turned them on. He was a master at seduction. He knew every move, every caress, every touch and stroke that would make his partner feel as if he was the most amazingly competent lover in the world.

But with Lily Archer he felt like he was starting all over again. He didn't have a clue. He felt out of his depth. He was floundering. Worried. Terrified he might hurt her or make her scared.

Her mouth felt like soft velvet under his. It was so responsive, hungry, searching and yet hesitant, as if she were still feeling her way with him. Relearning the steps, tasting, touching and feeling. Her shyness mixed with her simmering passion made his body throb and ache with need. The way she touched him, the way her arms came around his neck, the way her fingers threaded through his hair made his desire for her roar inside his loins.

She made little murmuring sounds of pleasure as he explored her mouth. But he had to keep a firm lid on his response. He was fully erect and aching to let go but she was nowhere near ready for him. He sensed it in the subtle ways she moved, jerking back, shifting, like a shying horse facing a jump that was too high.

'I'm not going to hurt you.' He stroked a finger down the curve of her cheek. 'Trust me, Lily.'

She gave him a tentative smile that was little more than a tiny flutter of her lips. 'I trust you.'

'If you want to stop at any point, then you just have to tell me.'

'I don't want you to stop.' She moved her pelvis against his. It was a subtle movement, probably more instinctive than conscious, but it caused a raging inferno to roar through his veins. 'I want you to make love to me.'

He moved a gentle hand over her breast. It fitted his palm perfectly, her nipple pressing against his flesh as if in search of his touch. He wanted to feel her skin on skin, to feel her silky heat against his, to feel the satin of her flesh against the rough rasp of his.

He slid a hand under her top, gauging her reaction, letting her dictate the terms, but if anything she encouraged his exploration. She arched her spine like a cat so her breasts would be in closer contact with his hands.

He lowered his mouth to the tight pink nubs of her nipples he'd exposed, savouring each one in turn. She bucked and writhed as he tantalised her senses, her hands grasping his head, her fingers digging into his scalp as he rolled his tongue over and around her sensitive flesh.

She suddenly eased back from him. 'Should I get, um, undressed?'

She looked so adorably out of her depth. He was used to women shrugging their clothes off before he got them through the door. He was used to women showing off their assets in clinging, revealing clothing that left nothing to the imagination. He was used to women telling him what they wanted and going out to get it, no holds barred.

Touch here. This hard. This slow; this fast.

It was so damned mechanical.

Lily Archer looked up at him with those big dark blue eyes and made him feel…like a man.

'I think that's my job.' His voice sounded like a croak. His hands felt like a fumbling teenager's on his first date. He peeled away her top, revealing her slim chest, small, pert breasts and her amazing abs and his breath stalled in his throat. 'Wow.'

She gave him a sheepish look. 'They look bigger when I'm wearing a push-up bra. It's sort of like false advertising.'

Raoul smiled as he laid a hand on the flat plane of her abdomen. 'Your breasts are beautiful.'

She shuddered under his touch. 'I like your hands. They're…gentle.'

'I like your body.' He stroked his hand down the length of her cotton-trouser-clad thigh.

Her gaze fell away from his. 'It's ugly.'

He pushed her chin up so her eyes met his again. 'It's not ugly. It's who you are now. You can't change it even if you wanted to.'

She gave him a frustrated, anguished look. 'I don't want to be like this. I wish I could get rid of my scars. It's not who I am now. I want to move on. I hate that I have this mark of who I was back then permanently etched on my body like a tattoo. I'm not that girl any more. I just got lost for a while and I've had to pay for it ever since.'

Raoul knew exactly what she was feeling. He wanted to move on, too. He didn't want to be trapped in his body, in a body that didn't represent him as a person, as a man. But what other choice did he have? What choice did she have? They were both trapped.

He brushed back her hair from her forehead. 'Do you think I want to live in my body the way it is? I lie awake at night terrified that this might be as good as it ever gets. You have some scars. I know that's hard to deal with, but they're only as permanent as you allow them to be.'

Wasn't there something in that he should be taking on board?

'I want to be normal.'

'You *are* normal.' His body registered just how normal by the way it was responding to hers. Hard, urgent, desperate.

She traced a fingertip over his bottom lip. 'Make me feel normal. Make me forget about anything but what's here and now.'

What was here and now was how wonderful, how magical her mouth felt beneath his. He gathered her close, delighting in the feel of her moulding herself to him as if she had been looking for him all of her life. There were no awkward shifts or adjustments. She moved into him like a key fitting into a tricky lock.

It felt so good to have her that close. Close enough to feel the contours of her body against his. He felt a sense of rightness that he had never felt before.

He tried to push the thought aside but it kept coming back, niggling at him, jostling him, urging him like an obsessed terrier dropping a tennis ball at its handler's feet.

He wanted this feeling to last.

Lily felt his hands moving over her so tenderly, so carefully. He was taking his time, peeling away her clothes piece by piece, kissing each part of her he exposed in warm, soft-as-air caresses that made her spine tingle like bubbles in a glass. He kissed each and every scar on her arms, his mouth and lips spreading a pathway of heat through her body.

He helped her get out of her cotton trousers, his mouth moving down her stomach, his tongue taking a little dip in the tiny pool of her belly button before coming to the top of her knickers.

She stiffened, her stomach churning. Was he thinking how awful the tops of her legs looked compared to his ex-fiancée's? She bet Clarissa Moncrieff's gorgeous long cellulite-free legs didn't have a single blemish on them. She bet his ex had waxed and exfoliated and spray-tanned regularly. Was he thinking how plain and sensible Lily's chain-store underwear was? Any moment now he would pull back in revulsion, make some excuse that this couldn't continue. Oh, God! Why had she asked him to make love to her? It was so desperate and gauche of her.

'Hey, hey, hey.' His voice was a soft, deep, soothing rumble, his hand gentle and steadying as it came to rest on her stomach. 'You're beautiful. I mean it, Lily. So very natural and beautiful.'

Her breath caught in her chest as he began stroking her thighs in long, smooth gentle caresses that made her tense muscles slowly relax. She stopped breathing altogether when he put his mouth to her left thigh, his lips moving over her scarred flesh like the brush of a teasing feather.

He did the same to her right thigh, moving tantalisingly close to the moist, swollen, pulsing heart of her. 'I want… I want…' She didn't know how to ask for the release she craved. She had never felt the need building quite like this before. It was rising to a crescendo in her body, every nerve tensing and twitching in feverish anticipation.

He stroked a lazy finger down the cotton-covered seam of her body. Close but not close enough. She gave a little whimper and arched her spine. 'I want *you.*'

He peeled away her knickers and traced her seam again. It made her gasp to feel the thickness of his finger against her moist heat. He brought his mouth to her, gently tasting her essence, teasing her until she was grasping his head like a drowning person with a rescuer. The sensations started as a ripple and then came smashing over her in a series of waves. She cried out in a breathless, gasping sobs, shaken to the core of her being by the out-of-control passion—not someone else's, but her own.

'You're very good at this.' *Did she sound unsophisticated?*

He gave her a smouldering smile. 'So are you.'

Lily shyly stroked a hand over his chest. Somehow while he had been kissing her she had managed to undo his shirt buttons but he was still fully clothed. Had he done that deliberately, to stop her from being overwhelmed by seeing his naked body? 'I want to touch you…'

He covered her hand with one of his. 'It might have to wait for some other time.'

Some other time?

Her stomach did that butter-churn thing again. He didn't want to make love to her? Was she so hideous?

But *surely* he wanted her? She'd felt his erection. She could *still* feel it pressing against her right thigh.

He doesn't want you. He wants his ex. His beautiful, perfect ex.

Lily slipped her hand out from under his and started to hunt for her clothes. 'Right; well, then. I wouldn't want to force you or anything. God, no; that would be ridiculously ironic, don't you think?'

'I don't have a condom.'

She stopped wrestling herself back into her trousers to look at him. 'Oh…'

He gave her a rueful look. 'I don't think Dominique would have packed one in the picnic basket, do you?'

She arched her brows cynically. 'I don't know. I'm sure if you'd asked her to she would have.'

He frowned at her. 'You think that's why I set up this picnic?'

'It was a way of riding two horses with one jockey, so to speak. You got me back in the saddle—both of them.'

'You've got it all wrong, Lily.' He raked a hand through his hair, making it look even more tousled. 'I didn't have any intention of sleeping with you.'

'You didn't sleep with me.' She threw him a flinty look. 'You *serviced* me.'

His mouth went into a tense line. 'If you think I'm the sort of man who would have sex with a vulnerable young woman without using a condom then you're even more—'

'What?' she flashed back before he could finish his sentence. 'Screwed up? Nutty? Crazy?'

His jaw moved in an out as if he was trying to control his temper. 'Stop putting words in my mouth.'

'It's what you're thinking, isn't it?' She stuffed her feet back in her shoes. 'It's what everyone thinks when they see my legs and arms.' She sent him another fiery glare. 'And, just for the record, I am *not* vulnerable.'

'Yes, you are. You're vulnerable and scared and you won't let anyone get close enough to help you.'

'You're a fine one to talk,' she threw back.

'I let *you* in, didn't I?'

'Grudgingly.'

There was a short, tense silence.

'You have helped me, Lily. You've helped me a lot.'

Lily felt her anger dissipating at his gruff tone. 'I have?'

'I think you're right about Rafe's wedding.' His mouth twisted resignedly. 'I need to be there, chair or no chair.'

She felt a wave of unexpected emotion swamp her. She blinked a couple of times to stop the tears that were threatening to spill. If nothing else, she had achieved what his brother had paid her for. Raoul was going to go to the wedding. It would be a big step for him to be out in public but it was an important one. 'I'm so glad, for you, for Rafe and Poppy.'

'Will you come with me?'

'I don't think it's my place to barge in on a—'

'I want you there.' His tone had a thread of steel to it. 'You're my physical therapist. I might need you to massage a tight muscle or stroke my ego or something.'

'Your *ego*?'

'Will you do it?'

She caught the inside of her mouth with her teeth. A family wedding. It was so...so *personal*. She would have to witness other people experiencing what she most desperately wanted for herself: love, commitment and a happy future. 'I don't know....'

'It's another ten days away. You have plenty of time to make up your mind.'

Lily wondered if he were asking her to accompany him for other reasons. It would be a very public gathering. There would be press everywhere. No doubt there would be speculation about his broken engagement. Was he looking for a way to divert public attention, having her pose as his stand-in date? 'I have to go back to London straight after. I have clients booked in. There's a waiting list.'

'I won't keep you longer than the month. After the wedding, you are free to leave.'

His words made her heart suddenly contract. He hadn't wanted her here in the first place. Why was she disappointed he was already planning for her departure?

'OK. Fine. Good.'

'We should do something about this food Dominique has prepared,' he said. 'She might not have packed condoms, but there is just about everything else inside this pack.'

Lily sat down on the blanket beside him. She couldn't think of a time when she had felt less like eating. She made a token effort but later she couldn't recall what she ate. The conversation was stilted. Awkward. She sensed Raoul couldn't wait for the evening to be over. Even the horses seemed to pick up on the restless mood. They twitched their tails and pricked their ears at the slightest sound.

Finally it was time to leave.

She made an attempt to pack up the picnic basket

but Raoul intercepted her. 'Leave it. Etienne will take it back to the château later.'

'Do you need a hand to get back on your—?'

He cut her off with a look. 'I'll be fine. Take Mardi back to the stables. One of the other stable hands will unsaddle her for you. I'll wait here for Etienne.'

Raoul was drowning. The water was over his head. His limbs were dead. His lungs were exploding. He thrashed against the restraint of the water but it didn't feel like water. It felt like fabric. He punched it away and he heard a choked-off cry.

He froze.

Woke up. Blinked. Realised he was in his bedroom and that Lily was sitting on the edge of his bed clutching her chin, her eyes as wide as dinner plates. 'Did I hurt you?' His insides turned to gravy. 'Tell me I didn't hurt you.'

'You didn't.' She dropped her hand from her face. 'Not really.'

He could see the red mark where his hand had glanced against her chin. He touched it gently with his finger. 'I'm sorry. I sometimes have terrible nightmares. I should've warned you.'

'I heard you shouting.'

Somehow his finger had gone from her chin to the soft pillow of her lower lip. 'Did I wake you?'

'I wasn't asleep.'

His gaze locked on hers. She looked so young and so…so unpretentious. Unprepared. Natural. Her hair was free about her shoulders. It smelt of honeysuckle and jasmine, familiar, homely yet exotic. He traced her top lip and then her bottom lip with his finger. 'Why weren't you able to sleep?'

Her eyes fell away from his. 'Just one of those nights, I guess…'

'I was having one of those myself.'

Her eyes came back to his. 'Can I get you a drink or something? Milk? Hot chocolate? Cocoa?'

'No.' He moved his thumb over her lip again. 'Thanks.'

Her lips shifted in an uncertain-looking on-off smile. 'I guess I should let you get back to bed…'

'Stay.'

She blinked a couple of times. 'Stay?'

'Talk to me. Keep me company. Distract me.'

She rolled her lips together. 'I don't think that's part of my job description…'

'I don't want you to stay here as my physical therapist.' He held her gaze with his. 'Stay for another reason.'

The tip of her tongue made a nervous dart out over her lips. 'What other reason could there be?'

He brought her closer, his mouth coming down to within a breath of hers. 'Think of one.' And then he covered her mouth with his.

It was a very good reason. The best *possible* reason. Lily couldn't think of any better reason to be in his bedroom and in his arms being kissed so soundly other than that it was exactly where she wanted to be.

His arms gathered her close to his body, his mouth moving on hers with devastatingly erotic expertise. His tongue slid into her mouth, stroking against hers, teasing it into duelling with his. Her belly flipped like a pancake as he deepened the kiss even further.

He pressed her backwards on the bed, his weight supported by his elbows, his lips and tongue working their magic on hers. 'You taste so damn good,' he groaned against her mouth.

Lily kissed him back with all the passion that had been ignited that evening of the picnic. It had been ignited from the first moment she had met him—that instant spark of attraction, that magnetic pull, that irresistible lure of polar opposites.

The need she felt for him was a throbbing ache that pulsed between her legs. She had never been more aware of her body. He had awakened the dormant sensations, making them explode like fireworks in front of a raw flame.

His hands moved over her, shaping her breasts, touching her, tantalising her with the promise of more. Her nipples were tight and sensitive, her flesh hungry for the hot, wet swirl of his tongue and the sexy graze of his teeth.

She gave a gasp as he pushed up her pyjama top, his hands warm and sure on her body. She shivered as his mouth closed over her nipple, the sucking motion making every hair on her head lift up at the roots. He was gentle yet determined, drawing from her a response she had not thought she was capable of giving. Her body writhed beneath his, looking for more connection, for flesh on flesh, for satiation.

'I don't want to rush you,' he said.

'You're not rushing me.' She kissed him, once, twice, three times. 'I want this. I want you.'

He smiled against her lips. 'At least this time I'm a bit better prepared.'

'Down at the lake… I thought you didn't want me.'

He pulled back to look down at her. 'How could you possibly think that?'

Lily looked at a point of stubble on his chin rather than meet his eyes. 'I thought it must be because of my scars. I guess I'm not used to men who are responsible enough to stop and think about using protection.'

He tipped up her chin. 'Not all men are irresponsible and selfish, *ma petite*. And you should stop worrying about your scars. They don't define you as a person. It's your behaviour, not your appearance, that does that.'

She touched his bottom lip with her fingertip. 'You've always dated such exquisitely beautiful women.'

'Some of the most beautiful women I've been with have also been the most boring. You, on the other hand, are captivating, intriguing and utterly irresistible.' He brought his mouth back to hers, pressing a lingering kiss to her lips until she forgot about her insecurities and thought of nothing but how he made her feel.

He made her feel good. Alive.

On fire.

Lily touched his chest, sliding her hands down over his taut abdomen shyly, hesitantly. She felt him suck in a breath as her hand came to the top of his groin. She felt the smooth head of his erection bump against her hand and a tight fist of intense longing grabbed at her insides.

She couldn't stop herself from exploring him. He was so thick and full, so strong yet contained. She had never really thought of a man's body as beautiful before, or at least not this part of a man's body. She ran her fingertip over the moist tip of his penis, that most primal signal of readiness. She felt her own intimate moisture; it was a silky reminder that she was just as aroused as he was. 'I want you inside me...'

'I want to be inside you.'

She shivered in anticipation as he reached for a condom. He came back over her, his weight balanced on his arms, his legs a sexy tangle with hers. He gently eased her thighs apart, hooking one leg over his hip as his mouth came back to hers.

She felt the probe of his body against her. It was subtle and yet urgent. She moved against him, silently giving him permission, wanting him so badly her body was aching with it.

'I'll take it slowly.' His words were a sexy rumble against her lips.

She arched her spine again, searching for his possession. She didn't want him slow. She wanted him fast. She wanted him to feel the same pressing need she felt building in her body.

He gave a guttural groan and slid partway inside, waiting for her to accommodate him. 'Are you OK?'

'I want *all* of you.' She dug her hands into his buttocks, urging him on. *'Now.'*

He went in a little deeper, still keeping control. 'It will be much better for you, the longer I prepare you.'

'I'm prepared.' She pressed her mouth to his, feeding off him hungrily while her inner muscles gripped him tightly. *I'm so prepared!*

He thrust deeper, his face burying against her neck as he fought for control. She caught his rhythm, feeling every movement, her senses going off into a tailspin when his fingers came into the action, caressing her intimately to trigger that final cataclysmic release.

She shattered into a million pieces, her body shaking and shuddering with an explosive orgasm that left her spent and limp in his arms.

'Good?'

She could barely speak. 'Wow...'

He brushed her hair back from her face, his look surprisingly tender. 'You did it.'

She pointed a finger at his chest. '*You* did it.'

'It takes two to tango, as they say. We *both* did it.'

'Not quite.' Lily used her inner muscles to squeeze him. 'You haven't...'

'I'm about to.'

She felt a shiver race down her spine at the smouldering look in his eyes. She felt him start to move again, the slow but steady build-up of thrusts that made her flesh tingle all over again. She didn't think it was possible for her body to experience another orgasm so soon after the previous one but within seconds she was flying away again. She clung to him as he buried his face into her neck as he pumped his way into oblivion.

It was a long moment before he moved away from her.

He had a little frown on his face as he disposed of the condom. He sat on the edge of the bed, his back turned to her. Lily wondered with a painful pang if he was thinking of his ex. How many times had they made love? How long had they been together? Was he comparing Lily's response to hers?

'I guess I should go back to my room.' She gave him a self-deprecating look when he turned to look at her. 'I'm not sure I want Dominique to find me slinking out of your bedroom first thing in the morning.'

'Don't go.'

She rolled her lips together, not sure what to make of his unfathomable expression. 'You want me to stay with you all night?'

A tiny muscle flicked in his jaw. 'Not just tonight. Every night until you go back to London.'

He was offering her a relationship. An affair. A temporary one.

Very temporary.

'Obviously I'm very flattered, but—'

'But you want more.' It was a statement not a question. 'The thing is, Lily, this is all I'm capable of right now.'

Would she sound terribly gauche, asking for more? What chance was there that a man like him would fall in love with someone like her?

Men like Raoul Caffarelli did not fall in love with shy plain Jane English girls with scars.

It just showed how hopelessly romantic she was. But a short affair was all he was going to offer her because he would not commit to anything else unless he was fully mobile. That was the sort of man he was. He could not envisage a future any other way. Could she risk her heart for a hope that might never come to fruition? He had undoubtedly improved in the last fortnight but that was no guarantee that he would regain his full mobility.

He was twice, *four* times the man of some of the able-bodied ones she'd met. He had so much to offer. He was not the least bit diminished by his physical limitations.

Why couldn't he see that?

Because he was so damned uncompromising and stubborn, that was why. He thought in terms of black or white, either-or. There were no shades of in between.

What if she said yes? It would give her a little under two weeks of memories that were certainly a whole lot better than the ones she had come with.

He was a passionate and skilled lover. He was a good

man, a decent, lovely man to be around. He was respectful and kind. Considerate.

And she was in love with him.

Which was why she should say no. Right now. Nip it in the bud. *Do not pass Go. Do not take another step. Do not stomp in where angels fear to tread.*

'I'll stay.'

CHAPTER TWELVE

'So how are things going with Miss Archer?' Rafe asked when he phoned a few days later.

'Fine.'

'Just "fine"?'

'Good.'

'So you're talking to her, then?'

Raoul didn't want to go into the details of his current relationship with Lily. He hadn't quite got his own head around it. All he knew was he enjoyed being with her. She was easy company, gentle and kind, caring. He enjoyed watching her wake up each morning, rub her sleepy eyes and give him that shy smile of hers. He loved the feel of her body nestled up against his when she slept.

He loved *watching* her sleep.

She looked like Sleeping Beauty, so pale and so beautiful. He loved the way she responded to him so passionately. She was far more confident now as a lover. He had never been with a partner who surprised and delighted him as much as she did. It was like discovering sensuality all over again. He was aware of his body in ways he had never been before. Her touch was like magic. He was sure it was one of the reasons he had improved his mobility.

He *felt* stronger.

'You *are* talking to her, aren't you?' Rafe's voice jolted him back to the moment.

'Of course I'm talking to her. So…how're the wedding plans going?'

'Whoa, quick subject change. What's going on?'

'Nothing.' Raoul gave himself a mental kick for answering too quickly. It was hard to pull the wool over Rafe's eyes, even over the phone. 'Nothing's going on.'

'You're not sleeping with the hired help, are you?'

He felt his back come up. 'Lily is not the hired help. She's—'

'So it's *Lily* now.' Rafe gave an amused little chuckle. 'I must say I didn't see that coming. I didn't think she was your type. Not compared to—'

'Shut the hell up.'

'You're not still cut up about that bimbo dumping you, are you? Come on, Raoul. She's not worth it. At your age you should be looking for love, not looks.'

Raoul clenched his jaw. 'I'm not interested in falling in love.'

'Famous last words.' Rafe chuckled again. 'I said them myself and look what happened—I fell hook, line, and sinker for Poppy and I couldn't be happier. I can't believe that this time next week we'll be man and wife.'

'Look, I'm happy for you. I really am. Just don't go expecting me to follow you down the aisle any time soon. Pick on Remy. He's the one who needs to settle down.'

'Has he been to see you? Called you? Texted? Emailed?'

'He came the day before you brought Lil…Miss Archer. I haven't heard from him since. Why, what's he up to?'

'I don't know.' A thread of concern seemed to un-
derpin Rafe's voice. 'I think he's having some sort of
showdown with Henri Marchand over one of his major
holdings or properties. I've heard on the grapevine that
Marchand is desperate for funds. He made a couple of
investments that didn't pay off.'

'Karma.'

'You could be right.' Rafe let out a breath. 'I just hope
Remy knows what he's doing. He's juggling a lot of finance just now. He's been trying to buy into the Mappleton hotel chain, as well. He's been working on the
negotiations for months. If he pulls it off it would be the
biggest coup of all of our careers. But apparently Robert
Mappleton is ultra-conservative. Word has it he refuses
to do business with Remy because he thinks Remy's too
much of a playboy.'

'I can't see Remy marrying someone just to nail a
deal, can you?' Raoul's tone was dry.

Rafe gave a laugh. 'Speaking of weddings… Are you
coming to mine?'

'Wild horses couldn't keep me away.'

Lily was in the garden picking flowers for the table when
Raoul came out to her. He was in his manual chair but he
had been up on his feet for at least a minute during their
gym session earlier. He had taken three steps—four, if
you counted the one before he had to grasp the rails. It
was an enormous leap forward. It was still too early to
say whether he would continue to improve, but she was
cautiously optimistic.

He looked tired now, however. He had lines of strain
around his mouth. She knew he still had a lot of pain but
he refused to take any medication. She knew he didn't

sleep properly. She had woken so many times to find him watching her with a frown on his face. Was it pain that put that frown there, or was it because she wasn't the woman he had thought would be sharing his bed?

'Did you want me?'

He gave her a sexily slanted smile. 'Always.'

Always? He wasn't offering always. He had offered her here and now. And here and now would be over in days. She had resigned herself to it. She would be going home and that would be it. She wouldn't see him again.

Her heart gave a painfully tight squeeze.

Ever.

'Dominique knows.'

'That I want you?'

'That you've *had* me.' She gave him a see-what-you've-done look. 'I tried to deny it, but my bed hasn't been slept in for over a week, so it wasn't like I could convince her otherwise.'

'And that bothers you?'

'Of course it bothers me. I'm not some scullery maid slipping upstairs for a bit of slap and tickle with the lord of the manor. I feel…awkward. Embarrassed. Ashamed.'

'Why?'

She tossed the roses she'd gathered into the basket she was holding. 'Dominique thinks it's all going to end up like some sort of fairytale. I think you should talk to her. Tell her how it is.'

His mouth tightened. 'I don't need to explain myself to my domestic staff.'

Explain it to me, then. Tell me *where I stand.*

'Fine.' She snapped another rose off and dropped it in the basket. 'But I'm not coming to the wedding with you. I think that's taking things way too far.'

'I want you with me.'

'Why?' She felt her heart contract again. 'So you can show everyone you've moved on from Clarissa?'

'It has *nothing* to do with Clarissa.'

'It has everything to do with her. You're not ready for a relationship.'

His jaw went down like a clamp.

'I've already made the arrangements. You can't *not* come.'

'I haven't got anything to wear.'

'I've got that covered.'

'You bought me clothes?' Lily glared at him. 'Is that what you did? *How could you?* How could you make me feel like some sort of tawdry kept mistress?'

His eyes hardened like diamonds. 'You're not my mistress.'

'No, of course not.' She gave him a testy look. 'I'm just your physical therapist with benefits.'

His mouth was pulled so tight it looked white around the edges. 'I don't want to have this conversation now.'

'Fine.' She tossed her head and went in hunt of another rose to pick. 'Don't have it, then.'

He blew out an audible breath. 'What is wrong with you? Why are you being so...so antagonistic all of a sudden? You knew how it was going to be. I didn't make any promises to you.'

Lily put the rose in her basket. The velvet petals and the savage thorns were a poignant reminder of what love was like: beautiful but excruciatingly painful.

No, he hadn't made any promises.

She was the one with the serious case of wishful thinking. A couple of times she'd caught him watching her when he had thought she was still asleep. He'd had a look of such tenderness and longing in his eyes it had made her wonder if he would open his heart to her. She was wrong. Clearly. 'No, that's right. You didn't.'

'Let's not fight now, Lily.' His jaw was set in an uncompromising line. 'Please…' His voice lost its harsh edge, showing a tiny glimpse of how vulnerable he was feeling, 'Not now.'

Lily felt herself caving in. What was she doing ruining their last few hours arguing with him? He had made up his mind.

She had better get used to it.

The Oxfordshire church was full of fragrant flowers. Raoul had to steel himself as he wheeled up the aisle. It reminded him of his parents' funeral. The cloying scent was overpowering. Sickening. Thank God there wasn't a choir.

He caught a glimpse of Lily sitting in one of the pews. She gave him a shy smile that tugged on his heart like stitches being pulled. She was wearing the designer outfit he had bought her. He couldn't make up his mind whether it suited her or not. Personally, he preferred her without clothes, but that was just his opinion. The slim-fitting, shell-pink suit clung to her neat figure like a glove. Her hair was swept up in an elegant twist on top of her head and she had put on a modest amount of make-up that highlighted her creamy complexion, regally high cheekbones and the deep blue of her eyes.

Rafe was standing at the altar, looking dashing if not a little nervous. Remy hadn't yet arrived, and no one was entirely sure if he would, but that was Remy for you.

'How're you doing?' Rafe asked as Raoul parked his chair alongside.

'I think that's supposed to be my line.'

'You made it.'

'I made it.'

Rafe swallowed a couple of times and then turned to face the front of the church. 'I feel a bit nervous.'

'I can tell.'

Rafe glanced at him. 'You can?'

'You keep tugging at your left sleeve. Dead giveaway.'

'Got that.'

Remy suddenly appeared at the portal of the church and did a last-minute adjustment to his bow tie as he ambled down the aisle. 'Were you guys waiting for me?'

Rafe gave him a look. 'Glad you could make it.'

Remy gave one of his renowned charming grins. 'Hey, Raoul, you're looking good. Walking yet?'

Raoul stretched his mouth into a rictus smile. 'Almost.'

The organist began playing. The beautiful cadences of Pachelbel's *Canon in D* swelled to the rafters.

'Here comes the bride....' Rafe's voice sounded hoarse with emotion.

Raoul looked at Poppy as she floated up the aisle. She only had eyes for his brother. Her face was glowing with love, with absolute rapture. He felt a pain in the middle of his chest. Would he ever see a bride come towards him with the same depth of love?

'Dearly beloved, we are gathered together...'

The sacred vows were a form of torture. To have and to hold. For richer for poorer...

In sickness and in health.

Did his brother realise what the hell he was promising? Did Poppy? There was only so much sickness a relationship could endure. It was too much to ask someone to stick by you no matter what. Life could throw some horrible curve balls. He had caught one fair in the middle of his gut. He was still reeling from it.

Could he ask someone—who was he kidding?—could he ask Lily—to stick with him through it? He didn't know how he would be in a week's, two weeks', two months' time, let alone a lifetime. Would it be fair to tie her down to such uncertainty?

'You may kiss the bride.'

Raoul looked at his hands where they were gripping the arms of his chair like claws. He was happy for Rafe. Of course he was. Rafe was a good brother. A great brother. He deserved to be happy after all he had done for Raoul and Remy. He had kept them together; sacrificed his own interests and at times his safety to keep them as a family.

But it was just so damned hard to be here like...*like this*.

He dragged his gaze towards the bride and groom. Rafe was grinning as if he had just won the lottery. Poppy was smiling with such love on her face it made Raoul feel sick with envy.

He wanted to be loved like that.

Did Lily love him like that?

Could he risk finding out?

The congregation erupted with spontaneous applause as the bride and groom walked back down the aisle as husband and wife.

Raoul felt every eye on him as he wheeled down after them as part of the official bridal procession. Cameras flashed, the frenzied click of shutters sounding like a round of artillery gunfire. His image would be plastered over every paper in the country and all over Europe tomorrow. His insides churned at the thought. What had he been thinking, coming here? Remy could have done just as good a job—better, actually. At least he'd been able to stand upright.

He caught Lily's eye as he came past her pew. She was biting her lower lip, her gaze concerned. Troubled. Uncertain.

He should never have crossed the boundary he'd crossed with her, but he hadn't been able to help himself. He had been spellbound by her feistiness, the way she stood up to him in spite of her initial reluctance to deal with him.

He forced himself to look away. He would speak to her later. When they were alone. He would ask her if she could love him like this.

If she *did* love him like this.

He *had* to know.

'I've been absolutely *dying* to meet you.' Poppy gave Lily a big, squishy hug. 'Rafe's been telling me how wonderful you've been for Raoul.'

'I don't know about that.' Lily felt her cheeks heating.

'He's doing really well,' Poppy said. 'I can't tell you how much it means to both of us to have him here. We thought he wouldn't come. He was so stubborn about it initially.'

'He can be pretty determined when he makes up his mind about something.'

Poppy gave her a conspiratorial look. 'It's a Caffarelli trait. Believe me; I know that first-hand. Have you met Vittorio, the grandfather?'

'No, I saw him at the ceremony, but not to speak to.'

'Don't go near him. He's out for blood. I can handle

most people, but he scares the living daylights out of me.' She gave a little shudder and then smiled widely as Rafe came over. 'Hello, darling.'

Rafe planted a kiss to her mouth. 'Hello, *ma chérie*. Is it time to leave? Please tell me it is. My face is aching from smiling so much.'

Poppy grinned as she linked her arm through one of his. 'We're not going anywhere until we've done the bridal waltz. I think I can hear the band warming up.' She turned and smiled at Lily. 'Will you excuse us? I think that's our cue.'

Raoul was on to his third glass of wine when the bridal waltz started. He wasn't interested in getting drunk or even tipsy. He wasn't trying to mask his pain. He just wanted to block out the smiling faces.

Everyone was so damned happy.

Rafe and Poppy took the floor. They moved together like poetry in motion. Rafe looked so strong and in control, Poppy so feminine and dainty. Their footwork was in perfect tune. No toes were being crushed. No legs were suddenly collapsing.

His stomach clenched.

He would never be able to do the bridal waltz. It was like a boulder hitting him out of nowhere. It crashed against his chest, almost making him double over in pain.

He hadn't been able to be a proper best man. How could he ever be a proper groom?

Raoul was wheeling his chair further away from the dance floor when he overheard two women talking behind one of the pillars. He stopped pushing and went very still, every muscle in his body tensing. Even his scalp pulled tight, making every hair stand up on end.

'Is that slim dark-haired girl Raoul Caffarelli's new mistress?'

'Quite a change from the last one.'

'I heard she's his physical therapist,' the first woman said. 'He must be more like his grandfather than the other two boys, eh?'

Raoul felt his stomach roil. He could not think of anything worse than being compared and likened to his grandfather.

The other woman made a sound of cynical assent. 'Sleeping with the help. Such a Vittorio thing to do. Mind you, that girl is obviously after Raoul for his money. I mean, he's good-looking and all that, but would you really want to spend the rest of your married life pushing him around in a chair?'

Raoul's stomach pitched again and a sickly sweat broke out over his brow.

'It would depend on whether he could still get it up.'

The two women shared a ribald cackle that grated on Raoul's nerves until he thought he would be physically sick.

'For that amount of money I wouldn't care if he *couldn't* get it up. Think of the other compensations: unlimited money to burn, jewellery, designer clothes to wear and luxury holidays to indulge in, not to mention that amazing château in France. What a life.'

'Yes, indeed,' the other woman said. 'No wonder she's got her claws in him so quickly. But how would he know if she loved him or not? Mind you, he probably doesn't care. Better to be with someone than no one when you're disabled. Got to feel sorry for him, though. I always thought he was the nicer of the three, didn't you?'

Raoul turned away in disgust. It was already happening. People were discussing him, talking about him, gossiping, conjecturing about him. It would be a thousand times worse once the press released all those photos of him from the ceremony.

The tragic invalid; the impotent, invalid brother.

He clenched his jaw so hard he thought his teeth would crack. How could his life have come to this?

People mocking him, feeling sorry for him, *pitying* him.

Remy swaggered over with a glass of whiskey in his hand. 'You're not out there to see their first dance. What's wrong with you?'

Raoul gave him a look that would have felled a three-hundred-year-old tree. 'You're not out there burning up the floor, either. No one taken your eye?'

'One of the bridesmaids is cute. I think her name is Chloe, but Poppy has warned her about me. I'm not making any inroads.'

'I feel your pain.'

Remy grinned. 'What's going on with you and your therapist?'

'She's *not* my therapist.'

Remy reared back as if Raoul had suddenly lunged at him with a sword. 'Whoa there, bro. Was that a raw nerve or what?'

'She's going back to London the day after tomorrow.'

'Why?'

'Because her time is up.'

Remy frowned. 'But she's helped you. You've done better with her than anyone else. You spent weeks in rehab and got nowhere. Four weeks with her and you're almost back on your feet. Why would you quit now?'

Raoul set his mouth. 'I'm not back on my feet.' *Half a minute standing without support is not back on my feet.* 'I might *never* get back on my feet.'

'You don't know that. You can't predict how you'll be. You know what the doctors said—it's a waiting game. It could take weeks or months or even years.'

'That's the whole point. I'm not prepared to wait.'

'So you're just going to send her away?'

'She's got nothing to offer me.'

'That's not what Dominique and Etienne say.'

Raoul narrowed his eyes to angry slits. 'Please don't tell me you've been gossiping about me with the domestic staff.' Was anyone *not* gossiping about him?

'They're not just domestic staff, they're like family to you. They care about you.'

'They're not paid to care about me.'

'Neither is Lily Archer, but she cares. She cares a lot.'

'What would you know?' Raoul said. 'You haven't even met her, or at least only in passing.'

'No, but I've spoken to everyone that has. She's like Poppy—warm, sweet and generous. I can't believe you're such a fool to walk away from someone like that.'

'Aren't you forgetting something?' Raoul gave his younger brother a cutting look. 'I can't walk away from her. I can't *walk* away from anyone.'

Remy put his whiskey glass down with a clunk. 'You're going to break her heart. Think very carefully before you do that.'

Raoul barked out a cynical laugh. 'I cannot believe you are preaching to me about breaking someone's heart. Have you taken a look at yourself lately? You haven't been with a woman more than a week in I don't know how long. That's fifty-two hearts you're breaking per year, right?'

Remy glowered at him. 'We're not talking about me here, we're talking about you.'

'I know what I'm doing.'

'We all think we know what we're doing…'

Raoul studied his younger brother's expression for a moment. 'Is everything all right with you?'

'Sure.' Remy gave him an overly bright smile. 'Everything's just fine.'

'Rafe told me you're dealing with Henri Marchand.'

'I've got it covered.'

'Sure?'

'Sure.'

Raoul wasn't so sure. There was something about Remy's expression that alerted him to an undercurrent of worry. Henri Marchand was a sly man, ruthless and conniving. He would sell his grandmother to make a buck. The only near relative he had was his daughter, Angelique, and God only knew what the price was on *her* head. He only hoped Remy wasn't the one who had to pay it. 'If ever you need an ear…'

Remy gave him a high five. 'I've got to get on the move. People to see. Deals to wheel.'

'What? You're not staying for the toss of the bouquet?'

Remy gave a visible shudder. 'Not my turn.' He landed a playful punch on Raoul's shoulder. 'You're next in line. *Ciao.*'

When Lily came back to the reception after freshening up in the ladies' room the crowd was jostling for the bridal bouquet toss. She stayed well back in the room, pretending a disinterest that was at odds with everything inside her. She would have loved to be up there pushing and shoving in the mad grab for the bouquet. It was such a high-spirited, girly thing to do.

But she watched from the sidelines, feeling disjointed, displaced, lonely.

'I've got it!'

'No, it's mine!'

'Get out of my way, you fat cow, it's mine.'

Lily moved aside as a wall of women surged towards her. She put up her hands to shield her face and suddenly found herself holding a bunch of flowers. Not just any bunch of flowers, either.

'Oh…'

Every single female eye in the room was on her. There was a massive round of applause and loud cheering.

'This is not meant for me.' Lily thrust the bouquet at the nearest pair of grasping hands. 'Excuse me…'

Raoul intercepted her as she left the reception room. His expression was dark and brooding, just like the first time she'd met him. His eyes were hard, his mouth was tight and his jaw was clenched. 'Did you do that on purpose?'

Lily felt a nervous flutter pass through her stomach. 'Pardon?'

'The bridal bouquet.' His gaze was bitter. 'A not-so-subtle hint to get me to come to the party, so to speak.'

'Party?' She looked at him blankly. 'What are you talking about?'

His mouth was so thin it looked almost cruel. 'You thought by catching that bouquet it would prompt me to ask you to stay with me, especially with the whole crowd watching and cheering.'

Lily opened and closed her mouth. *'What?'*

'It won't work, Lily.' His tone was hard, brittle, angry. 'I'm not asking you to stay with me. I'm asking you— no, strike that, I'm *telling* you—to leave.'

She could barely speak for the pain his words were causing. She hadn't been expecting him to ask her to stay but neither had she thought he would accuse her of such appallingly manipulative behaviour. Didn't he know her at all?

'You want me to leave, what, *now*?'

His expression was as cold and as hard as marble. 'It would seem rather stupid to fly back to France for forty-eight hours. Your contract with me is over. Consider your work with me done.'

Lily swallowed a painful lump in her throat. But her pride made it terribly important not to show how devastated she was by his heartless dismissal. Surely he could have done it differently? Given her some hope. Left things open-ended.

But no, he had cut her loose.

Cancelled her.

Finished with her.

'Right... Well, then, I guess this is goodbye.'

'Yes.' His answer was clipped. Decisive. Final.

Lily gave him one last smile, her bravest, unaffected, 'my heart isn't breaking into a thousand pieces' smile. 'I think you're a really lovely person, Raoul. I hope you get better. But, even if you don't, I want you to know that there are lots of really decent and genuine women out there who would be happy with you just the way you are.'

Something moved in his eyes. A muscle ticked in his cheek. She held her breath, wondering if he was going to change his mind.

The silence stretched…

But then an impenetrable mask came back down over his features. 'Goodbye, Lily.' And then he was gone.

The silence stretched.

The final, immaterial words came back down that line between... Gradually, he looked up at her, gazing...

CHAPTER THIRTEEN

'HAVE YOU HEARD how the honeymooners are doing?' Dominique asked as she poured Raoul's coffee two weeks later.

'They got back from Barbados yesterday.'

There was a little silence.

'Have you heard from Mademoiselle Archer?'

He clenched his teeth. 'No. Why should I? I'm just another client. Our time is over. She did all she could for me and it wasn't enough.'

Dominique pursed her lips in thought. 'Love is a funny thing. It can smack you in the face or it can slowly sneak up on you. But what you should never do is walk away from it. You might not get another chance.'

Raoul gave her a sour look. 'Is this a veiled way of hastening your retirement? I thought you wanted to work until you were sixty.'

'You love her. I know you do. I'm a Frenchwoman; I know about these things.'

'You're my housekeeper, not my life coach. I do not pay you to comment on my private life.'

'Mademoiselle Archer doesn't see the chair when she sees you. She just sees you, just like you see her without her scars.'

Raoul felt a lump come up in his throat. He'd been fighting this wretched loneliness for days. The château was oppressive without Lily here. The days were too long, the nights even more so. But how could he ask her to be with him? She would be signing up for a lifetime of caring.

That's what love is all about. Caring. Commitment.

Seeing Lily catching that bouquet at Rafe and Poppy's wedding had made him panic. He had done what he always did when he felt cornered—he had pushed back. Hard. Cruelly.

He had felt so trapped with everyone cheering and nudging each other. He'd felt claustrophobic, pressured, hemmed in at how everyone seemed to be waiting for him to come forward to claim Lily. He didn't want to be some sort of circus pony. He wanted time to think about what he would be asking her to do.

He wanted her.

He wanted it all: the caring and the commitment, the hope of children.

He wanted Lily so much it was an ache in his bones but he felt like he was going to ruin her life if he asked her to marry him.

What if she finds someone else?

His gut churned at the thought of someone else making love to her. Someone too rough and selfish, someone who wasn't sensitive and understanding about her scars. They would destroy her confidence, her self-esteem. She would go back to being that shy, prickly girl who hid behind layers of unflattering clothes.

You love her.

Of course he loved her. He had fallen in love with her the first time he had kissed her. Something had shifted inside him. And he couldn't shift it back. Making love with her had settled it once and for all.

He loved her and was always going to, chair or no chair.

Was it too late to ask her? Would she forgive him for pushing her away so publicly and so painfully? Everyone had been watching their interaction. He couldn't have chosen a worse place to bring things to an end. Was that why she had kept her features so stoic? So controlled? Had he broken her heart as Remy had warned?

Was it too late to undo that damage?

He looked up at his housekeeper. 'I'm going to London for a few days.'

Dominique beamed. 'I've already packed for you.'

He tried to frown at her but he couldn't quite pull it off. 'You did *what*?'

'I did it two weeks ago. I knew you would come to your senses. You're a good man. The *only* man for Lily. She won't be happy with anyone else and neither will you.'

Lily was filing paperwork when Valerie came into her office. 'You should've left an hour ago. You don't have to work overtime every day. You'll burn out.'

'I'm happy working.' Lily closed the drawer. *It distracts me. It's not like I've got anything better to do except sit at home and cry bucket loads of tears.*

'Has he called?'

Lily stiffened. 'Has who called?'

'You know who.'

She let out a rattling sigh. 'No. He won't. He's too stubborn. Once he makes up his mind, that's it. Game over.'

Valerie gave her a thoughtful look. 'He's been good for you. I've seen the change, Lily. Your clothes, your hair, that little touch of make-up. You look good.'

If only I felt good.

'Thanks.' Lily gave her a brief smile.

'Well, I'm off home.' Valerie gave a tired yawn. 'Thank God it's Friday. It's been a long week.'

It's been a lifetime.

Lily walked home even though the first chill of autumn had sharpened the air. It was another way to pass the time. It was an hour each way but she didn't mind the exercise. It was soothing to put one foot in front of the other and let her mind drift. She thought of Raoul even though she always made a promise to herself when she set off that she wouldn't. It was like a default setting inside her head. Her thoughts kept going back to him no matter how many distractions she put in the way.

She had even started imagining she saw him. Only two days ago she had seen a dark-haired man in a wheelchair at Piccadilly Circus. She'd blinked, her heart slamming against her ribcage, but when she had got closer she'd realised it was someone else.

Was that how her life was going to be now? Always wishing, hoping he would magically appear?

'Lily.'

Now she was hearing his voice. Maybe she really was nuts. Crazy.

Crazy in love.

'Lily. Wait.'

She spun around to see Raoul coming towards her. Her heart gave a lurch. She blinked. No, it was him. She wasn't dreaming. He was in his chair but he had a pair of crutches balanced along one side.

'Raoul...' Her voice was little more than a breath of sound.

He looked gorgeous, tired but gorgeous. He'd had his hair cut for the wedding but right now it looked like he hadn't combed it with anything but his fingers.

'I guess I should be on a white horse or something.' He gave her a lopsided smile. 'That's how it always happens in the fairytales, isn't it? I don't think I've read any with a guy showing up in a wheelchair, have you?'

Lily felt a bubble of hope swell in her chest. 'No, but that's not to say it couldn't happen. It's a fairytale, after all. Anything could happen.'

His gaze drank her in. There was a sudden brightness in his eyes and she almost forgot to breathe. 'Will you forgive me for telling you to leave the way I did?'

'You're apologising?'

His mouth tilted. 'I guess I am. How about that?'

'I forgive you.'

He let out a breath as if he'd been holding it in for ever. 'I was so wrong to react like that. It's a bad habit I have. I've been doing it since I was a kid. Pushing people away, hurting people before I get hurt. It's pathetic. It has to stop.'

'I've done it, too,' Lily said softly.

'I panicked at the wedding. I saw all those people staring at us. At *me*. I overheard two women earlier talking about us. It was awful. I couldn't get it out of my head. I couldn't bear the thought of people thinking you were with me out of pity.' He let out another breath. 'When I saw you holding that bouquet I shut down. It was like a reflex.'

'I didn't do it on purpose,' she said. 'I was trying to avoid it but it practically hit me in the face.'

Raoul smiled. 'Like love, *oui*? I have it on good authority that it can either sneak up on you or smack you in the face. I think it's been a bit of both.'

That bubble of hope in Lily's chest was growing by the second. 'What are you saying?'

'I love you,' he said. 'I've never said that to anyone other than my parents.'

She felt her own eyes fill with tears. She dropped to her knees in front of him and, wrapping her arms around him, buried her head against his chest. 'I love you, too.'

Raoul stroked her silky head as it lay pressed against his heart. 'I'm the one who is supposed to be kneeling in front of you. We're really murdering this fairytale thing, aren't we?'

Lily lifted her head to look at him. 'I can't believe you're here. I keep thinking I'm going to wake up and discover it's all been a dream.'

He stroked a finger down her cheek. 'You are my dream, *ma petite*. My dream come true. I know I'm not ideal husband material. I'm not going to be great at putting the garbage out or changing light bulbs. But, what the hell, I can pay people to do that. So will you marry me?'

Lily smiled through her tears. 'Yes.' She threw her arms around him again and hugged him tightly. 'Yes. Yes. *Yes.*'

Raoul lifted her chin up so he could see her face, her beautiful, loving face. 'You are the best thing that ever happened to me. I've hated every minute of being in this chair but if I hadn't been in it I would never have met you. I can't even imagine how awful my life would have been without you in it. I was physically able but emotionally crippled. You've made me see how important it is to be whole emotionally.' He wiped at his eyes with the back of one of his hands. 'Look, I'm even able to cry now.'

Lily tenderly blotted the pathway of his tears with a series of kisses. 'I love you. I love you. I love you.'

He captured her face in his hands and looked deep into her shining eyes. 'I can't carry you over the threshold, but do you think you could perch on my lap instead?'

Lily got up from the footpath and sat on his lap, winding her arms around his neck. 'Are we going to ride off into the sunset now?'

'You bet we are.' He grinned at her. 'Hold on, *ma chérie*. You're in for one hell of a ride.'

* * * * *

NEVER GAMBLE WITH A CAFFARELLI

BY
MELANIE MILBURNE

To my dear friend Heather Last, whom I met on the first day of kindergarten a very long time ago!

Thank you for always being my friend and for being one of the first people to say:

'You should write!' Much love. xx

CHAPTER ONE

'WHAT DO YOU mean you *lost* it?' Angelique stared at her father in abject horror.

Henri Marchand gave a negligent shrug but she could see his Adam's apple moving up and down as if he'd just had to swallow something unpleasant. But then, losing her late mother's ancestral home in the highlands of Scotland in a poker game in Las Vegas was about as bitter a flavour as you could taste, Angelique supposed.

'I was doing all right until Remy Caffarelli tricked me into thinking he was on a losing streak,' he said. 'We played for hours with him losing just about every hand. I thought I'd clean him up once and for all. I put down my best hand in a winner-takes-all deal but then he went and trumped it.'

Angelique felt her spine turn to ice and her blood heat to boiling. 'Tell me you did *not* lose Tarrantloch to Remy Caffarelli.' He was her worst enemy. The one man she would do anything to avoid—to avoid even thinking about!

'I'll win it back.' Her father spouted the problem gambler's credo with arrogant confidence. 'I'll challenge him to another game. I'll up the stakes. He won't be able to resist another—'

'And lose even *more*?' She threw him an exasperated

look. 'He set you up. Can't you see that? He's always had you in his sights but you made it a hundred times worse, sabotaging his hotel development in Spain. How could you have fallen for such a trick?'

'I'll outsmart him this time. You'll see. He thinks he's so clever but I'll get him back where it *really* hurts.'

Angelique rolled her eyes and turned away. Her stomach felt as if it had been scraped out with a rusty spoon. How could her father have lost her beloved mother's ancestral home to Remy Caffarelli? Tarrantloch wasn't even his to lose! It was supposed to be held in trust for her until she turned twenty-five, less than a year from now.

Her sanctuary. Her private bolthole. The one place she could be herself without hundreds of cameras flashing in her face.

Gone. Lost. Gambled away.

Now it was in the hands of her mortal enemy.

Oh, how Remy would be gloating! She could picture him in her mind: that cocky smirk of victory on his sensual mouth; those dark espresso-brown eyes glinting.

Oh, how her blood boiled!

He would be strutting around the whole of Europe telling everyone how he had finally got the better of Henri Marchand.

The bitter rivalry between her father and the Caffarellis went back a decade. Remy's grandfather Vittorio had been best friends and business partners with her father, but something had soured the relationship and at the last minute Henri had pulled out of a major business development he had been bankrolling for Vittorio. The Caffarellis' financial empire had been severely compromised, and the two men hadn't spoken a word to each other since.

Angelique had long expected it would be Remy who would pursue her father for revenge and not one of his brothers. Of the three Caffarelli brothers, Remy had had the most to do with his grandfather, but their relationship wasn't affectionate or even close. She suspected Remy was after his grandfather's approval, to win his respect, something neither of his older brothers had been able to do in spite of creating their own massive fortunes independent of the family empire.

But Angelique had clashed with Remy even before the fallout between their families and his dealings with her father. She thought him spoilt and reckless. He thought her attention-seeking. The eight-year difference in their ages hadn't helped, although she was the first to admit she hadn't been an easy person to be around, particularly after her mother had died.

Angelique turned back to her father who was washing the bitter taste of defeat down with a generous tumbler of brandy. 'Mum's probably spinning in her grave—and her parents and grandparents along with her. How could you be so…so *stupid*?'

Henri's eyes hardened and his thin lips thinned and whitened. 'Watch your mouth, young lady. I am your father. You will not speak to me as if I am an imbecile.'

She squared her shoulders and steeled her spine. 'What are you going to do? Call me a whole lot of nasty names like you did to Mum? Verbally and emotionally abuse me until I take an overdose just to get away from you?'

The silence was thick, pulsing, almost vibrating with menace.

Angelique knew it was dangerous to upset her father. To mention what must never be mentioned.

She had spent her childhood walking around on tiptoe to avoid triggering his ire. His temper could be vicious. As a young child she had witnessed how her mother's self-esteem had been eroded away, leaving her a wilted shadow of her former self.

But, while her father had never raised a hand either to her mother or to Angelique, the potential threat of it was there all the same. It hovered in the atmosphere. It crawled along her skin like a nasty, prickly-footed insect.

In the early years Angelique had tried hard to please him but nothing she had ever done had been good enough, or at least not good enough for his impossibly exacting standards.

In the end she had decided to do the opposite. Since the age of seventeen she had deliberately set out to embarrass him. To shock him. That was why she had pursued her career as a swimsuit model so determinedly. She knew how much it annoyed and embarrassed him that his little girl's body was displayed in magazines, catalogues and billboards all over Europe. She had even deliberately courted scandals in the press, not caring that they further cemented her reputation as a wild, spoilt little rich girl who loved nothing more than to party, and to party hard.

'If you're not careful I will disinherit you.' Her father issued the threat through clenched teeth. 'I will give every penny away to a dog's home.'

Angelique would have said, "Go on. Do it," but the fortune he threatened to give away had actually belonged to her mother. And she was going to do her darned hardest to get back what was rightfully hers.

Starting now.

The desert of Dharbiri was one of Remy's favourite places. One of his friends from his boarding-school days, Talib Firas Muhtadi, was a crown prince of the ancient province. The golden stretch of endless wind-rippled sands, the lonely sound of the whistling, pizza-oven-hot air; the vibrant colours of the sunset; the sense of isolation and the almost feudal laws and customs were such a stark change from his thoroughly modern twenty-first-century life.

No alcohol. No gambling. No unchaperoned women.

He loved his fast-paced life—there was absolutely no doubt about that—it was just that now and again he felt the need to unplug himself from it and recharge his batteries.

The hot, dry air was such a contrast to the chill of autumn that had come early back in Italy where he had spent a couple of days with his grandfather. No matter the season, Vittorio was a difficult person to be around, bitter and even at times violent. But Remy liked the sense of power it gave him to drop in with-out notice—which he knew annoyed the hell out of his grandfather—stay a couple of days and then breeze off without saying goodbye.

But while Remy loved Italy it was hard to decide where he felt most at home. His French-Italian heritage, on top of his English boarding-school education, had more or less made him a citizen of the world. Up until now he hadn't really had a base to call home. He'd lived in and out of suitcases and hotel suites. He liked that he didn't know where he was going to be from one week to the next. He would pick up a scent like a foxhound and go after a good deal. And nail it.

He liked to move around the globe, picking up busi-ness here and there, wheeling and dealing, winning the unwinnable.

He grinned.

Like winning that winner-takes-all hand with Henri Marchand in Vegas. It had been a masterstroke of genius on his part. He didn't like to be *too* smug about it but, truth be told, he did actually feel a little bit proud of himself.

He'd hit Henri Marchand where it hurt: he had taken that double-crossing cheat's Scottish castle off him.

Victory was more than sweet—it was ambrosial.

Remy had come out to Dharbiri so he could reflect on his prize. Tarrantloch was one of the most beautiful and prestigious estates in Scotland. It was isolated and private. It would make a fabulous base for him—a place he could call home. It would be the perfect haven to hunt, shoot, fish and hang out with his friends during his infamous week-long parties. He could have gone straight there to take ownership but he didn't want to appear *too* eager to take possession.

No, it was better to let Henri Marchand—and his spoilt little brattish daughter Angelique—think this was just like any other deal done and dusted.

There would be plenty of time to rub her retroussé little nose in it.

He couldn't wait.

Getting a flight to Dharbiri was hard enough. Getting access to where Remy Caffarelli was staying was like trying to get through an airport security check-in with a fistful of grenades or an AK47 in her hand luggage.

Angelique ground her teeth for the tenth time. Did she *look* like a security threat?

'I need to speak to Monsieur Caffarelli. It's a matter of great urgency. A family…er, crisis.'

Her family crisis.

The attendant on the reception desk was cool and disbelieving. Angelique could only suppose he was used to fielding off droves of female wannabes who would give an arm or a leg—or both—to have a few minutes with the staggeringly rich, heart-stoppingly gorgeous Remy Caffarelli.

As if *she* would ever sink so low.

'Monsieur Caffarelli is not available right now.' The attendant gave her a look that immediately categorised her as just another hopeful, starry-eyed wannabe. 'He is dining with the Crown Prince and his wife, and according to royal protocol he cannot be interrupted unless it is a matter of utmost political urgency.'

Angelique mentally rolled her eyes. It looked like she would have to try another tactic; find some other way of getting under the radar. But she was good at that sort of thing.

Outsmarting. Outmanoeuvring. Outwitting.

She smiled to herself.

That was her speciality.

It didn't take long to bribe a junior housemaid who recognised Angelique from a magazine shoot she'd done a couple of months ago. All it took was an autograph to get access to Remy's suite.

The young housemaid had mentioned how important it was Angelique wasn't seen in Remy's room other than by Remy himself. Apparently there were strict protocols on women and men socialising without appropriate supervision. As much as it annoyed her to have to hide until she knew for sure it was Remy entering the suite, Angelique decided to play things safe.

She scanned the room for a suitable hiding place.

Behind the curtains? No; she would be seen from outside.

The bathroom? No; a housemaid might come in to clean up the appalling mess Remy had left there.

Angelique looked at the wall-to-ceiling wardrobe running along one wall.

A little clichéd perhaps…

But perfect!

CHAPTER TWO

REMY FELT A strange sense of disquiet as soon as he entered his suite; unease; a sense that the place was not quite the way he had left it. He had cancelled the evening housekeeping visit because he hated people fussing around him all the time. Surely they hadn't gone against his wishes?

He closed the door and stilled.

Waited.

Listened.

His gaze scanned the luxuriously appointed suite for any signs of a disturbance. His laptop was still open on the desk and the screensaver was the same as when he'd left to have dinner. The can of soda he had half-drunk was still sitting where he'd left it, and a ring of moisture from the condensation had pooled around the bottom.

His gaze went further, to the open door of the palatial bedroom. The bed cover was slightly crumpled from where he had sat while he'd taken a call from one of his office staff in Monte Carlo. One of the towels he'd used when he'd showered was still lying on the floor. The clothes he'd worn earlier were in a messy pile nearby.

It was jet lag, that was all. He gave himself a mental shake, shrugged off his dinner jacket and threw it over the arm of the nearest sofa. He reached up and loosened his tie. It had been feeling a little tight all evening, but rules were rules, and he was happy to go along with them because out here he could forget he was the youngest son of the Caffarelli dynasty.

Here there was no one measuring him up against his older brothers or his impossible-to-please grandfather.

Out here he was as free as a desert falcon. He had the next few days to kick back and chill out in one of the hottest places on earth. Life could be pretty good when *he* was in the driving seat.

Angelique held her breath for so long she thought she would faint. But she knew she had to wait until Remy was well and truly inside the suite and in a relaxed mood before she came out of the closet—so to speak.

Not that there were too many of his clothes *in* the closet.

Most of them seemed to be on the floor of the bedroom or spilling haphazardly out of his lightweight travel bag. The en suite bathroom she'd scoped out earlier was just as bad. He'd left a dark ring of stubble in the marble basin when he'd shaved and there had been yet another wet towel on the floor.

It confirmed what she already knew: Remy Caffarelli was a spoilt playboy with more money than sense who had grown up with servants dancing around to satisfy his every whim.

It was a tiny bit ironic of her to point the finger at such a shiny black kettle as Remy when she too had grown up surrounded by wealth. But at least she knew how to pick up after herself and she could cook a three-course gourmet meal with one arm and her appetite tied behind her back.

Remy had never even boiled an egg.

He had probably never even boiled a kettle!

Angelique clenched her fists and her jaw.

He just boiled her blood.

She heard him moving about the suite. She heard the ring pull of a can being opened. It couldn't be alcohol, as this was a totally dry province. There were stiff penalties for bringing in or consuming contraband liquor.

She heard the click of his laptop being activated and then the sound of his fingers typing on the keyboard. She heard him a give a deep, throaty chuckle as if something he'd just read online or in an email had amused him.

Her belly gave a little flip-flop movement.

He had a *very* nice laugh. He had a *very* nice smile. He had a *very* nice mouth. She had spent most of her teenage years fantasising about that mouth.

Stop it right now, you silly little fool!

You are not going to think about his mouth, or any other part of his totally hot, totally amazing body.

Just as Angelique was about to step out of the wardrobe, she heard a sharp, businesslike knock at the door of the suite. Her heart gave a jerky kick against her breastbone.

Was he expecting someone?

One of his star-struck wannabes, perhaps? Oh God! If she had to listen to him having bed-wrecking sex with some bimbo who had been smuggled into his room…

'Monsieur Caffarelli?' an official-sounding voice called out. 'We wish to have a word with you.'

She heard Remy's footsteps as he moved across to open the door. 'Yes?' he said in that charming, 'I'm happy to help you' way he had down to a science.

The official cleared his throat as if he found what he was about to say quite difficult. 'We have received some information that you have a young woman in your room.'

'*Pardon?*' Remy's predominantly French accent made Angelique's belly do another little tumble.

'As you are well aware, Monsieur Caffarelli, the dictates of our province state that no single woman must be unchaperoned with a man unless she is his sister or his wife. We have reason to believe you have someone in your room who does not fit either of those categories.'

'Are you out of your mind?' Remy sounded incredulous. 'I know the rules. I've been coming here long enough. I would never do anything to insult Sheikh Muhtadi. Surely his officials—including you—know that?'

'A junior member of our housekeeping staff has tearfully confessed to allowing a young woman access to your room,' the official said. 'We wish to check on whether this is true or not.'

'Go on. Check.' Remy sounded supremely, arrogantly confident. 'You won't find anyone in here but me.'

Angelique heard the door of the suite being flung open and her breath screeched to a skidding halt in her throat. Her heart was pounding like a sledgehammer on a rocky surface. It actually felt like it was going to leap out of her chest. She shrank back inside the closet, hoping the shadows of the space would conceal her. She even closed her eyes, just like a little child playing hide and seek, thinking that if she couldn't see them, they couldn't see her.

She heard firm footsteps moving about the suite, doors being opened and closed. The curtains were swished back. Even the drawers of Remy's desk were opened and then shut.

A drawer? They thought she could fit in a *drawer*?

'See?' Remy's tone had a touch of irritability to it now. 'There's no one here but me.'

'The closet.' The more senior of the two officials spoke. Angelique could almost picture him giving a brisk nod towards her hidey-hole. 'Check the bedroom closet.'

'Are you joking?' Remy coughed out a laugh. 'Do you *really* think I would do something as clichéd as that?'

The mirrored door slid back on its tracks. Angelique raised her right hand and gave a little fingertip wave. 'Surprise!'

Remy could not believe his eyes. He blinked to make sure he wasn't imagining things. That could *not* be Angelique Marchand in his closet.

He opened his eyes and looked again.

It was.

'What the hell are you doing?' He glared at her so fiercely his eyes ached. 'What are the hell are you doing in my room? In my closet?'

She stepped out of the closet as if she was stepping out on to one of the catwalks she frequented all over Europe. She moved like a sinuous cat, all legs, arms, high, pert breasts and pouting full-lipped mouth. Her distinctive grey-blue eyes gave him a reproving look. 'That's not a very nice welcome, Remy. I thought you had better manners than that.'

Remy had never thought he had a temper until he'd had to deal with Angelique. He could feel his rage building up inside him like a cauldron on the boil. No one made him angrier than she did. She was willful, spoilt and a little too determined to get her own way. Did she have no sense of protocol or politeness? What the hell was she doing here? And in his room?

Did she have any idea of the trouble she could get him into?

She had made him look like a liar. Trust was everything in a place like Dharbiri. He might be a friend of the Crown Prince but flouting the rules out here was a definite no-no, friend or foe.

He could be deported.

Charged.

The blood suddenly ran ice-cold in his veins.

Flogged.

'You had better have a very good explanation for why you're in my room,' he said through gritted teeth.

She swept her thick, wavy, glossy black mane of hair over one slim shoulder. 'I came to see you about my house. You *have* to give it back.' She nailed him with a look that was diamond-hard. 'I'm not leaving your side until you sign me over the deeds to Tarrantloch.'

'Monsieur Caffarelli,' the older official spoke in a stern 'don't mess with me' tone. 'Would you please verify if this young woman is personally known or related to you? If not we will have her immediately evicted and the authorities will deal with her accordingly.'

Deal with her? Remy didn't like the sound of that. As much as he hated Angelique, he could not stand by and see her come to any harm. He took a deep breath and put on his best 'let's be cool about this' smile. 'I'm afraid there's been a little mix-up. I had no idea my fiancée was going to surprise me by turn—'

'Your fiancée?' Angelique and the senior official spoke in unison.

Remy gave the official a conciliatory smile. 'We've been trying to keep our engagement a secret. The press make such of fuss of this stuff at home.' He gave a Gallic shrug. 'You know how it is.'

The official straightened his shoulders, his expression as formal as a drill sergeant. 'This young woman may well be your fiancée, but it is against the laws of our land for her to be alone with you without a chaperone.'

'So, we'll get a chaperone,' Remy said. 'She won't be with me long in any case, will you, *ma chérie*?'

Angelique's eyes narrowed to hairpin slits but her voice had a false sort of sing-song quality to it that grated on Remy's already overstretched nerves. 'Only for as long as it takes, *mon trésor.*'

The official puffed himself up to his not considerable height. 'Due to the circumstances of your fiancée's… ahem…surprise visit, neither of you will be permitted to leave the province until you are legally married.'

'Married?' Angelique had joined Remy in a choked gasp of horror.

'You're joking?' Angelique gaped at the official with wide shocked eyes. 'You *have* to be joking!'

'He's not joking,' Remy muttered just low enough for her to hear it. 'Go along with it. Try and keep cool.'

Keep cool? Who was he kidding? He didn't feel cool. He'd never had to think so fast on his feet in his life. Pretending she was his fiancée had just popped into his head. And it still might not be enough to get them over the line.

'I'm not marrying you!' She flashed him a livid, blue-lightning look. 'I'd rather die!'

'Yes, well, you just might get that choice,' he said. 'We're not in France, Italy or England right now. Didn't you check out the Smart Traveller website before you came?'

Her throat rose and fell. 'I didn't think. I just…'

'Not thinking is something you do remarkably well.' Remy gave her a dressing-down look. 'You've made a lifetime's work of it.'

Her small hands clenched into tight fists and her eyes gave him another deadly glare. 'I thought you were best friends with the Crown Prince. Can't *he* do something?'

'Afraid not.' Remy had already had this debate with his friend during university. 'The royal family have a lot of power but not enough to overrule laws of the elder tribesmen of the province.'

'But that's ridiculous!'

Remy gave her a cautionary look. 'If you're going to stand there spluttering insults like a Roman candle firecracker, I'm not going to lay down my life for you.'

She opened and closed her mouth, seemingly lost for words. Not that it would last. He knew how quick and sharp her tongue could be. She always tried to get the last word.

He was the only person in her life who wouldn't let her have it.

'Monsieur Caffarelli?' The official stepped forward. 'We must leave now to make the necessary arrangements to conduct the ceremony first thing in the morning. We will arrange alternative accommodation for your fiancée. You will understand that she is not permitted to spend the night in your room.'

'But of course.' Remy gave him another charming smile. *I don't want her here in any case.* 'I understand completely. I sincerely apologise for my fiancée's impulsive behaviour. She is a little wilful and headstrong at times, but once we are married she will soon learn to toe the line. I'll make absolutely sure of it.'

Remy smiled to himself when he saw the two red-hot spots of colour pooling in Angelique's cheeks. She was standing rock-steady but he knew her well enough to know she was beyond livid with him. He could see it in her stormy eyes and in the clenched posture of her jaw. Too bad they had to have a chaperone. He would have quite liked to see what that anger looked like when it was finally unleashed.

Angelique turned to look at the senior official, her expression now meek and demure, those thick, impossibly long eyelashes batting up and down for good measure. 'Please may I have a private word with my, er, fiancé? Perhaps you could chaperone us from the lounge. We'll leave the door open here. Would that be acceptable?'

The official gave a formal nod and indicated with a jerk of his head for his sidekick to follow him out to the lounge area.

Remy got the full, fiery force of Angelique's gaze as she swung around to face him once the officials had gone. 'There's no point glaring at me like that,' he said before she could let fly. 'You're the one who brought this about.'

She visibly shook with rage. It reminded him of the shuddering of a small two-stroke engine on the back of a dingy.

'Fiancée?' She sounded like she was choking on the word. 'Why couldn't you have said I was your sister or…or even your cousin?'

'Because the whole world knows I'm one of three brothers who were orphaned when we were young. And since both of my parents were only children, I don't have any cousins.'

Her eyes fired another round of hatred at him. 'Did you have to make that comment about controlling me as if I'm some sort of waspish virago? You did it deliberately, didn't you? You just can't help yourself. Any chance you get, you like to thrust home the chauvinist dagger.'

Right now that wasn't the only thing Remy wanted to thrust home. He had always tried to ignore the sexual attraction he felt for her. In the past she had always been banned by his family or too involved with someone else. But it was hard to ignore the tingling that was stirring in his loins right now.

And if they had been in any other place he might well have done something about it.

'Got under your skin, did it, *ma petite*?'

'You set my father up, didn't you?' Her expression was tight with barely compressed rage. 'I know how your mind works. You wanted to hit him where it hurt most because of that stupid deal in Ibiza. But I'm not letting you get away with it. I'll fight you tooth and nail until you give me back my house.'

Remy gave her a cool and totally unaffected look because he knew how much it would annoy her. 'Fight me all you like. There's no way I'm giving it back. I won it fair and square. Your father knew what he was getting into—he knew the risks he was taking. But I must say, I think it's pretty pathetic of him to send you out here to try and butter me up.'

Her head jerked back. 'You think *that's* why I'm here? As if I would ever sink so low as that. You're the last man on earth I would ever consider seducing.'

'Likewise, *ma coeur*; you don't float my boat, either.'

A flicker of uncertainty came and went in her gaze and her perfectly aligned, beautiful white teeth sank into her bottom lip.

But just for a nanosecond.

She suddenly pulled herself upright, like an abandoned hand puppet that had just been reconnected with a firm hand. 'And as for marriage… Well, that's just totally ridiculous. It's out of the question. I *won't* do it.'

'It'll just be a formality,' Remy said. 'We don't have to take this seriously. It probably won't even be recognised as legal back home. We'll just do what they require and then we'll leave. Simple.'

'*Simple?*' Her eyes shot their fury at him again. 'Tell me what about this is simple. We'll be married—' she gave a little shudder as if the word was anathema to her '—or at least, we will be on paper. I don't care if it's legal or not. I don't want to be married to you. I can't think of anything worse.'

He gave her a smile. 'We'll get it annulled as soon as we get back to Europe.'

'This is outrageous! This is a…a *disaster*!'

'Of your own making.' He used his 'too cool for school' tone again. He loved the way it triggered something feral in her. She went off like a bomb every time.

She flattened her mouth into a thin white line, her eyes looking murderous. 'This is *no*t my fault. This is *your* fault for being so determined to score points. You don't need Tarrantloch; your family have properties bigger and better than that all over the world. Why did you have to take the one thing I love more than anything else?'

Remy felt a little niggle of guilt. Just a niggle; nothing major. Nothing he couldn't ignore.

He'd set himself a goal and he'd achieved it.

That was the Caffarelli credo—goal; focus; win.

Remy could have taken any one of the businesses in the Marchand Holdings portfolio if he'd been so inclined, but Tarrantloch was the one thing he knew Henri

Marchand would regret losing the most. He had a score to settle with Henri that had nothing to do with his grandfather's dealings with him.

It was far more personal.

Remy had just about got the Ibiza development in the bag when an anonymous email had spooked the vendor. It hadn't been too hard to find out who had sent it. Henri Marchand was devious but not particularly smart at covering his tracks. Remy had sworn he would get revenge, no matter how long it took.

Tarrantloch was Henri Marchand's most valued, prized possession. It was his ultimate status symbol. Henri liked to play Laird of the Highlands with a coterie of his overfed, overindulged, overweight corporate cronies by his side.

The fact that his daughter—his only child and heir—fancied herself in love with the place didn't come into it at all.

Not even a niggly bit.

Remy was running a business, not a charity, and the one person in the world he felt the least charitable towards was Angelique Marchand.

'It's mine now. Get over it.' He refused to allow sentimentality to mess with his head. 'It's not like you'll be homeless. You live in Paris most of the year, don't you?'

Her expression was so rigid with anger he could see a muscle moving in and out in her cheek. 'I planned to live at Tarrantloch after my retirement.'

He whistled through his teeth. 'That's some seriously long-term planning. You're what, twenty-five?'

Her teeth made a grinding noise. 'Twenty-four. I'll be twenty-five next year in May.'

'So, what age do swimsuit models retire?' He couldn't

stop his gaze sweeping over her body. To say she had a knockout figure was a bit of an understatement.

More than a bit, actually.

He could not think of a body he found more delightful to look at. Distracting. He had been distracted by it for the last few years, and so too had just about everyone throughout Europe. He still remembered the first time he had driven past a billboard with the then-nineteen-year-old Angelique on it. She had been draped along the edge of an infinity pool in some exotic tropical location, wearing a couple of miniscule triangles of fabric that left just enough to the imagination to cause serious discomfort in his nether regions.

To say she had a traffic-stopping figure was putting it rather mildly.

'I want to branch out into other areas of the business,' she said.

'Such as?'

She glowered at him. 'I'm not going to discuss my career plans with you. You'll just rubbish them. You'll tell me I'm wasting my time or to go and get a real job or something.'

Remy felt that little niggle of guilt again. He hadn't been exactly encouraging of her plans to pursue a modelling career. When he'd first heard she was going to quit school to sign up with a modelling agency, he'd put aside his grandfather's ban on contact with her and had called and told her to reconsider.

But listening to advice was not something Angelique was particularly good at doing.

'Monsieur Caffarelli?' The official spoke from the open doorway. 'The room is now ready for your fiancée.' He turned to Angelique. 'If you will come this way, *mademoiselle*? We have two chaperones to accompany you.'

Angelique glared at Remy as she stalked past him. He caught a whiff of her signature fragrance as she went by. It hovered about his nostrils, enticing him to breathe in deep. He had always associated the smell of sweetpeas with her—strong, heady and colourful.

His brain snapped back to attention like an elastic band being flicked by a finger.

Within hours they would be man and wife.

Usually whenever the 'M' word was mentioned to him he had a standard, stock phrase: *over my dead body*.

But somehow—right here and now—it didn't have quite the same ring to it.

CHAPTER THREE

ANGELIQUE COULD NOT even close her eyes, let alone get to sleep. She spent most of the night pacing the floor, cursing Remy, *hating* him. How could he have done this to her? He couldn't have thought of a worse punishment.

Married.

To him of all people!

It didn't matter if it was legal or not. She had sworn she would *never* marry. She would never allow someone else to have that sort of control over her, to have that sort of *commitment* from her.

She had seen first-hand her mother's commitment. Kate Tarrant had taken her marriage vows way too seriously. She had been browbeaten and submissive from day one. She had toed the line. She had obeyed. She had given up her freedom and her sense of self.

Angelique would *never* do that.

Marriage and all it represented nauseated her. Unlike most girls her age, she couldn't even bear the thought of wedding finery. Who wanted to dress up like a meringue, be smothered in a veil and be given away like a parcel to some man who would spend the next fifty years treating her like a household slave?

There was a knock on the door and when she opened it she found a maid holding a tray with fresh fruit, rolls and steaming hot, rather unusually fragrant coffee. 'Your breakfast, *mademoiselle*.'

Was this the time to announce that—despite her half-French bloodline—she actually loathed coffee and could only ever face tea first thing in the morning?

Probably not.

Not long after that maid left, another one much older one arrived, carrying a massive armful of wedding finery which she informed Angelique she would help her get into in preparation for the ceremony at ten.

'I'm not wearing that!' Angelique said as the maid laid out an outfit that looked more like a circus tent. A particularly beautiful circus tent, however. On closer inspection she saw there were fine threads of gold delicately woven into the fabric and hundreds of diamonds were stitched across the bodice.

'These are the official bridal robes of the province,' the maid said. 'The Princess Royal was married in them in July. It is a great honour that you have been given permission to wear them.'

I can't believe I'm doing this, Angelique thought as she stood and was wrapped in the voluminous folds. The irony wasn't lost on her. She made a living out of wearing the minimum of fabric. Now she was being wrapped in metres of it like some sort of glittering present.

Her blood simmered.

It boiled.

How could it be possible that within a less than an hour she would be married to Remy Caffarelli?

'Are we done?'

'Just about.' The maid came at her with a denser than normal veil dripping with even more diamonds and a train that was at least five metres long.

'Oh no.' Angelique shied away. 'Not that.'

The maid gave her a pragmatic look. 'Do you want to get out of here or don't you?'

'Are you OK with this?' Crown Prince Talib Firas Muhtadi said to Remy as he finished his second cup of thick, rich, aromatic cardamom-scented coffee. 'Things are really unstable right now in our province. The tribal elders are notoriously difficult to negotiate with and highly unpredictable. It's best to do things their way just to be on the safe side. We don't want a major uprising over an incident like this. Best to nip it in the bud and keep everyone happy.'

Remy mentally rolled his eyes as he put his cup back down on the saucer. 'No big deal. It's just a formality, right? It's not like this marriage—' he made the quotation marks with his fingers '—will be recognised at home.'

Talib looked at him for a long moment without speaking.

'You're joking, right?' Remy said, feeling a chill roll down his spine like an ice cube. *Please be joking.*

'Marriage is a very sacred institution in our culture,' Talib said. 'We don't enter into it lightly, nor do we leave it unless there are very good reasons for it.'

What about total unsuitability?

Being polar opposites?

Hating each other?

'I fought it too, Remy,' Talib added. 'But it's only since I met and married Abby that I realised what I've been missing out on. Oh, and yes, the marriage will be considered legal in your country.'

Damn.

Double damn.

* * *

The first thought Remy had was it could be anyone under that traditional wedding dress and long veil and he would not be any the wiser. But he instantly knew it was Angelique because of the way the robes were shaking, as if her rage was barely contained within the diamond-encrusted tent of the fabric that surrounded her slim body.

And her eyes.

How could he not recognise those stormy grey-blue eyes? They flashed with undiluted loathing through the gauze of the veil as she came to stand beside him.

He suddenly had a vision of his oldest brother Rafe's wedding day only a few weeks ago. The ceremony had been very traditional, and his bride, Poppy Silverton, had been quite stunningly beautiful and unmistakably in love. So too had Rafe, which had come as a bit of a surprise to Remy. He'd always thought Rafe was the show-no-emotion, feel-no-emotion type, but he'd actually seen moisture in Rafe's eyes as he'd slipped the wedding band on Poppy's finger, and his face had been a picture of devotion and pride.

His other brother Raoul was heading down the altar too, apparently just before Christmas. His bride-to-be, Lily Archer, had been employed to help rehabilitate Raoul after a water-skiing accident which had left him in a wheelchair. Remy had never seen Raoul happier since he'd announced his engagement to Lily, which was another big surprise, given how physically active Raoul had always been. But apparently love made up for all of that.

Not that Remy would know or ever wanted to know about love. He'd had his fair share of crushes, but as to falling in love…

Well, that was something he stayed well clear of and he intended to keep doing so.

Loving someone meant you could lose them. They could be there one minute and gone the next.

Like his parents.

Remy sometimes found it hard even to remember what his mother and father had looked like unless he jogged his memory with a photo or a home video. He had been seven years old when they had died, and as each year passed his memories of them faded even further. Listening to their voices and seeing them moving about on those home videos still seemed a little weird, as if a tiny part of his brain recognised them as people he had once known intimately but who were now little more than strangers.

He had completely forgotten their touch.

But there was one touch he was not going to forget in a hurry.

As soon as the cleric asked Remy to join hands with Angelique, he felt a lightning zap shoot up his from his hand, travel from the length of his arm and straight to his groin as if she had touched him there with her bare hands. He hadn't touched her even when her father had brought her with him when he had socialised with Remy's grandfather in the years before their fall out. Being eight years older than her, Remy had occasionally been left with the task of entertaining her during one of his grandfather's soirées. Even as a young teenager she had shown the promise of great beauty. That raven-black hair, those bewitching eyes, those lissom limbs and budding breasts had been a potent but forbidden temptation.

He had always made a point of *not* touching her.

Would the cleric expect him to kiss her? Not that

the idea didn't hold a certain appeal, but Remy would rather kiss her in private than in front of a small group of conservative tribesmen.

After all, he didn't want to offend them.

Angelique's hand was tiny. His hand almost swallowed it whole. But then the whole of her was tiny. Dainty. He felt a primal stirring in his loins when he thought of what it might be like to enter her. To possess her. To feel her sexy little body grip him tightly…

Whoa, keep it in your trousers. Remember, this is just an on-paper marriage.

The cleric went through the vows and Remy recited his lines as if he were an actor reading them from a script. No big deal. They were just words. Meaningless words.

When Angelique came to her lines she coughed them out like a cat with fur balls. She almost choked on the promise to obey him.

'I now pronounce you man and wife.' The cleric gave Remy a man-to-man smile. 'You may lift the veil and kiss your bride.'

Angelique's eyes flickered with something that looked like panic. 'I'd really rather not.'

Remy didn't give her time to finish her sentence in case she blew their cover. Besides, he'd kissed dozens of women. All he had to do was plant a perfunctory kiss on her lips and step back. Everyone would be happy.

Easy.

He lifted the heavy veil from her face and planted his mouth on hers.

Angelique had spent years during her teens imagining this very moment—the first time Remy kissed her. She had imagined it when other dates were kissing her, closing her eyes and dreaming it was actually Remy's mouth moving on hers, his hands touching her, his body wanting her. Quite frankly, those mind-wanderings of hers had made some of those kisses—not to mention some of her sexual encounters—a little more bearable.

But not one of her imaginings came anywhere near to the real deal.

Remy didn't kiss sloppily or wetly or inexpertly.

He kissed with purpose and potency.

The firm warmth of his lips, the taste of him, the feel of him was so…so *intensely* male, so addictive, she couldn't stop herself from pushing up on tiptoe to keep the connection going. His mouth hardened and then she felt his tongue push against her lips just as she opened them.

His tongue slid into her mouth and found hers.

She heard him smother a groan as her tongue tangled with his.

She felt his body stir against her as he gripped her by the hips and pulled her flush against him.

She heard the cleric clear his throat. 'Ahem…'

Remy dropped his hands. He looked slightly stunned for a moment, but then he seemed to give himself a mental shake before he grinned charmingly and rather cheekily at the cleric. 'Almost forgot where I was for a moment.'

The cleric gave him an understanding smile. 'It is very good to see an enthusiastic couple. It bodes well for a happy and fulfilling marriage.'

Angelique ground her teeth. Remy was enjoying this much more than he should. She could see the glint in his eyes as they reconnected with hers. She gave him an 'I'll get you for this later' look but he just grinned even wider and gave her a wink.

'The Crown Prince and his wife have a put on a special banquet in honour of your marriage,' the cleric said.

Oh no! Don't tell me there's going to be a reception with speeches.

But as it turned out it was more like a party. A dry party. Which was a crying shame, as right now Angelique needed a glass of something alcoholic—make that two glasses and to hell with the calories—because she was now officially *a married woman*.

Arrrggh!

The reception room was as big as a football field, or so it appeared to Angelique. How many friends did Remy have out here, or had someone rented a crowd? There were at least a thousand people. Who had a wedding that big? It was ridiculous! It was like a wedding extravaganza, a showpiece of what a celebrity wedding reception should be. The room was decked out in the most amazing array of satin ribbons, balloons and sparkly lights that hung from the high ceiling like diamonds. They probably *were* diamonds, she thought as she glanced up at the chandelier above her head. *Yep, diamonds.*

They were led to the top table where Angelique was finally introduced to the Crown Prince's wife, Abby, a fellow Englishwoman who had met and fallen in love with Talib earlier that year. A royal baby was due in a few months, which Abby explained had given an extra boost to the celebrations. It seemed Dharbiri was in party mode and an event like this could on for days. *Great.*

Remy took her hand and led her out to the dance floor for the bridal waltz. 'Loosen up, Angelique. You feel like a shop-window mannequin in my arms.'

Angelique suppressed a glare. 'Get your hands off my butt.'

He smoothed his hand over her hip and then tugged her against him. 'That better?'

She looked at him with slitted eyes. 'We're supposed to be dancing, not making out.'

'I thought you'd be great at dancing.'

'I *am* great at dancing.'

'Then show me your footwork.'

Angelique moved in against him and let him take the lead. The music was romantic with a flowing rhythm so she let her body move in time with it. She started to feel like a princess at a ball, or a star contestant on one of those reality dance shows. They moved in perfect unison around the dance floor. The other couples—and there were hundreds—swarmed backwards to give them more room.

'Nice work,' Remy said once it was over. 'Maybe we should do that again some time.'

'You trod on my toe.'

'Did not.'

'Did so.'

He gave her a grin as he pinched her cheek. 'Smile, *ma chérie.*'

She smiled through clenched teeth. 'I want to scratch your eyes out.'

'Did I tell you how beautiful you looked?'

'I can't breathe in this dress. And I have no idea how I'm going to fit in the bathroom. They'll have to take the door off or something.'

He grinned again and tapped her gently on the end of the nose. 'You'll find a way.'

Angelique let out a breath as she watched him turn

to speak to another guest. There were times when Remy took his charm into very dangerous territory…

'You have to try this,' Remy said as he came over with a loaded plate from the banquet a little while later.

Angelique breathed in the delicious smell of lamb with herbs and garlic. She couldn't stop her gaze from devouring everything on his plate. Along with the juicy lamb pieces, there was a couscous salad and some sort of potato dish and flatbread. The carbs would be astronomical. 'No.' She gave him a tight smile for the sake of anyone watching. 'I'm not hungry.'

'Here.' He forked a piece of lamb and held it in front of her mouth. 'You have to try this. It's amazing.'

'I don't want it.'

His eyes locked on hers, hard, determined. Implacable. 'Open your mouth.'

Angelique's belly shifted at his commanding tone but she was not going to let him win this. This was *her* battle, not his. She was the one who had to keep her body in top shape for her career. She had been counting calories and carbs since she had landed her first contract. Since before that, actually. It was the only thing she could control. She knew what she had to do to keep her body perfect. She was not going to allow anyone, and in particular Remy Caffarelli, to sabotage her efforts.

She gave him a flinty look. 'I said I'm not hungry.'

'You're lying.'

She felt the penetrating probe of his dark-brown eyes as they tussled with hers. Heat came up from deep inside her, a liquid molten heat that had nothing to do with food but everything to with hunger.

Sexual hunger.

Angelique knew one taste would not be enough. She

would end up bingeing on him and then where would that get her?

His kiss had already done enough damage.

And that dirty dance routine...

She could not afford to let herself be that vulnerable again. She was in control of her passions. She did not slavishly follow her desires. She had self-control and discipline.

She did *not* want him or his food or his fancy footwork.

Angelique pulled out an old excuse but a good one; she was nothing if not a great actress when the need arose. She put a hand to her temple and gave him a part-sheepish, part-apologetic look. 'I'm sorry, Remy, it's just I've been fighting a tension headache ever since I got up. Well, actually, I didn't get up, because I didn't go to bed in the first place. I couldn't sleep a wink.'

He studied her for a moment as if weighing up whether to believe her or not. 'Maybe you're dehydrated. Have you had enough to drink?'

'I could kill for a glass of wine.'

He gave her a wry look. 'You could get killed for having it.'

Angelique felt a cold hand of panic clutch at her insides. 'We *are* safe now, aren't we? I mean now we're—' she gave a mental gulp '—married?'

Remy's expression sobered for a moment, which made that fist of panic grip a little tighter. 'We're safe as long as we act as if this is a real marriage. It would be foolish to let our guard down until we're on the plane home.'

Angelique swallowed as she cast a nervous eye over the crowd of people who had joined in the wedding celebration. They looked friendly and innocuous enough, but how could she be sure one or more of them weren't waiting for her to make a slip up?

Her stomach pitched with dread.

Never in her wildest dreams had she ever thought something like this would happen. She had wanted a face-to-face with Remy. She hadn't given a thought to where he was or whom he was with or whether it would be convenient or politic *or safe*. She had focused solely on her goal to get him to hand back the deeds to Tarrantloch.

Now she was pretending to be married to him.

Not pretending, a little voice reminded her. *You* are *married to him*.

Angelique turned back to look up at Remy. 'Why do you come out here? It's not the sort of place I thought you would be drawn to. It doesn't really suit your party-boy image.'

He gave a shrug of one broad shoulder. 'The Crown Prince is a friend of mine. We went to university together. I like to visit him now and again.'

'Do you come here often?' Angelique gave herself a mental kick for not rephrasing that a little less suggestively.

He gave her a wicked look. 'No single, unchaperoned women in my room, remember?'

She compressed her lips. 'I'm being serious. How many times do you, er, visit?'

He put his plate down on a nearby table. 'Not as often as I'd like. I only get out here once a year. Two, if I'm lucky, like this year when I came out for Talib and Abby's wedding.'

Angelique's eyes widened to the size of the plate he'd just put down. 'But…but *why*? What's so great about it?

I don't see anything that's relaxing or beautiful about it. It's just a bunch of boring old sand dunes.'

He put his hand on her elbow and led her away to a quieter area. 'Will you please keep your opinions to yourself until we're out of danger?' he hissed out of the corner of his mouth.

Angelique wriggled out of his hold, not because she found it unpleasant, but because she found she rather liked it. *A lot.* She hadn't realised until now how much she had come to rely on him protecting her. To come to her rescue. She had blundered into a minefield and yet he had remained calm and steady throughout. Even cracking jokes about it.

Was *he* scared?

If so, he had shown little sign of it until now.

'I'm sorry, but I'm not used to this,' she said. 'You've been coming here for ages. This is my first time. I'm what you would call a desert virgin.'

'What about that bikini shot of you I saw in New York a couple of years back? You were draped over a sand dune with a couple of camels in the background.'

Angelique mentally raised her brows. So he'd seen that, had he? And taken note of it. 'It was staged. The sand dunes were in Mexico and the camels were cranky and smelly. One of them even tried to bite me. It was a horrible shoot. The designer was impossible to please and I ended up with a massive migraine from sunstroke.'

A frown appeared between his eyes. 'Why do you do it?'

She felt her back come up. She'd heard this lecture before, too many times to count. The most memorable one had been from him. 'Why do I do what?'

'Model. Put yourself out there in nothing but a couple of scraps of fabric.' His tone sounded starchy and disapproving. Old-fashioned. *Conservative*. 'You're capable of so much more than being some gorgeous too-perfect-to-believe image young guys jerk off to when they're in the shower.'

Angelique gave him an arch look. 'Is that what *you* do?'

His eyes hardened. His mouth flattened. A muscle ticked in his jaw. On-off. On-off. 'No.' His tone was clipped. *Too* clipped. 'I don't think of you like that.'

He was lying.

Just like she had been lying about her hunger.

How…*interesting*.

The thought of him being turned on by *her*, orgasming because of *her*, was deliciously shocking. It made her flesh tingle. It made her juices run. It made her need pulse and ache to feel him come to completion with her, *the real her*, not some airbrushed image that didn't even come close.

Are you out of your mind? The sensible part of her brain kicked in again.

You are not *going to sleep with Remy. Whether he wants to or you want to.*

Angelique looked up at him, noting the dull flush that had flagged both of his aristocratic cheekbones. 'So, when do we get to step out of this charade? We can leave for the airport once this is over, can't we? I've got my bag packed all ready to go. All you have to do is say the word and I'm out of here with bells on. Not the wedding variety, of course.'

His dark-brown eyes seemed to go a shade darker as they held hers. 'We're not leaving tonight.'

Angelique felt that fist of panic come back, but now it was two fists.

Two very big, very *strong* fists.

'But why not? You have a private jet, don't you? You can leave whenever you want.' She swallowed and looked up at him hopefully. Desperately. 'C-can't you?'

Remy turned his back so anyone nearby couldn't see his expression, his voice sounding low and deep, like a rumble of an imminent earthquake under the ocean floor. 'There is a tradition we have to uphold. We can't leave until we officially consummate the marriage.'

Angelique jerked back from him. 'You're joking. You *have* to be joking! There's no way we have to do *that*! How would anyone know if we, um, did it or not?'

He gave her a levelling look. 'We'd have to prove it.'

Her brows went up. Her eyes went wide. Her heart started to gallop. Her inner core got hot. *Very hot.* 'You mean like witnesses or something? Oh my God, I can't believe this! I'm so not a threesome person. I'm not even a twosome person. I—' She clamped her mouth shut. She had given away too much as it was.

'We'll need evidence that you're a virgin.'

Angelique blinked. *'Pardon?'*

'Blood.' He had his poker face on. 'On the sheets. We have to display them the next morning.'

She gave him a narrowed look. 'Whose blood?'

His mouth cracked in a half-smile. 'Yours.'

Angelique sent him a fulminating glare. 'I just *knew* you were going to say that. The only blood I want to see spilled right now is yours.'

'You're really hating this, aren't you?' His expression was amused.

Her eyes went to slits again. 'By "this" I suppose you mean this ridiculous subservience.'

He gave one of his loose, get-over-it shrugs. 'It's the way things are done here.'

She shook with outrage. 'But it's the wrong way!'

'The women here are happy.' His voice was calm, measured. 'They don't have to do anything but be who they are. They don't have to primp and preen. They don't have to have a spray tan every week or put on false nails or colour their hair. They don't have to pretend they're not hungry when they're starving, because they're not going to be judged solely on their appearance. It is who they are on the inside that matters.'

He was describing a paradise...or was he?

She set her mouth. 'That's only because they probably don't know what they're missing. If just one woman gets a glimpse of what she could have, you could have total anarchy out here.'

An amused quirk tilted his mouth. 'And I suppose you'd be out front and leading the charge of that particular riot?'

She gave him a beady look. 'You'd better believe it.'

CHAPTER FOUR

REMY WAS ENJOYING every minute of his 'marriage' so far. It was so amusing to press all of Angelique's hot buttons. He knew exactly what to say and how to say it—even the way to look at her to get a rise out of her. The reason he knew was because deep down he felt exactly the same.

Marriage was a trap.

It was stultifying. Restraining. A freedom-taking institution that worked better for some than for others.

And he was one of the others.

He didn't like answering to anyone. He had spent too much of his life living under the shadow of his brothers and his grandfather. He wanted to make his own way, to be his own person. To be known as something more than a Caffarelli brother or grandson.

He didn't want to be someone's husband.

And as for being someone's father… Well, he was leaving that to his two older brothers, who seemed pretty keen on the idea of procreating.

Remy was not interested in babies with scrunched-up faces and dirty nappies; sleepless nights, running noses, temper tantrums. Not for him. *No way*.

He was interested in having a good time. Playing

the field. Working the turf. Sowing his oats—the wild variety, that was.

And at times his life could get pretty wild.

He loved the element of risk in what he did—scoping out failing businesses, taking chances, rolling the dice. Chasing success, running it down, holding it in his hands and relishing the victory of yet another deal signed and delivered.

He was a gambler at heart, but not an irresponsible one. He knew where to draw the line, how to measure the stakes and to raise or lower them when he needed to.

And he was a firm believer in the golden rule of gambling: he only ever lost what he could afford to lose.

Besides, he'd already suffered the worst loss of all. Losing his parents so suddenly had been shattering. He still remembered the crushing sense of loss when Rafe had told him about their parents' accident: the panic; the fear; the terror. It had made Remy feel that life was little more than a roll of a dice. Fate was a cruel mistress. Your life could be perfect and full one day, and terrifyingly empty the next.

Remy looked down at Angelique who was trying to disguise her fury at the little 'proof of virginity' story he'd spun her. He wondered how long he could spin it out. She looked so infuriated he thought she was going to explode. She probably had no idea how gorgeous she looked when she was spitting at him like a wild cat. He wouldn't mind having those sharp little claws digging into his back as he rocked them both to paradise.

Are you out of your mind?

If you sleep with her you won't be able to annul the marriage as soon as you get home.

Right. They would have to share a room—there

would be no avoiding that—but he could always sleep on the sofa.

There had better be a sofa or you're toast.

'Right.'

Angelique looked up at him and Remy realised he'd spoken aloud. 'Pardon?' she said.

'How's your headache?'

She looked at him blankly for a moment. 'My…? Oh yes; terrible. Absolutely excruciating.' She put a hand to her temple again. 'I'm getting blurred vision and I think I'm seeing an aura.'

'We'd better get you to bed, then.'

The words dropped into the silence, suspended there, echoing with erotic undercurrents that were impossible to ignore.

'To sleep,' Remy said. 'Just in case you were getting the wrong idea.' Like his body had. It was already hard. Getting harder. *Deep breath.*

She angled her head at him suspiciously. 'Why do I get the feeling you're playing with me?'

He wanted to play with her all right. His body said yes but his mind kept saying no, or at least it was saying no so far. But how long would he be able to keep his hands off her? Theoretically she was the last woman in the world he wanted anything to do with. She was too high-maintenance. Too wild.

But, theory aside, when it came down to practice, well, he was only human. And she *was* hot. He normally preferred blondes but there was something about Angelique's raven hair and creamy skin that had a touch of old-world Hollywood glamour about it. She walked into a room like a movie star. He didn't think it was put on or something she'd learned on the catwalk. He'd seen her do it since she was a kid. *She made an entrance.* It was like she was making a statement: *I'm here. What are you going to do about it?*

She was here all right.

She was right, smack bang in the middle of his life and he couldn't wait to get her out of it.

'You take life too seriously, Angelique.'

'That stuff about the sheets...' She chewed her bottom lip for a moment. 'That's not really true, is it?'

Remy felt a sudden urge to ruffle her hair or pinch her cheeks like he would a little kid. She was so cute when she let her guard down. He couldn't remember ever seeing her look that vulnerable and uncertain before. Angry, annoyed, irritated, yes—but vulnerable? No. If she felt it, she covered it well, but then who was he to talk?

'Why?' He kept his face deadpan. 'Aren't you still a virgin?'

She gave him a pert look. 'Aren't you?'

He laughed. 'An emotional one, maybe, in that I've never been in love. But I've been around a few times.'

She gave her eyes a little roll. 'I can just imagine.'

'How many?'

'How many...what?'

'Lovers.'

She stilled, every muscle on her face seeming to momentarily freeze. But then she gave a little toss of her head and sent him haughty look. 'I fail to see why that should be of any interest to you.'

'I'm your husband.'

One.

Two.

Three.

Blast off.

Remy could time her down to a nanosecond. Her face

went rigid again, her teeth clenching together, her eyes flashing at him like a turbulent gun-metal-grey ocean. 'You're enjoying every minute of this, aren't you?' she hissed at him. 'I bet you can't wait to get back to Italy or France, or wherever it is you live these days, to tell everyone how you tricked me into marrying you. You'll be dining out on this and how you got Tarrantloch off my father for decades, won't you?'

'Calm down.' Remy held up a hand like a stop sign. 'I'm not the one who brought about this marriage. You're the last person I would consider marrying if I was considering marriage, which I'm not, nor ever will be.'

'Ditto.'

'Fine. Then at least we're square on that.' He pushed his sleeve back and glanced impatiently at his watch. 'I think it's time this party was over. Come on. Let's get out of here.'

Angelique followed him with feigned meekness as they said their goodnights to the other guests and officials. Her little white lie about her headache was now lamentably and rather painfully true. Her temples were pounding by the time she got to the suite with Remy. She felt nauseous and lightheaded and her heart began to pound once he closed the door and they were finally alone.

Alone.

In the bridal suite.

She affected a light and breezy tone. 'Do you want to toss a coin for the bed?'

His dark-brown eyes looked darker than they had during the reception. She couldn't make out the shape of his irises at all. He took a coin out of his pocket without breaking his gaze from hers and laid it on the back of his left hand, covered by his right. 'Heads or tails?'

'Heads.'

He flipped the coin high in the air and deftly caught it as it came back down, his gaze still locked on hers. 'Want to change your mind?'

Angelique raised her chin. 'Once my mind is made up I *never* change it.'

His mouth kicked up a little on one side, those dark-chocolate eyes gleaming. 'Ditto.'

She leaned forward to see how the coin had fallen but he hadn't uncovered it. He held it in his closed palm in the space between them. 'Go on. Show me.' Her voice sounded huskier than normal but she put that down to the fact he was in her personal body space. She could smell his citrus, wood and male smell. She could see the rise of fresh dark stubble on his jaw.

She could feel his desire.

It was pulsing in the air like sound waves. There was an answering throb in her body like an echo. Her inner core shifted. Tensed. Clenched. *Hungered.*

She suddenly became aware of her breasts inside the lacy cage of her bra. She became aware of her tongue as it moved out over her lips, depositing moisture to their surface. She saw his hooded gaze follow its passage and something in her stomach unfurled, as if a satin ribbon was being pulled out of its centre.

She took a little swallow. 'Um…the coin?'

His gaze was still fixated on her mouth as if it were the most fascinating mouth in the whole wide world. 'What about it?' His voice sounded deep and rough around the edges.

'I want to know who won.'

'I did.'

Angelique frowned at his confident tone. 'You can't possibly know that without looking.'

His mouth went up at the corners again. 'I have a sixth sense about this sort of stuff. I won. You lost.'

She coughed out a little sound of scorn. 'You think I'm going to fall for that without seeing the evidence? Open your palm.'

His eyes locked back on hers; they seemed to be glinting at the challenge she had laid down. 'Want to make me?' he said.

The floor of her belly shivered. He was near to impossible to resist in this mood. Was that how he bedded so many women? No wonder they fell like ninepins around him. He was just simply irresistible in this playful mood.

But Angelique didn't do alpha males and Remy was very definitely an alpha male. It was in his blood. Had been born and bred to rule, to take charge, to take control and hold onto it no matter what. To lead, not to follow. He was too commanding, too sure of himself, too ruthless and way too sexy.

Too much a Caffarelli.

Too much of an enemy.

Too much of everything.

She hitched up her chin and squared her shoulders. 'Thanks but no.'

His eyes glinted some more, moving slowly between her mouth and her gaze, burning, searing all the way. 'Shame. I was looking forward to a little tussle for possession. It could've been fun.'

Angelique knew he wasn't talking about the coin. She blew out an uneven breath. 'You have the bed. You're much taller than me.' That was an understatement. He'd had to stoop through every door they'd been through so far. 'I can curl up on the sofa.'

'What sofa?'

She chewed her lip as she glanced around the suite. It had everything *but* a sofa. 'Oh... Well, then...'

'The bed is big enough for both of us. You stick to your side. I'll stick to mine. It's only for one night.'

Angelique tried to read his expression but he had his poker face back on. 'I hope you don't snore or talk in your sleep.'

'If I do just give me a shove in the ribs.'

She gave him a frosty look. 'I'm not going to go anywhere near you.'

A sexy smile tilted his mouth. 'Then you'd be the first woman I've shared a bed with who hasn't.'

Angelique spent an inordinate amount of time in the *en suite* cleansing her face and brushing her teeth. She even brushed her hair for a hundred strokes to delay going back into the bedroom. But when she came out of the bathroom there was no sign of Remy. He hadn't even bothered to leave her a note to tell her where he had gone or when he would be back... Or whom he was with.

Careful; you're starting to sound like a wife.

She shook off the thought and pulled back the covers on the massive bed. The tension of the last twenty-four hours—seventy-two if she counted the time since she'd found out Tarrantloch had been lost—had finally caught up with her. As soon as her limbs felt the smooth, cool embrace of the impossibly fine linen she felt every muscle in her body let go. She melted into the mattress, even though it was far too firm for her, and closed her eyes on an exhausted sigh...

* * *

Remy came back to the suite at three in the morning to find Angelique fast asleep.

Right in the middle of the bed.

Her mane of glossy black hair surrounded her head like a cloud. Her blood-red lips were soft and slightly parted, her skin now without its armour of artfully applied make-up. Now she had lost the layer of worldly sophistication she looked young and tiny, almost fragile. There were dark shadows underneath her eyes that her make-up must have hidden earlier. Her slim body—personally he thought she was *too* slim—was curled up like a comma, the sharpness of her hipbone jutting out from beneath the covering of the bed linen.

He could see the spaghetti-thin straps of her nightie, an ivory white that was a perfect foil for the creamy tone of her skin. The upper curves of her breasts were showing just above the sheet. He'd always thought of them as Goldilocks breasts—not too big, not too small, but just right.

He gave himself a mental shake and turned away from the sight of the temptation lying there.

Hands off, remember?

He rubbed a tired hand over the back of his head and down to the knotted muscles in his neck. He'd had to pull some strings to get out of Dharbiri by first light. He didn't want to spend any more time than he had to 'married' to her. If the press got wind of this back home, it would go viral in no time. He didn't want to be made into a laughing stock. He could just imagine the headlines: *World's biggest playboy gets hitched. The last of the Caffarelli rakes bites the dust.*

He wanted to erase it from the record. Wipe it from his memory. Get back to normal.

Get her out of his life.

Remy looked at her again. She murmured something in her sleep and stretched out her arms and legs like a cat—and not just any old moggy—a beautiful, exotic cat that was begging to be stroked.

He wondered who her latest lover was. He hadn't read anything just lately in the press about her, which was surprising, as hardly a month or two went by without some mention of her caught up in some scandal or other. He often wondered how much of it was true. He knew from his own experience that not everything that was reported was accurate. But how she was keeping her head below the parapet was a mystery if not a miracle. It was not an easy feat to stay under the radar when around every corner was a camera phone. You didn't have to be a member of the paparazzi to get a shot of a celebrity or any other high profile person these days.

He'd had a few candid camera shots he'd rather weren't out in the public domain. The press always made it look far worse than it was. He wasn't a heavy drinker, and he had never and would never touch party drugs. But somehow he had been portrayed as a hard-partying, hard-drinking playboy.

The playboy bit was true.

He wasn't going to deny the fact he'd bedded a lot of women. And he wasn't going to stop any time soon. Which was why he had to get this marriage annulled as soon as possible. Call him old-fashioned but, on-paper marriage or no, he was not going to betray those promises he'd made. As far as he was concerned, infidelity was a deal breaker even in his most casual relationships. Sleeping around on a partner was not what a real man would do.

Talking of sleeping… He smothered a yawn as he

heeled off his shoes and unbuttoned his shirt. He tossed it in the vague direction of a chair and put his hands on the waistband of his trousers.

Nah, better keep them on.

He could do with a few more barriers between him and Sleeping Beauty right now. He just hoped two layers—three, if you counted hers—would be enough to keep him out of danger.

CHAPTER FIVE

ANGELIQUE ROLLED OVER and breathed in the scent of lavender-scented sheets, citrus and wood and…warm, sleepy male.

Her heart gave a little flip-flop as she looked at the tanned arm lying across her stomach. It looked so dark, hairy and foreign against the ivory white of her satin nightie. It felt like an iron bar was holding her in place.

His strongly muscled legs were entangled with hers, just loosely, but they felt rough and strong. Powerful.

Had they…? She gulped. *Had sex?*

No.

No!

Hang on a minute… Her body didn't feel any different. She knew without a doubt she would feel *very* different if Remy had made love to her.

She would feel…*satisfied.*

Because she couldn't imagine him not doing the job properly. There would be no half-measures with him. He would know his way around a woman's body like a curator knew their way around a museum. Interesting—some might say Freudian—choice of metaphor, as it felt like an aeon since she'd been intimate with anyone; but still.

Sex had always been a bit of a disappointment to her.

She tried to enjoy it but she had never felt truly comfortable with any of her partners. Not that she'd had as many as the press liked to make out.

Her first experience of sex had been when she had gone to New York to sign with the agency. A photographer had hooked up with her for a couple of months but she hadn't really felt valued as a person; rather, she'd felt more of a commodity, a bit of arm candy to be paraded around to gain Brownie points with his colleagues. That relationship, as well as one or two others, had made her come to the conclusion that sex was something men *did* to her, rather than something she experienced *with* them. She had always been able to separate herself from the act, to keep her mind to one side, to be the impartial observer.

She had talked to girlfriends about it and they had assured her she just hadn't met the right partner. That it was all a matter of chemistry and timing. Animal attraction.

It was ironic that Angelique had one of the most looked-at bodies in the world, yet she felt a stranger to it in terms of passion. She knew how to pleasure herself but it wasn't something she did with any regularity. She didn't have the inclination or the desire. She wondered if she was just one of those people with little or no sex drive.

Remy's arm tightened across her middle and he nuzzled against the sensitive skin of her neck. 'Mmm...' he murmured sleepily.

The sex drive Angelique thought was non-existent suddenly made an appearance. It was centre-stage and wanted to be noticed. She felt it stir within her core, a tugging sensation, a needy little ache that wouldn't go away. Her breasts tingled from the brush of his arm as he shifted position again. His legs were entwined with hers and his erection—*his rock-hard erection*—was pressing against her thigh.

Was he even awake?

Maybe he was so practised at this he could do it in his sleep. She mentally rolled her eyes. It wouldn't surprise her.

One of his hands moved up and gently cupped the globe of her breast. Even through the satin of her nightie she felt his warmth and the electricity of his touch. It made her hungry for more, to feel that large, firm hand on her, skin to skin.

He rolled his thumb back and forth over her nipple, making it ache and tingle with pleasure.

OK, so he *had* to be awake.

The sensible part of Angelique knew this was the time to step in and remind him of the hands-off nature of their relationship, but the newly awakened *sensual* part of her was saying the opposite.

She wanted hands-on.

His mouth found the super-sensitive area just behind her earlobe. Angelique shivered as his tongue moved over the area in slow, lazy strokes. His hand moved up from her knee to the top of her thigh in one smooth caress that made her inner core clench tight with longing, triggering a rush of dewy moisture between her thighs.

He shifted position again, rolling her further on to her back as his body moved over hers.

You really should stop him.

Not yet! Not yet!

His hooded eyes slowly opened and then he flinched back from her as he let out a rather appropriate profanity. 'What the hell do you think you're doing?'

Angelique gave him a pointed look. 'What am *I* doing? You're the one with my breast in your hand.'

He frowned and looked down at his hand as if he had only just realised it was attached to his body and that he was the one with control over it. He dropped it from her and moved away and up off the bed.

He scraped the same hand through the thick black tousle of his hair and turned to glare at her. 'You should've woken me.'

She arched a brow. 'So you really *can* do it in your sleep.'

He gave her an irritated frown. 'Looks like you were running on automatic pilot as well. When were you going to call a halt?'

Some little demon inside Angelique decided it was time to rattle *his* cage for a change. She gave him a sultry look from beneath her lashes, her 1950s Hollywood movie-star look. 'Maybe I wasn't.'

A cynical look came into his eyes and his mouth hardened. 'It won't work, Angelique. I'm not staying married to you for a minute longer than I have to, so you can forget about your plans to snare yourself a rich husband. I'm not playing ball.'

She decided to press him a little further. *This was so much fun!* She had never seen him look quite so furious. His jaw was clenched and his hands were fisted. Where was his puerile sense of humour now? 'But you want me. You can hardly deny that.' She glanced at the tented fabric of his boxer shorts before giving him another smouldering smile.

His brows snapped together. 'You are *such* a piece of work. Is this how you hook your claws into every man who crosses your path?'

Angelique slowly stroked her right foot down over

her left ankle, her chest arched back as she rested on her elbows. 'You're hardly one to talk. Women run each other down to get into your bed. I didn't run to get here. I didn't even walk. I got here by default.'

'And now you're getting out of it.' He stepped forward and ripped the bed linen off her like a magician pulling a cloth from a table.

Angelique gave a startled squeal as he grabbed one of her ankles and tugged her towards him. 'Get your hands off me!'

'That's not what you were saying a minute ago.' He pulled her upright but she stumbled and would have fallen except for his arms coming around her to steady her.

She thought he would let her go but he didn't. If anything his firm grip on her hips tightened. She felt every imprint of his fingers pressing into her skin; she even wondered if they would leave marks.

She looked at his mouth, always a big mistake, but there you go. She couldn't seem to help herself. Her gaze was drawn like a tiny piece of metal to a powerful magnet.

Their bodies were touching, feeling, *discovering* each other's contours.

Angelique felt the heft, weight and heat of his erection pressing against her belly. It stirred her senses into a madcap frenzy of longing that took over her whole body. She felt the rush of heat from her core, the liquid of lust that was outside of her control.

'This is not what I want,' he ground out but still he didn't let her go.

'I don't want it either.' *You liar. You do want it. You want him.*

He suddenly put her from him, stepping back and

raking a hand through his hair again. 'OK… Let's get some time out here.'

Time out?

I want time in!

Angelique's little demon wasn't quite ready to back down. 'You're scared. You're worried you might get to like having me around, aren't you, Remy? You're not used to that feeling. You're the one who hires and fires your bedmates week by week. You don't form lasting attachments. You form convenient, casual alliances that temporarily scratch your itch.'

He glowered at her again. 'I do *not* want you around. You're nothing but trouble. You attract it and you revel in it. I don't want it.'

'Then give me back Tarrantloch and I'll be out of your life as soon as you can say blackjack.'

The silence vibrated with palpable tension.

'No.' His one-word answer was clipped and determined. *Very* determined. *Caffarelli* determined.

Angelique hitched up her chin. 'Then you're stuck with me. I'm not leaving your side until you give me what I want.'

'You don't want Tarrantloch.' His lip curled mockingly. 'What you want is a pat on the back from your father.'

'Ha ha,' she scoffed. 'And what *you* want is a big tick of approval from your grandfather. You think by taking possession of Tarrantloch that it will somehow win favour with him.'

He gave a harsh bark of laughter. 'I do not need my aging grandfather's approval to get on in life. I've made my own way. I don't need anyone's tick of approval to be happy.'

'You're not happy. That's why you're so restless. You

can't settle because you're not happy with who you are on the inside.' *Just like I'm not happy.*

His eyes flashed with ire. 'Oh, and you're an expert on that, are you? The woman who doesn't eat in case she puts on a gram of flesh. Don't make me laugh.'

Angelique hated that he knew so much about her, about her insecurities. How did he *do* that? They had barely seen each other for years, yet within such a short time he had summed her up in a sentence. 'I have a contract—'

'That insists you parade yourself in front of people who don't give a damn about you, to make millions of dollars for *them*. *You're* not important to them, only your body is. They don't want what's inside you, they're only interested in what they can get out of you.'

It was true.

It was painfully, agonizingly true.

It was a blunt truth she had come to acknowledge only very recently, which was why she was so keen to get out of the industry, to come at it from a different angle—the design and marketing angle.

But her confidence had always been the kicker and now it was even more so. She hadn't gone to university. She had no business degree or diploma. She hadn't even finished school. She had no official qualifications. What sort of ability did she have to run her own business?

She would be such a babe in the woods. It was cut-throat and dog-eat-dog out there. She had seen it first-hand. People with good intentions, with good skills and awesome talent were pushed aside by the power brokers, the money men who were only interested in the profit line.

'I'm not planning on modelling for too much longer.'

His gaze hardened. 'So am I part of the back-up

plan? The rich husband to bankroll your—' he made quotation marks with his fingers '—retirement plan?'

'I have my own designs.'

He looked at her for a moment in silence, a frown deepening across his forehead.

'Designs?'

Angelique let out a little breath. She had told no one about her plans. It seemed strange, almost ironic, she would be telling *him*. 'Not every woman is a size zero. There are women out there with post-baby bodies, with scars, who've had mastectomies, or with the track marks of age. None of us are perfect.'

'I can't believe you just said that.'

Her shoulders went down on a sigh. 'I'm tired of being the poster girl for perfection. It takes a lot of hard work to look this good.'

'You look pretty damn good.'

Angelique felt a frisson of delight at his comment. He *liked* the way she looked?

But it's not real.

If she ate properly she would be a size—maybe even two sizes—bigger. Would he—and the rest of the world—find her so attractive then?

She was a physical fraud.

And an even bigger emotional one.

Angelique hadn't been in touch with her emotions since the day she had stumbled across her mother's unconscious body when she was ten years old. She could still see the glass of water with the faint trace of her mother's lipstick around the rim.

The pill bottle that had been empty.

The silence.

Not even a heartbeat.

No pulse.

No mother.

Angelique had locked down her emotions and acted like a puppet ever since.

'I want to launch my own swim and leisurewear label. I've wanted to do it for a while. I want more control over my life and my career.'

'You'll need money to do that.'

'I know. I have some savings put aside, but it's not quite enough. I have do it properly or it will fold before it gets off the ground.'

'Is anyone offering to back you?'

'I've approached a couple of people but they were a little gun-shy.' She let out a little sigh. 'I think my reputation as a bit of a hell-raiser put them off.'

'How much of it is true?'

Angelique looked at him. 'The gun-shy people?'

'The hell-raising.'

Her shoulders went down in a little slump. 'I'm no angel…I've never tried to be. It's just the press make it out to be a hundred times worse than it is. I only have to be standing next to someone at a party or a nightclub or social gathering to be linked to them in some sort of salacious scandal.'

'You never defend yourself.' His expression was inscrutable, as if he was still making up his mind about her, whether to believe her or not. 'You've never asked for a retraction of any of the statements made about you.'

'What would be the point? Defensiveness only makes it worse.' She let out another sign. 'Anyway, to begin with I welcomed the gossip. I figured any publicity is good publicity. Some of the most famous models in the world are known for their behaviour as much as their looks.'

He rubbed a hand over his jaw. The raspy sound was loud in the silence. 'I have a couple of contacts who might be able to help you with launching your designs. I'd have to look at what you've got on the table first. I'm not going to recommend anything that hasn't got a chance of flying. I prefer to back winners, not losers.'

Angelique felt a little piqued that he didn't instantly believe in her. She hadn't realised until now how much she wanted him to have faith in her ability. To believe that she wasn't just another pretty face without any substance behind it. 'I wouldn't dream of putting your precious money at risk.' Her words were sharp, clipped with resentment.

He gave her a levelling look. 'I might love a gamble, Angelique, but at the end of the day I'm a businessman. I can't allow emotions to get in the way of a good business decision.'

She sent him a chilly glare. 'You didn't worry too much about your emotions when you tricked my father out of Tarrantloch. That wasn't a business decision. It was a personal vendetta and I'll never forgive you for it.'

'I admit I wanted to pay him back for what he did to my grandfather. We almost lost everything because of what he did.' His look was darkly scathing. 'But it wasn't just about that. I bet he didn't tell you the details of his underhand behaviour over the Ibiza account I was about to close? He would have put a completely different spin on it for his precious little girl.'

His precious little girl.

Angelique had to choke back a laugh. If only Remy knew how much her father despised her. He never showed it in public. He couldn't afford to tarnish his reputation as a devoted father. He put on a good show when the need arose but as soon as the doors were closed Henri would revert back to his autocratic, boor-ish, hyper-critical ways. She had always known her fa-ther had wanted a son as his firstborn but her mother had failed to deliver one.

Angelique was a living, daily reminder of that fail-ure.

'I know my father isn't a plaster saint but neither is your grandfather,' she tossed back.

'I never said he was. I know how difficult he can be.'

She folded her arms across her chest. 'I don't want your money, Remy. I want you to give me back what is mine. That's all I want from you.'

'Not going to happen, *ma chérie*.' He gave her an in-tractable look. 'And, just for the record, I haven't fin-ished with your father. Tarrantloch is nothing compared to what he did to me in all but defaming me online. I'm not stopping until I get the justice I want.'

Angelique curled her lip. 'Is that why you jumped at the fiancée charade that led to this ridiculous mar-riage? You saw a perfect opportunity for revenge. For rough justice. Forcing my hand in a marriage neither of us wants in order to score points. That's so...*pathetic* I want to throw up. '

His brows jammed together. 'Do you really think I'd go that far? Come on, Angelique, you're not think-ing straight. I don't want to be married to anyone, let alone you. If by any remote chance I choose to settle down with someone it won't be with someone like you.'

She gave him a huffy scowl. '*Like me?* What does that mean? What's wrong with me?'

He let out a breath as he pushed a hand through his hair. 'Nothing's wrong with you… It's just, I don't see you as wife material.'

'Because?'

'Because you're not the "marriage and babies" type.'

Angelique raised her brows. 'You want...*babies*?'

He reared back from her as if she'd asked him if he wanted a deadly disease. 'No! God, no. I'm just saying...'

She gave him another scowl. 'I'm not sure what you're saying. Maybe you could elaborate a bit. Fill in the blanks for me.'

He looked about as flustered as she'd ever seen him. It was a rare sight. He was normally so in control—joking around. Having a laugh at everyone else's expense. Now he seemed to be back-pedalling as if he had stepped on a land mine and wasn't quite sure how to step off it without an explosion. 'It's not that I don't think you'd be a great mother.'

'But you think I'd be rubbish at being a wife.'

'I think you'd find it hard to compromise.'

Angelique blurted out a laugh. 'And *you* don't? Oh, for God's sake, Remy. You really are unbelievable. You're the least compromising person I've ever met. If I'd make a rotten wife, then you'd make an even worse husband.'

'Then thank God we'll be able to stop being a husband and wife as soon as we get back to England.'

'You really think it will be *that* simple?' Angelique asked. 'What if someone hears about this? A journalist or someone with contacts in the media? Did you see how many people were at our wedding? What if someone took a photo? What if *everyone* took a photo?'

His expression locked down, leaving just one muscle moving in and out on the left side of his jaw. 'No one is going to find out. We can annul this as soon as we land. I've already spoken to my lawyer in London. We can go straight to his office from the airport. It will be over and we can both move on with our lives as if it never happened.'

Good luck with that, Angelique thought. She'd been lucky lately in keeping her face out of the gossip pages but she knew it wouldn't last. If a journalist got a whiff of what had happened in Dharbiri she and Remy would be besieged by the media as soon as they landed. But then, anyone with a camera phone could snap a picture of them together and email or text it to a newspaper.

Even arriving at Heathrow together was going to cause a stir because there were always people coming back from holidays from tropical locations where her body had been on yet another billboard.

Oh joy...

CHAPTER SIX

REMY COULD NOT believe the sort of attention Angelique attracted. Even before they had cleared Customs people were nudging each other and pointing. Several came up and asked for autographs. Some took photos, even though the signs in the customs area strictly forbade the use of phones or cameras.

'Do you have to be so damn nice to everybody?' he said in a low, gruff tone as he ushered her through to where a driver was waiting to collect them. 'Can't you pretend you're not you? Let them think they've got the wrong person or something. I've done that heaps of times. It works like a charm.'

'*You've* got the wrong person if you think I'd be rude to someone who paid a lot of money for a swimsuit I've modelled.' She smiled at another fan who came over with a pen and a boarding pass for her to sign.

Remy could feel his blood pressure rising. Was she doing this on purpose? People were looking at *him* now, trying to figure out who he was and how he fitted into her life. How long before they recognised him and put two and two together?

He took her firmly by the elbow. 'We have to go. *Now.*'

'Hold your horses.' She winked up at him cheekily. 'Or your camels.'

She smiled again as yet another person came over and told her how much they admired her, and that they didn't believe for a second all that rubbish about her and the English banker who was married, and how it wasn't her fault the marriage had broken up because it was obviously doomed from the outset, blah, blah, blah.

Remy had to wait until they were in the car before he asked, 'Did you know the banker was married when you hooked up with him?'

'I didn't hook up with him.' She flicked some imaginary lint off her clothing. 'I was photographed next to him in a hotel lobby. I was waiting for the porter to bring out my luggage.'

He frowned at her. 'Are you seriously telling me you didn't have anything to do with him? That you didn't have a secret love tryst with him in that hotel?'

She gave him a bored look. 'Does every woman you speak to end up sharing your bed?' She held up her hand and gave her eyes a little roll. 'No, don't answer that. I already know. If they're under the age of thirty, they probably do.'

'I don't do married women. I might be a playboy but I do have *some* standards.'

'Good to know.' There was something about her tone and the exaggerated way she inspected her perfectly manicured nails that irked him.

'What do you mean?'

'It's very reassuring, that's all.'

He frowned again. He could sense she was up to something. 'What is?'

'That you don't *do* married women.'

'Why's that?'

Her look was arch when she turned to look at him. 'Because I'm married.'

A surge of hot, unbridled lust rose in his loins. He could not think of a woman he wanted more than her right now. It was pounding through him like an unstoppable tide. It tapped into every thread of desire he had ever felt for her, thickening it, swelling it, *reinforcing* it.

He covered it with a laugh. 'But not for much longer.'

She put her chin in the air and inspected her nails again. 'That annulment can't happen soon enough.' She lowered her hand back down to her lap and studied it for a moment. 'I can't think of a worse forty-eight hours in my life.'

'Hell of a short marriage,' he said after a little pause. 'Do you think that's some sort of record?'

She shrugged one of her slim shoulders a little without looking at him. 'Maybe.'

Another silence.

'Are you heading back to Paris after this?' Remy asked. 'This' being the sign-off of their brief marriage. He didn't want to admit it but he would miss her. A bit. A niggly bit. She was incredibly annoying but vastly entertaining. He could think of worse things to do with his time than spar with her. She stimulated him physically and intellectually. Not many women did that.

In fact, he couldn't think of the last one that had…

'I have a shoot in Barbados.' Her shoulders went down dejectedly. 'I have to lose at least three pounds before then.'

'You're joking, surely?'

She gave him a resigned look. 'No one wants to see a bloated belly in a bikini they're going to pay a hundred and fifty pounds for, are they?'

'But you've got an amazing belly.' He'd been having

shower fantasies about it for years. He compared other women to her. He knew it was wrong but he couldn't help it. She was his benchmark. That billboard in New York all those years ago had nailed it for him. No one even came close.

He suddenly found himself imagining her belly swelling…growing larger with the bloom of a child… *his* child…

Whoa! What are you thinking?

She pressed her lips together. 'I've got a belly like every other woman. It has its good days and its bad days.'

Remy studied her for a moment. 'Is that why you don't eat?'

She visibly bristled. 'I *do* eat.'

He gave a disparaging grunt. 'Not enough to keep a gnat alive.'

She sent him a flinty glare. 'So you keep a catalogue of all your lovers' food intakes, do you?'

'You're not my lover.' A fact his body was reminding him of virtually non-stop. Why wasn't it letting up?

'No.' Her chin hitched up until she was eyeball to eyeball with him. 'I'm just your wife.'

Remy felt his back come up at the way she said the word. It was like she was spitting out a nasty object, something foul and distasteful. 'Why are you so against being a wife? Your parents were happily married, weren't they? Everyone said how devastated your father was when your mother died. He was inconsolable.'

'Yes, he was…' Her expression clouded and her teeth nipped into her bottom lip.

He wondered if he should have mentioned her mother's death. Suicide was a touchy subject. Kate March-and had taken an overdose after a bout of depression, which had supposedly been accidental, and rumour had it Angelique had found her body.

She had been ten years old.

The same age his brother Rafe had been when their parents had been killed.

Remy had seen first-hand what a child with an over-blown sense of responsibility went through. It had only been since Rafe had met Poppy that he had let that sense of responsibility ease. Rafe had taken stock of his life and was a better and happier man for it.

Raoul had done much the same, recognising his life would not be complete without Lily Archer, the woman who had shown him that physical wholeness was not as important as emotional wholeness.

But what could Angelique teach Remy other than patience and self-control?

Remy wondered if finding her mother like that was why she was such a tearaway. Losing her mother in such a way must have hit her hard. Had she blamed herself?

He looked at her sitting with her arms folded across her middle, her gaze focused on the tote bag on her lap. A frown was pulling on her forehead and her teeth were savaging her lower lip. She looked far younger than her years. Vulnerable.

'Did you blame yourself for your mother's death?'

'A bit, I suppose. What child wouldn't?' She started plucking at the stitches in the leather of her bag strap, tugging at the tiny threads as if to unpick them one by one. 'If I'd got home earlier I might've been able to save her. But I'd stopped at a friend's house on the way home from school. I'd never done that before.' She stopped picking to look at him. 'Needless to say, I never did it again.'

There was a lot of pain in her eyes. She covered it

well but it was there lurking in the depths. Remy saw it in the way she held herself, a braced posture, guarded, prepared. Vigilant. There was so much about her that annoyed him, yet how much of that was a ruse to cover her true nature? Her brash wilfulness, her impulsiveness, her refusal to obey instructions could well be a shield to hide how vulnerable and alone she felt.

'Monsieur Caffarelli?'

Remy had almost forgotten they were still in the car until it came to a halt and the driver opened the partition that separated the driver from the passengers.

'There are paparazzi outside,' his driver said. 'Do you want me to drive another block or two?'

'Yes, do that.' Remy took out his phone. 'I'll give my lawyer a call to see if he can meet us somewhere else.'

'How did they know we were going to your lawyer's office?' Angelique asked.

'God knows.' He put his phone to his ear. 'Brad. You looked out of your window lately?'

'I was just about to call you,' Brad said. 'I've just had Robert Mappleton on the line. He heard a rumour you're married to Henri Marchand's daughter and—'

'Where the hell did he hear that?' Remy barked.

'Not sure,' Brad said. 'Maybe someone in Dharbiri spoke to the press. All I know is this is like winning the lottery for you right now.'

'What are you talking about?' Remy said.

'Have you forgotten? You've been trying to win this guy over for months. *The* Bob Mappleton of Mappleton Hotels?'

'That crusty old bastard who refused to even discuss a takeover bid, even though the shareholders are threatening to call in the administrators?' Remy curled his lip. *All because of that inflammatory email Henri March-*

and had circulated. 'Yeah, how could I forget? He'd rather face total bankruptcy than strike a deal with me.'

'Well, here's the thing,' Brad said. 'He just called and said he's changed his mind. He wasn't prepared to do business with a hard-partying playboy, but now you're married to Henri Marchand's daughter he figures that stuff Marchand said about you last year can't have been true. He wants to set up a meeting. He's as old-school and conservative as they come but this marriage of yours couldn't have come at a better time.'

Remy felt his scalp start to tingle. The biggest take-over bid of his career: a chain of run-down hotels he knew he could make into the most luxurious and popular in the world. The Ibiza development was child's play compared to this.

The catch?

He had to stay married in order to nail it.

He looked at Angelique who was giving him the evil eye. He could see the storm brewing in her grey-blue eyes. He could feel the air tightening along with her body. Every muscle in her face had turned to stone. 'Call him and set up a meeting for the end of next week,' he said to Brad.

'Why next week? Why not this week? Why not today?' Brad asked.

Remy grinned. 'Because I'm going on my honeymoon.' And then he closed his phone and started counting.

One.

Two…

'What?' Angelique spluttered. 'I'm not staying married to you!'

'Has anyone ever told you how cute you look when you're angry?'

Her eyes iced and narrowed, her voice coming out through clenched teeth. 'Don't try your charm on me, Remy Caffarelli. It won't work. I'm not staying married to you, so you can just call your lawyer right back and tell him we'll be up there in a less than a minute to sign on the dotted—'

'What if you were to get something out of it?'

Her head slanted at a suspicious angle. 'Such as?'

'I'll back your label,' Remy said. 'With my connections and guaranteed finance you could really take your designs places. You'll become a global brand overnight.'

She wavered like a wary dog being offered a treat from someone it didn't quite trust. 'How long would we have to stay married?'

He gave a shrug. 'A couple of months tops. We can get the wheels rolling on our business ventures and then call it quits. Easy.'

'It's still going to be a paper marriage, right?'

Remy found himself wondering if he could tweak the rules a tad. Just a tad, mind. A couple of months with Angelique in his bed could certainly make the temporary sacrifice of his freedom worthwhile.

Besides, it wasn't as if he could sleep with anyone else while he was officially married to her. It went against everything he believed in.

'That would depend.'

'On what?'

'On whether you wanted to be celibate for two months or whether you wanted a paper marriage with benefits,' he said.

An insolent spark lit her gaze. 'Is that the only choice I have? Celibacy or you?'

Remy gave her a winning smile. 'I know; it's a tough one. But wait. There's more. I'll set up a business plan and employ accounting staff to see to the details while you get on with designing and sourcing fabrics.' It was like reeling a fish on the line. He could practically see her mouth watering. *He was going to win this*.

'It's not enough.'

He frowned. 'What do you mean, it's not enough? I'm the one taking a risk here. I haven't even seen one of your designs. You could be rubbish at designing for all I know.'

Her small chin came up. 'I want more.'

More what? Money? Sex? He could tick both those boxes several times over. 'I won't sleep around on you, if that's what's worrying you,' Remy said. 'I'm a one-at-a-time man and I'd expect the same commitment from you. I won't settle for anything else.'

Her eyes held his a challenging little lockdown that made the base of his spine shift like sand moving in an hourglass. 'I'm not going to sleep with you, Remy.'

Sure you're not, Remy thought. He could feel her attraction for him ringing in the air like a high-pitched radio frequency. She wanted him but she didn't want to be the first one to give in to it.

He saw it in those looks she gave him when she thought he wasn't looking: hungry, yearning, lustful. She was proud and defiant, determined to withstand the temptation he was dangling before her.

He was used to women caving in to his first smile. Angelique's resistance to his charm was doing the opposite of what she probably intended. Instead of making him want her less, it made him want her more. She was a challenge. A goal to score. A prize to claim.

A bet to win.

'Do you want to put money on that?' he asked.

She gave him a mordant look. 'Thanks, but no.'

'You're definitely not your father's daughter.'

'Ah, but that's where you're wrong,' she said, still eyeballing him with those stormcloud eyes.

Remy could feel his desire for her thundering through his blood. How he loved a woman with spirit, and they didn't come much more spirited than Angelique. He would relish every single moment of having her finally succumb to him. The chase would be fun but the catch would be magnificent. He could already taste the victory. He could feel it in his blood and in his bones.

He would have her.

He would have her right where he had always secretly wanted her.

In his bed.

Her beautiful face was held at a regal height, her eyes glittering with an implacable purpose. 'I think you'll find I'm very much my father's daughter.'

'Because you don't know when to quit when failure is staring you in the face?' He gave an amused chuckle. 'That would certainly be a case of the apple not falling far from the tree.'

Her chin stayed at that haughty level, her mouth set in a tight line. 'I'll stay married to you on one condition and one condition only.'

Remy felt a warning tingle course through his blood; even the back of his neck started to prickle. 'Go on.'

The corner of her mouth lifted as if she knew she had this in the bag. 'I want Tarrantloch at the end of it.'

CHAPTER SEVEN

REMY DREW IN a breath. Why couldn't she want a life-long stipend or a bank vault of diamonds? But no, not Angelique; instead she had insisted on the one thing he didn't want to relinquish. Would *never* relinquish.

Tarrantloch was a trophy. He wasn't prepared to hand it over before he'd enjoyed everything it represented: *success. Revenge. Justice.*

He leaned forward to give the driver instructions to take him to his regular hotel in Paddington. He wanted time to plan a counter-move. He wasn't going to let her manipulate him. His mind shuffled through the ways he could turn this to his advantage. She didn't want the property half as much as she wanted to beat him at his own game. This was another one of her power plays.

'You drive a hard bargain,' he said when he sat back again.

She acknowledged that with an aristocratic tilt of her head. 'You want me to be your wife? That's the price you have to pay.'

Remy knew he could turn this around. Easily. Besides, she had got under his skin with her haughty airs and don't-touch-me looks.

He knew she wanted him.

It was in the air between them every time they were

alone. It had been there for years, truth be told. Now he could act on the desire he had always suppressed for her. He could finally indulge his senses, binge on her body until she was out of his system and out of his head. It would not be much of a hardship spending a month or two with her in a red-hot affair. He would be the envy of every man with a pulse.

Remy smiled a secret smile. He would be the one to finally tame the temptress, the wild and sultry Angelique Marchand.

'I don't know…' He rubbed at his jaw as if thinking it over. 'Tarrantloch for a couple of months of pretence? Doesn't seem fair to me.'

'Fair?' she shot back incredulously. 'Of course it's fair. I never wanted to be anyone's wife either, for real or pretend. It will just about kill me to spend two months acting like I feel something for you other than loathing.'

Remy had never wanted to make her eat those words more than at that moment. She didn't hate him as much as she made out. She hated that he saw through her game-playing and manipulative attempts to outsmart him.

But he would *always* win.

Losing was not an option for him.

'Like you, I want more.'

Her eyes suddenly flared. 'How much more?'

He gave her a smouldering look. 'I think you know how much more.'

She tried to disguise a swallow. 'You're joking.'

'It's a big house,' he said. 'I put a lot at risk to acquire it. I'm not going to relinquish it unless I think it's well and truly worth it.'

She gave him a gimlet glare. 'I think I should've faced the gallows or the firing squad or a public flogging back in that godforsaken place we just left. It would've been preferable to this…this *outrageous* proposition of yours.'

Remy laid his arm along the back of her seat, his fingers close enough to touch the nape of her neck. 'What's so outrageous about making love with someone you've desired for years?'

'I don't desire you. I've *never* desired you.' Her eyes flashed pure venom at him. 'I detest you.'

He caught a coil of her hair and tethered her to him. He watched as her grey-blue eyes flared and her tongue swept over her lips again. 'I could make you eat those words, *ma belle*.'

Her mouth was pinched tight. 'You can't make me eat anything.'

There was something incredibly arousing about her defiant stance. She pulled against his push. She had always stood up to him. Challenged him. Annoyed him. Goaded him. 'I'll have you eating out of my hand soon enough.' He gave her a confident smile. 'You won't be able to resist.'

She grabbed her hair and tugged it out of his hold even though it must have hurt. 'I hate you for this.'

He gave a negligent shrug. 'So what's new?'

Her eyes narrowed to slits. 'I mean I'll *really* hate you.'

'So.' He curled his lip mockingly. 'You've only been pretending up until now?'

'I can't believe you're being so ruthless about this.' She continued to glare at him. 'You don't want me at all. You just want to win the upper hand.'

He caught her hand and brought it to his groin, holding it against his throbbing heat. 'Oh, I want you all right, princess,' he drawled. 'Make no mistake about that. And what I want, I get. Every. Single. Time.'

She snatched her hand back and glowered at him. 'Then you've met your match, Remy Caffarelli, because I bend my will to no man. If you want to sleep with me, then you'll have to tie me to the bed first.'

Remy smiled a sinful smile. 'I can hardly wait.'

Angelique seethed as she waited for him to come round to open her door when they arrived at his hotel. The press must have been given a tip-off as they surged towards him, but he just gave them one of his butter-wouldn't-melt smiles.

'Mr Caffarelli, the news of your marriage to Angelique Marchand has surprised everyone. Have you any comment to make on your whirlwind relationship?'

'No comment other than to say I haven't even told my family about it yet.' Remy grinned at the television camera. 'Rafe, Raoul, if you're watching this—sorry I didn't tell you guys first. You too, *Nonno*. Bet you didn't see that coming. But I wanted to surprise you all. Who would have thought it? Me, head over heels in love.'

Angelique mentally rolled her eyes as Remy helped her out of the car. 'Do you have to be so…?'

'Smile for the cameras, *ma chérie*,' he said as he took her by the hand in a firm, almost crushing grip.

'But I—'

'Miss Marchand.' A journalist thrust a recording device at her. 'Your marriage to Remy Caffarelli is the biggest scoop our network has had in decades. There are photos going viral with you in that gorgeous, ancient wedding dress. Can you tell us about your secret wedding?'

'It was very romantic,' Remy said before Angelique

could answer. 'Very traditional too, wasn't it, *mon amour*?'

'Very.' Angelique stretched her mouth into a smile. 'In fact, you would not believe quite *how* traditional it—'

Remy pulled her tightly against his shoulder. 'Right, show's over, folks. We've got things to do.'

'Miss Marchand, there's been some speculation going around on whether or not Remy has followed the example of his older brothers in not making his bride sign a pre-nuptial agreement. That's surprising, given the Caffarellis' wealth. Is that true in your case?'

Angelique felt Remy's hold on her tighten to the point of pain. But then he seemed to force himself to relax, although she could still feel the tension in him as he stood with his arm loosely around her shoulders. 'Yes, that's true,' she said in dulcet tones. Two could play at this game. 'It just goes to show how much he loves and trusts me.'

'Will you show us your rings?' a female journalist said.

'No rings as yet,' Remy said. 'We're still waiting for them to be finished. I'm afraid I didn't give the designer enough notice.'

Angelique looked up at him with feigned affection. 'It was an impulsive, spur-of-the-moment proposal, wasn't it, *mon cher*? You just couldn't hold it in any longer, could you?'

His dark-brown eyes warned her she would be paying for this later but right now Angelique didn't care. 'That's right,' he said. 'I couldn't wait to make her my wife. Now, if you'll excuse us…'

'One last question, Miss Marchand,' the female journalist said. 'Does your marriage to Remy Caffarelli mean there is now an end to the bitter feud between your father and Remy's grandfather, or are you star-crossed lovers?'

'Um…'

'I'm sure Henri Marchand will be thrilled to know his daughter has married a man who worships the ground she walks on,' Remy said smoothly.

'So you didn't ask his permission, then?' the female journalist asked with a cheeky smile.

Remy gave the journalist a level look. 'I did not believe that was necessary. Angelique is an adult and does not need her father's permission to do anything, much less marry the man she has loved since she was a teenager.'

'Is that true, Miss Marchand?' The journalist swung the recording device back to Angelique. 'Have you been in love with Remy since you were a girl?'

Angelique felt her teeth grind together behind her smile. 'Absolutely. Head over heels. Besotted. Totally, utterly smitten.'

Remy held up a hand to field off further questions. 'That's all, folks. No further comment.'

He practically dragged her into the building with him. 'Hey, not so fast,' Angelique said, almost stumbling over the pavement. 'I'm wearing heels.'

He slowed his pace but his grip on her hand didn't loosen. 'Behave yourself, Angelique, or you might find your time with me unnecessarily unpleasant.'

She threw him a caustic look. 'More than it is already?'

His expression was deceptively cool and composed but she knew she had riled him to the edge of his control. She felt it in the tense grip of his fingers. 'If you want to get your way at the end of this then you'll have to play the part of the happy bride, especially in public. Do you understand?'

'So, you agree to give me Tarrantloch?'

A steely glint came into his eyes. 'We'll see.'

Angelique narrowed her gaze in anger. 'If you don't give me a straight yes or no then I'm going to walk back out there and tell those journalists this is nothing but a sham.'

His hold on her wrist tightened like a vice. 'You're not going anywhere, young lady. For once in your life, you're going to do as you're told. That will make a refreshing change for you, *n'est-ce pas*?'

'Welcome back, Mr Caffarelli,' the hotel manager said as he came over to shake Remy's hand. 'A little bird tells me congratulations are in order. On behalf of all of us here, may I wish you both a very happy future together.'

'Merci,' Remy said with a polished smile.

Angelique had to bite her tongue not to blurt out the truth but she knew in the end she would be the one to look foolish. Remy had a knack for turning things to his advantage. Didn't the last twenty-four hours prove it? He was going to make the most of being married to her.

Damn him!

'How long are you staying with us?' the manager asked.

'Just tonight,' Remy said. 'We'll be moving on first thing in the morning. If you could keep the press away from us, I would greatly appreciate it, Thomas.'

'Will do, sir.' Thomas beamed. 'We took the liberty of preparing the bridal suite for you.'

Not another one!

'That was indeed very kind of you,' Remy said with a glinting smile. 'I'll make sure we do it justice.'

Angelique had to wait until they were in the lift and alone before she could give him a piece of her mind. 'I can't believe you said that. Now they'll be sniggering down there imagining us up here doing…it.'

He hooked a dark brow upwards. 'It?'

She folded her arms and glowered at him. 'I bet it's a pretty regular occurrence, you bringing scores of women upstairs to have sex with them.'

'Never in the bridal suite, however, and only one at a time.'

She flickered her eyelids in disgust. 'You're unbelievable.'

The lift doors pinged open and he waved for her to go ahead of him. 'Jealous, *ma belle*?'

Angelique made a rude vomiting noise as she breezed past him. 'You have *got* to be joking.'

He opened the suite door but blocked the entrance with his body. 'This is the fun part.'

'Pardon?'

He held out his arms. 'I get to carry you over the threshold.'

Angelique backed away. 'Oh, no you don't. You're not putting your hands anywhere on me—

'*Hey!* What are you doing? *Put me down this instant!*'

Remy's arms were like steel cables around her as they carried her into the suite. Angelique kicked her legs and pummelled his chest with her fists but it was like a goldfish trying to fight off a tiger shark. 'Is that the best you can do?' he taunted as he kicked the door shut with his foot.

Angelique grabbed a fistful of his hair and pulled. *Hard.* 'I'm just starting, so don't say I didn't warn you.'

He slid her down the entire length of his rock-hard

body, leaving her in no doubt of his red-hot desire for her. 'So am I,' he drawled and covered her mouth with the blistering heat of his.

It was a hard kiss, an almost crushing one, but it stirred an ember inside Angelique into a suddenly combustible flame. It didn't matter that she was supposed to be fighting him off for the sake of her pride. All that was important now was keeping his mouth locked on hers as her senses spun, twirled and reeled in delight.

His hands were rough as they gripped her by the hips, his erection heavy and urgent against her feminine mound. She felt the tug and drag of desire deep and low in her belly, that restless urge to be closer to him, to be possessed by his thick, hot length, was almost unbearable.

Every lustful thought or dream she'd had about him was making her giddy with the anticipation of finally experiencing his possession. Was that why she had continued to niggle and goad him—to push his buttons? To make him lose control and do what they had always wanted to do to each other even though, if asked, both would have flatly denied it?

She kissed him back with primal heat, using her teeth and her tongue, her hands still tightly fisted in his hair, her breasts jammed up against his chest, making her nipples ache and tingle as they were abraded by the fabric of his shirt.

His tongue duelled with hers until she was making needy, hungry little whimpering noises in the back of her throat. One of his hands went to the zip at the back of her dress and lowered it in one swift but smooth slide, his warm hand cupping her bottom through the cobweb lace of her knickers as he pulled her even closer to his turgid length.

An inferno seemed to be raging inside her body. It was lighting spot fires all over her flesh, burning her, searing her with the need to feel him skin on skin.

'Damn you,' he growled against her lips, making them vibrate with lust.

She tugged at his lower lip with her teeth, tasting blood but not sure if it was hers or his. 'Damn you right back.'

He sucked in a breath and crushed his mouth to hers again, harder this time, going deeper with his tongue until no corner of her mouth was undiscovered. He was consuming her like a hungry man does a feast and she was doing exactly the same. He was a sensual banquet she couldn't resist. Would she ever have enough of his mouth, of his electrifying touch?

His hands shoved her dress away from her shoulders, letting it puddle at her feet. He unhooked her bra and cupped her right breast in his hand as his other kept her locked against his pulsing heat. His thumb moved over her tight nipple in a mesmerising back-and-forth motion that made her spine loosen like oil poured into a rusty lock.

Angelique slid a hand between their bodies so she could unzip him. Ever since that shocking moment in the car when he'd pushed her hand against him, her palm had been tingling to feel him without the barrier of clothes.

He groaned with approval against her mouth as she freed him from his underwear. She shaped him with her fingers first, getting to know the feel, length and weight of him. Then she started rubbing up and down his silky shaft, registering every guttural sound he made, delighting in every flinch or movement of pleasure he made. She felt the beading of his pre-ejaculatory moisture and rolled it around the head of his penis, inciting him, urging him on. Daring him. Wanting him. Aching for him.

He was on his own sensual mission to get her naked. Her knickers were soon dispensed with and she had barely stepped away from the tiny circle of them when his fingers found her hot wetness. She gasped as he slipped them inside her; it was the sweetest torture to have him but not have him quite the way she wanted him. She moved against the blissful friction, making throaty little pleas against his plundering mouth.

'Condom.' The word sounded like it was wrung out of him.

'Have you got one?' *Dumb question.* He probably had hundreds on him. Maybe even thousands. He probably had his own insignia on them.

'In my back pocket.' He walked her backwards further into the suite, his mouth still fused to hers as his hand searched for the protection in the pocket of his jeans.

Angelique took the foil packet off him and saw to the business end of things. She tried not to fumble in her haste but her hands were shaking in anticipation. For most of her adult life she had dreamed and fantasised about feeling this level of lust.

It was overpowering.

Totally consuming.

Unstoppable.

It was as if every nerve in her body was standing up on its tiptoes and screaming out for release. *Now! Now! Now!*

It made every single encounter she had had—not that there had been many—pale in comparison.

'You are so damn hot and wet and ready for me,' he

said as he tumbled with her onto the king-sized bed in a sexy tangle of limbs.

'Yes.' One word was all she could manage. Her heart was racing, her blood pumping and her flesh tingling as he came over her with his weight.

He hitched up one of her legs over his hip and entered her so deeply she cried out as his thickened flesh stretched hers to capacity. He immediately stilled and looked down at her with a frown knitting his brows together. 'Am I rushing you?'

Angelique let out a little breath. 'No... Sorry, I'm a bit out of practice. It's been a while.'

His dark eyes searched hers. 'How long?'

'A few weeks... Months...'

His gaze was still locked on hers. 'Months?'

'OK, a year...and a bit. Two, actually...'

'But the press...'

'Get it wrong occasionally.'

His frown was still tugging at his forehead like stitches being pulled beneath the skin. 'Why do you let people say all that stuff about you when it isn't true?'

Angelique stroked a finger down his sternum, focusing on its journey rather than staying connected with his gaze. 'I don't care what people think. I know what's true. That's all that matters to me.'

'Stop distracting me.' He captured her hand and held it firmly in the cage of his. 'I want to talk to you.'

She couldn't help an exaggerated little eye-roll. 'I bet that's what you say to all the girls.'

His frown deepened. 'Will you stop it, for God's sake? I'm trying to have a sensible conversation with you.'

'While your body is doing what it's doing to mine?' Angelique writhed beneath him. 'Can't you feel that?'

He bit back a curse and moved within her. Deeply. Roughly. Urgently. 'I can't stop myself from wanting you. I hate myself for it.'

She grabbed at his buttocks and dug her fingers in to hold him in place. 'I hate myself for it too. I hate *you* for it. For how you make me feel.'

His mouth curved in an indolent smile. 'How do I make you feel?'

She tried to glare at him but it didn't quite work with his body still intimately connected with hers. Instead, she pushed out her bottom lip in a pout. 'Mad.'

'I like it when you're mad at me.' He gave one slow, deep thrust. 'It turns me on.'

Angelique felt her belly do a funny little shuffle like the pages of a book being thumbed. Her body was fully aware of him. Excruciatingly so. Every nerve ending was primed for his next thrust. She felt the tension building in her flesh with every erotic movement of his body in hers. He increased the pace and her pleasure rapidly climbed with the pulsating throb of her swollen, sensitised tissues as they each clamoured for release.

He hitched her leg higher over his hip and drove even deeper.

It was like detonating an explosive device.

Angelique felt the explosion deep in her body, radiating out in pulsing waves that ricocheted through her. She shuddered and screamed, a raw, primal-sounding scream that was unlike any other sound she had ever made before. But then she had never felt anything like this before either. She bucked beneath his rocking body to keep the exquisite sensations going for as long as she could. Finally they faded and she was left in a blissful state of lassitude.

But he wasn't finished with her yet.

He shifted position slightly, slowing his pace until her body was crawling with need once more. She felt the tingling start all over again, the tightening of muscles, the pulse of longing and the steady climb to the summit that was tantalisingly just out of reach.

He slipped a hand underneath her buttocks and raised her as he thrust deeper and faster. She looked at his face, at the taut set to his features as he fought for control. His eyes were hooded, his jaw like honed steel, his breathing sounding harsh and laboured. She had never seen a more erotic sight. A beautifully cut and carved man in full arousal, poised to explode, waiting for that final trigger.

Angelique lifted and then rolled her hips. He grimaced as he tried to hold back but then she rolled her pelvis again. She felt the exact moment when his control slipped. He stiffened and then let out a shout, the pumping action of his body triggering another wave of pleasure through her body that travelled all the way to her fingertips and toes.

He slumped over her, burying his head to the side of her neck, his warm breath and stubbly skin a deliciously sensual caress against hers.

Angelique was so used to sparring with him that this new connectedness was faintly disturbing. If he could read her body so well, how well could he read her mind?

She wasn't used to feeling such powerful sensations during sex. She had never felt that level of desire or need before. She had never orgasmed with a partner before. She'd always pretended and got away with it.

This was so new and exciting. Breathtaking. Tantalising. Addictive.

Dangerous.

Remy finally lifted his head and looked at her. 'Was that good for you?'

His arrogant confidence made her retort 'Average.'

His brown eyes glinted as if he knew she was lying. 'Then maybe I should try and improve my rating.' He stroked a lazy finger down between her breasts where a tiny slick of sweat had pooled. 'You're incredibly beautiful.'

She gave him one of her bored looks. 'Do you know how many times I've heard that?'

His eyes tethered hers; dark, probing, penetrating. 'Ah, but do you believe it?'

Angelique felt as if he had already cracked open a corner of her mind and was examining the contents with a high-beam searchlight. She put her hands on his chest and pushed him away. 'I have to get up. I don't want the condom to leak.'

He got up and dealt with the disposal of the condom while she went in search of her clothes. She felt foolish and somehow sordid, scrabbling about the room, picking up her underwear and redressing while all he had to do was straighten his clothes and zip up his trousers.

Was it somehow indicative of the imbalance of their relationship? She would always be the one who felt naked and exposed while he would only reveal what he wanted her to see.

He was in control.

She wasn't.

'Is this yours?' Remy asked, holding up a diamond pendant swinging on a fine gold chain.

Angelique went to take it off him but he held it just out of her reach. 'Give it to me.'

His mouth was curved in a sarcastic smile. 'Where are your manners, *mon amour*?'

She ground her teeth and flashed him a resentful look. 'Please.'

'Not good enough.' He held the pendant higher as she took another swipe at it. 'I want to hear you ask nicely.'

She felt a ripple of annoyance course through her, tightening every muscle to snapping point. 'Give it to me, *please*.'

His chocolate-brown eyes contained a goading glint. 'You can do better than that, *ma belle*. I want to hear you beg.'

Angelique felt the sudden rush of her fury as it unleashed itself from the tight restraints she had spent a lifetime keeping in place.

She would *not* beg.

She would *not* plead.

She would *not* give in to his command like a servant who had no rights. She would scratch his eyes out before she did that.

She flew at him like a dervish, calling him every foul name she could think of. It all came bubbling out like poison—the rage, the hatred, the feeling of impotence, the shame at being under his control when she had worked so hard not be under any man's control.

He had subdued her sensually.

He had ambushed her.

Disarmed her.

Now he wanted to break her spirit just like her father had done to her mother.

Of course, she was no match for him. He took control of her flailing fists before they could even land a punch. 'What the hell is wrong with you?' he asked, frowning at her.

Angelique pulled against his iron-like hold. 'Let go of me, you…you *bastard*!'

'Not until you simmer down.' His tone was calm but implacable. 'You're going to hurt yourself carrying on like that. What's got into you?'

Tears started and burned in her eyes. It was the greatest shame of all to be snivelling like a child in front of him but there was nothing she could do to stop the flow once it had started. She choked back a sob but another one soon followed, and then another, and another until she finally bowed her head and gave in to the storm of weeping. It was lowering to find herself in such a vulnerable state. How could she have let this happen? What was wrong with her? Where was her pride and determination? Had his powerful love-making undone her completely? How would she get herself together again?

Remy released her wrists but he gathered her to him, putting his arms around her so the wall of his body supported her. One of his hands went to the back of her head and gently stroked her hair as she shook with sobs against him. 'I've upset you.' His voice was very deep and sounded surprised. Perhaps even a little shocked.

Angelique gave an almighty sniff, and as if by magic a neatly folded white handkerchief with an embroidered black *C* on it was handed to her. 'Thanks.'

'Don't mention it.'

She blew her nose and scrunched the handkerchief into a ball inside her hand. 'I'm fine now.' She took a ragged breath and glanced up at him with an attempt at wryness. 'Bet you don't think I'm so beautiful now.'

His expression was clouded with concern as he looked down at her. 'I was only teasing. You do know that, don't you, *ma petite*?'

Why did he have to keep calling her those wonderful endearments in that sexy accent of his? It made it so much harder to hate him.

You don't hate him.

Angelique skirted around the thought and gave him a small self-deprecating smile. 'It's a bit of a hot button for me. A red rag, if you like. I don't beg. Ever. For anything.'

'I'll make a note of it.'

The silence thrummed for a moment.

She tucked a tendril of hair back behind her ear. 'Um…I guess I should go and clean up.'

He handed her the pendant, his expression now inscrutable. 'It's very nice. Was it a gift from one of your lovers?'

The fine chain tickled Angelique's palm as it coiled there. 'It was my mother's.' She raised her chin a fraction. 'Just for the record, I don't accept gifts from my lovers. Ever.'

He held her gaze for a beat or two, his still dark and unfathomable. 'Apart from Scottish mansions, of course.'

She pursed her lips at his counter-move. Would he end up giving her back Tarrantloch? He hadn't made any promises. Nothing was written down or signed. They had consummated their relationship, but did that mean anything to him other than yet another sexual conquest?

Angelique gave a little shrug of her shoulder as if it didn't matter to her either way. 'I'm sure you'll do the right thing when it comes to the end of our relationship.' She met his gaze again with a bold look. 'Have you got a date in mind or are we just going to wing it?'

The screen was still down over his eyes but a tiny muscle tightened near his mouth. 'Don't worry. I'll give you plenty of notice.'

She smiled a saccharine-sweet smile. 'Big of you.'

He let out an audible breath. 'You have first shower. I have some things to see to. We'll eat out at nine.'

'But I—'

The door clipped shut and after a moment Angelique dropped her shoulders on a sigh. He had a nasty habit of getting in the last word.

She would have to break him of it.

CHAPTER EIGHT

REMY HAD BARELY stepped out of the hotel when his mobile buzzed. He looked at the screen and winced. 'Rafe, I was just about to call you and—'

'Tell me I did not just see you telling the press you've married the devil's spawn, Angelique Marchand,' Rafe said.

Remy glanced around to see if anyone was close enough to listen in. 'That's not a very nice way to speak of your brand new sister-in-law, bro.'

Rafe let out a curse. 'Are you out of your mind? What the hell are you playing at?'

'Hey, it's not Angelique's fault her old man is a double-crossing tool.' Remy couldn't help thinking how ironic it was to find himself defending her when normally he was finding any excuse to criticise her.

'Don't tell me you're in love with her, because I don't believe it for a second. The only person you love is yourself.'

'That's a bit harsh. I love lots of people. Even you.'

'Come on, Remy, this is me—Rafe. I know you. You would never fall in love with Angelique. She's as far away from your ideal woman as she could be. You've always said what a little slutty shrew she is. What's going on? Has Henri Marchand done the dirty on you? Forced you to marry her? Set up some sort of dodgy deal?'

'None of the above,' Remy said. 'Angelique followed me to Dharbiri and, to cut a long story short, she was found in my room and I had to marry her to keep from causing a public riot which might have ended up in one or both of us losing the skin off our backs. I decided not the take the chance.'

'Are you kidding me?' Rafe asked.

'Not at all,' Remy said.

'You said she followed you to Dharbiri. Why didn't you say something earlier if you were involved with her? Why let us find out like this?'

'I wasn't involved with her. Before this I hadn't seen or even spoken to her in years. She came to see me about her father's house. Remember Tarrantloch in Scotland? I won it off Henri Marchand in a bet.'

Rafe swore again but this time it was more a sound of admiration. 'So, it's just a marriage on paper, right?'

Another little silence, while Remy thought of how to answer. He didn't want to lie to his brother but neither did he want to discuss what had happened not ten minutes ago. His body was still singing from what was one of the most—if not *the* most—exciting sexual encounter of his life.

'You haven't,' Rafe said, sounding stern and incredulous at the same time.

'Hey, what *is* this?' Remy said. 'I don't ask you about your sex life with Poppy. Back off. I know what I'm doing.' *Sort of.* 'It's cool. Everything's cool.'

'You married our family's worst enemy's daughter without a pre-nup,' Rafe said. 'I don't think that's cool; I think that's outright stupidity. You're jeopardising everything we've worked for, just like *Nonno* did. Have you learned nothing in your thirty-two years on this planet?'

'What was I supposed to do?' Remy felt his hackles come up. 'Let her take the rap for being discovered in my room? I had to think, and think fast. There wasn't time to draw up a pre-nup. I did what I thought was the best and safest thing.'

'Being legally tied to Angelique Marchand is *not* safe,' Rafe said.

Tell me about it. 'I won't stay married to her for any longer than I have to,' Remy said. 'I'm working it to my advantage. Remember the Mappleton hotel chain I've been trying to buy for months? Henri Marchand's rumours about me turned old man Mappleton off, but now I'm married to Angelique he wants to play ball. I'm meeting with him next week. If I nail that deal, it will be worth any minor inconvenience of being married.'

'I can't help thinking this could blow up in your face.'

'You always think that about me,' Remy said. 'I like taking chances. Going with the gut. I always land on my feet. Always. Goal. Focus. Win. Remember?'

Rafe let out a long breath. 'Watch your back, Remy. Keeping your enemies close is wise, but sleeping with them is not.'

Sleeping with them is the fun part, Remy thought as he ended the call.

In fact, he couldn't wait to do it again.

Angelique was putting the finishing touches to her make-up when her mobile phone rang. She glanced at the screen to see it was her manager, Mackenzie Hillstrom, from her New York modelling agency. 'Hi, Mac, I was going to call you but—'

'Darling girl, I should hate you for not inviting me to your totally awesome desert wedding, and for not even telling me you were dating one of the most eligible and gorgeous men on this planet, but I forgive you, because you've just landed yourself the biggest contract of all time,' Mackenzie said.

'I…I have?'

'Forget Barbados and bikinis and bum-biting camels in Mexico. You are now the new poster girl for designer bridal wear. Every top designer wants you on his or her books! There's a bidding war going on as we speak. You looked absolutely amazing in that traditional garb. No one but you could pull that exotic look off. You've created the biggest sensation in bridal wear since the royal wedding.'

Bridal wear?

Was this fate's idea of a twisted joke? 'Um… Wow, that's great.' Should she tell her manager her marriage to Remy was only temporary, a charade unlikely to last longer than it took him to nail the Mappleton account?

'This is the big break you've been waiting for,' Mackenzie went on in her fast-paced New York accent. 'You're our golden girl now. You'll earn millions out of this. It will set you up for life—me too, when it comes to that. I'll email you the contract. Get it back to me as soon as you can. Take the next couple of weeks off while I sort the spring schedule out. Shanae will fill in for you on the Barbados shoot. Any questions?'

'No…that sounds wonderful.' *I think.*

Angelique put the phone down on the dressing table. She looked at it for a long moment, wondering if she should call her manager straight back and tell her she didn't want to take up the offer. Her life seemed to be spinning out of control in an alarming manner. A part of her wanted the money that was being put on the table, but the fame and constant exposure that would go with it gave her a troubling sense of unease. She had planned for months to get out of modelling. She was tired of living in the false world of perfection.

Her body was tired.

She had notebooks and slips of paper with designs doodled all over them. When would she have time to pursue her dream if she was caught up in a hectic shooting schedule? She didn't believe in doing things in half-measures. If they wanted her to be the next it girl in bridal wear, then her designs would have to wait…

Angelique was made up, coiffed and poised when Remy came back to the suite. She felt much more in charge when she had her professional armour on. It seemed important to give Remy the impression their love-making had made little or no impact on her. But it was hard to ignore the way her senses jumped to attention as soon as he came in the door, even harder to ignore the way her skin tightened all over and the way her inner core contracted. 'Nice walk?' she said.

His espresso gaze moved over her in a lazy sweep that tightened her skin and her inner core another notch. 'I wonder how long it would take me to get you out of that dress?'

She squared her shoulders even as her belly flipped over. 'What happened before was a mistake. I'd rather not repeat it.'

A hint of a smile lifted the corner of his mouth. 'You're not a very good liar, *ma chérie*. What happened before is going to happen again. And soon and often.'

Angelique felt a shiver course down her spine at the dark glitter of unbridled lust in his eyes. 'I think it would be foolish to complicate things with that level of involvement. We don't even like each other. It's rather unseemly to be going at each other like wild animals.'

His smile tilted a little further. 'Unseemly?'

She willed herself to hold his gaze for as long as she could. 'Primitive.'

He closed the distance between them in an easy stride or two. She knew she should have stepped back but her feet seemed to be bolted to the floor. She drew in a sharp breath when he put a hand to the nape of her neck. His warm palm was slightly rough against her soft skin and a shower of sensations spiralled through her at the delicious contact.

His eyes were so dark they looked like bottomless black pools. His mouth was so sexy, so sensually con-toured, her insides shifted restlessly and her own mouth started to tingle.

'The thing is, *ma belle*, I feel very primitive when I'm around you.' His hand cupped her left cheek, his thumb pad giving one stroke over her lips that sent every nerve into a frantic dance.

Angelique's heart skipped a beat as his thighs brushed against hers. She felt the bulge of his erec-tion. It spoke to everything that was female in her. Her senses were not sleeping or dormant now; they were wide awake and hungry for his touch. Ravenous. 'Find yourself another plaything.' She was really rather proud of how curt and cold she sounded. 'I will not be used by you.'

His thumb pad moved back over her lips, his eyes still locked on hers. 'Is that really what you want? To go back to a hands-off arrangement?'

No! 'Yes.' Angelique moistened her lips and tasted salty male. It was like tasting a powerfully addictive drug. She wanted more. Now. *Right now.*

His gaze searched hers for a pulsing moment. 'Fine.' He dropped his hand from her face and moved away.

Fine? She looked at him in numb shock. *Fine?* Why wasn't he challenging her? Why wasn't he making her eat her words? Damn it! She wanted him to make her eat her words!

He glanced at his designer watch. 'We should get going. I don't want to lose our booking; I had to pull some strings to get a table at such short notice.'

'I find that very hard to believe.' Angelique curled her lip as she picked up her purse. 'The Caffarelli name can get you a table just about anywhere, I would've thought.' *Let's see if I can push a few more of those buttons of his.* 'Maybe I'll change mine and see if I can cash in on some of the benefits.'

His expression hardened to stone. 'Don't get ahead of yourself, Angelique. This is not permanent. Don't kid yourself that it will be anything but what it is right now.'

'A war zone?' she quipped.

'Temporary.' He held the door open with a pointed look. 'Shall we?'

It was a popular restaurant owned and operated by one of Britain's celebrity chefs, which meant it was a famous-person hot spot, so the paparazzi were nearly always on hand.

Angelique quailed at the thought of fending off another round of intrusive questions. She was a pretty good actor but any body-language expert worth his or her credentials would be able to see Remy was still angry with her. He hadn't spoken a word to her during the short trip to the restaurant. He had spent the entire time tapping emails into his phone.

'Couldn't we have stayed and dined in the hotel?' she asked as he helped her from the limousine.

'No.' His hand was firm as it took hers.

'But surely we should be avoiding all this attention as much as possible?' She gave him a pouty glance. 'Anyway, what will people think? We're supposed to be on our honeymoon. Eating's supposed to be the last thing on our minds.'

'Yes, well, it's probably the last thing on *your* mind, but I'm starving. I need food and I need it now.'

Angelique rolled one shoulder haughtily. 'Why are men at the mercy of their basest desires?'

He gave her a glinting look. 'Why do women deny their needs as if it's something to be ashamed of? It's not wrong to feel hungry or horny. It's completely natural.'

'You know something?' She frowned at him. 'I've always really hated that word.'

'What, hungry?'

'Horny. It's sounds…I don't know. Coarse.'

A mocking smile angled his mouth. 'So underneath that brash, streetwise exterior is a sweet old-fashioned girl? Don't make me laugh.'

Angelique glared at him. 'You don't know me. Not the real me.' *No one knows the real me.*

He tucked her arm through one of his as he led her into the restaurant. 'Maybe now's a good time to start.'

Dining out for Angelique was like sharing a room with Remy—full of wicked temptation. Being tired and emotionally out of sorts made it much harder for her to rely on her steely resolve to keep to her strict diet. Just like kissing or touching Remy, one taste was enough to throw caution to the wind. Making love with him had changed everything. It was like trying to eat one peanut or one French fry: it was impossible; she would always want more. More of him. *All* of him. But how could she have him when he didn't want this arrangement to last any longer than it took to seal his latest business coup?

The Caffarelli brothers—before Rafe had married and Raoul had become engaged—had written the rule-book for rakes. Of the three of them, Remy had the worst reputation for the rate of turnover of partners. He had never had a relationship last more than a week or two.

But then, why would he?

He was spoilt for choice. Women adored him and flocked about him like bees around blossom. He was never in one place longer than a week at a time, which of course made it easy for him to be casual about his hook-ups.

Did he ever want more than just sex? Did he ever think about the companionship and loyalty his brothers were now experiencing? Did he think about the prom-ise of stability and a love that would last through good times and bad? To have someone to share the bond of children with, to watch as they grew from babies to children to adulthood? To love and protect them, nur-ture them and teach them how to be good, trustwor-thy citizens?

Angelique's brow furrowed as she looked down at the menu. Instead of the words printed there, she started to picture a tiny baby with a shock of jet-black hair and big brown eyes fringed with dark lashes.

Remy said he didn't want children.

She had said the same. Many times.

But it wasn't quite true...

'By the way.' Remy looked up from the menu he was perusing. 'We are not leaving this restaurant until I've seen you eat something. Understood?'

Angelique's back prickled. 'I have to think of my figure, especially now.'

'Why especially now?'

She gave him an imperious look. 'You're not the only one getting a ratings boost from our marriage.'

He cocked his head in interest. 'Oh, really?'

'My manager is firming up a new contract for me to consider. Once I sign it, I'm going to be booked up for months and months.'

'Tell them to wait. Tell them you're not available until after Christmas. I want you with me for the next month or two at the very least.'

Angelique felt her heart give a little skip at the thought of him wanting her with him but then she remembered his precious business deal. He wanted her for show, not for her.

It was an act.

A game of charades.

Even though technically she was free to be with him while her manager negotiated the schedule, she resented him arrogantly assuming she would drop everything just because he told her to.

She was *not* going to be ordered about by him.

'Do you really think you can just march into my life and take control as if I have no mind or will of my own?'

He gave her a knowing look. 'I didn't come marching into your life. You came blundering into mine. Now it's time for you to take responsibility for it.'

'By following you around like a stupid little lapdog?' She gave an exaggerated shudder of distaste before curling her lip at him. 'I don't think so.'

His mouth flattened and his eyes flashed her a warning. 'You will do as I say or I'll take everything off your father. Do you hear me? Everything. There won't be a penny left for you to inherit once I'm done with him. Don't say I didn't warn you.'

Angelique pressed her spine back against the supports of her chair. 'Do you really think I will respond to threats?'

'You will if you know what's good for you.'

What would be good for me would be to put as much distance between you and me as is globally possible.

It was too dangerous being with him. How soon before she caved in and fell into his arms again? She had to get away. She had to think. Clear her head.

Protect her heart.

Angelique put her napkin down on the table and pushed back her chair. 'Will you excuse me?'

His brows snapped together. 'Where are you going?'

'I'm going to the powder room.' She gave him a lofty look. She didn't have to tell him *which* powder room. *Like one several thousand kilometres away.* 'Do I need to ask your permission first?'

His dark, unreadable eyes measured hers for a moment. 'Fine. Go and powder your nose. But if you're not back here in two minutes I'll come and find you.'

I'll be miles away by then.

Angelique only got as far as the street when she was stopped, not by Remy but by her father. He came striding towards her from the cab he had just vacated. His cheeks were puce and his brows were joined over his formidable nose.

'Is it true?' he asked. 'Have you married Remy Caffarelli?'

It was probably perverse of her, but she felt a strange sense of satisfaction at having done something so shocking and outrageously disappointing to her father. He looked like he was having a conniption. 'News certainly travels fast in this city,' she said lightly. 'How did you find out?'

He gave her a poisonous glare. 'Do you have any idea of the utter fool you've made of me? I was at my club when one of my colleagues informed me. He read a tweet about it. There was a photo of you in a wedding outfit that looked like something out of *The Arabian Nights*. How could you do this to me? You couldn't have thought of a worse punishment, you silly little cow. Have you no brain in that stupid, big, fat ugly head of yours?'

'Apologise to my wife or I'll flatten you.'

Angelique spun around to see Remy standing there. He had a grim look on his face and his fists were clenching as if he was already rehearsing his first punch. 'Don't.' She put her hand on his arm. 'It's not worth it.'

He gently but firmly unpeeled her fingers from his wrist and faced her father. He spoke in French and it wasn't pretty. Angelique watched as her father's face went from puce to bright crimson and then back to puce. Even the tips of his ears were bright red, as if he was going to explode on the spot.

'She is my daughter,' Henri said through tight lips. 'I'll speak to her any way I like.'

Remy suddenly seemed so incredibly tall as he stared down her father. 'She is my wife and no one gets to speak to her like that.' His tone was commanding, authoritative. Intractable. 'Apologise now or suffer the consequences.'

Her father huffed and puffed but finally he muttered what one could only very loosely describe as an apology before he sloped off back into his cab like a chastened dog being sent to its kennel.

Remy put a protective arm around Angelique's waist. 'Does he normally speak to you like that?'

She pressed her lips together as she watched the lights of the cab fade into the distance. She felt a sudden desire to cry and had to blink a few times to get control. No one had ever come to her defence before. Her mother had been too weak; the household staff too scared of losing their jobs.

'Ma petite?'

Angelique looked up at him. Had he ever looked more handsome, more dashing and gorgeous than right now? How could she ever have thought she hated him? She quickly shielded her gaze. 'We don't have the best relationship. His short fuse and my smart mouth aren't a good combination for familial harmony.'

He brushed her cheek with a light-as-air glide of his finger. 'Has he ever laid a hand on you?'

'No. But he uses words just as lethally. He did it to my mother. I'm sure it caused her breakdown. She just couldn't take it any more.'

His expression flashed with disgust. 'Why didn't you say something earlier? I would have sorted him out years ago.'

Angelique gave a weary sigh. 'I wanted to plenty of times but who would've believed me? It would blot his copybook too much to be seen as anything but a devoted father. The fact that he bawled me out like that in such a public place is a testament to how much he hates you. He would normally never speak to me like that if there was an audience.'

Remy took her hands and gave them a light squeeze. 'Promise me something.'

'What?'

'Don't ever be alone with him. Ever. Do you under-stand? Never.'

Right at this very moment, Angelique would have promised him anything. 'I promise.'

'Good girl.' He brought her hands up to his mouth and kissed both of them in turn, his eyes still holding hers. 'So, tell me about this new contract. You didn't get round to telling what it was about.'

She gave her eyes a little roll. 'You're not going to believe what they want me to do.'

His brows snapped together. 'Not a naked shoot?'

Angelique laughed at his fierce expression. 'No, nothing like that. I'm to be the new poster girl for de-signer bridal wear.'

'Bridal wear?'

'Yes. How ironic is that? I never even wanted to be a bride and now I'm going to be wearing frothy wedding dresses and voluminous veils every day of the week, and earning millions for the privilege.'

His dark gaze searched hers for a moment. 'And you're pleased?'

Angelique pasted on her brightest smile. 'But of course. For one thing, I won't have to diet so strin-gently. Just think of the multitude of sins I can hide under a hoop skirt.'

A smile kicked up the corners of his mouth. 'This calls for a celebration. Want to go back to the hotel and order in room service?'

'But what about the table you had to work so hard to secure?'

He gave a shrug. 'Personally, I think the place is overrated. My brother Rafe's wife, Poppy, would prob-ably agree with me. Did I tell you she's a cook?'

'I think I read that somewhere.' She fell into step

beside him as they walked along the footpath. 'What's she like?'

'Gorgeous.' He gave her a sudden grin. 'I mean that in a brother-in-law kind of way, of course. She reminds me of my mother. So does Raoul's fiancée, Lily. They're both really lovely girls. A bit too homespun for me, but still, each to his own.'

'Careful, Remy, you're starting to sound envious.'

He shook his head, his smile fading away. 'I'm not cut out for that domestic scene. I'm like you; I like my freedom too much. Babies seem such smelly, noisy things. And then they grow up and become annoying smart-mouthed tearaways who keep their parents up all night worrying about them. No. Not for me. Definitely not.'

Angelique gave him a playful little shoulder-bump. 'I'm sure not all children turn out horribly spoilt, obnoxious brats like you and me.'

He gave her a crooked grin as he gently shoulder-bumped her back. 'God forbid.'

CHAPTER NINE

REMY WATCHED an hour later in their suite as Angelique nibbled at an undressed green salad and took occasional sips from a glass of Chianti. When she wasn't acting tough and being lippy, she was surprisingly good company. Quirky. Funny. Engaging.

Something had shifted in their relationship outside the restaurant.

He had been brought up to defend and protect women. Not by his grandfather, who exploited them any chance he could, but by his father before he had died and his two older brothers. Remy didn't mind the occasional verbal brawl, but insulting a woman and calling her names was not something he could ever tolerate.

He had never liked Angelique's father, even when Henri had been a regular visitor at his grandfather's villa in Rome, well before he had come across him in business. Remy had always found him two-faced, sly and conniving. The fact that Henri had been verbally abusing his wife and daughter disgusted Remy but it didn't surprise him. Men like Henri Marchand used power in dishonourable ways. They snatched at it whenever they could and gave little thought to the harm they were causing others.

Remy wondered if Angelique's wilful and at times

reckless behaviour was a reaction to the tyranny she had lived under for so long. While she didn't live with her father, and hadn't for a long time, he still seemed to have power to hurt her. He'd seen the way she'd flinched at Henri's horrible words. It was no wonder she was so adamantly opposed to marriage since the example set for her had been so appalling.

Protecting her had been an automatic reaction for Remy. He had been prepared to use force if he'd had to, although generally he didn't condone physical violence. His anger at her escaping from the restaurant had turned so quickly into something else.

He still wasn't quite sure exactly what it was…

'Do you want some more wine?'

Angelique shook her head. 'No, one is enough. I'm not a big drinker. Too many calories.'

Remy frowned as he looked at her barely touched meal. 'This new contract… How does that fit in with your plans to focus on designing?'

She put her glass back down and met his gaze. 'It'll take ages, possibly months or even up to a year, to get to the manufacturing and selling stage. I'll need an income in the meantime. I can't live on air.'

He gave her a dry look. 'You're doing a pretty fine job of it so far. You've only taken a couple of nibbles of that piece of lettuce.'

'I don't need a lot of food.' She gave his empty plate a baleful glance. 'Unlike some people, who have disgustingly voracious appetites and seemingly hollow legs.'

'I'm not a glutton. I just love food.'

She arched a neatly groomed eyebrow in a worldly manner. 'And sex.'

He gave her a glinting smile. 'That too.'

There was a little silence.

She passed the tip of her tongue over her lush lips and an arrow of lust speared Remy in the groin. Was she thinking of their passionate union earlier?

He hadn't *stopped* thinking about it.

He hadn't stopped feeling it tingling in his flesh like aftershocks in the wake of an earthquake. He could still taste her sweet vanilla and milk taste. He could still feel the softness of her lips, the boldness of her clever little tongue, the smooth glide of her hands and fingers.

He suppressed a shudder as he thought of what that mouth and those hands could do to him. What that gorgeously tight, feminine body *had* done to him.

Made him lose control.

'We're going to have to share that bed,' Remy said. 'Maybe we should put down some ground rules first.'

'What do you suggest?' Her expression was pert. 'A chalk line down the middle?'

'I was thinking more of a roll of pillows or a bolster.'

'How about a barbed wire fence?'

Remy felt another arrow hit bull's-eye. 'I wouldn't want you to get hurt when you head over to my side.'

She gave him an arch look. 'What makes you think I would come over to your side?'

'You think we can keep this thing between us on ice? Seriously, how long do you think that's going to last? You're hot for me. You can deny it all you like, but I know you want me. You've always wanted me.' *Like I've always wanted you.*

She flickered her eyes upwards. 'I can't believe the size of your ego. I might have wanted you, but I've *had* you, and quite frankly once is more than enough.'

Remy felt the rush of a fresh challenge fire through his blood. She was playing hard to get. It was another point-scoring game to her. She had sensed his weakness and was going in for the kill.

Did she want him to beg?

He would *never* do that.

He could live without sex—for a while. Sure he could. Monks did it all the time. It was supposed to be good for the mind. It was supposed to be mentally cleansing…or something.

'So, what are you saying? I didn't float your boat or something?'

'The sails gave a little flutter but that was about it.'

She was lying. He had felt her spasms and he had heard her cries. Unless she was a very good actress, she'd had the orgasm of her life. Why then was she so keen not to repeat it? 'If you change your mind then just lean over and tap me on the shoulder,' he said. 'I'll be happy to get your motor started.'

She gave him a withering look. 'Don't hold your breath.'

Angelique came out of the bathroom half an hour later to find Remy lying on his back with an e-reader flopped down on his chest. His eyes were closed, his breathing was steady and even, his body naked from the waist up. She wasn't sure if he was naked below the waist, because the sheet was covering him, but she had a feeling he wasn't the type of guy to wear pyjamas to bed.

She let her eyes feast on his naked chest and broad shoulders. Each muscle was so perfectly contoured, toned and taut with not an ounce of excess flesh on him anywhere. His hair was tousled, as if he had not long ago run his fingers through it, and his face was shadowed with evening stubble.

All of the Caffarelli brothers were staggeringly gorgeous but Angelique had always found Remy's dark features particularly so. It was something about his chocolate-brown eyes, the way they glinted with amusement or mockery even when he was doing his deadpan thing. It was the way his mouth was fashioned, the lower lip fuller than the top one. The chiselled leanness of his jaw; the way he always looked like he hadn't shaved closely enough. It was something about his hands with their long, tanned fingers that felt like a Taser zap when they touched her.

Angelique carefully approached his side of the bed and lifted the e-reader off his chest. He made a low murmur and she paused before she put the e-reader on the bedside table. She tiptoed round to her side of the bed, gently peeled back the covers, slipped in and huddled right on the edge so no part of her body was anywhere near his. She closed her eyes and willed herself to sleep but the citrus scent of his aftershave stirred her senses. She could feel the warmth of his body; it seemed to be reaching out to her, enveloping her…*tempting her.*

She jammed her eyes even tighter together and brought the covers right up to her chin.

She would not touch him!

Angelique must have drifted off eventually because she when she opened her eyes it was light and Remy was already up, showered and dressed. He'd dropped the towel he'd used over the back of the velvet covered chair he was now sitting on as he typed something into his phone, a heavy frown between his brows.

'Don't you *ever* pick up after yourself?'

'Hmm?' His tone was absent and he didn't even look her way as he kept typing.

Angelique swung her legs over the side of the bed,

slipped her arms through her wrap and tied it around her body. She came over to where he was sitting, picked up the damp towel and held it between two fingers. 'Do you ever spare a thought for the person who has to come in and service your room?'

'What?' He glanced at her then, his expression still dark with a frown.

'You leave stuff everywhere. The least you could do is hang your towel up or leave it in the tub or the shower cubicle if you're not going to use it again.' She put her hands on her hips and glowered at him. 'Stop typing when I'm talking to you!'

'You're not talking to me, you're nagging me.'

'Yes, well, that's what wives are forced to do, because their lazy husbands don't see the hours of invisible work that goes on behind the scenes to keep a house running smoothly.'

He rose to his feet and Angelique took a little step back. Without her heels he towered over her and she had to crick her neck to keep eye contact. His expression was mocking as he looked down at her. 'And just how many houses have you run, *ma chérie*?'

She pursed her lips. 'I'm just saying...'

He held her gaze for a long moment. He seemed to be thinking about something. She could see his mouth shifting from side to side in a contemplative manner. 'Can you cook?'

'Yes. I've been to cookery schools in France, Italy and Thailand. Why?'

'Would you cook a dinner for me?'

Angelique frowned. 'What, you mean every day, like in a traditional marriage?'

'No, nothing like that. I want to entertain Robert Mappleton—you know, the guy I've been trying to win over? He's ultra-conservative and traditional. He's been wined and dined thousands of times in the best restaurants across the globe. What I think would really impress him is a home-cooked dinner in a private setting. Will you do it?'

She caught her lower lip between her teeth. The sooner she helped Remy nail his deal, the sooner they could go their separate ways. That certainly wasn't half as attractive as it had been a day or so ago. She had her own contract to consider now. Would the top-end designers currently courting her still want her if she was divorced?

Probably not.

'Which private setting did you have in mind?'

'Tarrantloch.'

Angelique glared at him. 'You insensitive bastard!'

'What?'

She narrowed her gaze to slits. 'You really are the most unfeeling jerk I've ever come across. How much more do you want to rub my nose in it? You stole my house and now you want me to play the 1950s housewife in it? Arrggh!'

'I guess that's a no?'

Angelique glowered at him. 'You're damn right it's a no. How could you be so cruel?'

'I was actually thinking of you,' he said. 'I thought you'd be more comfortable cooking in a familiar kitchen.'

'I'd be more comfortable if the deeds to my home were back in my hands where they belong.'

He gave her a dry look. 'Then perhaps you need to work on charming me into changing my mind, *ma petite*, hmm?'

Angelique felt a traitorous spurt of longing assail her.

How did he do that to her with just one look? Those dark eyes smouldered and she was instantly aflame. How was she going to resist him when all she wanted was to be back in his arms?

But she wasn't going to let him know that.

She narrowed her eyes even further. 'Are you blackmailing me?'

'I prefer to call it negotiating.'

'Negotiating my foot! You want me to sleep with you. Why don't you come right out and say it?'

His eyes scorched hers. 'I want to sleep with you.'

Angelique's inner core contracted. Her breasts tingled. Her heart skipped and then raced. She ran her tongue over her suddenly dry mouth. She saw the raw, naked lust in his dark eyes. She felt it in the crackling air she was trying to drag into her lungs. She felt it in the firm grip of his steely hands as they captured her by the hips and pulled her against him.

Heat against heat.

His mouth came down, hovering just above hers. 'This is what I want.' He toyed with her lips in a tantalising little tug-and-release game that made her spine turn to liquid.

I want it too. So, so much!

'And this…' He stroked the seam of her mouth with his tongue, teasing the sensitive flesh, taking possession as soon as she opened to him.

She tried to smother a whimper but her bones were melting like an ice sculpture in the Dharbiri desert sun as he explored every corner in intimate detail. One of his hands went to the small of her back, pushing her closer to his hot, hard heat, the other deftly untying the ties of her wrap and unpeeling it from her body.

He pushed aside the satin straps of her nightgown

and it slipped off her body and pooled at her feet. His hand cupped her breast, her nipple brushing against his palm, making her senses hum with delight. Need unfurled in her body, stretching like a sun-warmed cat, reaching into all of her limbs, making them soft and pliant as he crushed her to him.

Angelique tugged his shirt out of his trousers and blindly undid the buttons as her mouth fed off his. She unhitched his belt, undid his waistband, rolled down his zipper and then boldly took possession of him. He groaned into her mouth as he kicked off his shoes and stepped out of his trousers.

They stumbled back towards the bed, knocking one of the table lamps over in the process. He came down over her, his thighs trapping hers, his mouth still working its heady magic on hers.

Angelique arched her back as he left her mouth to concentrate on her breasts. The feel of his tongue and teeth on her flesh was a blissful torture. She writhed and gasped and clutched at his head.

He didn't stop at her breasts. He went lower to the cave of her belly button, dipping in and out with his moist tongue, laving her flesh, trailing even lower.

She automatically tensed. This was so personal. So very intimate.

He calmed her with a gentle hand on her thigh. 'Not comfortable with this?'

Angelique felt a blush crawl into her cheeks. He thought she was so hip and worldly but this was the one thing she had never felt comfortable sharing with any partner. It was all very well, pretending to have an orgasm when someone was rocking and humping above her, but *this* was something else. 'Um…'

'It's fine, *ma petite*. You don't have to do anything you're not comfortable with.'

Was it the fact he had given her the freedom to say no that made her now want to say yes? She slowly met his dark gaze. 'I've never done this with a partner...'

Something moved in his eyes. A flicker of surprise? Delight? 'Do you trust me to make it good for you?'

Angelique suddenly realised she did. Hadn't he already shown her what her body was capable of in terms of pleasure? She had never experienced anything like the supremely passionate response she had felt in his arms with anyone else. She wanted to experience *this* with him; this incredible intimacy would leave her with something precious and unique to remember when their marriage was over. 'Yes...'

He gently caressed her thighs, waiting until she was open and relaxed before he traced her folds with his tongue. All of her nerves writhed and danced, twirled and fretted for more. He did it again, separating her this time, tasting her, briefly touching her clitoris to give it time to get accustomed to the sensation. He slowly built the movements of his tongue against her swollen flesh, making her shiver all over as tiny ripples began to course through her. He was patient and gentle. Experimental. Gauging her response, learning her body's secrets and indulging her senses until she was suspended on a precipice, hovering, wanting, aching, but not quite able to take that final plunge.

'Come for me, *ma petite*,' he coaxed her softly. 'Don't hold back.'

'I want to but I can't.'

'Yes you can.' He stroked her tensed up thighs until they released. 'You can do it. Just stop thinking and let go.'

Angelique felt the flickering of his tongue against her and a wave of pleasure came rolling up from deep inside her. She felt every muscle in her body tighten before the final lift off. She went careening into oblivion, shuddering and shaking as the tide of release passed through her like a powerful relaxant.

Remy came back over her and pushed her wild hair back off her face. 'Average?'

Angelique couldn't stop a coy smile. 'How do I know, since I don't have anything to compare it to?'

His gave her one of his smouldering looks. 'I can soon fix that.'

'Wait.' She put a hand on his chest, her gaze sultry. 'There's something I have to see to first.'

He drew in an audible breath as her hand moved down his body. But she wasn't content with just stroking and caressing him. She wanted to taste him as he had tasted her. This was another act she had shied away from in the past, but right now it seemed perfectly natural to pleasure him with her lips and tongue.

She pressed a pathway of kisses down his chest, swirling her tongue into his belly button before going inexorably lower. She felt his abdominal muscles contract the closer she got to her target. She breathed over his erection at first, letting him feel the dance of her breath, letting him experience the anticipation of her imminent possession.

'I usually put a condom on at this point.' His voice sounded rough. Gravelly.

Angelique gave him a seductive look from beneath her lashes. 'There isn't time.'

'But I— *Oh God*.' He sucked in another breath as she set to work on him.

It was thrilling to have him so in her power. She

had never realised how arousing it was to feel him and hear him struggle for control. She was ruthless as she drew on him, not giving him a chance to pull away. She tasted the hot essence of him against her tongue, felt the tension in him against her lips as she moved them up and down his shaft.

He grabbed at her head with both of his hands, presumably to push her away, but she refused to budge. She hummed against his swollen flesh and he gave a quickly muttered curse and then spilled.

After it was over he fell on the bed on his back, his chest rising and falling as he tried to get his breathing under control.

Angelique trailed a light fingertip up and down his chest. 'Better than average?'

He turned his head and gave her a sinfully erotic look. 'The best.'

'Are you just saying that?'

'No.'

Wow. Oh wow. Her fingertip came back up and circled one of his flat, dark nipples. 'How soon before you can go again?'

'Why do you ask?'

She gave a casual little shrug. 'Just wondering.'

He rolled her back over and trapped her within the cage of his arms. 'You still want to play, *mon trésor*?'

She traced his lower lip with her fingertip. 'Might as well make the most of our time together.'

He stopped the pathway of her finger by holding her hand in his. 'Just so we're clear on this—I'm not making any promises about Tarrantloch. I won it fair and square. I don't do sentimentality or guilt trips. You need to understand and accept that.'

'But I thought you said—'

'If we continue to sleep together, it's because we want to satisfy the mutual attraction we feel. It's not about and should not be about anything else.'

Angelique knew how determined he could be, but then so could she. Clearly locking horns with him wasn't going to work. It had never worked before. She would be better served in finding another way to appeal to his sense of fairness—assuming he had one, of course. Charm him. Woo him. Beguile him. *Outsmart him.*

She tiptoed a fingertip down his sternum again. 'Do you ever *not* get your way?'

He gave her a lazy smile. 'Giving in is about as much in my nature as submission and demureness is in yours.'

'I don't know about that.' Angelique gave a little sinuous movement beneath him. 'I'm feeling pretty submissive right now.'

His eyes glinted as his hands pinned her arms either side of her head, his strong thighs trapping hers with erotic intent. 'Then I'd better make the most of it.'

And he did.

CHAPTER TEN

ANGELIQUE BREATHED IN the sharp, clean air of the high-lands as Remy helped her out of the car the following day. Tarrantloch in autumn was bleak and cold but that was part of the raw beauty of it. The turreted grey stone mansion had been in her mother's family for over three-hundred years. It was set in a large verdant clearing in the middle of a forest and had its own lake and a burn that ran with ice-cold water full of salmon and trout.

She had spent some of her happiest times here as a child before her mother had turned into a browbeaten shadow of her former self. Coming here had been some-thing Angelique and her mother had done together in the early days to spend time with her maternal grand-parents while Henri had been busy with his business affairs in Europe.

But, once her grandparents had passed away within a year of each other, Tarrantloch had been left idle with just a handful of servants, as her father had insisted on living in his homeland of France so he could commute more easily to Italy, where he had his major business interests, including those with Vittorio Caffarelli.

Over the last couple of years, however, he had come back and taken up residence, strutting around like a proud peacock as he conducted various house parties with his business cronies. It disgusted Angelique to see her mother's home exploited by her father and she had mostly kept well away unless she knew he was abroad on business.

Angelique hadn't been to Tarrantloch since the summer when she'd had a ten-day break from her schedule. It seemed surreal to be here now, officially married to Remy, knowing the house was no longer hers.

Might never be hers again.

Remy had decided he wanted it as a trophy. What else could it be to him other than a prize to gloat over? He had luxury homes all over Europe and the Mediterranean. Besides, if he wanted to see snow he could go to his chalet in the Swiss Alps.

No, Tarrantloch was his way of publicly claiming victory over her father. What pained her the most was Remy could so easily turn around and sell it once it had served its purpose. And, one thing she knew for certain, he wouldn't be offering it to her for mate's rates. He was a ruthless, hard-nosed businessman. He wouldn't allow sentimentality or emotions to influence him.

But she was not going to give up until she had exhausted every possible avenue to get it back.

Angelique walked with Remy over the pebbled driveway to the front door. 'Have you kept on any of my father's staff?' she asked.

'None, apart from the gardener, and he's on notice.'

She raised a brow. 'Why not?'

'Because not one of them was doing a proper day's work.' He took out the keys he had in his pocket and unlocked the heavy door. 'I'm going to conduct some interviews while we're here. I want to employ locals, people who know the house and want it to be preserved. Your father surrounded himself with a motley crew of sycophants who didn't do much more than take up space.'

Angelique was inclined to agree with him. More than inclined. She had never liked the obsequious butler and housekeeper her father had hired. The devoted staff her grandparents had employed had left in dribs and drabs over the years, either through retirement, death or disenchantment. 'So who's here now?'

'Just us.'

She blinked. 'What? No one at all? Just us?' *Alone?*

He gave her a wickedly sexy smile. 'It's our honeymoon, *ma chérie*. We're not supposed to have people with us.'

Her belly gave a little quivery swoop. 'But what about the dinner with Robert Mappleton? After all, isn't that why we're here?'

'That's not until the end of next week.'

'Why not get it over with this week?'

'Ah, but that would appear too eager, *n'est-ce pas*? Better to let him think I'm in no great hurry to play ball.'

Angelique sent him a wry look. 'I can see why you've accumulated the wealth you have at such a young age: you're as cunning as a fox.'

He grinned as he held the door open for her. 'No point in being too predictable. Where's the fun in that? No, my philosophy is to keep them guessing for as long as you can and then reel them in when they least expect it.'

Is that what you're doing with me? Angelique wondered as she followed him inside. Hadn't she already been reeled in? She had been so determined to keep out of his bed, to keep immune to his potent charm, but as soon as he'd kissed her at the wedding ceremony in

Dharbiri her fate had been sealed. What hope did she have resisting him when his passionate possession made her feel so alive and vital as a woman?

Coming here with him for a two-week 'honeymoon' was only going to make her need of him all the more entrenched. She knew that, but had come anyway, even though she could have made up some excuse to do with her new contract. She had signed and emailed it earlier that day. Her manager had already lined up a shoot with three of the biggest names in haute couture in Paris.

Angelique rubbed her hands up and down her arms as the chilly air of the old house goose-bumped her skin. 'Right now I'm kind of wishing I had gone to Barbados.'

Remy flashed her a quick grin. 'Where's your sense of adventure, *ma petite*? It won't take long to lay a fire.'

'There's central heating. The main switch is over there.'

'I'll see to it and the luggage while you have a wander around. Make yourself at home.'

She gave him a flinty look. 'Excuse me, but up until a few days ago this *was* my home.'

'Then you won't need me to take you on a guided tour, will you?'

Angelique glowered at him. 'Why are you doing this? Why are you rubbing my nose in it like this? I realise you have issues with my father over what happened between him and your grandfather but that's nothing to do with me. I didn't do any dodgy deals. Why am I the scapegoat?'

His look was brooding and intractable. 'This isn't about you, Angelique. Last year your father circulated rumours about me that cost me millions. I don't take that sort of stuff lying down. I wanted revenge, not just for myself but also for what happened to my family. My grandfather almost lost everything when your father pulled the rug from under him.'

'You don't even like your grandfather!' Angelique threw back. 'Why are you so keen to get justice for him?'

'I'm not getting it for him,' Remy said. 'I'm getting it for Rafe. He worked harder than any of us to rebuild our assets. Rafe has always shouldered the responsibility of looking after Raoul and me. I wanted to do my bit to show him his sacrifice hadn't gone unnoticed or been taken for granted.'

'Don't you care that you're hurting me in the process?'

'How am I hurting you?' His expression turned mocking. 'You're the one who just landed a multimillion-dollar contract simply because you're married to me. I have yet to reap any benefits, especially if this Mappleton deal falls through.'

But I don't even want that contract. I shouldn't have signed it. I wish I hadn't.

Angelique pushed the errant thoughts back and planted her hands on her hips. 'I seem to recollect you got some fringe benefits last night.'

His eyes started to smoulder as he closed the distance between them in a couple of lazy strides. 'I didn't hear you complaining.'

She pushed her bottom lip out in a pout. 'I have bruises.'

A frown flickered across his forehead. 'Where?'

Angelique turned over her wrists to show him where his fingers had faintly marked her skin when he'd held her down the night before. Every time she saw the tiny marks she felt a shudder of remembered pleasure go through her. It had been like being branded by him.

Owned by him. Controlled by him. She had been more than willing, which somehow made it worse. She didn't want to need him in such an intensely physical way. She had always been the one in control with men in the past. Being dominated by Remy, even playfully during sex, made her feel as if she was relinquishing all power to him, especially when he still hadn't told her if he was going to give her back her home.

He took her left wrist, brought it up to his mouth and gently brushed his lips against the almost imperceptible mark. 'I'm sorry. I didn't realise I'd hurt you.'

She felt a traitorous ribbon of desire unfurl inside her. 'You didn't hurt me. I just have a tendency to bruise easily.'

His thumb moved over her pulse point. 'Maybe you should be the one who does the tying up next time.'

Angelique arched a brow. 'You'd let me do that?'

His eyes smouldered some more. 'Only if I knew I could get out of it.'

Like our marriage.

It wasn't for ever. He wanted to be free as soon as his business deal was signed and secured. The bitter irony was *she* was going to help him achieve it. She would be breaking her own heart. Trashing her dreams. Ruining her hopes.

There would be no happy-ever-after with Remy.

It was foolish to dream of black-haired babies with chocolate-brown eyes. It was crazy to think Remy would ever utter an endearment he actually meant. It was madness to want him to fall in love with her.

It was madness to have fallen in love with him.

She would have to fall out of love with him. Quick smart. It would be the ultimate in humiliation to have him find out how she felt. It sounded so pathetic, being hopelessly in love with someone since you were sixteen.

Unrequited love.

Obsessive love.

That was all it was—a fantasy. A teenage infatuation that had grown into an adult fixation.

The sooner she got over it the better.

Angelique stepped back from him with a casual air. 'What plans have you made about food and so on? I'm pretty sure my father wouldn't have left anything healthy and nutritious in the pantry.'

'I've organised a food parcel from our hotel in London. It's in the car with our luggage. I'll do some more shopping tomorrow.'

She widened her eyes in mock surprise. 'You actually *know* how to shop for food?'

'I do occasionally pick up the odd item or two. I quite enjoy it.' He turned to the thermostat on the wall and began adjusting the temperature settings. 'My mother used to take us shopping with her. She was keen for us to experience as normal a life as possible because she hadn't been born to money or privilege. If we behaved well, she'd buy us a *gelato* at the end.' His hand dropped from the panel and he turned. He had a wistful expression on his face. 'Rafe would always have chocolate, Raoul would always have lemon, but I used to have a different flavour each time…'

Angelique studied him for a moment. He looked like he was mentally recalling each and every one of those outings with his mother. The boating accident on the French Riviera that had killed his parents had occurred the year before she had been born. She had only ever known the Caffarelli brothers as orphans. From her youthful perspective they had always seemed terribly sophisticated and racy, with their eye-popping good looks and wealthy lifestyle. But behind the trappings of wealth and privilege was a tragedy that had robbed three little boys of their loving parents.

Angelique remembered too well the shock of feeling alone. The utter desperation she had felt at seeing her mother's body lowered into the ground on the dismally wet and grey morning of the funeral was something she would never forget. The build-up of emotion inside her chest had felt like a tsunami about to break. But somehow she had kept it in because she hadn't wanted to disappoint her father. He had said she must be brave and so she was. But inside a part of her had died and gone with her mother into that cold, black hole in the ground.

Angelique blinked away the memory and said, 'It must have been devastating for you when your parents were killed.'

A screen came down over his face. 'I got over it.' He moved past her to go back outside to get their bags. 'Stay inside out of the cold. I won't be long.'

Had he really got over it? He had only been seven years old. It was young for any child to lose a parent, yet he had not lost one but both. Angelique suspected that, like her, his restlessness and wild, partying lifestyle had come out of that deep pain of being abandoned so suddenly and so young. He was anchorless and yet shied away from anything that would tie him down.

His grandfather Vittorio could not be described as a nurturer. He was a cold, hard, bitter man with a tendency to lose his temper at the least provocation. She hadn't seen Vittorio for a number of years, but in the old days when she and her father had been regular visitors to the Caffarelli villa in Rome she had given him a wide berth.

Of the three boys Remy seemed the most willing to deal with his grandfather. He visited him more often than his brothers and seemed to have a better relationship with him than either Rafe or Raoul, possibly because Remy had always relied on his natural charm to win people over.

Angelique wondered if Vittorio had found out about their marriage yet. It had been three days and as far as she knew Remy hadn't called or spoken to him other than what he'd said on camera when the press had stormed them.

What did his brothers think? Had they contacted him and told him what a fool he was for marrying someone like her? She had always been a bit frightened of Rafe, who was so much older, but Raoul had always been nice to her.

Would he too think it was the worst disaster in the world for Remy to be locked in a marriage with her?

Remy was dusting the snow off his shoulders as he came inside when his phone rang. He knew it was his grandfather because he had set a particular ringtone to Vittorio's number. He deliberately hadn't called Vittorio before now to talk about his marriage to Angelique because that was what his grandfather would have expected, and Remy had learned over time that it was more tactical to do what he *didn't* expect. It gave him more leverage with the old man and, he liked to think, a measure of respect. '*Nonno*, nice of you to call. What's new?'

'I have a newspaper in front of me that says you've married Angelique Marchand.' His grandfather's voice had that thread of steel in it that used to terrify Remy as a young child. 'There's also a photo of you together outside some hotel in London.'

'Is it a nice photo?' Remy asked. 'She'll be hell to live with if it isn't.'

He heard Vittorio's intake of breath. 'Is this a set-up? One of your pranks to gain publicity or something?'

'It's no prank. We're married and we're staying married.' *Until I have that Mappleton deal in the bag.* Not that he could tell his grandfather that. If old man Mappleton got a hint that Remy's marriage to Angelique wasn't authentic, he would pull the plug on any negotiations.

'You always did have a thing for that girl,' Vittorio said.

Remy hadn't realised he'd been so transparent about lusting over her in the past. He'd thought he'd done a pretty good job of disguising it. 'Yes, well, you've seen what she looks like. I'm only human.'

'Why didn't you just screw her and get her out of your system?' Vittorio continued. 'Why on earth did you marry her? Have you got her pregnant or something?'

Remy gave himself a mental shake when an image of Angelique with a baby bump came to mind. 'No, I did not get her pregnant. I'm in love with her.' *Ouch. That hurt. Not sure I want to say that again. It might make it happen.*

Perish the thought!

Vittorio gave a disdainful laugh. 'The day you fall in love is the day hell freezes over or I get accepted into heaven. Take your pick; neither of them is going to happen. You don't have the capacity to love. You're exactly like me in that regard. Love is for emotionally weak people who can't survive without being propped up by someone else.'

Remy knew his grandfather was scathing about his brothers for falling in love. He mocked them any chance he could, picking Poppy and Lily to pieces as if they were not real people with feelings but department-store items Rafe and Raoul had picked up that, in Vittorio's opinion, were somehow faulty.

Remy didn't like admitting it but deep down he was starting to feel a little envious of how happy his brothers were. How settled; secure; anchored. His life of flying in and flying out of cities and relationships had always seemed so exciting and satisfying up until now.

He shook off the thought like the snow he'd just brushed off his shoulders. 'Be that as it may, you have to admit she's great to look at. What more could a man ask for than a stunningly beautiful wife who loves him?'

'She's stunning but she's Henri Marchand's daughter. Do you really want to mix your blood with the likes of him?'

What was his grandfather's obsession about babies? It was making Remy distinctly uneasy. 'We're leaving the breeding to Rafe and Raoul. Angelique wants to keep her figure.'

Vittorio grunted. 'She won't stay with you. You mark my words. Next thing you know, she'll slap divorce papers on you and take half your assets. You're a fool to enter a marriage without a pre-nuptial agreement. I thought you had more sense than your brothers. Seems I was wrong.'

It did worry Remy about the lack of a pre-nup but he wasn't going to dwell on it while he had other more pressing matters to deal with. Besides, Angelique had her own reasons for wanting the marriage to continue.

The bridal-wear gig was huge. He'd already seen hundreds of tweets about it. It was amusingly ironic to think of her modelling the one type of outfit she loathed more than any other.

'How's that new housemaid working out?' Remy asked.

'She's got a face like a monkey.'

Remy rolled his eyes. Some things never changed. 'I might pop over in a couple of weeks to see you once I've sorted out a few business issues. I'll bring Angelique with me.'

Vittorio gave another cynical grunt. 'That's if she's still with you by then.'

CHAPTER ELEVEN

ANGELIQUE CAME DOWN to the large sitting room where Remy was stoking a roaring fire. Warmth was spreading throughout the house now the heating was on but the sound of the flames crackling and spitting in the fireplace reminded her of cosy times with her grandparents when she was young.

The removals company had obviously come and taken away her father's personal belongings, leaving just the original furniture. Without Henri's things here it was like stepping back in time to a happier period in her life.

But it still annoyed her that Remy had possession of her family home and was so determined to keep it. It was all very well sleeping with him and fancying herself in love with him, but at the end of the day she had to get her home back.

Her goal was to get the deeds to Tarrantloch back where they belonged. Nothing else was supposed to distract her from that.

Not Remy with his smouldering looks, spine-loosening smile, his magical touch and mind-blowing love-making. She could indulge in an affair with him for the period of their marriage but it had to end with her achieving her mission.

Tarrantloch was meant to be hers and she would not be satisfied until she had it back in her possession.

Remy stood up and glanced at her over his shoulder. 'Warming up?'

'You certainly move fast.' Angelique walked further into the room. 'You've had every trace of my father's occupation of the place removed.'

He kicked a piece of charcoal back into the fire with the side of his shoe before he looked at her again. 'That's normally what a new owner does, is it not?'

Angelique set her jaw. Did he have to rub it in every chance he got? 'What do you plan to do with it?'

'I want to base myself here.' He dusted off his hands from having placed another log on the fire. 'It's private and far enough away from a major city to put off the paparazzi.'

She frowned at him. 'But you're a big city man. You spend most of your time in casinos and clubs. You'd be bored out of your mind up here in the highlands with nothing but the wind and the rain and the snow for company.'

'I don't know about that…' He nudged absently at the fire with the poker. 'Rafe's been raving about the mansion he bought in Oxfordshire—the one that Poppy's grandmother used to work in when she was growing up.' He put the poker back in its holder and faced her again. 'He originally planned to turn it into a luxury hotel for the rich and famous but now he's living there with Poppy. It's home to them now, it's where they plan to bring up a family.'

'That's all very well and good, but you're not a family man,' Angelique pointed out. 'You're going to get lonely up here unless you regularly fly in some party girls to while away the long winter nights.'

He shrugged a shoulder and kicked at another piece of charcoal that had fallen out of the fire. 'It may surprise you, but I don't spend all of my time partying and gambling. That's one of the reasons I love Dharbiri so much. It's so different from the life I live in the city.'

'It's certainly different.' Her tone was wry. 'It's not a place I'm going to forget in a hurry.'

He met her gaze across the glow of the firelight. 'Apart from the sand and the heat it's much the same as here. It has a bleak sort of raw beauty about it. You can hear the silence.'

She gave him a knowing look. 'It might be isolated and a little bleak up here but no one's going to come barging in threatening to flay you alive if you have an unchaperoned woman in your room.'

He acknowledged that with little incline of his head. 'Perhaps not, but I bet there are quaint old ways and customs up here in the highlands and on some of the west coast islands.'

'I still don't think you'll last a winter up here.' Angelique sat down on the sofa and curled her legs underneath her body. 'It can get snowbound for weeks and the wind can bore ice-pick holes in your chest. And don't get me started about the rain in summer. It goes on for weeks at a time. Quite frankly, I don't even know why they bother calling it summer. It should be called the wet season, like in the tropics.' She flicked her hair back behind her shoulders. 'Oh, and did I mention the midges and mosquitoes? They're as big as Clydesdales.'

He crossed one ankle over the other as he leaned against the mantelpiece, a lazy smile curving his lips. 'If it's as bad as you say then why do you love it up here so much?'

She looked at the flickering flames before she answered. 'I spent some of the happiest days of my life up here when I was a child.'

'You came here with your parents?'

'My mother,' Angelique said. 'It was her parents', my grandparents', home. My father never used to come because he was always too busy with work. I think the truth was he didn't get on with my grandparents. They didn't like him. I was too young to remember specific conversations but I got the impression they thought he was two-faced.' She looked back at the fire again. 'They were right. Everything changed when my nanna died. The grief hit my mother hard and then my granddad died less than a year later. It was devastating for my mother. That's when things started to get a little crazy at home.'

Remy was frowning when she looked at him again. 'That's when she became depressed?'

Angelique nodded. 'She must have felt so lonely once her parents were gone. She was shy and lacked confidence, which was probably why my father was attracted to her in the first place. He saw her as someone he could control.'

Remy's frown was more of anger than anything. 'I wish I'd flattened him when I had the chance. What a cowardly son of a bitch.'

'You hurt him far more by taking Tarrantloch off him,' Angelique said. 'And of course by marrying me. That really stung. He won't get over that in a hurry.'

His expression turned rueful. 'Yes, well, my grandfather isn't too happy about it either.'

'You've spoken to him?'

'He called when I was bringing in the bags. And it wasn't to congratulate me.'

'No, I expect not.' She hooked her hands around her

knees. 'I guess the congratulations will come in thick and fast once we divorce.'

The silence was broken only by the hiss and crackle of the flames in the fireplace.

Angelique chanced a glance at him but he was staring into the fire as if it were the most befuddling thing he'd ever seen. Was he worried about their lack of a pre-nup? It was certainly a worrying thing for a man with wealth—or a woman, for that matter—to be exposed to the possibility of a financial carve-up in the event of a divorce.

The only way to avoid it would be to *stay* married.

Which was not something Remy would be likely to suggest, even to keep control of his fortune. He didn't do love and commitment. He was the epitome of the freedom-loving playboy. Tying him down would be like trying to tame a lion with a toothpick.

It wasn't going to happen.

Remy turned from the fire. 'I don't suppose there's any point in asking if you're hungry?'

Angelique unhooked her hands from around her legs. 'I am, actually. It must be the cold wintry air. I used to eat heaps when I came here as a kid. My nanna was a fabulous cook.'

'Your grandparents didn't have a housekeeper?'

'Yes, but nanna still did most of the cooking. I used to help her. I can still make a mean batch of oat cakes and flapjacks.'

He smiled a sexy smile as he held out his hand to her. 'I'm told it can sometimes get very hot in the kitchen.'

Angelique felt a tingle in her core as his strong fingers wrapped around hers. She gave him a sultry look. 'If you think it's going to be too hot for you, then you should stay out of there.'

He brought her up against his body, his *aroused* body. Another tingle coursed through her, making her nipples stand to attention. His gaze zeroed in on her mouth for a pulsing beat. 'I'm pretty sure I can handle it.'

She moved against him, just the once, but it made his eyes go almost black with desire. 'You think?'

He swept her up in his arms and carried her towards the door. 'Let's go and find out.'

Remy slid her down his body once they got to the kitchen. Her body inflamed his; he had been burning for her ever since they'd arrived. It seemed years since he'd last made love with her but it had only been last night. And what a night that had been.

He craved her.

Ached for her.

His groin was tight with longing; he wanted to sink into her and lose himself. Block his thoughts—the rational, sensible ones, that was. He wanted to feel the magic of her touch, the way her body clenched so tightly around him as if she never wanted to let him go. He could not remember a more passionate, exciting lover. It felt different somehow...more intense; as if his skin had developed a new, overly sensitive layer that only responded to her touch.

Remy started playing with her lower lip in little tug-and-release bites. 'How's the heat so far?'

She snaked her arms up around his neck and threaded her fingers through his hair. 'Not hot enough.' She slid her tongue into his mouth and he nearly disgraced himself then and there.

He took control of the kiss, deepening the thrusts of his tongue as it chased and subdued hers. She gave little gasps and encouraging groans, her body pressing as close as she physically could. He felt her mound rubbing against his erection, a tantalising tease of the delights to come.

He lifted her up on to the kitchen bench and stood between her spread thighs. 'You're wearing too many clothes,' he growled against her mouth.

She nibbled at his lips. 'That would be because it's below freezing outside.'

He grabbed at the back of his cashmere sweater and tugged it over his head. Next came his shirt, which lost a button or two in the process. 'Now let's start on you.'

She gave him a seductive look as she undid the tiny pearl buttons of her designer cardigan. She was wearing a black lacy camisole underneath that showed the shadow of her cleavage and the perfect globes of her breasts. 'I'm not wearing a bra.'

His groin tightened another notch. 'I can see that.'

She peeled the shoestring straps over her shoulders, one by one, lowering the lacy garment slowly, like a high-class stripper. 'You want to touch me, don't you?'

I want to do more than touch you. 'What gives you that idea?' Remy did his deadpan face.

Her lips curved upwards in a siren's smile. 'I'm not going to let you touch me until I'm good and ready. You have to be a good boy and wait.' She lowered her camisole a little further, revealing a tightly budded pink nipple. 'Do you think you can do that?'

Remy had to count backwards to stop himself from jumping the gun. His need was pulsating with such relentless force it was painful. 'I'll wait, but you do realise at some point in the future you're going to pay for this, don't you?'

She gave a little mock shiver. 'Ooh! Is that supposed to scare me?'

'Be scared,' he growled. 'Be very scared.'

She exposed her other breast, all the while holding his gaze with the dancing, mischievous heat of hers. She glided her hand down over her belly to the waistband of her pencil-thin designer jeans. 'I'm wet. I bet you want to feel how wet, don't you?'

Remy had never been so turned on. He was fighting to keep his hands off her. He couldn't think about anything but the need to thrust into her to the hilt and explode. 'I'm hard. I bet you want to feel how hard, huh?'

Her eyes sparkled as she traced a fingertip down the ridge of his erection through the fabric of his trousers. 'Mmm; impressive.' She took the same fingertip and traced it down the denim-covered seam of her body. 'I guess I should get out of my jeans. Would you like that?'

I would love that. 'Take your time.'

She slithered down off the bench, pushing him back with a fingertip. 'Not so close, big boy. You don't get to touch until I give the go ahead.'

Remy mentally gulped. This was going to end badly if she didn't speed things up a bit. He could feel his erection straining against his jeans. He just hoped the fabric was strong enough to hold him in.

She was definitely going to pay for this.

And it would involve a leather whip and handcuffs.

Angelique locked gazes with him and slowly undid her zipper. The sound of it going down was magnified in the throbbing silence. She stepped out of her heels and then she peeled the jeans off her legs. Once they were off she stepped back into her heels, leaving just the black lace of her knickers on. 'So…' She ran the tip of her tongue over her lower lip leaving it wet and glistening. 'Are you getting excited?'

Way, way beyond that. 'What do you think?'

She traced his erection again, her eyes still holding his in a sexy little lock that made his blood heat to boiling. 'How badly do you want me?'

Off the scale. 'Let's put it this way. Right now I could do you in five seconds flat.'

Her eyes flared and then her lips pushed forwards in a pout. 'That sounds like I would be left high and dry.'

'Don't worry. I'd take you along for the ride.'

She put that teasing fingertip to work again. 'What if I was to strike up a little deal with you?'

Remy marvelled at her self-control. He'd always thought he was a master at keeping his desire under his command but she had pushed him to the very limit. His body was a mass of twitching nerve endings and primal urgings. But he was still in enough control—only just—to recognise manipulation when he saw it. 'What sort of deal?'

She slowly lowered his zipper. 'A deal where we both get what we want.'

He sucked in a breath as her fingers tugged his underwear aside. It was hard to think straight when she was touching him, stroking him to the very edge, but he was not going to be tricked or manoeuvred into giving away what he had spent years fighting to gain.

Besides, he hadn't just done it for himself: he had done it for his brothers. It wasn't his prize to give away. It represented far more than a victory over a double-crossing enemy. Taking ownership of Tarrantloch was finally setting right the wrongs of the past. Handing it over to the sole heir of the man who had almost destroyed his family's fortune was the very last thing he would consider doing, no matter what his relationship with Angelique was. Or wasn't.

He pushed her hand away and stepped back from her.

'Game over, *ma belle*. I'm not giving you Tarrantloch in exchange for a quick screw up against the kitchen bench. I'm not *that* desperate.'

Her expression switched from sexy siren to outraged virago within a heartbeat. 'You bastard.'

'*Orphan* is the correct term.'

She came at him then like a spitting cat, all claws, snarls and scratches. 'I hate you!'

Remy restrained her by holding both of her flailing arms behind her back, which rather delightfully pushed her pelvis into blistering contact with his. 'You don't hate me. You want me.'

Her grey-blue eyes flashed venom at him. 'Why won't you give me what I want?'

He ripped her knickers down with a ruthless jerk of his hand. 'What do you want the most?' He probed her folds with his painfully erect penis. 'Tell me. Right now, what do you want the most?'

He heard her swallow as he made contact with her slippery moistness. 'I want what's rightfully mine.'

'Then at least we're on the same page,' he said and then he sealed her mouth roughly with his.

Angelique lost herself in his kiss. To be truthful she had lost herself the day she had flown to Dharbiri. Remy had taken control of not just the situation, but also her life and perhaps even her destiny. He had introduced passion and excitement to her and now there was no going back. She didn't want to go back.

How was she going to live without this rush of excitement every time his mouth met with hers?

She had thought she would play him at his own game: up the stakes, tantalise him, tease him until he gave in, but he had turned her efforts around to his advantage.

He was not going to be hoodwinked out of relinquishing Tarrantloch. Nothing she did or offered was going to change his mind.

Tarrantloch was his talisman of success.

His only weakness that she could see was that he wanted her. But even that need was under his tight control. She had ramped up his desire to the point where she thought he would agree to anything.

But it seemed she was the one who was the more desperate.

His mouth was hard against hers but she worked at softening it with little pull-backs and strokes of her tongue. Once he'd eased off a bit she nipped at his lower lip with her teeth, and then laved it with the glide of her tongue.

She felt him rummaging around for a condom, his hands leaving her in order to apply it, but his mouth didn't budge from plundering hers.

He was at her entrance and nudging to possess her. She opened her legs and stood up on tiptoe to welcome him. He surged so thickly and so forcefully she felt her back bump the bench behind. He set a furious pace but her body was so wet, and aching so much, it was a blessed and welcome assault of her senses to feel him pumping so hard. She came almost immediately, not even needing the coaxing stroke of his fingers. All it took was a little roll and tilt of her pelvis and she was flying off into the stratosphere, screaming and sobbing all the way.

He didn't waste time waiting for her to come back to earth. He rocketed after her with a deep, primal grunt as he unloaded. She felt the rise of goose bumps over his back as she held him against her, his hectic breathing a harsh sound in the silence.

Angelique wanted to hate him for turning the tables on her but somehow she couldn't access that emotion right now. So instead she held him and stroked her hands over his back and shoulders, planting soft little teasing kisses to his neck and behind his earlobes.

He eased back from her but only so he could rest his forehead against hers. Their breaths mingled intimately in the space between their mouths. 'I wasn't too rough, was I?' His voice sounded gruff, almost apologetic.

Angelique trailed a fingertip over his bottom lip. 'I wanted you any way I could have you.'

His dark gaze meshed with hers. 'You really turn me on like no other woman I've ever been with, but I have a feeling but you already know that.'

She smiled a little smile and did another circuit with her finger, this time pushing it into his mouth so he could suck on it. It sent a shudder down her spine when he did. His mouth was hot and moist, and his tongue a sexy rasp against her soft skin. When she pulled it out she said in a voice that wasn't quite even. 'You do a pretty fine job of lighting my fire too.'

He held her gaze for an interminable moment. 'We should do something about a meal. I don't want you fading away on me. I have plans for you and, believe me, you're going to need your stamina.'

She traced each of his eyebrows in turn, a playful smile pushing up the corners of her mouth. 'When you look at me like that, I get a wobbly feeling in my girly bits.'

His eyes glinted dangerously as he tugged her back against him. 'And so you damn well should,' he said and brought his mouth down to hers.

CHAPTER TWELVE

REMY WATCHED AS Angelique slept in the tumble of sheets, pillows and bedcoverings that had become their love-making nest over the last three weeks. He had extended their stay because a sudden snowfall had made it impossible for Robert Mappleton to get to their meeting so Remy had to postpone it until the roads cleared.

And what a time it had been.

He and Angelique had made love not just in the bedroom but the bathroom and the sofa in the sitting room; the morning room; the linen room; the utilities room and the kitchen four or five times over. Angelique had delighted him, shocked him, teased and tantalised him until he only had to look at her and his body would swell with lust.

He had lit a fire in the master bedroom. The flickering flames were casting their usual golden glow over the room. There was another fluttering of snow outside; he could see it falling silently past the windows in ghostly handfuls. It had been snowing on and off for a couple of days now but the roads were open again. He felt a niggling sense of disappointment as he had secretly harboured a fantasy of being snowed in with her for weeks on end. Maybe right up to and including Christmas.

Every couple of days they had driven to the village

to buy supplies at the local store. He liked the normality of it, the hunting and gathering that was an everyday occurrence for most people. Angelique knew a few of the locals and had stopped and chatted to them, introducing him as her husband with a naturalness that made him feel like a fraud. If she felt the same way, she showed no sign of it.

Robert Mappleton had left by helicopter that afternoon after an overnight stay. Angelique had shown the class and grace he had come to expect from her. It seemed she could be whatever he wanted or needed her to be: a playful, adventurous lover; an intrepid hiker across the moors or through the forest; a gourmet cook in the kitchen and an engaging, convivial hostess. She had made the old man feel at home, plying him with fabulous home-cooked food and old-fashioned highland hospitality. Mappleton had been charmed—besotted would have been closer to the mark. He had spent most of the time chatting to Angelique and had only given Remy his attention—and cursorily, at that—to sign the papers to hand over the Mappleton chain for a princely sum.

Remy knew he should be feeling happy. Proud. Satisfied. Victorious.

But his mind was restless.

It was time to put an end to this madness but Angelique had a photo shoot lined up in Paris the following day to kick-start her new modelling career. He could hardly walk out on her when so much was at stake for her. As least modelling bridal wear would be better for her than swimwear. There would be less pressure on her to be rail-thin all the time. Over the last few days he had noticed her eating a little more than usual. It had delighted him to see her enjoy her food instead of seeing it as an enemy.

Talking of enemies...

He was having more and more trouble thinking of her as an opponent. He looked at her lying next to him; at the way the light fell on her cheekbone as she was lying with her head resting on one of her hands. She looked so peaceful. Relaxed and sated.

He felt a little free-fall inside his stomach as he recalled the way she had crawled all over him earlier that night. His body was still humming with the aftershocks of having her ride him.

Was there no end to this driving lust he felt for her? He kept waiting to feel that flat feeling of boredom, the tinge of irritation that nearly always occurred about now in his relationships. He would look at the woman in his bed and wonder: *what was I thinking?*

But when he looked at Angelique in his bed, he thought: *how can I keep her there?*

Angelique made a sleepy sound from the tangle of sheets and then opened her eyes. 'What time is it?'

'Late. Or early. I guess it depends on whether you're a night owl or a lark.'

She sat up and pushed her dark hair back over her naked shoulders. 'I'm not sure what I am any more. I think I've crossed too many time zones or something.'

Remy pushed himself away from the mantelpiece. 'I'm cooking breakfast this morning. I think it's time you had a break from the kitchen.'

Her brows lifted. 'Wonders will never cease. I never thought I'd see the day when you put on an apron.'

He grinned at her. 'Not only that, I actually picked up a towel and hung it back on the rack. How's that for becoming domesticated?'

She gave him a beady look. 'Toilet seat?'

'Down.'

She gave a slow smile. 'Wow. That's pretty impressive. Maybe there's hope for you as a husband after all. Some girl in the future is really going to thank me for training you.' She tapped her finger against her lips musingly. 'Maybe I should think about opening a school for future husbands. There could be a big market for that: *give me your man and I'll whip him into shape.* What do you think?'

'Did you say *whip*?'

'I meant that metaphorically.'

'Pity.'

Her eyes danced with mischief and his blood raced. 'You don't really want me to beat you, do you?' she asked.

He came over to the bed and tipped up her chin with the end of his finger. 'I sometimes wonder if I'll ever know the real you. You're full of surprises.'

Her look was all sexy siren. 'Who do you want me to be?'

He dropped his hand from her chin. He felt strangely dissatisfied by her answer. He was all for playing games when it suited him, but he wanted to *know* her: the *real* Angelique Marchand. What she felt and thought and believed in. What she valued.

Who she loved.

It was ironic but in many ways she reminded him of himself. She had forged a reputation for herself as scatty and irresponsible, as a wild tearaway who had no intention of putting down roots. She had shied away from commitment like he did. She had hated the thought of the formality and entrapment of marriage. She was a free spirit who wanted to live and enjoy life on her terms.

But was that who she really was? Or was it what she thought people expected her to be?

Remy tried to think of another girl who would be in his bed in the flickering firelight some time in the future and couldn't quite do it. He kept seeing Angelique with her fragrant cloud of dark hair, her arresting grey-blue eyes and her bee-stung mouth with its lush, kiss-me ripeness…

He gave himself a mental shake.

He wasn't interested in a future with her. He wasn't interested in a future with anyone.

He was interested in the here and now.

Today and tomorrow were his only focus.

He didn't want to think any further ahead.

Angelique swung her legs over the edge of the bed, but as she stood up she tottered for a moment and went a ghastly shade of white. He put out a hand to steady her. 'Are you all right?'

She looked a little dazed for a moment or two but then her colour slowly returned. 'Whoa, that was strange. I thought I was going to faint. It's not like I've not been eating enough. I still feel full from all that chocolate pudding I had last night.'

He pushed a tiny tendril of hair back from her face. 'Maybe I've been keeping you up too late.'

She smiled cheekily as she danced her fingertips down his bare forearm. He felt the electric shock of her touch all the way to his groin. 'I'm the one who's been keeping you up.'

He was up right now—painfully so. But she was still looking peaky even if she was putting on a brave front. He knew that about her if nothing else. She was excellent at hiding behind various masks. He gently patted her on the behind. 'Have your shower while I rustle up some breakfast. How does bacon and eggs sound?'

The colour drained from her face again and she quickly thrust a hand to her mouth and bolted for the *en suite*. Remy followed her to find her hunched over the toilet seat, retching without actually bringing anything up. 'Oh, *ma petite*, why didn't you say you were feeling sick?' he said.

She wiped her mouth on the face cloth he handed her. 'I didn't feel sick until you mentioned… Urgh.' She gave a little shudder. 'I'm not even going to say the words.'

'Shall I call a doctor?'

'What on earth for?' She got to her feet and grabbed her hair and, using its length, tied it in a loose knot behind her head. 'It's just a stomach bug. I've had them before. It'll pass in twenty-four hours or so.'

He reached for her forehead but it was clammy rather than hot. 'Do you want to go back to bed?'

She pushed his hand away, a little frown creasing her forehead. 'Stop fussing, Remy. I'm fine.'

'You look pale.'

'I haven't got my make-up on.'

'Personally, I prefer you without it.' He followed her back into the bedroom. 'Are you sure you don't want me to call a doctor?'

'And make me look like a drama queen for dragging him or her out here to diagnose a virus? No thanks.'

Remy pulled back the covers on the bed. 'In. Rest for an hour and see how you feel.'

She rolled her eyes and flopped back down on the bed. 'You should keep well away from me. It might be catching.'

'I'll risk it.'

'I should probably warn you, I'm not a very good nurse. I have no patience or compassion.'

He smiled as he touched her cheek with a lazy finger. 'I think you'd make a very good nurse. You'd look hot in a uniform too.'

She cranked one eye open. 'I thought you preferred me without clothes?'

He gave her hand a gentle squeeze. 'Right now I'd prefer you to rest up. We have to get you to Paris in tip-top shape.'

'And after Paris?'

'We have Raoul and Lily's wedding.'

A little frown pulled at her brow. 'Are you sure I should go to that?'

'I want you there.' He meant it, which was a little surprising. Worrying, actually. He had to let her go at some point; no point dragging this on too long.

'But I thought once your business deal with Robert Mappleton was done we were going to go our separate ways.'

Remy searched her gaze but he wasn't sure what he was looking for. 'It would look a bit suspicious if we parted within a day or two of the contract being signed. And your manager is going to be pretty pissed with you if you suddenly announce you're getting a divorce. I think we should leave things as they are until after Raoul and Lily's wedding. It's only a matter of weeks. We can reassess things in the New Year.'

'What have you told your brothers about us? Surely they know the truth?'

'Yes, but that's not the point. I don't want a big press fest on our break-up occurring right in the middle of Raoul and Lily's wedding.'

Remy had spoken to Raoul not long after Rafe had

called. But, rather than berate him for marrying Angelique, he had said what his grandfather had said—that he'd always sensed Remy had a thing for her and that his little spin about her being hell on heels didn't ring true with him. It had annoyed Remy to think he hadn't disguised his feelings as well as he'd thought. What would Raoul make of his feelings now?

Angelique's gaze narrowed. 'You're not falling in love with me, are you?'

He coughed out a laugh. 'Are you joking? I've never fallen in love in my life.'

'Good.' She closed her eyes again. 'I don't want any hearts broken when this is over.'

Remy got up from the bed. 'I'll come and check on you in an hour.'

'I'll be back in the ring and punching by then.'

'I'll look forward to it.'

He walked to the door but when he turned back to look at her she had turned her back and was huddled into a tight ball.

Something shifted in his chest: a slippage; a gear not quite meshing with its cogs.

He shook off the feeling and walked out, closing the door softly behind him.

Angelique rolled over to her back, pressing a hand to her churning stomach. She was due for a period. She had taken herself off the pill months ago because she felt the brand she'd been on was making her put on weight. She hadn't bothered renewing her prescription because she hadn't been dating anyone. But she didn't feel period pain, just this wretched, churning nausea. That near-faint had happened a few times before when she hadn't eaten enough. But she could hardly use the lack of food as an excuse because she had been eating normally over the last couple of weeks. The thought of not having to bare her body all the time in a bikini was like being let out of prison. She was almost getting excited about the Paris shoot. Almost.

She swung her legs over the edge of the bed again and tested her balance. So far so good. Her stomach was uneasy but her head was more or less clear. She padded back to the bathroom and stepped into the shower. She closed her eyes as the water cascaded down and mentally calculated when her last period had been—was it four weeks or five?

She was occasionally overdue; disruptions came with the stress of dieting and travelling.

Anyway, they'd used condoms. The failure rate was miniscule…but enough to be slightly worrying. Terrifyingly worrying.

Angelique put a hand to her concave belly. It wasn't possible. She wasn't the type of girl to get herself pregnant. It just couldn't happen.

She thought of the first time when Remy had taken for ever to withdraw. Had some of his Olympic-strong swimmers sneaked out past the barrier of the condom and gone in search of one of her desperate little eggs?

Oh, traitorous body and even more traitorous hormones!

Panic set in. She felt it clutch at her insides. She felt it move over her skin like a clammy shiver. She felt it hammering in her chest.

She couldn't be pregnant. *She couldn't be.*

Buying a pregnancy test in a village this small was out of the question. She would have to wait until she got to Paris. And then after Paris, baby or no baby, she would have to attend Raoul and Lily's wedding and pretend everything was normal in front of their family and friends. It seemed so tacky to be attending a romantic wedding when theirs had been so extravagant yet so meaningless.

Angelique felt a pang of envy for Raoul's bride-to-be, Lily. How excited she must be getting prepared for her wedding. Doing all the girly things to make her day so special. Angelique cringed when she thought of her wedding to Remy. The whole thing had been nothing but a big, overblown sham. She was a fraud. A fake bride. A fake wife. And this was a fake honeymoon.

If she was pregnant would Remy insist on her staying with him for the sake of the child? He would end up hating her for tying him down. He might even end up hating the child.

Angelique bit her lip as she looked in the mirror at her body. For years she had denied her body, punished her body, controlled her body, but now it would not just be hers but the shelter in which her baby—hers and Remy's baby—would grow and develop.

She could not think of getting rid of it. It was certainly an option and one she felt other women were entitled to make. But it wasn't for her.

She put a hand to her flat belly. How could it be possible that she and Remy had made a baby? He didn't even like her.

Well, maybe that wasn't quite true. He certainly didn't hate her any more. She had seen him looking at her with lust, longing, amusement, and even annoyance when she got in the last word, but not hatred.

Their relationship had changed over the last three weeks. They still bickered occasionally but it was a sort of foreplay. They were both strong-willed and determined and didn't like losing an argument or debate. It was foolish of her to have fallen in love with him but it had happened so long ago it was pointless flagellating herself about it now. She had fallen in love with him at the age of fifteen.

She still remembered the day it had happened. She had gone with her father to Vittorio's villa for a function. Remy had been home for a visit and he'd been assigned the task of keeping her entertained while her father and Vittorio had a business meeting before dinner. She had been waiting in the home entertainment room, idly leafing through one of her fashion magazines, when Remy had come in. She hadn't seen him in a year or two. Her heart had quite literally stopped when he had come in. He had been so tall and so staggeringly handsome, with that lazy smile that had travelled all the way to his eyes.

But as soon as she had stood up his smile had disappeared. He'd seemed a little taken aback seeing her dressed in a short denim skirt and a clinging top that revealed a generous amount of cleavage due to the brand-new push-up bra she'd bought.

He had cleared his throat, walked briskly over to the television, selected a movie and set it running. 'There, that should keep you happy for a while.'

'I'm not twelve,' she'd said with a pout.

He'd pushed a hand through his thick overly long hair. 'It's a good movie. It won two Oscar nomination and three Golden Globes.'

She had put on her beseeching face. 'Will you watch it with me?'

He had muttered something that sounded very much like an English swear word before he had sat down on the sofa furthest away from her. But he had stayed and watched it with her. He'd even laughed at the funny bits, and at one point paused the movie to go and get some popcorn he'd charmed one of the housemaids to make.

Yes, falling in love with him had been the easy bit. *Falling out of love was going to be the kicker.*

CHAPTER THIRTEEN

'ARE YOU SURE you're all right?' Remy asked Angelique when they landed in Paris. 'You've been so quiet and you still look a little pale.'

'I'm fine.' She gave him a tight smile. 'I'm just nervous. The thought of all those wedding dresses is enough to make my insides churn.'

He put an arm around her waist as they walked out to the waiting car. 'You'll blow everyone away as soon as you walk up that aisle.'

Angelique hadn't been sick for the last couple of days but she still felt queasy in the stomach. She had managed to keep it from Remy but then saw a pharmacy ahead and wondered how she could sneak in and get a testing kit without him noticing. But just then his phone rang and she seized the opportunity. She pointed to the ladies' room and mouthed the words to him about needing to take a pit stop. He nodded and turned away, plugging one ear so he could hear the conversation without all the noise of the busy airport terminal.

Angelique walked briskly into the shop and bought tampons—that was her positive thinking working overtime—and a pregnancy kit. She put both items in her tote bag and came out with her heart thumping so loudly she could feel it in her throat.

Remy was still talking on the phone and only turned around when she appeared by his side. He ended the call and slipped his arm back around her waist. 'That was Robert Mappleton. He said to say hi.'

'He's a very nice man,' Angelique said, falling in step beside him as they made their way out to the waiting car. 'He really misses his wife. She died eight years ago after a long struggle with breast cancer. They'd been married for forty-nine years. She used to do a lot of the background work in the business. I think that's why it went downhill so badly. He's been grieving all this time.'

Remy glanced down at her. 'He told you all that?'

She nodded. 'We talked about the grieving process—the denial, the anger, the bargaining, transition and then acceptance. I told him how lost I'd felt when my mother died. He was very understanding. He and his wife couldn't have children.' She gave a little sigh. 'Wouldn't it be cool if we could choose our parents? I would've loved a father like Robert Mappleton instead of my own.'

Remy's arm tightened protectively. 'I wish I could have mine back, just for a day, to tell him how much he meant to me. And my mother.'

Angelique leaned against his shoulder. 'They'd be very proud of you and your brothers.'

His expression clouded and he looked away. 'Of Rafe and Raoul maybe, but me? I'm not so sure.'

'But why? You've just nailed the biggest deal of your career. It's bigger than anything your brothers have done.'

He looked at her again. It was a hard look: cynical; jaded. 'It's just another deal.' He dropped his arm from her waist and took her hand instead. 'Come on. We'd better get you to the church on time.'

Remy stood at the back of the photo shoot in one of Paris's gothic cathedrals as Angelique was photographed in a variety of bridal outfits. She looked stunning in every one of them. It made him think of their wedding back in Dharbiri. She had looked fabulous then too, but nothing about that day had been real.

He couldn't help imagining her as a real bride, walking down the aisle not to a crowd of photographers but to him.

He blinked and shook his head. It was definitely too hot and stuffy in here or something.

He looked back at the action playing out in front of him. The photographers, all six of them, issued commands and directions, which Angelique followed tirelessly like the consummate professional she was. Her manager had come over and introduced herself earlier, telling him how Angelique's star was set to shine brighter than any model she had represented before.

Remy felt proud of Angelique in a way he had never quite expected to feel. He had always thought her spoilt and wilful, yet seeing how she treated the more junior staff on the shoot with respect and kindness made him realise he had seriously misjudged her.

You're falling for her.

No, I'm not.

Yes, you are. Big time.

Remy's phone vibrated in his pocket but instead of ignoring it he welcomed the distraction. He didn't even check the screen to see who was calling as he stepped outside the cathedral to answer it. 'Remy Caffarelli.'

'I want you and your brothers here tomorrow for a family meeting,' Vittorio said.

Typical. His grandfather always expected everyone to dance around him at a moment's notice. Remy would go when he was good and ready and not before. 'I can't drop everything just because you fancy a family get-together.'

'Where are you?'

'In Paris with Angelique. She's working.'

'She wouldn't know how to work unless it was flat on her back.'

Anger tightened every muscle in Remy's spine. 'That's my wife you're insulting. I won't have you or anyone speak about her like that.'

'If you don't come here tomorrow I'll tell the press your marriage to that little black-haired slut is nothing but a sham.'

Remy felt a cold hand of dread grab at his guts. It wasn't the deal with Robert Mappleton he was most worried about. What would happen to Angelique's new-found career if that sort of leak got out before her first shoot was even over?

How on earth had Vittorio found out? His brothers would never have betrayed him. He had sworn them to secrecy.

There could only be one person who would want to do the dirty on him even if it hurt his only daughter in the process.

Henri Marchand.

Angelique came over to where Remy was standing at the back of the church once her shoot was over for the day. 'I didn't expect you to stay the whole time. You must be bored out of your brain. There's nothing more tediously boring than watching mascara dry— Hey, is something wrong? Why are you frowning like that? Are you cross with me?'

Remy forcibly relaxed his frown. 'Sorry, *ma petite*. It's not you. It's my grandfather. He's insisting on a family meeting tomorrow. He won't take no for an answer. Can you ask for a day off? I know it's short notice.'

She frowned at him. 'He wants *me* there? But why?'

'I'll explain it later. I don't want anyone listening in. Do you think you can get tomorrow off?'

'I'm sure it'll be fine. There's been a delay on the next collection. Mackenzie just told me about it. We're shooting at a private château in Vichy the day after tomorrow so I'm all yours till then.'

Remy put his arm around her shoulders and hugged her close. 'Best news I've had all day.'

Angelique didn't have time to do anything about the pregnancy test because Remy had organised a flight straight to Rome. She tried to put her worries to the back of her mind. She was probably imagining her symptoms anyway. Stress always made her stomach churn. And being late with a period was certainly not unusual; it came with the territory of dieting and travelling across time zones.

And, to be fair, Remy had been keeping her up late at night, not that she was complaining. The nights in his arms were the highlight of her day. Not that he had restricted their passionate interludes to the evenings: mornings, mid-morning, lunchtimes, afternoons and evenings had been spent in a variety of activities that had made every cell in her body shudder with delight.

It worried her that it might soon be over. His deal was done and dusted. The only thing keeping them together was her modelling contract—a contract she didn't even want.

Rafe and Poppy arrived just as they were getting out of the car at Vittorio's villa, so there was no chance of slipping away and finding out one way or the other about the result.

Rafe was distinctly cool with Angelique but Poppy was anything but. She wrapped her arms around Angelique and gave her a warm hug. 'It's so lovely to meet you.' She pulled back to look at her. 'Oh. My. God. You're *so* beautiful! I'm having such a fan moment. I feel I should be asking for your autograph or something.'

Angelique loved her already. 'Congratulations on your marriage.' It was the first thing she thought of to say.

Poppy's toffee-brown eyes twinkled. 'Congratulations on yours.' She leaned in close so the boys couldn't hear. 'And all that rubbish about it being a sham just to save your necks doesn't fool me for a second.'

Angelique quickly schooled her features. She wasn't ready to play confidante just yet, even if Poppy was the sort of girl she longed to have as a best friend. 'Sorry to burst your bubble, but I'm not in love with him. We're just making the most of being stuck together. I've always fancied him, but then what girl with a pulse wouldn't?'

'Oh, well…sorry. I just thought… Never mind.' Poppy's flustered look was replaced with a smile. 'Just wait until you meet Lily, Raoul's fiancée. She's a darling. She's quite shy but once you get to know her I'm sure you'll adore her.'

'I'm not worried about Lily or Raoul,' Angelique

said. 'It's Vittorio I'm concerned with. I've always been a little terrified of him.'

Poppy rolled her eyes. 'Tell me about it. I avoid him as much as possible. So do Rafe and Raoul. I think Remy is the only one who can crack a smile out of him. But you know him, don't you? Rafe told me you used to come here a lot when your father and Vittorio were business partners.'

'Yes, but it was a long time ago, and there's been a lot of dirty water under the bridge since then.'

Poppy gave her a friendly smile. 'Maybe, but you weren't the one to put it there. Now, let's go and meet Lily and Raoul. That's their car arriving. See?'

Angelique watched as a slim ash-brown-haired young woman stepped out of the car to go around to the driver's side with a pair of crutches. 'I thought Raoul couldn't walk any more?'

'He can take a few steps now,' Poppy said. 'Lily's been amazing for him. They're just the most adorable couple. Check out the way he looks at her. It just makes me melt.'

Angelique felt an ache around her heart when she saw Raoul take the crutches from Lily. He smiled a smile that was so much more than a smile. It was the smile of a man hopelessly in love. But when she looked at Lily she saw the same thing: Lily was besotted with Raoul and was not one bit ashamed about showing it.

They came over to where the rest of them were standing. Raoul leaned heavily on his crutches to offer a hand to Angelique. 'Welcome to the family, Angelique. It's good to have you here again. It's been a long time. Too long.'

Angelique felt a sudden rush of emotion. Raoul had

always been the nicest to her. '*Merci*. I'm sorry about your accident. I sent a card. Did you get it?'

He gave her a warm smile. 'It meant a lot to me. It made me smile, which I wasn't doing a lot of back then.' He rebalanced on his crutches so he could get Lily to step forward. '*Ma chérie*, this is Angelique, an old family friend and now Remy's wife. Angelique, this is my fiancée, Lily Archer.'

Angelique took Lily's hand. 'I'm very pleased to meet you.'

'And you,' Lily said with a shy smile. 'Wow, you really are as stunning as you are on those billboards and in those magazines.'

'You should see me before breakfast,' Angelique said. 'I spend a fortune on cover-up and I'm on a constant diet. How I look is totally fake.' *I'm a fake.*

Lily's smile said she didn't believe it for a second. 'Maybe you could give me some make-up tips for my wedding. I'm not very good at that stuff.'

'I would be happy to. You have amazing blue eyes. They're so incredibly dark. Has anyone ever told you that?'

Lily smiled and glanced at Raoul who was looking at her with such a tender look it made Angelique's heart suddenly contract. 'Yes; yes, they have. Many times.'

There was a rumble from inside the villa like a dragon emerging from his cave. Vittorio suddenly appeared at the front door with a savage frown between his brows as his gaze fell on Angelique. 'I always knew you'd be trouble. You're just like your two-faced father.'

Angelique stepped forward with her shoulders back and her chin at a combative height. 'I don't think it's fair that I should be judged for the wrongs my father did to you and your family. I had nothing to do with it. I'm an innocent party.'

Vittorio glared at her. 'There's not too much about you that's innocent.'

Angelique stared him down. 'Yes, well, perhaps there's some truth in that, given what your grandson has been doing with me over the last three or four weeks.'

'You shameless hussy!' Vittorio spat at her. 'I bet your double-dealing father put you up to this. No wonder he couldn't wait to crow about it when he called me the other day. You tricked Remy into marrying you so you could carve up his assets when you bail out of it.'

Remy stepped up and put an arm around Angelique's waist. 'I've already warned you about speaking about or to Angelique in a disrespectful manner. She is my wife, and you will treat her with the respect accorded to that position.'

Vittorio curled his top lip. 'How long are you going to keep her? She's not going to stay with you. She'll do the dirty on you first chance she gets. You've left yourself wide open. She's a witch. A Jezebel. You're crazy to think she's going to stick by you. She'll take half of what you own because you've been thinking with your—'

'I'm not taking anything that isn't rightly mine,' Angelique said.

Vittorio laughed. 'Do you think my grandson will hand that castle over just because you opened your legs for him? He's not that much of a fool. His winning that property off your father was the one time I felt proud to call him my grandson. He won't relinquish a prize like that. He's too much like me to give in just because a beautiful woman bats her eyelashes at him.'

'That's enough!' Remy barked. 'Stop it right there.'

Poppy came to the rescue. 'I think it's time for us

girls to get to know one another over some devil's food cake, which strangely enough seems rather appropriate just now. You boys can have your family meeting. We want no part of it.'

Lily touched Angelique's hand. 'Maybe this would be a good time to swap make-up tips.'

'You could be right,' Angelique said.

Rafe took Remy aside after Vittorio had stormed off in a temper. 'You OK?'

Remy clenched and unclenched his fists. 'I swear to God I could have punched him for that.'

'Yes, well, maybe you're feeling hot under the collar because there's a bit of truth in what he said.'

Remy glared at his brother. 'Don't you start. I'm nothing like him.'

Rafe gave him his 'older and wiser' look. 'We're all a bit like him, Remy. There's no point trying to hide from it. It's best to face it and deal with it. We've all used people to get what we want. We've learned it off him. But it doesn't mean we have to go on being like that. I know I've always taught you and Raoul to set goals and to focus, but I've come to realise that winning at any cost is not always the right or the wisest thing to do.'

'I know what I'm doing.' Remy tightened his jaw. 'I don't need your advice or guidance any more.'

Rafe gave his shoulder a squeeze. 'Sorry. I have this lifetime habit of feeling responsible for you. You're old enough to make your own decisions.'

And take full responsibility for them, Remy thought.

'Is Angelique all right?' Raoul asked as he came over once Rafe had left to join Poppy and the girls. 'She looked really pale and fragile. You haven't been giving her a hard time, have you?'

Remy slid his brother a look. 'Trust you to be the softie. She's fine. She's had a stomach bug and the shoot she was on yesterday was long and tiring.'

'What's going on with you two? Is it true what she said to *Nonno*?'

'You know what Angelique's like,' Remy said. 'She likes centre stage. The bigger the scene she makes, the better.'

Raoul's mouth tightened in reproach. 'She's a nice kid, Remy. I've always thought so. A bit messed up because of her mother dying so young and all, but she's a got a good heart. Just because she's got an asshole for a father isn't her fault. She didn't screw us over. Henri did.'

'And I got him back,' Remy said through tight lips.

'Yes, by taking the one thing Angelique loves above everything else.' Raoul readjusted his crutches under his arms. 'You should give Tarrantloch back to her. It doesn't belong to you, bet or no bet. It belongs to her.'

'How do you know I wasn't planning to do that once our marriage comes to an end?'

Raoul gave him a levelling look. 'That's some parting gift, bro. But have you considered she might not want it to end?'

Remy gave a short bark of cynical laughter. 'Can't see that happening. She hates being married to me. She's only sticking with it while she gets her new modelling gig off the ground. She thinks marriage is an outdated institution that serves the interests of men rather than women.'

'Yes, well, it's certainly served your interests,' Raoul said.

'What's that supposed to mean?'

'You didn't have to sleep with her. You could have

got her out of Dharbiri and annulled the marriage once you got home.'

Remy flashed a glare his middle brother's way. 'Since when is who I sleep with your business?'

Raoul held his glare. 'If you divorce her, all hell could break loose. She could take half of your assets.'

'I thought you said she was a nice kid?'

'She is, but that's not to say she wouldn't want to get back at you for breaking her heart.'

'I'm not breaking her heart, OK?' Remy said in an exasperated tone. 'What is it with you and Rafe? You fall in love and expect everyone else to do the same. She doesn't even like me. I can't help thinking she's biding her time to turn things on their head. She's smart that way. She likes having the last word and she'll do anything to get it.'

'Have you really got so cynical you can't see what's right in front of your nose?'

'What? You think she loves me or something?' Remy said. 'Sorry to disappoint you, but Angelique's a great actress. She's no more in love with me than I am with her.'

Raoul gave him a look.

'What?' Remy gave another bark of a laugh but even to his ears it sounded hollow. 'You think *I'm* in love with *her*? Come on. No offence to you and Rafe, but falling in love is not on my list of things to do. I don't have that particular gene.'

'It's not a matter of genetics,' Raoul said. 'It's a matter of choice. If you're open to it, that is.'

'Well, I choose not to be open to it. I don't want that sort of complication in my life. I'm fine just the way I am.'

'You'll end up like *Nonno*,' Raoul said. 'Stuck with a

houseful of obsequious servants who pretend they like him when all they do is laugh and snigger about him behind his back.'

'I know what I'm doing, Raoul.'

'Yeah, and you're doing a damn fine job of it too. But, if you're so sure of Angelique's motives, why don't you give her Tarrantloch now and see if she still wants to stay with you? Take a gamble, Remy—or are you too scared of losing where it matters most?'

Remy let out a tight breath as his brother limped away to join Lily, who was looking at them with a worried frown.

Poppy came over with a cup of coffee and a slice cake for Remy. 'Have you seen Angelique?' she asked. 'She said she was going to the bathroom but she's been ages. Is she OK?'

'She's fine. She had a stomach bug a couple of days ago.' *How many times do I have to say this?* 'She's still getting over it.'

Poppy's expression flickered with something. 'Oh. I just wondered…'

'What?'

'Nothing.' She pinched her lips together as if afraid of speaking out of turn. She put a protective hand over her belly as a rosy blush spread over her cheeks.

Remy felt like someone had just slammed him in the solar plexus. It was a moment before he could get his breath back. His mind was reeling.

'Excuse me…' He almost pushed Poppy out of the way as he moved past.

CHAPTER FOURTEEN

ANGELIQUE LOOKED AT the dipstick.

Negative.

Why was she feeling so disappointed? It was ridiculous of her to feel so deflated. Why was she thinking about little dark-haired babies when she stood to gain squillions from parading around in bridal wear on every catwalk in Europe?

Because she didn't want to be a pretend bride.

Not on the catwalk. Not in a photo shoot. Not in magazines and billboards.

She wanted to be a real bride, a real wife and a real mother.

'Angelique?' There was a sharp rap at the door.

She quickly stuffed the packaging and results in the nearest drawer underneath the basin. ' Just a second…'

She checked her appearance in the mirror. She looked like she'd just auditioned for a walk-on part as a ghost in a horror movie.

The door handled rattled. 'Open this door,' Remy commanded. 'I want to talk to you.'

Angelique stalked over, snipped the lock back and opened the door. 'Do you mind? What does a girl have to do to get some privacy around here?'

He glanced to either side of her. 'What are you doing in there?'

She gave him a look. 'What do you think I was doing? What do you do when you go to the bathroom? No, on second thought, don't answer that.' She brushed past him. 'I know what you guys do.'

He captured her arm and turned her to face him. 'Are you pregnant?'

Angelique blinked at him in shock. 'What?'

His mouth was set in a grim line. 'I asked you a simple question. Are you pregnant?'

'No.'

'But you thought you were?'

She waited a beat before answering. 'Yes…'

He frowned so heavily his eyebrows met. 'And you didn't think to mention it to me?'

'I wanted to make sure first.'

'So you could do what? Announce it to the press? Post a tweet about it? Drop it on me to force me to keep our marriage going indefinitely?'

Angelique pushed past him. 'That's just so damn typical of you. You think everyone is going to do the dirty on you.'

'Do you realise how insulting this is?' He swung around to follow her. 'Don't you think I had the right to know you suspected you were carrying my child? This is something we should've been facing together. You had no right to keep that information to yourself.'

'You seem pretty certain it's your child,' Angelique said. ' How do you know I wasn't trying to foist another man's baby on you? You should watch your back, Remy. You think you're so smart, but I could have tricked you and you wouldn't have suspected a thing.'

'I don't believe you would sink to that level. You like

to act streetwise and tough but that's not who you really are. Your father might be a double-crossing cheat but you're not cut from the same cloth.'

'You don't know me.'

'I know you can't wait to get out of this marriage.' His jaw was locked tight with tension. 'Well, guess what? You got your wish. I'm releasing you. You're free to go as of now. I won't have anyone tell me I'm exploiting you by sleeping with you or getting you pregnant against your will, or keeping your precious castle just for kicks. Just go. Leave. Tarrantloch is yours. I'll send you the deeds.'

Angelique had dreamed of this moment, the moment when she would have Tarrantloch back in her possession. Why then did she feel like she was losing something even more valuable? 'You want me to leave?'

'That's what *you* want, isn't it?'

Here is your chance.

Tell him what you want.

But the words were stuck behind a wall of pride. What if she told him she loved him and wanted to stay with him for ever? He had never given any sign of being in love with her. Lust was his language. She had made it her own. If he loved her, wouldn't he have said so?

'Yes.' The word felt like a dry stone in her mouth. 'That's what I want.'

'Fine.' He let out a breath that sounded horribly, *distressingly* like relief. 'I won't make any announcements to the press until after Christmas. I don't want to compromise your modelling contract.'

That was the least of Angelique's worries. She was already trying to think of a way out of it. 'Thank you.' She pressed her lips together as she gathered up her bag. She would not cry. She would not beg him to let her stay. She would not tell him she loved him only to have him mock her. 'Will you say goodbye to the others for me? I don't want to create a scene.'

He gave a rough-sounding laugh. 'What? No big dramatic exit? You surprise me. That's not the Angelique Marchand I know.'

Angelique turned at the door and gave him a glacial look. 'Then perhaps you don't know me as well as you thought.'

As exit lines went, it was a good one. The only trouble was she could barely see where she was going for the tears that blurred her vision.

But she resolutely blinked them back and walked out of the villa and out of Remy's life without anyone stopping her.

And she wouldn't be coming back.

CHAPTER FIFTEEN

'BUT YOU CAN'T possibly spend Christmas on your own!' Poppy said. 'Rafe, darling, will you tell your impossibly stubborn brother he's got to be with us? He won't listen to me.' Her bottom lip quivered as tears shimmered in her eyes. 'I can't bear the thought of anyone spending Christmas all alone.'

'It's nothing to get upset about,' Remy said, feeling like a heel for triggering Poppy's meltdown. 'I just don't feel like socialising, that's all.'

Rafe put his arm around Poppy and drew her close. 'Poppy's feeling a bit emotional just now, aren't you, *ma petite*?'

'I think we should tell him,' Poppy said with a little sniff.

'Tell me what?' Remy said, looking between the two of them.

'We're having a baby,' Rafe said with a proud smile. 'We found out a few weeks ago but didn't want to overshadow Raoul and Lily's wedding. We were going to wait until they got back from their honeymoon to announce it at Christmas.'

Remy's smile pulled on the tight ache in his chest that had been there since he had set Angelique free. 'Congratulations. I'm happy for you. That's great news.'

He even managed a short laugh. 'How about that? I'm going to be an uncle.'

'Will you *please* come to us for Christmas?' Poppy pleaded. 'I know you don't want to be anywhere near your grandfather just now, but we're supposed to be a family. It won't be the same without you there.'

It won't be the same without Angelique there.

Remy thought of the cosy family scene Poppy was so keen to orchestrate: wonderful cooking smells and warm fires in every room. A fresh pine-scented Christmas tree decorated with colourful bells and tinsel with thoughtfully chosen and artfully wrapped presents for everyone beneath it. His brothers and their wives would be talking non-stop about brides and honeymoons and babies. The photos from Raoul and Lily's wedding—where Angelique's absence in them would cause him even more pain—would be pored over and he would sit there being the odd one out—along with his grandfather, of course.

He'd rather be on his own than suffer that.

'Sorry, but I have other plans.'

'I wonder what Angelique has planned,' Poppy said as she handed back Rafe's handkerchief. 'Maybe I'll invite her. Do you think she'd come now that you're not going to be there?'

Remy frowned. 'Why would you invite her?'

'Why shouldn't I invite her?' Poppy gave him a haughty look. 'I loved her the minute I met her. So did Lily.'

'You spent all of five minutes with her!'

'Maybe, but it was enough to know she's a lovely person.'

'I never said she wasn't.' Remy caught his brother's look. 'Lately, I mean.'

'Did you know she's cancelled the bridal wear contract?' Rafe said. 'It will cost her a fortune to get out of. One of the designers is threatening to sue.'

Remy felt his stomach drop. 'Where did you hear that?'

'Social media,' Rafe said. 'Where else?'

Angelique stood back and inspected the tree she had set up in the sitting room of Tarrantloch. The scent of pine filled the air with a pleasantly sharp, clean tang. It brought back wonderful memories of Christmas with her grandparents all those years ago. She had even found in the attic the decorations they had used back then—miraculously overlooked by the ruthlessly efficient removal men—including the angel she had loved so much as a child. The angel was looking a little the worse for wear with her yellowed robes and moth-eaten wings but Angelique didn't have the heart to replace her.

The festive season was the worst time to be alone. She had spent far too many of them in hotel rooms or with people she didn't particularly know or like to do it again this year.

Poppy had invited her to spend it with her and Rafe in Oxfordshire, with Lily, Raoul and Vittorio, but she'd politely declined, even when Poppy had assured her Remy wasn't going to be there. Angelique hadn't asked where he would be spending Christmas or who he'd be spending it with.

She didn't want to know.

The sound of helicopter blades outside gave her a little start. Robert Mappleton wasn't due to arrive until tomorrow, on Christmas Eve. She had invited him because she'd found out he had spent every Christmas alone since his wife had died.

Angelique peered out of the window, but it wasn't Robert who got out of the helicopter. Her heart banged against her chest as Remy came through the icy wind towards the house. She dusted off the tinsel sparkles clinging to her yoga pants before opening the front door. 'What are you doing here?'

'I want to talk to you.'

She folded her arms. 'So talk.'

'Aren't you going to invite me in?'

She put her chin up. 'I'm expecting company.'

He flinched as if she'd just struck him. 'Who?'

Angelique saw his throat move up and down. His eyes looked tired. He needed a shave more than usual. 'Robert Mappleton.'

His expression turned to stone. Unreadable stone. 'I guess I should've guessed that.'

Angelique unfolded her arms. 'Why aren't you spending Christmas with your family?'

He gave her a brooding look. 'I don't trust myself in the same room as my grandfather. Every time I see him I want to punch him.'

'I told my father I *would* punch him if he came anywhere near me.'

Remy stood looking at her for a beat of silence. 'So…I guess I should leave you to it…' He raked a hand through his windblown hair. He was too late. He'd left it too late. His gamble hadn't paid off. She had moved on with her life. Robert Mappleton was far too old for her but she was probably searching for a father figure, given hers was so appalling.

He was too late.

'Why are you here?' Angelique asked.

Remy was sick of all the game playing, the pretence

and subterfuge. He decided to take one last gamble. His pride was on the table but it was a small price to pay.

It was the price he was prepared to pay.

'I wanted to tell you I love you.'

Her eyelids flickered. 'You…*love* me?'

Remy gave her a self-deprecating look. 'You looked shocked.'

'But you never said a word… You sent me away.' She narrowed her gaze at him, her cheeks firing up with red-hot anger. 'How could you *do* that to me?'

Remy took umbrage at her cutting tone. 'I thought that's what you wanted. For God's sake, I asked you straight out what you wanted. You said you only wanted Tarrantloch.'

'I was pretending!' Angelique said. 'How could you think I would want a big old, draughty castle instead of love?'

Now it was his turn to look shocked. 'You want love?'

Angelique felt tears prickling at the back of her throat. 'I want love and marriage and…and a baby.'

Remy blinked. 'You want a baby?'

She brushed at her eyes with the back of her hand. 'I know you're going to think this is utterly ridiculous, but I was bitterly disappointed when that pregnancy test was negative.'

'Why?'

'Because without it I had no reason to stay with you.'

'But what about your modelling contract?'

'You just don't get it, do you?' Angelique said. 'You don't get me at all. I *hate* being a model. I hate having to look perfect all the time. I only ever got into it because I knew it would annoy my father. I want to design clothes, not parade around in them.'

Remy took her by the shoulders. 'You want to stay with me? Is that what you're saying?'

Angelique looked up into his dark brown eyes. 'I've wanted to stay with you since the night you put on *The Lion King* when I was fifteen and watched it with me.'

Remy's fingers tightened. He was frightened to let go of her in case this was all a dream. 'You love me?'

'Desperately.'

'Then why the hell didn't you say so?' He glared at her. 'Do you realise the torture you've put me through? I could put you over my knee and spank you.'

Angelique gave him a cheeky smile. 'Is that a promise?'

He clutched her to his chest, almost crushing her in the process. 'I thought I'd lost you. I thought it was too late. I thought *I* was too late. When Rafe told me he'd heard a rumour you were trying to get out of your contract I started to think...*to hope*...it was because you weren't happy with your life.' He pulled back to look at her. 'Tell me I'm not dreaming this.'

She smoothed away the frown between his brows with her fingertip. 'Do you think we're always going to fight?'

He captured her finger and kissed its tip. 'I hope so. It's so much fun making up.'

Angelique's eyes sparkled. 'Do you think Robert Mappleton would mind if we have a slight change of venue for Christmas?'

'What did you have in mind?'

She toyed with his shirt collar. 'Well...it sounds like Poppy's gone to a lot of trouble and it would be really nice to have a proper family Christmas for once. And I really want to see Raoul and Lily's wedding photos and hear all about their honeymoon.' She lifted her gaze to his. 'Would you mind?'

'For you, *mon amour*, I would agree to anything. But first I have something to give you.' He took out a box from his anorak pocket and handed it to her.

Angelique opened the box to find an engagement and wedding ring ensemble that was so exquisitely and yet so simply crafted it took her breath away. She blinked away a sudden rush of tears and looked up into his gaze. 'It's perfect! It's absolutely gorgeous! How did you know I would love this so much?'

He gave her a twinkling smile as he scooped her up into his arms. 'I took a gamble.'

EPILOGUE

REMY LOOKED AROUND the sitting room of Dalrymple House where his family was gathered for Christmas. His grandfather was sitting grumbling about the stock market fluctuations with a very patient Robert Mappleton. Raoul was sitting on the sofa with his legs up on an ottoman. Lily was tucked in close to his side, looking up at him with such rapt attention it made Remy's chest feel warm. Rafe was helping Poppy carry in egg nog and nibbles but stopped in the doorway to give her a lingering kiss under the mistletoe.

Remy looked across at Angelique who was on the floor in front of the Christmas tree cuddling all three of Poppy's cute little dogs. Chutney, Pickles and Relish were instantly besotted with her and had no shame about showing it. Pickles—who according to Rafe was a hard nut to crack—had even snuck in an extra couple of licks.

Angelique laughed as she got off the floor to come over to Remy. 'Did you see that, darling? I won Pickles over straight away. He couldn't resist me.'

'I saw you sneak him a treat,' Remy said. 'In my book, that's cheating.'

She gave him a grin as she wound her arms around

his middle. 'You're just jealous because you didn't think of it first.'

'I'm not jealous.'

'Yes you are.'

'Am not.'

'Will someone tell those two to stop bickering?' Rafe said from over by the mistletoe.

'They're not bickering,' Raoul said from the sofa. 'They're just warming up for a kiss. See, what did I tell you? Any second now. *Bingo.*'

* * * * *

Give a 12 month subscription to a friend today!

Call Customer Services
0844 844 1358*

or visit
millsandboon.co.uk/subscriptions

MILLS & BOON®

Why shop at millsandboon.co.uk?

Each year, thousands of romance readers find their perfect read at millsandboon.co.uk. That's because we're passionate about bringing you the very best romantic fiction. Here are some of the advantages of shopping at www.millsandboon.co.uk:

* **Get new books first**—you'll be able to buy your favourite books one month before they hit the shops

* **Get exclusive discounts**—you'll also be able to buy our specially created monthly collections, with up to 50% off the RRP

* **Find your favourite authors**—latest news, interviews and new releases for all your favourite authors and series on our website, plus ideas for what to try next

* **Join in**—once you've bought your favourite books, don't forget to register with us to rate, review and join in the discussions

Visit **www.millsandboon.co.uk**
for all this and more today!

MILLS_WEB